UNEASY STREET

A SONS OF SCANDAL ROMANCE

BECKY WADE

Romances by Becky Wade

SONS OF SCANDAL ROMANCE SERIES

#1 Memory Lane

#2 Rocky Road

MISTY RIVER ROMANCE SERIES

#1 Stay with Me

#2 Let It Be Me

#3 Turn to Me

BRADFORD SISTERS ROMANCE SERIES

#1 True to You

#2 Falling for You

#3 Sweet on You

PORTER FAMILY SERIES

#1 Undeniably Yours

#2 Meant to Be Mine

#3 A Love Like Ours

#4 Her One and Only

STAND-ALONE NOVEL

My Stubborn Heart

for Mom and Dad

I've been the beneficiary of a lifetime's worth of your love and support. And that's made all the difference. Thank you for the big things, the small things, and everything in between.
Love, Becky

Chapter One

I've waited four years for this day, and it's finally here.

That was the thought that dropped into Max's head the split second he came awake in his luxurious bed. His eyes flicked open. And a slow smile moved across his lips.

Today was the day. He was not a patient person and so the time between when he'd learned that Sloane was coming back to Maine and now had moved as slowly as a sailboat without wind.

Even so, time had finally done what time did.

It had passed.

And today, though she did not know it, he'd see her again.

For the next four months of her life, Sloane would be living with two males who terrified her.

Namely, a pair of rats named Kevin and Ricky. Due to Sloane's (extremely reasonable) fear of rodents, very, very few things in life would have convinced her to share square footage with two of them. Come to think of it, there was only *one thing* in life that could have convinced her—the fifteen-year-old girl shrieking with joy and running toward her now.

"Ivy!" Sloane opened her arms. It had been six months since she'd seen her niece.

"Aunt Sloane!"

They hugged. A ball of emotion formed in Sloane's throat as she breathed in the peppermint scent of Ivy's shampoo. Deep love. Happiness. A sense of completeness.

Her alarm clock back home in Los Angeles had jolted her awake this morning at 3:45 a.m. She'd flown to Chicago. Changed planes. Flown to Bangor. Jumped into the 2015 white Suburban that Brooke had left for her in the airport's long-term parking. Now here she was in the quaint town of Groomsport, Maine, collecting her niece and her niece's beloved pet rats. Sloane was less than a minute into her time with Ivy and already everything that had gone into making this trip possible—the planning, the prep for working remotely, today's travel—was worth it.

They stepped apart.

"You look beautiful," Sloane said.

The girl beamed. "Thank you."

Ivy's appearance always reminded Sloane in the best possible way of the phrase "peaches and cream." Her long hair was the peaches part, a mellow shade of red. Her complexion was cream, dotted with auburn freckles. At this age, her almond-shaped brown eyes, as well as her nose and mouth, appeared to be a bit too large for her petite face. Almost as if Ivy's bone structure was lagging behind her features in a race— huffing, puffing, and entreating her features to slow down until it could catch up. Ivy had dressed her five-foot-two frame in a T-shirt emblazoned with a smiling rat on the front, Nike shorts, and Birkenstocks.

"I missed you," Sloane told her honestly.

"I missed you! Thank you so, *so* much for coming to Maine to stay with me."

"You're welcome. I'm excited about it." *Excited about everything, that is, except the rodents.*

"I really did think at first that I wanted to go with Mom and Dad to the Middle East." Her parents were both geologists and from time to time accepted overseas assignments. "But then my church invited me to volunteer as an intern at their summer camps in the mornings. And I'm taking driver's ed. I don't want to leave my friends, and it would be a bummer not to start my sophomore year when everyone else does." She paused to inhale. "But mostly I changed my mind about the Middle East after becoming a rat mom. When I received Kevin and Ricky as my birthday gifts I was like, 'There's no way I can go overseas.' And Mom was like, 'You're the only child left in my nest. There's no way you and Kevin and Ricky can stay in the States alone.' And I was like, 'What if Aunt Sloane came to stay with me?'"

"And here I am."

"You're my hero! Come meet the rats."

They walked up the path toward the cute historic house where Ivy had been staying the past two nights, with her friend Faith.

Ivy was the only child of Sloane's only sibling, an older sister named Harper. Harper had placed Ivy with a family through open adoption when Ivy was a baby. Back then, Brooke and Jared Ray had become Ivy's parents and Ivy had become the youngest of their four children. Brooke and Jared, who operated under the worldview of "the more the merrier," had also welcomed Harper and Sloane into their family, inviting them to be as involved as they wished to be with Ivy. Sloane had joyfully taken them up on that and *thank God for*

Ivy. Since her birth the girl had been a ray of sunshine in Sloane's life.

"I'm sorry I wasn't able to make it to Groomsport in time to see your parents," Sloane said. They'd departed for the Middle East on Saturday, and it was now Monday.

"They would have loved that. It's okay, though. You had a big etiquette training event this past weekend, right?"

"Right."

They entered the foyer and Ivy flourished both hands toward a large, two-story cage. "Here they are."

A shudder darted down Sloane's spine at the sight of two white rats with pink eyes and long tails. They were scurrying over enough mini toys to stock a preschool.

"They're smart and sweet."

"Ah."

"I'm sure they'll warm up to you right away."

Sloane highly doubted that but saw no reason to voice that thought. "Nice to meet you, Kevin and Ricky."

"Nice to meet you, too," Ivy answered for them in a high-pitched rat voice.

Faith and her dad emerged to help load Ivy's suitcases and rat condominium into the Suburban. Ivy secured the cage with a seat belt "for their safety" and draped some towels over it in order to "keep them from feeling anxious" during the car ride.

Sloane plugged the address of their apartment into the Maps app on her phone and then she and Ivy were coasting along Groomsport's main street. Storefronts showed off muted shades of red, blue, green, cream, and gray. As picturesque as ever, the historic town nestled amid hills that funneled down to the harbor, where boats of all shapes and sizes bobbed on the swells.

The car windows open, breeze rushed against Sloane's skin. Today was July eighth and her home state of Maine was basking in a quintessential, mid-summer, Down East day. With two hours to go before sunset, it was still warm enough for short sleeves. But barely, seeing as how the air here carried a crisp, bracing, salty tang.

Groomsport had begun as a ship-building village in the late 1700s. One hundred years later—thanks to the natural beauty of its mountains, rivers, and lakes—wealthy families had begun to build summer cottages here. This was one of the prettiest spots in one of the prettiest states in America and the charm of Groomsport was a good representation of the charm of Ivy's overall life—so different from the hardscrabble beginning Sloane and Harper had experienced. They'd been raised thirty minutes inland from here in the working-class town of Waldoboro, yet their childhood might as well have taken place a continent away from Ivy's childhood.

It had been a long time since Sloane had spent four straight months in Maine. In fact, she hadn't spent that much consecutive time here since leaving the state at eighteen to attend the University of Pennsylvania on a full ride. She'd remained in Philadelphia for six years after graduation, then moved to California, where she'd been for the last four.

Since relocating to the West Coast, she'd seen Ivy as much as she could manage, but less than she'd wanted to, and certainly less than she had when she lived on the East Coast. Plus, she loved Maine best at this time of year. So her heart had begun saying *yes* even before Brooke had finished asking Sloane if she'd be willing to stay with Ivy.

Her phone's map drew them north, parallel to the ocean. The buildings and houses became more infrequent. On the outskirts of town, the map voice prompted her to turn left into a driveway.

"This is exciting." Sloane leaned forward in her seat.

Ordinarily, Sloane stayed at Ivy's parents' house when she

came to Groomsport. They weren't going that route this time because back when Brooke and Jared had accepted the Middle East assignment, they'd made their rambling farmhouse available on a house-swapping site. It had booked immediately.

When Ivy had chosen not to join her parents overseas, Brooke had rented a garage apartment for Sloane and Ivy and been happy to do so since she and Jared were making out like bandits on their house-swapping arrangement. As far as Sloane was concerned, the apartment was the best-case scenario. For one thing, Ivy's house was jammed with decades of stuff. For another thing, this apartment wasn't Sloane's California house or Ivy's Maine house. Because it was set apart from their usual routines, staying here felt special.

Residents of this region of Maine might not know that this property was formally named The Gables. But she'd bet they'd all seen the house on this piece of land. From Route 1, the Victorian mansion was partially visible through the woods and so magnificent that you slowed your car when you drove past, or made up fairytales about it in your imagination, or ran searches about it online. It had long been owned by a couple named the Brewsters, who were patrons of everything from school fundraising auctions, to food kitchens, to local theaters. Sloane had a vivid, star-struck memory of the Brewsters giving a speech at her high school once.

The pavement took them on a curving route through spruce trees. Ivy sighed dreamily as they passed the mansion.

"Harper and I used to call it The Prince's House," Sloane said.

"Oh? Chelsea, Caleb, Jordan, and I called it The Make-Believe House."

A distance behind and to the side of the main house stood the free-standing building where Sloane and Ivy would be staying. The first floor contained a four-car garage. The second floor, their apartment.

The garage had been built in the same general style as the one-hundred-and-thirty-year-old mansion and was painted the same colors. Dark green, medium green, brown, beige. However, this structure smacked of new construction. Three dormer windows jutted from an A-line roof covered in slate shingles. At the base of each window, flower boxes burst with white geraniums and ivy.

Sloane peered at their apartment through the windshield, enchanted.

"It's even cuter inside," Ivy assured her. She and her mom had toured it a few months back before signing the rental papers.

Sloane carried one edge of the rat condominium up the exterior staircase, Ivy carrying the other. This proximity to rats was spurring a case of full-body shivers of revulsion.

The landing that served as the entrance to the apartment was just big enough for a café table and two outdoor chairs. They set the condominium on the little table while Sloane punched the code she'd been given into the keypad. The lock whirred open, then they carefully set the condominium inside.

"Isn't this apartment *so* nice?" Ivy asked.

"It's beyond perfect."

Ivy crossed to a doorway on the far side of the space. "This is the room with the twin bed, so this one's mine." She disappeared inside.

Sloane took in the open-concept living areas. Most of the walls were white, except for the living room's accent wall, which was covered in striped light-blue-and-white wallpaper. Oak hardwood floors. A pastel rug supported furniture accented with bright, patterned pillows. The kitchen's white countertops and backsplash offset yellow cabinets. The overall effect was feminine, stylish, and serene.

Sloane arrived at her bedroom, which contained a queen bed, a nightstand, and a narrow desk facing the dormer window. The air smelled of fresh paint and grapefruit. Everything looked brand new.

Were she and Ivy the first people to stay here?

When Brooke had sent her pictures of this place, Sloane had responded with amazement. Ivy's parents did fine financially, but it had been clear to her that this apartment was beyond their budget. Brooke had explained with enthusiasm that they'd gotten a killer deal because the owners of The Gables were very picky about who they'd let stay on the property. They were only open to renting it to friends of friends. Since the real estate agent Jennifer was a friend of Brooke's, the apartment had gone to Brooke, which felt outrageously fortunate.

The beautiful bedding reminded Sloane how exhausted she was—sending her into a daydream that included her silk pajamas and sliding between those sheets—

"Aunt Sloane?"

She startled. "Hmm?"

"I just tried to wash my hands in the bathroom but there's no water."

Sloane stepped to the shiny bathroom positioned between the two bedrooms.

Ivy moved the sink handle back and forth. Nothing happened. She glanced at Sloane like, *Are you seeing this?*

"Let me check the kitchen." Sloane tried the faucet there. No water.

Ivy returned to her room as Sloane pulled her phone from her purse to text Jennifer, who'd been friendly and efficient via email and text messages.

SLOANE

The apartment is absolutely wonderful, and we entered without any issues. Thanks! We just discovered that there's no running water. Is there a way for me to turn that on?

Leaning wearily against the kitchen counter, she waited for an answering text. She'd put on this fitted black-and-white-striped top, this wide knee-length skirt, and these flats what felt like a week ago—way, way back when her day had begun. She was rumpled and, in the bathroom mirror a second ago, she'd seen that her hair was flat. She'd spilled coffee on her skirt and had been dogged by the scent of coffee ever since. She could *not conceive* of ending this day with anything other than a shower.

JENNIFER

Head to the main house and knock. Explain the situation and I'm sure the owner will be able to get it running ASAP!

"Ivy," she called, "I'm going to the main house to discuss the water situation. I'll be right back and then we'll finish unpacking the car."

"Cool."

The stairs she'd come up minutes ago, she now took in the opposite direction. A flagstone path led her through grounds lush with purple hydrangeas and white roses. When the path forked—one direction leading to the back patio, one direction leading toward the front door—she took the one toward the front.

Now that she was up close, she saw that the mansion had been superbly maintained. Not an inch of flaking paint or splintered wood anywhere. Its earth-tone colors gave it a rich, masculine vibe.

Well done, Brewsters.

She didn't see a doorbell, so she knocked. Almost at once, she heard answering footsteps approach.

Though she was not at her absolute best, she was certainly presentable. Sloane straightened her posture and assumed a friendly, I'm-sorry-to-be-interrupting-you expression.

The door swung open.

And there . . . In the opening . . .

Was Max Cirillo.

In real life. Actually him.

Her expression dropped as she stared at him with confusion and shock.

He did not look confused or shocked. He regarded her with a hard, angry, and satisfied glint in his eyes.

Chapter Two

Sloane's brain scrambled, cherry picking elements of him. The thick, black hair and olive complexion that spoke of his mother's Greek heritage. The unusual pale green eyes that had come to him through his father. Dark stubble covered the lower part of his face and jaw. His six-foot two height seemed taller in this moment than it had back when she'd been accustomed to it. Lips—soft yet cynical. Body—fit and strong.

For three years, he'd been her college friend. Then for six years, her business partner. But four years had passed since she'd seen or spoken to him and now Max was both wildly familiar and completely foreign.

He held a strangely shaped metal object at his side and wore a gray crewneck sweater, jeans, and expensive-looking sneakers. She'd never seen these clothes on him before.

What a nonsensical thought. *Of course* she'd never seen these clothes on him.

Max.

She'd determined never to interact with him again. Yet here

he was in a place he should not be. What in the world was happening right now? Her brain was reeling—

"Strange," he said, "that an etiquette expert would knock on a door and then say absolutely nothing to the person who answers."

Obviously, he knew about her business, My Fair Lady Etiquette. "Etiquette does not apply to you and me," she said tightly.

"Oh? I'd no idea there were things in your world to which etiquette does not apply."

"Just one thing." She gave him a telling look.

He had the gall to *wink*.

She drew back her shoulders. "I'm here to speak with Mr. and Mrs. Brewster."

"That will be difficult seeing as how Mr. and Mrs. Brewster are deceased."

"Deceased?"

"You're remembering them from when you were in high school. They were getting up in years then and that was fifteen years ago."

A blush rushed up her cheeks. Now that she thought about it, the Brewsters had been quite old when she was in high school. "In that case, I'm here to speak to the current owners."

"Owner. Singular." He appeared to be relishing this painful exchange. "You're speaking to him."

His statement was too awful to absorb. It hung in her ears, going round and round. *Please let him be toying with me. Please let someone else own this estate.* "You've had your fun. Now I'd very much like to speak to the owners so that I may address an issue with them."

"What's your issue?"

"There's no running water in the garage apartment."

"Oh?" he said, droll. With fake surprise, he lifted the metal object he held. "Look what I have here. The tool needed to get water flowing to the garage apartment." He stared at her dead-on, one eyebrow raised.

He'd answered the door carrying the tool to turn on the water. Because he'd known she'd be coming to complain about the lack of water. Because he'd *purposely* turned off the flow. "You knew that Ivy and I were the ones moving into the garage apartment," she concluded.

He said nothing. His smug expression was answer enough.

"How did this happen?" she asked. "How did Ivy and I end up in an apartment that you own?"

"Fate?"

Dawning understanding was coursing through her in hot ripples. She'd once known Max very well. He was cunning and the type of person who'd buy a well-known property like The Gables purely to prove to the world that he was wealthy enough to do so. "You did this. Somehow you arranged it so that Brooke would rent this particular apartment."

"Don't give me too much credit—"

"—I give you no credit—"

"—because it wasn't hard. When I heard that you were coming back, I remembered that Brooke's friend Jennifer works in real estate. I mentioned to Jennifer that I was considering renting out my apartment for an *incredibly cheap* price, but only to renters who she knew personally and who would stay at least four months. I've had more difficulty putting on a T-shirt than I had arranging this."

Anger pounded against her temples. "Why would you want me and Ivy living in the garage apartment?"

"I've always liked Ivy a lot, as you know. But her living in the apartment is just incidental. It's you I want there."

"For what purpose?"

"Closure."

She glared at him.

He made a *tsk* sound. "Glaring is not good etiquette."

"What do you mean by *closure*?"

"An explanation. And an apology." His tone was extremely smooth and casual. The more smooth and casual Max's delivery, the less he liked you.

"You will not be receiving either of those things from me." She was known for her calm and poise. They were hallmarks of her personality. Yet in this moment, Sloane could feel her grip on calm and poise disintegrating. Holding her head high, she strode off the porch.

"I thought you wanted your water turned back on."

"No need." She didn't look back. "Ivy and I are moving out."

"You bet. Go ahead and do that if you want to stick Brooke and Jared with a giant bill."

Her steps whipped to a halt, which sent her long skirt rushing forward before falling against her shins. She forced her chin in his direction.

"The rental agreement they signed," he explained, "has lots of very fine print but is completely legal. Breaking the lease carries a sizeable penalty."

Her blood pressure skyrocketed. "I'll need to see a copy of that agreement."

He grinned. In his contradictory way, he *liked* that she'd made that demand. It showed how wily and untrusting she'd become, thanks in large part to her history with him.

He lifted papers off the entry table, met her where she stood, and handed over the agreement. This, too, he had anticipated.

She glanced over it. No way was she going to read the whole thing with him as her audience. But she definitely *would* read the whole thing. Every word. "What's your plan?" she asked, looking up. "To force me to stay in an apartment with no running water?"

"What kind of monster do you think I am? I'm a benevolent landlord and will gladly turn on your water." He walked to a spot near the driveway and lifted a lid off what she assumed was the main water valve. As always, his body moved with athletic grace and easy confidence.

Clutching the papers, she made her way toward the apartment like a train thundering along tracks.

"Happy housewarming," he called mockingly. The sound of his amused chuckle followed her.

She shut the door behind her and locked it with a snap.

This was a disaster.

The summer and fall Sloane had envisioned was folding in on itself like the papers she was unconsciously folding into smaller and smaller rectangles.

This was a disaster.

Max adjusted the valve to allow for the flow of water, then straightened.

He'd lost numerous things in his life. He'd lost the home he'd lived in up until the age of fourteen. He'd lost his anonymity. He'd lost his family's good name. But losing Sloane was the loss that had cut him the deepest.

Back inside his house, he set the tool aside and walked straight through to the den at the back. From here, a wall of sliding doors gave him a clear view of the garage.

Sloane was back. And not just back but living steps from

his house. Satisfaction filled his chest as he crossed his arms. The payoff of this was even greater than he'd anticipated.

Memories of the night he'd met her circled like a whirlpool, clearer in some ways than things that had happened to him yesterday.

It had been near the end of his freshman year at Penn. He'd just finished dinner with friends at a Philadelphia restaurant within walking distance of a Coldplay concert. As usual, he ordered the cheapest thing on the menu—a hot dog and chips that night. And, as usual, he hoped no one would notice he'd ordered the cheapest thing. The restaurant had been packed with people who, unlike him, could afford tickets to the concert. Lots of Coldplay T-shirts and excited talking and drinking. As the concert's start time neared, the place emptied in a rush.

"Sure you don't want to at least walk over there with us?" his buddy asked. "There might be someone scalping a ticket you could buy."

"Nah, I need to study." A lie.

His friends slapped him on the back, gave him fist bumps, then left him standing next to a bus-stop pole.

A pack of college girls exited the restaurant and he watched almost the exact same goodbye scene play out between a brunette and her friends. The rest of the girls made their way toward the concert. The brunette stayed behind.

Suddenly it was the two of them waiting for the bus in surroundings that turned quieter and quieter. She gave Max the small, noncommittal smile you give strangers in response to brief eye contact before looking away.

She had a pale oval face and generous lips. Her brown hair was parted in the middle and hung past her shoulders. It had volume but no curl. Dark eyes. Very little makeup. Her white shirt collar folded neatly over the neckline of her navy sweater.

Her height was average—not tall, not short. Thanks to her skinny jeans, he could see that she had a good body.

His first impression? Unremarkable. Pretty but not beautiful. There was kindness in her face and modesty in her clothes. She reminded him of the neighborhood girls he'd known back home, who were nice and who you liked just fine but never dated.

He didn't see a reason to bother making conversation with her.

Except . . .

He was noticing there *were* a few unusual things about her. Almost every girl her age he knew would pass time at a bus stop looking down at her phone. Her chin was up, face turned to the side, feet planted exactly together. She held herself very still. She was polished, in the way that some of the rich girls he knew were polished. Yet if she was rich, she'd be going to the concert.

"Are you in college around here?" he asked, deciding conversation with her might be worth the effort.

She looked over, revealing slight surprise that he'd spoken. "I am. At Penn."

"Same here. What year are you?"

"Freshman."

"Me too."

"What's your major?" she asked.

"Business."

"I'm also a business major."

"Huh. Lots of similarities." He smiled. "Next you're going to tell me that you're from Maine."

Her eyes rounded and he saw that she had long, thick eyelashes. "I actually *am* from Maine."

"No."

She released a huff of amusement. "I truly am. I know for a

fact, though, that you're not from my hometown of Waldoboro. I'm familiar with everyone in Waldoboro who's my age."

"I'm from Groomsport originally but moved to Montville for high school."

"I know Groomsport well. My little niece lives there."

"You're basically the female version of me."

"Or maybe," she said with gentle teasing, "you're the male version of me."

He stuck out his hand. "I'm Max Cirillo."

She showed no sign of recognizing his name, which was good. "Sloane Madison." She had a solid handshake. Firm and brief. "It's a pleasure."

They'd talked easily while they'd waited. When the bus came, he took the seat in front of hers, then twisted to face her so they could continue talking on the ride to campus.

Max only went out with girls who were beautiful, knew they were beautiful, and advertised their beauty. He felt sexual chemistry with girls who wore low-cut tops and high-cut skirts. He didn't feel sexual chemistry toward Sloane. But he did like her.

At Penn, he'd walked her to her dorm. They'd said goodnight without exchanging numbers. But then, two days later, in the lecture hall for Economics, he'd noticed her sitting a few rows below and to the right of him. The next time he'd entered that class, he'd sat next to her. When finals rolled around, they'd studied together.

Fall of their sophomore year, they'd had two classes together and shared more and more study sessions. When one of them had to miss class, the other would supply notes. When professors assigned group projects, they paired up.

Over time, he'd learned that his joking comment—that she was basically the female version of him—was truer than he could have imagined. They had the same personality—both driven, success-oriented, sensible. Both personable and confident. The two of them were at the top of their class, Sloane even more so than he was. They both had brains built to excel at business.

Max's phone vibrated in his pocket. Though he didn't pull his phone free, the buzzing jolted him back to the present.

Sloane hadn't changed much in the past four years. Her expressive brown eyes were exactly the same, glittering the way they always had. She was the type of person who never varied her hairstyle. She'd added some caramel-colored highlights to the front, which were flattering. But otherwise her hair was still the color and length he remembered.

Her face and body were slightly more lean. Was she eating enough?

She wore pale pink lipstick now, which suited her.

She'd switched her perfume. It smelled of coffee.

Nothing romantic had ever passed between them. Yet his relationship with her had been longer-lasting and far more important to him than any of his romances had been. Right up until Sloane had stabbed him in the back.

He didn't care enough about any of his past girlfriends to pull the strings needed to land one of them in his garage apartment. But with Sloane?

The opposite was true.

Sloane delighted in her morning ritual.

When the weather permitted, which it did the majority of the time in California, she started her day with a cup of coffee outdoors. By the time her mug was empty, she'd have read her devotional, prayed, and done a paragraph or two of journaling.

On this, her first morning in Darth Vader's apartment, she

carried her mug, devotional, Bible, and journal to the café table on her landing. Savoring her first sip of coffee, she soaked in Maine's summer splendor—

Her vision intersected with the sight of Max.

The coffee went down the wrong way and she ended up coughing to clear droplets from her airway.

In a mocking salute, he raised his mug from where he sat at the outdoor table on his expansive patio, wearing a white T-shirt and plaid pajama pants. Sloane herself had on silk pajamas beneath a pink chenille robe. Even with the robe, the weather was on the chilly side for her. Max was only wearing the T-shirt. But then, Max had always been warm-natured—

Ignore him.

He knew about her morning ritual. He'd come outside to ruin it for her. She scooted her chair around so that instead of facing the larger view of The Gables, she faced the landing's half wall and treetops. Well. Treetops were also lovely to look at in the morning.

She opened her devotional and tried to process the first sentence, but the meaning wouldn't penetrate. She could *feel* Max's attention, beating against her back.

She'd yet to even *begin* to reconcile herself to the fact that she'd be spending the next four months in a garage apartment that he owned. She'd not made peace with that. Not accepted it. She had, however, gone over the rental agreement. Clearly, Brooke and Jared had signed it without reading it. They'd certainly never have consented to such a large monetary penalty for breaking the lease. Sloane had called the law firm listed, and they'd confirmed the document to be legitimate.

Max's footfalls crunched near her position.

"I slept better last night," he called up to her, "than I've slept since you moved to California."

She said nothing.

"How did you sleep?" he asked.

She slid her chin in his direction, observing him the way she'd observe a cockroach on her bathroom floor. Max came to a stop on the lawn below, his hair in disarray. Unfairly, his features had hardened and matured with age in such a way that he was even more handsome now than he'd been when younger. And he'd been mysterious-looking and gorgeous back then. Max's face, coloring, and charisma came together in such a way that they'd always tugged at the romantic dreams of women. She'd seen the evidence of that a thousand times.

Fortunately for her, she'd always recognized that *Max* recognized exactly how appealing he was. Which had helped her remain immune. They were both now thirty-two, him six months older than she. Max's understanding of his appeal had likely grown tenfold because at this age he wasn't merely handsome. He'd become both handsome *and* a multimillionaire. Which was supremely irritating.

"I slept poorly," she said.

"I had the garage apartment designed for my mom with the best of everything. So I know you didn't sleep poorly because of the quality of the mattress or sheets."

"It wasn't the mattress or sheets," she said meaningfully.

He chuckled, pleased to have destroyed her rest. "Enjoying your coffee more than your night's sleep?"

"I only enjoy my coffee when I'm left to do so in solitude."

Ivy emerged from the apartment in a voluminous sweatshirt and leggings. She followed Sloane's attention downward. "*Max?*"

"Ivy." He opened his arms.

She dashed downstairs and hugged him.

"I remember toddler Ivy," he said as they separated, "and elementary school Ivy but this version is your best yet."

"I think I was eleven the last time I saw you. I'm fifteen now."

"Try not to break the heart of every boy at your high school, okay? Have pity."

Ivy glowed. "Boys aren't really that interested in me."

"Only because they're intimidated by your greatness."

"What are you . . ." Ivy glanced with confusion at Sloane, then back to Max. "What brings you here?"

"I live here."

Her jaw dropped. "You live at The Gables?"

"Yes. Just so you know, my company is thriving so I'm hugely wealthy."

"Wow!"

"He's also pig-headed and untrustworthy," Sloane added. She hadn't felt up to explaining the identity of their landlord to Ivy yet. She'd intended to do so later in the day. Her way, after coffee. Add that to the list of things Max had destroyed.

"You two had a big fight years ago, right?" Ivy asked Sloane.

"Yes," Sloane answered, crisp.

"Have you guys made up?"

"No."

"Ooh." Ivy bit her bottom lip and winced at Max. "Awkward."

"Only for her," Max said.

Simultaneously, Sloane said, "Only for him."

"I'd do anything for you, Ivy." Max disarmed females with over-the-top statements like that one. "Please let me know if there's anything you need to make your stay with me more comfortable. Gucci purse, Tiffany bracelet—"

"Do not take that bait," Sloane warned her niece.

Ivy laughed. She'd always been a huge fan of Max. "Your apartment is really great. I love it. I don't think there's anything we're going to need."

"Except a security gate to keep intruders away from the apartment," Sloane murmured.

His attention sliced to Sloane. He had the hearing of a fox. "Owners can't be intruders."

"Until just this moment, I would have concurred with that."

Ivy giggled nervously.

"See you soon, Ivy." He moved off.

"See you soon, Max."

Ivy ascended, coming to a stop next to Sloane's table.

Across the garden, Max resumed his seat on his patio, his focus still fixed on Sloane.

"Did you know he was the owner of this property?" Ivy asked in a stage whisper.

"I found out yesterday afternoon."

"Why didn't you tell me?"

"Because I was trying to come to terms with it first. He orchestrated things so that we'd move in here."

Ivy whistled. "Why'd he do that?"

"He says he wants closure."

Ivy's smile communicated encouragement. "I really liked it when you two were friends. Maybe, living so close together, you'll both get closure and be able to forgive each other."

"Maybe." Sloane couldn't very well scream *NEVER!* to the concept of forgiveness with a Bible sitting inches away.

"There's this . . . spark-y vibe between you and Max." Ivy flashed her hands open and closed to demonstrate.

"I don't know what you mean."

"I mean spark-y." More flashing hands. "Being near you guys right now reminded me that the vibe was there between you guys before, too."

Sloane had been a reserved fifteen-year-old who wouldn't have insisted to her adult aunt that she had a spark-y vibe with a man. Yet she *loved* that her niece was spunky enough to speak her mind.

It wasn't that Ivy was indestructibly assertive. Ivy frequently exhibited self-consciousness and shyness. However, she usually pushed past those in order to say and do whatever was true to her. That was Ivy at this age—a charming mix of gawky and brave. Also sweet, goofy, impatient, and enthusiastic.

"It's been a long time since you were near Max and me simultaneously," Sloane said calmly. "You would have been in elementary school."

"But I was a smart elementary schooler. Smart enough to notice sparks." Ivy peeked toward The Gables. "He's looking at you like he's a panther who wants to eat you."

"If he's looking at me like he wants to eat me, it's because he hates me and wants to kill me."

Ivy shrugged—the universal teenage symbol of willingness to dismiss one topic and move to another. She dropped into the empty chair. "Is this a good time to talk about my big summer plan?"

"Sure. Do you mean working at the church and taking driver's ed and spending time at the beach with your doting aunt?"

"No, my *bigger* summer plan." Ivy lifted her eyebrows a few times. "Mom said she told you about how I want to find my birth father."

Sloane braced inwardly. The topic of Ivy's parentage was an emotional one for her. "Your mom did tell me about that, yes."

"Okay. So, I've been thinking about my birth father a lot lately. I can't really explain why. Except that I feel a sense of incompleteness. I . . . *need* to know more. I'm hoping to find out who he is so I can meet him."

"All right, but I feel honor bound to ask how it will affect you if he's not ready to meet you? Or doesn't turn out to be a good guy?"

"If that happens, I'll deal. I really want to give this a try. You'll help me?"

"I'll always help and support you in any way that I can."

"Thank you." Ivy hopped to her feet. "I'll be right back with food. Do you want anything?"

"Fresh coffee?"

"Yep." Ivy swiped up Sloane's mug and sailed indoors.

The stereotypical oldest child was high-achieving and rule following. In Sloane's family, those traits had somehow skipped over Harper, older by two years, and landed on Sloane. Harper had been beautiful, sensitive, free-wheeling, creative. Unfortunately, she'd also been wounded, unreliable, and self-destructive.

Growing up, Sloane and Harper had been close. Then Harper had graduated from high school, left home the day after, and moved to Boston. For the next year and a half, Sloane's contact with her had been scant. Until the day Harper called out of the blue and bluntly announced that she'd given birth to a baby girl.

Sloane had been shocked.

Dad had been shocked.

They'd driven to Harper's apartment in Boston and met five-day-old baby Ivy.

On that late-fall day, Sloane had been seventeen years old, a studious girl with a singular aim—get a scholarship to college so she could better her circumstances in life.

Instantly, though, when she'd held her niece in her arms and looked down into that rosebud face, her world had expanded to encompass Ivy. Even then, Ivy's hair had been ginger, her skin milky, her temperament sunny. For Sloane it had been love at first sight.

Here, Sloane had thought, *is at last a family member who might love me, who might stay, who might be kind, who might care.*

In the weeks and months that followed, Sloane had made several weekend trips to visit Harper and Ivy. Harper had needed *a lot* of help and Sloane had tried to give it. It hadn't been enough. Or even close to enough. On one of those Boston weekends when Ivy was five months old, Harper had sat Sloane down and informed her that she wasn't cut out for motherhood.

Sloane remembered where she'd been sitting during that conversation. On the crummy blue sofa in Harper's efficiency apartment. There'd been rain on the windows, the warm weight of Ivy asleep on Sloane's shoulder, dismay in Sloane's heart.

Harper had gone on to say many things. That she wanted Ivy to have the best life possible but knew she couldn't provide that for her daughter. That she'd found a couple who were older, married, settled. They already had a biological daughter followed by two adopted sons of different ethnicities.

"The parents are named Brooke and Jared Ray," Harper had told her. *"They're cool with open adoption, so we can see Ivy a lot. It'll be good for Ivy to grow up with lots of siblings. They live in Maine, so it will be like a do-over for Ivy. She'll get to have the childhood in Maine I wish we'd had."*

Sloane had been sick with grief.

Ivy was supposed to have been the one who loved Sloane. The one who stayed. She'd felt like a starving person presented with a meal, only to have the meal jerked away after just one bite.

But Harper's mind had been made up.

The Rays had swiftly adopted Ivy.

Teenaged Sloane hadn't known the thing that the passage of years had proven absolutely to be true. Namely, that Ivy's adoption had been the very, very best thing.

For all of them.

Brooke and Jared were laid-back, warm, and outgoing. Their house brimmed with exuberant commotion. Their door had *always* been wide open to the birth family members of their three adopted children. The Rays' generosity meant that Sloane had been able to see and spend time with Ivy. Which had become easier to do seeing as how the Rays' house in Groomsport was a short drive from Waldoboro—much closer than Boston.

The most surprising blessing of all was that Brooke had taken one look at Sloane and immediately recognized her pain and loneliness. Brooke had a big heart. Big enough to mother her four children and to make room under her wing for Sloane, too.

Even now, Sloane teared up when she thought about it. More than once, she'd tried to express her gratitude to Brooke. Brooke would listen and indicate that she understood. Yet because Brooke and Jared hadn't walked Sloane's path, they could never *fully* understand. Brooke and Jared both had happily married parents. They had close-knit, "white-picket-fence" extended families. So, no. They could never fully understand how much Sloane's relationship with Ivy and with them meant to her.

Ivy returned with a bowl of Cheerios and milk topped with banana slices. She handed Sloane her mug, settled at the table, and downed a few bites of cereal.

Harper's long ago wish for her daughter, that Ivy would have the best life possible? It had come true.

"So," Ivy said, "back to my big summer plan! You're the

only person left who knew me during the first five months of my life."

The statement landed heavy on Sloane because of why it was true. It was true because Harper had died of an overdose four years ago and because Sloane's father had never attempted to know Ivy.

"Is there anything you can tell me about my biological father?" Ivy asked.

"I can tell you that he was not around during your first five months. He was already out of the picture by then." Sloane took a swallow of coffee, tasting its dark, chocolatey flavors. "I asked Harper about him, but she didn't tell me much. Only that he'd been a short-term boyfriend."

"She didn't say his name?"

"No."

"Anything else you know about him?"

"I'm guessing he had red or ginger hair. For which I will forever be grateful." Fondly, she tugged a lock of Ivy's hair.

"I must look like him, right? Because I don't look like Harper."

This, too, landed heavy. Sloane loved Ivy's look. Yet it was true that she didn't resemble Harper very much. "Your eyes are brown like Harper's were." Though, Harper's eyes had been world-weary. Ivy's were open and trusting. "And Harper had freckles like you do."

"But her face was really different. Sort of hard and pointy." Ivy took another bite of cereal. "My face is soft."

"Wonderfully so," Sloane said staunchly. As always, Sloane did not mention Ivy's etiquette lapses. At present: hunched posture and elbows on the table.

"Harper was a brunette." Ivy continued to list the differences between herself and her biological mother. "And my lips are puffier than hers were. More like yours, actually."

"Matching lips." Sloane blew Ivy a kiss.

Ivy blew Sloane a kiss back. "Any ideas how we could find my biological dad?"

Before Ivy's parents had gone overseas, Sloane and Brooke had talked at length about Ivy's interest in finding her birth father. Brooke, in her relaxed and imperturbable way, had made it clear that she and Jared viewed Ivy's desire to meet her biological father as perfectly natural. They understood, too, why Ivy wanted Sloane's assistance with her search. To Ivy, Brooke and Jared were Mom and Dad. But Sloane was her younger, cool auntie as well as the sister of Ivy's biological mother. As such, it made sense that Ivy would view Sloane as her ally in all things related to her biological relatives.

Brooke had told Sloane that she had their full blessing and permission to help Ivy with the search while they were away. And, in turn, Sloane had promised that she and Ivy would keep Brooke informed every step of the way.

Secretly, though, Sloane had been hoping Ivy would change her mind about finding her birth father. Selfishly, Sloane didn't want to share her niece with a man who'd invested nothing in Ivy except his DNA. More than that, she worried that this search would end in disappointment for Ivy, and she'd prefer to shield her from that.

"I suppose," Sloane said, "that your biological father's name might be on your adoption documents or birth certificate."

Thoughtfully, Ivy chewed cereal. "But a group of like ten Italian people have moved into my house. So I can't look for those documents there."

"When Harper passed away . . ." Would it always be painful to speak that sentence? Or would there come a day when she could say it with only gratitude for the years she'd had with her sister? "Dad and I put all of Harper's important belongings into storage containers." Two, to be factual. Harper's existence—reduced to two containers. "Those containers are at my dad's place. Any documents she would have had about your adoption or birth would be there."

Ivy straightened, brightening. "Oh! Can we go by there and look?"

"Sure. Maybe next week?" It would take that long for Sloane to pep-talk herself into seeing her father. "I'll call to see which day works for him."

"Perfect."

Chapter Three

The text had come in early this morning. Max had ignored it, hoping silence would serve as his answer.

An hour ago, near the end of his workday, Max had received another text from Felix that was a word-for-word replica of the first text. Max's biological father was letting Max know that he wouldn't be ignored.

The quickest way to get rid of this? To have the meeting Felix was requesting. So he'd told Felix he'd stop by Maple Lane when he left the office and was driving there now.

He'd much rather be driving home. He'd eaten breakfast outside again this morning during Sloane's coffee ritual, just like he had yesterday on her first morning at the apartment. That had been something, but not enough. The sooner he got home, the sooner he'd have a chance to spar with her again.

Max steered his Porsche along a wide, uphill curve. In the

eighteen years that had passed since he'd learned he was Felix's son, the knot of resentment he harbored toward Felix had never diminished in size. These days, though, he and Felix could be in the same room when the situation called for it, like it had this spring after Jude had been injured and they'd both gone to the hospital in New York. When they talked, they did so with the detachment of acquaintances, not with father/son closeness.

As a rule, they texted only when necessary.

This was the first time Felix had summoned Max for a one-on-one. Which was strange. What did Felix want?

Max coasted past Maple Lane's iron gates, currently standing open. As the estate's name suggested, the drive leading to the house was lined on both sides with maples. They were green now but would turn orange-red in the fall.

Max had loved this place when he was a kid, back when his mom had been the housekeeper here. The biggest perk of that job had been the opportunity to live rent-free on the estate. Their house—the house where he'd spent his childhood—had been out of sight of the main house, but just a short walk away. It was a historic three-bedroom that had been built for servants yet had been nicer than the houses of most Americans. Certainly nicer than the houses of his mom's parents and siblings.

The field where he and Jeremiah and Jude had played flag football passed on the right. To the left, behind those trees, a stream flowed. They'd fished there whenever the water ran high.

Usually, when you'd loved a place once, returning to it was pleasant. But for him, returning here was a bitter pill to swallow.

The enormous white stone mansion came into view.

The Camden family's banking empire had begun in the Gilded Age thanks to their Irish ancestor Finbar Camden. In subsequent generations, Finbar's sons and grandsons had spread out across America, establishing more and more banks. Maple Lane was built in 1905 by the descendant who'd brought the family's kingdom to the far northeast. Camdens had been living in this part of the country ever since.

Max parked on the circle drive, followed steps to the grand front door, and pressed the doorbell.

It didn't take Felix long to answer. "Good evening."

"Good evening."

As usual, Felix looked fit and impressive for a man in his sixties. Unlike Max, who preferred to dress casually and comfortably, Felix dressed like he was modeling for a tailor-shop ad. Today he wore black suit pants, a white business shirt, and a Hermes belt.

"Thank you for coming by." The older man led Max to his extravagant home office. "Please take a seat."

Max did so. "What can I do for you?" No point wasting time on chitchat.

"I wanted to talk to you about a piece of jewelry." Felix lowered into his chair on the far side of the desk.

Max tilted his head, waiting for an explanation.

"A tiara, specifically." Felix pushed a photograph toward him.

Max picked it up. He wasn't a jewelry person, but he didn't have to be a jewelry person to recognize that the tiara was extraordinary. A top and bottom row of square diamonds enclosed an inner pattern of diamonds that formed blocky, interlocking spirals. The top center of the tiara was wider than the sides, coming up to a gentle point. "It looks Greek."

"Yes. It's a Greek design called a meander tiara. This particular one was made by a jeweler named Bapst in 1856 for Empress Eugenie of France. At the time, she was married to Napoleon the third, the last Emperor of France. It contains six hundred and twelve diamonds. Three hundred and twenty carats' worth."

Max placed the photo back on the desk.

"When this tiara was made," Felix went on, "it contained at its center one of the most famous stones in the world, the Regent Diamond. That particular diamond is well over three hundred years old and has a long, dramatic history. At one point, it was placed in the hilt of Napoleon Bonaparte's sword. Later his nephew, Napoleon the third, set it in this tiara for his wife. The Regent Diamond remained in the tiara for eleven years before it was removed, and the tiara took on its final shape. The shape in this picture."

Max could not fathom what any of this had to do with him. "Where is the Regent Diamond now?"

"On display at the Louvre."

"And the tiara?"

"France no longer had monarchs by 1887. So Eugenie's tiara, along with many of the French crown jewels, were sold at auction that year. One-third of those jewels were purchased by Charles Lewis Tiffany of Tiffany and Co. Some he bought on behalf of clients, others he purchased to resell. After he transported them all back to New York, an ancestor of mine purchased Eugenie's tiara from Tiffany as a wedding gift for his bride. She wore it on their wedding day." He slid another photo to Max.

This picture showed a black-and-white image of a serious-looking couple. The man was in tails, the woman in an ornate white gown. The tiara was set into the puff of hair on top of her elegant head.

Max returned the photo. Looking at long-ago, rich Camdens wasn't his favorite pastime.

"The tiara has been passed down through my line of the

family since then," Felix said. "It's a part of Maple Lane's permanent art collection."

"Okay." Max waited, an ominous feeling coming over him.

"It's missing."

Max let a few moments of silence pass. "Missing?"

"It went missing when you and your mother moved away."

In a flash, Max *did* see what this tiara had to do with him. Anger lit a fuse inside him. "You think I stole this?"

"No."

"You think my mother stole this?"

"I do." Holding Max's gaze, Felix interlaced his hands. "Eugenie's tiara was displayed, along with other pieces of jewelry, in Maple Lane's library, in a display case that was also a safe of sorts. It was made of tempered glass. It had locking mechanisms. I unlocked it for Nicole so that she could dust and clean the jewelry. This was something she'd done many, many times before. But later that same day, she and Fiona had their fight. The next day, everything blew up. You two were gone. And so was the tiara."

A pause lengthened between them while Max's stomach gradually turned to stone. The nerve of this man to accuse his mother of this.

Felix Camden, former NFL quarterback and owner of three Super Bowl rings, had been America's golden boy. The famous family, the athletic ability, the looks. He'd been idolized. Women coveted him. Men were jealous of him. His first wedding to supermodel Isobel O'Sullivan had been televised live, which had lifted Felix and Isobel's fame even higher.

When it came out a few years later that Felix had been cheating on Isobel with her sister Fiona and that Fiona was pregnant, the scandal had been huge, setting off a gossip earthquake nationwide.

Max's mom, Nicole, had begun working here soon after. By

then, Felix had divorced Isobel and married Fiona, and they were expecting their first child, Jeremiah. Two years later, Jude had been born. Then a few months after Jude, Max had been born to Nicole.

In addition to cleaning and laundry, Mom had handled grocery shopping and most of the cooking at Maple Lane. Max couldn't remember anyone telling him that he was the employee's son. That's just how it had always been, from his first conscious thoughts. It was the only thing he'd known. All he was used to. He'd been too busy enjoying his childhood to waste time feeling resentful about his position in Maple Lane's pecking order.

Jude was his best friend, and he was close with Jeremiah, too. They'd grown up together—roaming Maple Lane's acres, playing sports, mastering video games, going to the same private schools.

His idyllic setup had ended when he was fourteen. After the fight Felix had referenced between Mom and Fiona, Mom had called a reporter and told that reporter something she'd never once told Max.

That Felix was his biological father.

Another scandal had followed. Also huge. Another gossip earthquake. From that point on, Max had had plenty of years to feel resentful.

Fiona had fired Mom, expelling her from Maple Lane. Max and his mother moved to a duplex in Montville where his high school years had been hard, rocky, and humiliating.

Felix had begun paying Mom child support. Eventually, he'd written checks to cover Max's tuition, room, and board at Penn. Felix had been willing to write many more checks. For example, he'd made clear that he would've given Max a generous allowance at college, would have provided a car, would have assisted with living costs in the years following graduation. But Max had been too proud to accept any of that from him. And when Max had rebuffed Felix's early attempts to establish a relationship between them, Felix had been too proud to continue trying.

Since Fiona had divorced Felix, Felix had lived at Maple Lane alone.

"Why couldn't Fiona have taken it?" Max asked coldly. "She had a bone to pick with you when it came out that you'd fathered a child with your housekeeper."

"She did have a bone to pick with me," Felix acknowledged. "But Fiona was my wife at the time, so she had money and expensive jewelry of her own. She knew that, even if she divorced me, her settlement would be enormous. Which it was."

"So, because my mother wasn't rich, she's your prime suspect?"

"That's partly why she's my prime suspect," Felix answered, unruffled. "Like I said, she also had access. And motivation. She was furious with this entire family and taking the tiara was a good form of revenge."

"If you suspected her, why didn't you come after her right away?"

"In Maple Lane's collection there are several other pieces that are of equal and even greater value. I was content to let Nicole keep the tiara for a time. I knew it would help her feel secure, help her feel she'd made me pay for my sins. But now she has other reasons to feel secure." Felix motioned toward Max. "You've built a successful company."

Max nodded.

"Jeremiah and Remy just got engaged," Felix continued. "I'd like to offer the tiara to Remy to wear on her wedding day if she desires. In order to do that, I need my property back."

Max held his silence.

"I'd be glad, of course," Felix said, "to also make it available to your bride on your wedding day. And to any granddaughters I might one day have on their wedding days."

Max set his teeth together.

"I've had my people keep an eye on Nicole, in case she tried to sell the tiara. We've never seen evidence of that. She still has it." Felix rose and went to stand at his window. "I have an appraiser coming to examine the full collection November first, so I'll need Eugenie's tiara back before then." He straightened an already straight curtain. "I could hire a private investigator. Or I could hand this story over to the media. But I've never wanted to go those routes for your sake. I think the two of us can handle this privately, don't you?"

"I don't believe my mother has it." His mom wasn't perfect, but she wasn't a thief.

Felix's expression took on a pitying tinge. "I think the two of us can handle this privately," he repeated. "Don't you?"

"I'll do what I can." Max left without another word.

Sloane had been looking forward to a relaxing Friday night in. However, before that could begin, she'd need to bring this Zoom meeting to a close. At the moment, she was positioned at her desk in the bedroom discussing the logistics of My Fair Lady's upcoming etiquette courses with a few of the freelancers who worked for her. They all lived on the West Coast. It was 3:00 p.m. in LA, which meant 6:00 p.m. in Groomsport.

Back in middle school, some of the girls in Sloane's grade had complained about having to go to cotillion class, where they learned things like manners and dancing. Sloane had been intrigued. Classes about manners? Dancing? She'd have adored the chance to take classes on those subjects but cotillion cost money her dad wasn't willing to pay. So she'd gone to the library and checked out books on etiquette.

From the first page of that first book, she'd been enamored with etiquette. It had blown her mind that she, a thirteen-year-old girl living in a small town in Maine, could learn the same manners used by kings and queens of international countries. She requested more books on the subject, which the librarians had transferred in for her from other libraries far and wide. She'd read voraciously. She'd practiced her newfound knowledge.

Etiquette had given Sloane a sense of power over her life. The first true sense of power she'd ever tasted. Ultimately, it had changed not only how others perceived her but, even more importantly, how she perceived herself.

After the crushing disappointment of everything that had gone down between her and Max, she'd fled to California because at that time Brooke and Jared's family had been there for a two-month-long assignment. When the Rays returned to Maine, Sloane stayed in Los Angeles.

Needing to invent a new career for herself from scratch, she'd naturally turned to her long-time hobby. Friends and acquaintances had come to her often over the years with etiquette questions, so she knew from experience how much she enjoyed coaching people in the subject. It had been a game changer to develop herself through etiquette. She was positive etiquette could be a game changer for others. She'd plunged in, naming her business My Fair Lady because she related so fully to Eliza Doolittle's life story.

She'd spoken with every hotel and every event planner in LA who would take a meeting with her. Soon, she was giving in-person sessions at hotels, country clubs, social clubs, businesses, and rec centers. She taught on afternoon tea, table manners, social etiquette, business etiquette, children's etiquette, teen etiquette, and etiquette for service-industry employees.

From there, she'd started recording her courses so that they could be purchased and viewed online. Because numerous clients asked for private lessons, she'd begun offering those, too.

She'd been working on My Fair Lady full-time for four years. While her income was incredibly modest compared to Max's income, she earned enough to support herself and provide herself with the sense of safety she craved.

During the upcoming months in Maine, she'd opted to work a lot less than usual. She'd paused the private lessons until her return. She'd hired and trained two women to teach the in-person LA events while she was away. The online side of her business would continue full force.

Sloane brought the meeting to a close by thanking everyone and extending a polite goodbye. She gave the others time to respond with polite goodbyes, then hit the button to end the session.

With that, she'd just completed her first week of working remotely while caring for Ivy. It had required problem solving, ingenuity, and adjusting. It had also been wonderful.

Sweet, restful solitude surrounded her. From her desk, she had a view of the driveway, The Gables, and nature all around. Tonight the sky looked like a watercolor painted with dusky blues and creamy whites.

Her attention drifted to the four framed items she'd brought with her from California and arranged next to her computer. A picture of herself and Harper as girls sitting side by side, their feet submerged in the run-down pool of the apartment complex where they'd lived at the time. Both of them were looking up and to the side at the camera, smiling. Two brown-haired sisters in summertime.

A picture of herself and Ivy from two years ago, when they'd visited Disneyland with Ivy's family.

A picture of Sloane's greatest inspiration—Her Royal Highness, the Princess of Wales. Also known as Catherine, the Countess of Chester. Also known as Kate Middleton.

Sloane changed out the photo in this particular frame annually on Kate's birthday, always updating it with one of the princess's epic style moments from the past year. The current picture showed Kate smiling in a sequined gown she'd paired with Queen Mary's Lover's Knot tiara. In one hand, she held a clutch. As always, Kate's posture was faultless, and she was making an art form of high heels and aspirational hair.

The final frame on Sloane's desk surrounded a cross-stitch of one of Kate's most famous quotes. *With grace and elegance, anything is possible.* Words Sloane lived by.

A faint squeaking sound reached her. Knowing what that sound meant, she made her way to the doorway of Ivy's room and peeked in. Ivy was away, at driver's ed. But, of course, the rats were here and one of them was running on his wheel. He was really going for it, his pale body sprinting so fast that his legs were a blur.

"Excellent cardio."

Sloane felt it best to handle Kevin and Ricky two ways. With compliments and distance. She had an irrational fear of them prying their cage open, hunting her down, and attacking. More than once the past few nights, when trying to fall asleep, she'd imagined she heard scuttling rat nails, which always brought to mind an image of rat teeth sinking into her skin. Thoroughly spooked, she'd turned on the lights. Only to see there was no need to repel an invading rat.

Kevin and Ricky had yet to make an escape. But should they ever do so, she wanted to have buttered them up with so much flattery that they'd treat her with mercy.

In the kitchen, she contemplated the inside of her fridge, trying to decide what sounded best for dinner. She preferred to consume food the way she did everything else. With class. Years ago, she'd learned that all aspects of life could be made more luxurious and fancier without much additional effort. For example, showers could be made more luxurious with beautiful-smelling bath products. Coffee could be made more luxurious with a frother. Sleepwear could be made more luxurious with choice of fabric. When it came to eating, this philosophy meant she didn't typically rely on frozen food, microwaved food, or fast food.

Tonight . . . maybe rosemary focaccia bread with slices of tomato and Manchego cheese?

She assembled her plate artfully, set a linen napkin next to it, then stuck her glass into the water dispenser mounted within the refrigerator door.

A rasping spurt of water made her jump. Then nothing. No flow of water.

She furrowed her brow—

Max had shut off the water again.

Pursing her lips, she went to the sink and tested the faucet. Which confirmed it.

This was his way of—of . . .

Summoning her. And irritating her.

Truth be told, Darth was doing an excellent job of irritating her even when their flow of water *wasn't* interrupted. He'd sat at his outdoor table every morning this week at the exact same time that she was outside. He hadn't spoken to her since that first morning. Even so, she'd found it almost impossible to turn her mind to her devotional while he was staring daggers at her back.

She'd been trying to ignore him. Trying *not* to think about him. *Not* look at his house. *Not* remember snippets of their past. *Not* hear his cars when they rumbled up and parked directly beneath the apartment.

It would be fantastic if she could blot Max out from the next four months of her life the way that thick black lines blotted out sensitive portions of classified documents. But no one had ever used the word *unassuming* to describe Max Cirillo. He'd rather cut off her water supply than let her blot him out.

Groaning with frustration, she made her way to her closet. Today's beige dress tied at the waist with a bow. Since it seemed she was incapable of donning footwear that *didn't* complement her dress—even when en route to deal with her difficult landlord—she eased her feet into slip-on sandals with raffia straps.

It didn't take her long to reach Max's front porch. For the second time in a week, she knocked.

Unlike the first time, on this occasion she knew well and good to prepare for a fight.

Chapter Four

Max opened his door to a stiff and irate Sloane. In response, he experienced an immediate rush of happiness.

Her clothing was as prissy and formal as ever. He had motion-sensor cameras mounted on the exterior of his house and so he knew that she'd only left the property in the Suburban twice today. She'd likely spent the rest of her day working inside the apartment. Even so, she was dressed like she was on her way to a baby shower. A white fabric headband that tied in a knot on top held back her hair with obedient precision. Her makeup didn't have a single smudge.

However, if she'd been a cartoon character, she'd have had steam coming out of her ears and eyebrows slashing down at the center. Take the prissy clothing and the cartoon anger, stir them up, and looking at Sloane in this moment was like looking at a furious teacup poodle.

Highly entertaining.

"I have no water," she stated, "at the apartment."

"Please come in."

"Is the resumption of water contingent on me coming inside?"

"It absolutely is."

She entered with the dignity of a queen on the way to her own beheading.

He led her past the staircase on one side and the formal dining room on the other. "May I get you something to drink or eat?" he asked.

"No, thank you."

"Care to sit?" He motioned to the den.

"No."

He'd overseen a major renovation and now his house had the feel of an art gallery—wood floors, white walls, paintings illuminated by their own individual lights.

Because she'd turned down food, drink, and a chair, they were facing each other in the no-man's-land between the kitchen, den, and back porch. Which felt like a metaphor for the no-man's-land location of what had once been their partnership.

"In case you're unaware," Sloane said, "landlords are required by Maine law to provide running water."

"Seeing as how you've only been without running water for twenty minutes, I don't think you'll have success charging me with uninhabitable living conditions."

"Without water," she went on as if he'd said nothing, "we'll dehydrate and die. Is that what you'd like to happen to Ivy and me?"

He made a show of contemplating that. "Not to Ivy."

She scowled, again reminding him of the teacup poodle.

"What needs to happen in order for you to turn our water back on?" she asked.

"I've already told you what I want. You moved in on Monday. It's Friday. I still have no closure."

She straightened. "If you have questions for me, ask them."

He held her eye contact steadily, knowing he could win any staring contest she was willing to offer. "I want your version of what happened four years ago."

She went to cross her arms, then stopped herself. No doubt crossed arms weren't good etiquette. She settled on clasping her hands in front of her waist.

"Well?" he prodded.

"Since you're the one who wants to rehash all of this, why don't you tell your version of what happened, and I'll interject my version when applicable?"

"Four years ago," he said in a matter-of-fact tone, "Libri was struggling."

Their final year of college they'd taken an entrepreneurship class that had tasked them with creating a business plan for a brand-new company.

Sloane, an avid childhood reader, had suggested they build a company that would function as a digital library to the entire English-speaking world. For a reasonable monthly fee, subscribers would receive unlimited access to ebooks, audiobooks, magazines, newspapers, sheet music, and podcasts. It would be affordable because Sloane knew from personal experience that a tremendous number of people didn't have much money to spend on those items. And it would be convenient—all content immediately accessible via phones, tablets, and computers.

Max had caught her vision. They'd named their company Libri, the plural form of the Latin word *liber* for "book." By the time they'd completed college, both of them in caps and gowns receiving their diplomas during the same graduation ceremony, Libri had become a passion for them, and they'd committed to making it a reality.

They stayed in Philadelphia, each working at full-time,

entry-level jobs during the week and working on Libri the rest of the time. They received $110,000 in seed funding from a venture capitalist. Nine months later, they'd raised one and a half million from two other VC groups, at which time they quit their day jobs.

They'd rolled almost every dime Libri made back into the company—investing in additional employees, in tech, in marketing. They'd worked intense hours and battled obstacle after obstacle as they'd sought to enter into deals with the "big five" publishing companies. It had been an uphill slog. Many times the two of them had inched Libri forward out of nothing but sheer, stubborn persistence.

"The business was at an inflection point," he went on. "The annual general meeting that year was arguably the most important AGM we'd had. Three weeks before, I was preparing for it, you were preparing for it. And then, overnight, you changed. Your body was still present at the office some of the time, but it was like the rest of you was MIA. For the first time ever, your work slipped. You started dropping responsibilities. When I asked you what was happening, you said 'family issues.' That was it. That was all you told me."

He paused. When she didn't contradict him or add anything, he continued. "I offered to take your presentation at the AGM off your plate. I told you that the rest of the team would pick up the slack for you. But for three weeks you insisted, repeatedly, that you were fine. That you'd present as usual at the AGM."

She inclined her chin, agreeing with the facts he'd laid out so far.

"Twenty minutes before your presentation, the board of directors, the auditors, and the shareholders were arriving. I get a text from you saying, 'Sorry, I can't do it.' Five words. I tried to call you, over and over, but you wouldn't answer. Time ran out and I was forced to go up and present in your place. I looked like an idiot in front of some of the most powerful people in the Northeast. I was uninformed, disorganized, unprepared. It was the worst day in the history of my career and as soon as it ended, I drove to your apartment."

"If you recall," Sloane said tightly, "when you got there, I immediately tried to apologize to you. You ignored my apology. You didn't want to hear anything except your own ranting. How could I sabotage you like that? How could I tank our company? And on and on. You were furious."

"Yes. I was furious. Justifiably."

"I'd committed an unforgivable sin when I hurt your pride by making you give that presentation."

"No," he responded flatly. "It was later that you committed the unforgivable sin."

"And later still that you did the same to me."

"You kicked me out of your apartment"—Max returned to the sequence of events—"and the next morning at work Nate tells me your sister died. That was the family issue you'd been dealing with for three weeks. *Harper* had *died*. Of an overdose. He tells me that your grief has been terrible and explains that immediately before the presentation you had a panic attack. Which is why you couldn't do it. I had to hear all of this very important, very relevant information about what had been going on with my business partner from Nate. *One of our coders* knew about Harper's death and I did not."

"Nate was my boyfriend at the time."

Max's temper spiked. "You'd known Nate for how long? Five minutes? Nate had the significance of a gnat compared to me. I'd spent nine years earning the right to be at the top of the list of people who mattered to you. As your partner and friend, you should have told me about Harper's death miles before you told Nate."

"I'm private when it comes to my family."

"That explanation isn't good enough."

"It's going to have to be."

"Why didn't you tell me, Sloane?" he demanded.

She drew her shoulders back. "I'm private when it comes to my family," she said again with steely calm. "I didn't tell you about Harper because I wanted my personal life to remain separate from my professional life. I told myself I could keep my grief from crossing over and affecting Libri. Unfortunately for me, I was wrong about that . . . as the panic attack proved."

"If I'd known you were grieving your sister, I would have handled everything differently."

Her brown eyes narrowed. "That statement in no way exonerates you in my eyes."

It seemed he'd gotten a little spoiled. These days, almost no one stood up to him the way she was doing now. He'd become accustomed to telling people what to do and receiving little pushback.

But here was Sloane, jutting her delicate chin and pushing back hard. A part of him didn't like it at all. Another part of him relished it. That part of him was saying *finally* and causing all his synapses to fire.

"The argument at your apartment was the last time we spoke," Max said. "So, to this day, I've never heard what was going through your head during those weeks between Harper's death and the AGM. I want to hear it now."

"That won't help anything at this point—"

"Closure." He gave her a look like, *Tell me.*

Every inch of her communicated reluctance. He worried she'd storm away. But instead, she shifted position. Feet side by side, she straightened one arm and clasped the elbow of that arm with her other hand. It was the type of pose only used by royalty and celebrities on the red carpet. He knew her well enough to know that she employed etiquette as armor. This ladylike pose was her chain mail.

"Harper's death devastated me," she said. "Even more than I realized at the time. I survived the days following her overdose by focusing on the things that needed to be done . . . choosing a casket, flowers, a cemetery. Organizing the funeral service. We buried her on a Sunday, and I was back at my desk on Monday. Since our senior year, Libri had been my passion. It had consumed every empty space in my life, and I didn't mind. In fact, I liked it that way. I had more than enough energy and love to give it. But after Harper died, something shifted." She looked toward the windows. Light slid along her cheekbone and neck.

He waited.

"All of a sudden, I didn't have any gas left in my tank. Grief was a physical thing for me." She turned her face back to him. "During those weeks leading up to the AGM it felt like I was living with a heavy blanket weighing me down. I believed that if I could press through the sadness, things would return to normal, and I was desperate for things to return to normal. So I held on to Libri like a life preserver—which is why I didn't let you take responsibilities off my plate. Some days I felt slightly better, like the old Sloane, the one who had a sister. Other days I felt blue. On the worst days, my life seemed pointless."

Max focused wholly on her. A helicopter could have crashed to the earth outside and he wouldn't have glanced its way.

"The morning of the AGM, I woke up consumed with anxiety. I reassured myself that it was okay, that I could and would give the presentation. I dressed. I had all my materials ready. But the anxiety kept mounting and mounting. Eventually my attempts to overcome it failed and a full-fledged panic attack set in. My heart was thundering, and I was gasping for breath. I had this out-of-body moment when I thought, *I can't do this. I literally cannot give this presentation.* Which is when I texted you."

His mouth formed a thin line.

"When you arrived at my apartment, I was weak and shaky and overwhelmed with guilt about leaving you in the lurch the way I had. But then you immediately came at me with fury, which I'd never been less prepared to handle." She blew out a slow exhale. "In response, I went into self-preservation mode. It was all too painful and too stressful, and I knew I couldn't deal with you anymore. So I forced you to go and then I packed a suitcase and got in my car. I drove aimlessly. Slept in a hotel that night. Drove aimlessly the next day. Slept in another hotel. Then found an inn in North Carolina with several tiny cabins spread out in the forest. I stayed in one of them for the next month."

Max was not the type to let emotion sit in the driver's seat and take the wheel of his life. Now that something that might be remorse was twisting inside him, he recalled why he didn't let emotion sit in the driver's seat. He *hated* how this felt. He shoved remorse aside and kept a tight grip on his anger. "After Nate explained what was going on, I was determined to get you, me, and Libri back on course. I tried everything to reach you." He counted actions off on one hand. "I tried calling you. I tried texting you. I tried emailing you. I returned to your apartment, but you were gone, and no one would tell me how to get in touch with you or where to find you."

"Like I said, I knew I couldn't deal with you anymore."

"Libri descended into chaos. No one was trained to do the things you did. I barely slept that month, trying to do my job and your job."

She tilted her head. "You can't seriously expect my pity. Can you?"

"I went to your dad, but he had no idea where you were.

Then I went to Brooke and Jared. Brooke wouldn't tell me anything, but as Jared was walking me out to my car, he said that Titan had made you an offer to buy your shares in Libri. And that you were considering selling." A visceral memory of that night came to him—the blindsided betrayal he'd experienced at Jared's words. Sloane owned twenty percent of Libri. Max owned twenty. Their investors owned the rest. "I was ready to believe that Jared, who'd always been a decent guy, had turned into a lunatic and a liar. Because that seemed more plausible to me than the idea that you'd sell your stake to our biggest competitor."

"None of what happened was Jared's fault, yet he still hasn't forgiven himself for telling you about Titan's offer." Sloane used a pinky finger to reposition a lock of hair. "Jared trusted you. He thought you had my best interests at heart, that the information about Titan would motivate you to find me and patch things up with me. He never imagined that the information would cause you to see me as a threat. Or that you'd sacrifice me because of it."

"I saw you as a threat because you *were* a threat to me. Titan would have started with your twenty percent, then bought out other shareholders, until they had enough for a hostile takeover. Neither of us would have had a company then." Max could hear bitterness creeping into his tone. That was too telling, so he checked himself and reverted to a detached tone. "Titan would have ripped Libri away from me. So, explain. Explain how you were willing to throw away the business we started."

Silence bubbled between them like lava.

Accepting disappointment had never been easy for Max. But his disappointment in Sloane had been the most impossible to accept of them all.

"I answered the phone when Titan called me," she said.

"Of course I did. I wasn't willing to throw Libri away, I was simply weighing my options because the number Titan offered for my stake was a bigger sum than I'd ever seen in my life. Any savvy businessperson would have done the same. Any savvy businessperson in that circumstance would have taken time to weigh their options."

"Let's be clear. You were weighing the option of handing our competitor the ammunition *for a hostile takeover*."

"I was burned out at the time. Vulnerable."

"Up until that point, I'd have sworn that my smart, trustworthy partner would *never* turn on Libri like that. No matter how burned out or vulnerable."

"And I'd have sworn that my smart, trustworthy partner would never have turned on me the way that you did. I knew success was critically important to you. But I failed to realize that it was the only thing in the world you care about."

"I'd invested six years of work into Libri—"

"As had I. In the end, you didn't find me and try to patch things up with me as Jared had expected. You didn't even give me the autonomy to decide on Titan's offer. Instead, you went to our shareholders. You made them afraid of me. Called for a vote. And had me removed." She set her palm against her chest. "From Libri, the business that had begun as *my* idea. I'd put just as much blood, sweat, and tears into it as you had. But when you were done scheming, I had zero ownership."

"You left me no choice."

"Oh? Does telling yourself that help you sleep at night? I found out about what you'd done from Nate and returned home in a panic. I met with an attorney, who handed me a check for the valuation you and the other shareholders had determined my share was worth, which was less than Titan's offer. The rest of you divided my shares and washed your hands of me. *That's* how you ended things. That's how you cut me out of Libri."

"You left me no choice—"

"My check from Libri was just enough to buy a little house and a little car in LA." She sliced a hand through the air. "So then I'm out in California, going to therapy in an attempt to wrap my head around what you did to me, and starting a new small business from scratch. And while I'm grinding away at that, Libri is gaining traction, taking off, and becoming a winner."

"Proving that selling to Titan would have been catastrophic."

"You returned to Maine as a victorious prince and moved the headquarters here." Her words were picking up pace and steam. "Libri is now a billion-dollar company, which means my share, was it still mine, would amount to *two hundred million dollars*. It's laughable that you're acting as though you're entitled to closure from me when you should be down on your knees kissing my feet in gratitude."

"Gratitude?"

"For creating a scenario that enabled you to evict me from my own company at a bargain basement price. Bravo, Max."

He'd grown Libri into what it was today. He wouldn't minimize the satisfaction of that. The satisfaction of that was enormous. However, the past four years had revealed that in winning his way with Libri, he'd lost something crucial.

Sloane.

"That was more than enough closure," she stated, "to justify the resumption of water at the garage apartment."

"I'll be the judge of that."

"Turn the water back on," she ordered.

He wasn't ready for her to go. But before he could think of

something to say to keep her with him, the front door snapped closed behind her.

Sloane was still awake at 1:24 a.m., trying *not* to think about Max and the conversation they'd had earlier.

Why, she wondered, did giving him real estate in her head make her feel so wretched?

Perhaps because Max was forcing her to face the mistakes she'd made. She'd go to the grave insisting that Max's sins toward her were worse than hers toward him. After all, only one of them had ended up as the super-rich CEO of Libri. And it wasn't her, so she rested her case.

Nonetheless, she had made some foolish choices while sick with grief over her sister's death. In going back over the events of four years ago, she couldn't hide from those foolish choices. Or from her own fallibility. Or from regret.

No doubt giving Max real estate in her head also made her feel wretched because he was a living, breathing reminder of the things she'd once had. And didn't have any longer.

She'd once had Libri. It had been more than a career. It had been her dream, the work she loved, her community. Most of her friends back then had been co-workers, all of them rowing in sync toward the same goals.

Because of Libri, she'd once had a reason to live in this corner of the United States—the East Coast region where she'd been born and raised.

And because of Libri, she'd once had Max as her partner. He was a formidable enemy, but he'd been an even more formidable ally.

When they'd first become friends in college, he'd been more ruthless, less emotionally available, and more smoothly charming than she. But they'd both been college kids determined to better themselves and their prospects in life. She'd understood what made him tick and vice versa. She'd appreciated his sense of humor, his smarts, his work ethic.

Almost every college girl she'd known had been infatuated with him because of his looks. But she'd always had a window past his looks to the person beneath. And for a long, long time she'd liked the person beneath a great deal.

Perhaps even sweeter than her appreciation of him, though, had been *his* appreciation of *her*. Max had never said, "Our friendship means the world to me." Even so, his actions had convinced her of that very thing.

He'd shown up for her. He'd prioritized her. Whenever she communicated with him for any reason important or unimportant, she heard back from him right away. If they planned to do something together and his guy friends or his girlfriend-of-the-month made plans the same night, he always chose her.

She and Max did the lousy jobs no one but true friends were willing to do—like moving each other into and out of college apartments, driving the other home to Maine, sitting through boring ceremonies during which one of them received a recognition. If either of them got sick, the other delivered prescriptions and Gatorade and food.

Once, during the winter of her senior year, she'd gone to a frat party with a friend. Her friend had snuck off with a boy and Sloane had suddenly found herself alone and outnumbered. One drunk boy in particular kept insisting she dance with him. Not wanting to trudge at night through the ice and snow back to her apartment, she'd texted Max to ask if he could give her a ride. Within minutes, he'd arrived, put his arm protectively around her shoulders, and steered her out of there. When the drunk boy had tried to block their retreat, Max had shoved him roughly to the side.

It had been heady, the favored status he'd granted her.

Sloane knew and accepted that she was not extraordinarily beautiful. Nor extraordinarily special.

In terms of weaknesses—she'd been abandoned by her mother and neglected by her father. She'd come from a poor family. Those hardships had been the sewing machine that stitched her together in the sturdiest of ways.

In terms of strengths—she was intelligent and industrious. Mannerly and gracious. A faithful aunt to Ivy. She had integrity. Though her brand of determination was more composed than Max's brand of determination, they were equals in that respect.

Somehow . . . way back at Penn, handsome Max Cirillo— the illegitimate son of famous and wealthy Felix Camden—had seen who Sloane was and had valued her greatly. Knowing she had Max so staunchly in her corner . . .

Well.

Once upon a time, that had been a powerful thing.

After graduation, in Libri's early years, their role in one another's lives had felt even more magnified. Perhaps that had been because Sloane had not had a serious boyfriend and Max had not taken any of his girlfriends seriously. He wouldn't stoop to loving any of those women, so while the women had sometimes irritated Sloane, they'd never truly bothered her because they'd never truly threatened her—

Wait. Was that the *scritch-scratch* of rat feet?

She jerked upright, listening.

No, it was raining. That was just the sound of rain.

Sloane socked her pillow, annoyed by her fear of rats, annoyed that she was awake at this hour, annoyed because now that she was being so honest with herself, she should admit something she did not like to admit. Namely that there had been a few forbidden and ill-advised moments across her years with Max when she'd found herself almost unbearably attracted to him.

She flopped onto her mattress face-up, limbs open like a starfish.

She'd been too wise to act on those wayward moments. Too unwilling to wreck her life, her company, and their friendship by falling for a man who ran through women like water.

It had been one such wayward moment that had motivated her to keep her personal life and professional life separate. A year before Harper's death, she and Max had been working late in the boardroom, hunched over a spreadsheet. He'd stood and used a dry-erase marker to slash numbers across the white-board. She'd rushed to her feet and pulled the marker out of his hand.

Her intention had been to immediately begin using the marker herself, but all at once, she'd been caught in the crosshairs of his nearness and his masculine physicality. She'd been close enough to see the gradient of color in his irises and catch a whiff of the soap he used, which always made her think, *This is what Greece must smell like.* Ocean, trees, sun.

Time turned heavy as honey. He'd gazed at her with heat. And Sloane had *longed* for him.

She'd come back to her senses in time to save herself. But the near miss had frightened her. She'd determined that it was dangerous to be so chummy with Max Cirillo. Naïve. Reckless. For all their sakes, for Libri's sake, she needed to treat him less like her best friend and more like she treated the other male members of the board of directors—with the utmost profession-alism. From that day forward, she'd put that into practice.

Which was why she hadn't blurted out the truth to Max when Harper died. Why she hadn't cried on his shoulder. Why she'd shut him out during her weeks at the cabin. All of which had ultimately resulted in him shutting her out of their company.

To her great frustration, her anger at Max hadn't prevented her from dreaming of him from time to time the past four years. Whenever her subconscious turned traitor and allowed him to visit her in her sleep, it was to do things he'd never done in real life. To whisper words of love to her, to hold her, to kiss her.

In the name of all that was right and holy, she wished she didn't feel Max's magnetism.

But ridiculously, she *still* did.

Even after all this time.

Chapter Five

More than anything at present, Max wanted the freedom to stew over Sloane without distractions.

What he did not want? To bother with The Case of the Missing Tiara that Felix had dropped in his lap. His research into Eugenie's tiara had proven the historical facts about it that Felix had relayed. It was a priceless artifact. And to protect his mother from getting arrested for stealing it, he had no choice other than to bother with it.

Saturday, the day following his confrontation with Sloane, he slept in, worked out, went to the office, then drove to his mother's house—arriving in time for dinner.

He made his way up her front walk.

Back when the two of them had been ordered to leave Maple Lane, they'd relocated to the small town of Montville, forty minutes from Groomsport. Mom was very close to her Greek immigrant parents, her sister Melissa, and her brother Greg. They all lived in Groomsport and forty minutes from them was as far as she'd been willing to go.

He and Mom had moved into a rented duplex and she'd

worked at a soap manufacturing company. She'd kept that job all the way up until three years ago, at which point Max had amassed enough money to ensure his ability to provide for her for the remainder of her life. He'd encouraged her to retire, which she had. He'd offered to buy her a house anywhere she wanted but she'd chosen to stay in Montville, close to her network of friends.

She'd selected a house she loved. She loved it so much, in fact, that she'd only stayed overnight at The Gables a couple of times. Back when Max had been renovating his property, he'd added the garage apartment, thinking that if his mother came to stay for extended periods of time, she (and he) might prefer for her to have a space of her own. However, she had yet to stay for an extended period of time.

She was expecting him, so he let himself in with his own key. "I'm here."

"*Yios!*" she called from the direction of the kitchen. The word meant "son" in Greek and had always been her term of endearment for him.

She rushed into the entry area, embracing him in a hug that smelled pleasantly of basil. She grew many of her own herbs but typically smelled of this particular one.

After landing a smacking kiss on his cheek, she stepped back, smiling.

When she was young, her hair had been a mass of thick, jet-black curls. Now, at sixty-two, her hair was still curly, but gray, and worn in a long bob.

"You must be starving!" she said. "Come, let's have dinner."

He'd been endlessly hungry during his middle school, teenage, and college years. Ever since, she'd assumed the same was still true even though his metabolism had slowed. He hadn't corrected her because she enjoyed feeding him and he enjoyed being fed. They had their love of Greek food in common, which made meals the easiest part of their relationship.

He trailed her into the bright kitchen.

"I'm serving moussaka. You can make yourself useful by adding dressing to the salad and tossing it."

He washed his hands and went to work, which gave him a sense of déjà vu. When he was a kid, the two of them used to return home around the same time of day. She'd prepare dinner. He'd serve as her sous chef.

"It's amazing to me now," he said, "that you had the energy to cook dinner almost every night when I was growing up." She'd always been physically strong. But so was he. And even though he wasn't a single parent like she'd been, he didn't have the energy to cook dinner.

"We didn't have the budget for restaurant food. Besides, a meal cooked at home always tastes the best." She pulled on oven mitts and lifted a casserole dish onto the stovetop. It released mouth-watering scents of ground beef, cheese, potatoes, and spices.

Once she'd cut the moussaka, they filled their plates, poured drinks, and took seats at her kitchen table. He had a view through to her living room of a comfortable sofa and a rectangular wooden side table.

She said grace.

"Amen." He dug into the food.

She ate a bite. Then another. Brought her napkin to her lips. "I'm glad you came by."

"I am, too."

"Are you here for any particular reason?"

"Do I have to have a reason to visit my mother?"

"Definitely not. But you *do* have a reason because you rarely come by without one."

Her statement was blunt but accurate. He saw her once a

week or so, usually in Groomsport with a group that included his grandparents, aunt and uncle, cousins, or all of the above. One gathering a week with the Cirillos was about right for him, seeing as how it took him approximately six days to recover.

He set his fork on the edge of his plate. "You're not going to like today's reason," he warned.

She went still, waiting.

"Felix Camden asked me to meet with him."

Her jaw stiffened. Whatever heights of love or desire she'd once felt for Felix—to that same degree, she now hated him. Felix had a knack for inspiring that effect in women. His two wives—Isobel and Fiona—felt the same way about him.

"What did he want?" she asked.

"To tell me that a piece of jewelry called Empress Eugenie's tiara went missing around the time that you and I left Maple Lane. He believes that you stole it."

The next few seconds were so quiet that they made the whir of the cooling oven sound loud.

"He believes," she repeated slowly, "that I stole it."

"Yes. Did you?"

"*No*." Her chair screeched back. "Of all the idiotic, egotistical, untrustworthy things that Felix has ever said, saying that I stole his tiara has to be the worst."

His mother was a what-you-see-is-what-you-get person. Genuine. Affectionate. Opinionated. Mischievous, with an off-color sense of humor and a deep laugh. Her temper didn't flare that often, but when it did, it flared very hot. She could be bossy. And, if wronged, she held a grudge and didn't easily forgive.

"What's his purpose," she demanded, "in accusing me of this? Is he trying to turn you against me?"

"No. My read is that he's certain that you have his tiara. He simply wants it back. He's going to bring private investigators or the media in on this if it's not returned to him in a few months."

"Let him."

Max frowned. The very last thing he would let Felix do? Publicize the story of the missing tiara. If that happened, negative media speculation would fall once again on his mother and him. "Felix can't go public with this story," he said calmly but firmly. "I'm Libri's CEO. It would hurt the company."

"Why? I thought I was the suspect here."

"If this goes to the court of public opinion, they'll suspect me of stealing the tiara, too. I had motive."

"Of course you didn't take it!" She threw up her hands. "That man has numerous pieces of art and jewelry. One tiara is nothing to him."

"Oh, it's something to him," he assured her. "Do you remember this particular piece of jewelry?"

"I do."

"So you might recall that it contains over six hundred diamonds?"

"It could contain six thousand diamonds for all I care. That wouldn't change the fact that I didn't take it."

He considered her words, her features, her body language. He believed her. "Any idea who did take it?"

She gave an angry shrug. "Fiona? Jeremiah? Jude? They were all mad at Felix around the time you and I left Maple Lane."

"Jude definitely didn't take it. He's too ethical for that."

"The Camdens had staff at Maple Lane all the time. The nanny. The pool guy. The gardener. Workmen—to fix appliances or to deep clean the carpets. Any of them could have taken it." Her dark eyes blazed. "A big part of me hopes Felix never gets the tiara back. It would serve him right to go without something for once in his life."

How was it possible, Fiona Camden wondered, that her youngest child was thirty-three years old?

She'd had Jeremiah and Jude young. But still.

Jude's birthday was prompting her to think back over all his earlier stages. Infancy. Preschool years. Elementary and middle school years. Jude as a teenager, so dutiful and helpful. Moving him into his college dorm room. The celebratory trip they'd taken when he'd completed law school. Jude nobly (and somewhat bizarrely, let's be honest) leaving the prospect of private practice behind in favor of becoming an FBI agent.

When Fiona played the movie reel of images from all those different seasons, then yes, she could see that it *was* possible for Jude to be the age he was. Herself as the mother of a thirty-three-year-old man, however? That's when she hit a mental stumbling block.

She was not a fan of aging. It was better than the alternative but only if the alternative was literally death. Aging was definitely *not* better than the alternative if the alternative was her younger self.

She did not condone the way her skin wanted to sag. Or the way her body wanted to simultaneously droop and put on pounds . . . droopy pounds. Or the way her eyes wanted to puff, or her joints wanted to ache.

So, no. She was not a fan of aging. But she *was* a fan of events like this one that celebrated one of her sons. Jeremiah and Jude were both deeply deserving of celebration. And, as their mother, she was always granted a pleasing amount of attention and applause herself at gatherings like these.

She, her sons, her sons' girlfriends, and Max Cirillo were currently enjoying a ride on Jeremiah's refurbished 1950s boat, the *Camdenball*. He was at the helm, steering them along the channel between the mainland and Maine's nearest islands. Fiona sat gracefully in the open air on the long seat spanning the back of the boat. From beneath the brim of the sun hat that kept the wind from doing too much damage to her blow-out, she could observe the others, feel the briny air against her face, and enjoy the stunning view of ocean, sky, and land.

Had it been up to her, she would've marked Jude's birthday by hosting a large and more formal party at her home. She embraced reasons to employ a caterer and get dressed up. However, Jude did not like to call attention to himself—a facet of his personality so completely unlike both herself and his father that it puzzled her afresh each year when he leaned toward a birthday celebration that included very few people.

This time, he and his girlfriend, Gemma, would be taking Felix's plane to Prince Edward Island tomorrow, on his actual birthday. They planned to spend the day biking, kayaking, and eating. Of those three, only the eating appealed to Fiona. Jude had suggested to her that he mark this birthday with the PEI trip and nothing more, but Fiona had insisted on a family gathering as well. So here they were.

Felix was in Aspen this weekend doubtless being admired and kissed up to. Her ex-husband's schedule often prevented him from attending family get-togethers so Fiona had decided early on that they would not bother to reschedule simply because Felix couldn't make an event. Admittedly, the policy was self-serving. Fiona had long practice at interacting with Felix when necessary. But honestly, the less she had to deal with him, the better.

"This goat cheese and hot pepper jelly is delicious, Fiona," Gemma said, holding a cracker loaded with the dip aloft. The curvy redhead was an easy conversationalist, both funny and warm.

"I'm so glad you like it," Fiona replied. The rest of this

group were all Millennials, bless their hearts, and so *of course* Fiona had provided lunch, champagne, cake, candles, and the rest of the necessities for today's cruise.

Fiona raised her champagne flute, which bubbled with Dom Perignon. "To the guest of honor, Jude. Happy birthday, darling. You've brought me so much joy over the years and I'm very thankful for you."

The rest of them—Remy sitting beside Fiona and everyone else standing—raised their glasses.

Jude had been seriously injured while working a case two months ago. He still moved more slowly and carefully than he had before. But other than that, he radiated health. He was young, strong, vital. Praise God, his body had rebounded with amazing speed.

The group took turns toasting Jude.

Max joined in, though her sons' half-brother seemed distracted today. At the moment, he was leaning against the side of the boat, the wind flapping the hem of his black T-shirt against the waistband of his jeans.

For the first fourteen years of Max's life, Fiona had known him as two things. One, the son of their housekeeper (and her very good friend), Nicole. Two, Fiona's sons' playmate. Max had spent great chunks of time under Fiona's roof or rambling across Maple Lane's woods with Jeremiah and Jude. Max had been a sporty kid—brave, persistent, quick-witted. Back then, Fiona had felt simple, undiluted affection toward him.

Then she'd learned that he was the product of an affair between her then-husband Felix and Nicole, an affair which had lasted for several months during her second pregnancy right under Fiona's nose. Which had made Fiona's feelings toward Max less simple. The unpleasant truth of Max's parentage hovered at the forefront of Fiona's mind every time he was near.

Nevertheless, he'd continued as a frequent presence in her life because he'd remained close to her sons. Thankfully, she and he had both made an effort to keep their interactions courteous.

"Thank you," Jude told them all with sincerity. "And now I'd like to toast Jeremiah and Remy. Congratulations on your engagement."

"I'd love to hear more details about that," Gemma encouraged.

Jeremiah swiveled on his captain's chair to face them more fully. "I've been carrying around the engagement ring for the last two months, waiting for a moment when it seemed like I had a chance of Remy saying yes to me."

That was very sweet and all, but it needled Fiona when Jeremiah spoke with this kind of humility about his romance. He seemed to think he was the luckiest man in the world when anyone with even a mediocre IQ would rank him as the most eligible bachelor in the state of Maine.

"I considered an elaborate proposal," Jeremiah continued. "But I didn't think Remy would like anything too staged."

"You were right," Remy said.

Dimples dug into Jeremiah's cheeks. "Man, I love it on those rare occasions when you say that I'm right."

Remy smiled. "Don't get used to it."

Fiona, for one, greatly appreciated the staged proposals so prevalent on social media. Mostly because the mothers were often on site to dole out hugs and excitement. That was not what had happened with her son's recent engagement.

"A week ago we went on one of our favorite hikes on Islehaven," Remy said. "When we reached Restoration Point, I walked out in front of Jeremiah. Islehaven is one of my favorite places on earth and that particular spot is the best of the best. Jeremiah was being quiet—"

"That's rare," Jude joked.

Remy swung a glance brimming with camaraderie and wry amusement toward Jude. "When I turned around, I saw that Jeremiah was down on one knee, holding a ring box. There wasn't another soul around. Just the two of us and the sound of waves and birds. I was dressed in leggings with my hair in a top knot."

"I couldn't wait any longer to propose to you," Jeremiah said. "I finally saw a moment to ask. And so I asked."

"And I said yes. It was a perfect proposal, actually. For me, it couldn't have been more wonderful." Remy's face glowed. Even on days like today when she was wearing makeup, she wore very little. She had a lovely ivory complexion, wavy blond hair, and a body that managed to look slender even in the voluminous sundress she had on. If Fiona were to don that sundress, she'd resemble a bowling ball.

Jeremiah and Remy had called Fiona soon after they'd returned from the hike to Remy's cottage. Secretly, she'd felt testy over the fact that not only had she not been included in the proposal, but she also hadn't been told that a proposal was in the works. She'd refrained from verbalizing any of that, though, discretion being the better part of valor.

Upon further reflection, Fiona had decided to view Jeremiah's heartfelt, impromptu proposal in an approving light. His first proposal to his wife Alexis, a social media influencer, had been enormously showy. Jeremiah had not found contentment with Alexis. Remy was as far from Alexis as a person could get and Fiona had every expectation that her firstborn *would* find contentment with Remy. So if Remy preferred to be proposed to on the edge of nowhere dressed in leggings, then the least Fiona could do was make peace with it.

"May I have a closer look at your ring?" Gemma asked, making her way to Remy.

Remy proffered her left hand.

Fiona had received her engagement ring from Felix in the eighties, a time when everything had been ostentatious, including her ring. She'd adored it.

Remy was a wood-carving artist and not very enamored with material things. For her, Jeremiah had selected a ring composed of small diamonds the same size all the way around. They were invisibly set so that it looked as if the diamonds formed a magical fairy ring around her delicate finger.

"I love my ring," Remy announced.

"I can see why," Gemma said. "It's *stunning*."

"Have you thought yet about when you might like to get married?" Jude asked.

"If it were up to me, I'd marry her at a justice of the peace tomorrow, before she changes her mind—"

"No justices of the peace allowed!" Fiona crowed, genuinely horrified.

"To answer your question," Remy said to Jude. "We haven't thought about when we might like to get married yet. We've both just been enjoying being engaged."

"The sooner, the better," Fiona encouraged. For one thing, she knew that's what Jeremiah wanted. For another, the quicker they wed, the quicker the grandbabies. If a woman's biological clock could tick loudly for grandchildren, then Fiona's clock was ticking at the volume of a Guns N' Roses' concert. "I could pull together a very grand wedding this winter," Fiona said. "Wouldn't a winter wedding be lovely?"

"I don't think Remy wants anything grand," Jeremiah said.

"That's true." Remy glanced at Fiona. "However, I don't hate the idea of a winter wedding."

"Really?" Jeremiah asked hopefully.

"It's something to ponder," Remy told him.

"Think of it!" Fiona clapped her palms together. "We could

swag garlands of pine down the pews. You could go with a woodsy, natural theme. Or a gold and glittery theme. No matter what, lots of candles. It would be magical."

Remy nodded thoughtfully. She actually seemed receptive to this idea!

"How many people are you thinking of inviting?" Fiona pressed.

"Only close friends and family."

"Perhaps two hundred?"

"No, no," Remy hurried to say. "Perhaps forty."

"Ah. That is *very* small—"

"Mom," Jeremiah cautioned.

"Yet a delightful size for a wedding which will be organized in short order," Fiona added, once again choosing to view their preferences in an approving light. "If you'd like my assistance, please let me know. I'd be thrilled to help. Party planning is one of my favorite hobbies." That and gardening, drinking wine, massages, golf, Botox, and cheering for the Patriots.

"Thank you for offering, Fiona," Remy said.

"You're welcome, dear."

"How's Burke doing?" Jeremiah asked her.

He was referring to her friend Burke Ainsley. "Very well."

"Did you invite him to join us today?"

"I didn't." She refrained from mentioning that doing so would have been odd, seeing as how the only non-family members here were involved in romances with her sons.

"You're welcome to include him anytime," Jeremiah said.

"Yeah," Jude said. "I really like him."

"Are you and Burke dating?" Max asked.

That was an overly personal question for Max to ask, but then sensitivity wasn't his strong suit. Fiona adjusted her hat. "No."

"I think they should give dating a try," Jude said.

She needed dating advice from her children even less than she needed a hot flash. "We're friends." Charming, though, of her sons to imagine that she could give her heart to a man again after the way their father had demolished her trust. She could not.

"How are Grandma, Grandpa, and the rest of the O'Sullivans?" Jude asked.

"They're doing beautifully." Fiona saw her parents, siblings, and nieces and nephews often.

Talk turned to Remy and Gemma's families and Fiona's attention snagged on a distant sailboat.

The *one* fly in the ointment of Fiona's family at present? Her failure to restore communication between herself and her estranged sister, Isobel. She'd invited Isobel—both face-to-face and through letters—to come to Groomsport in early October so they could experience a total solar eclipse together.

Back when they were eight and ten years old, they'd traveled with their family to the path of a total solar eclipse in Suriname, South America. She and Isobel had stood side by side for that eclipse. It had awed them both and they'd made a solemn pinky-promise to watch the total eclipse coming to Maine decades in the future together, too.

So far, Fiona had received nothing but stony silence from her sister in response to her invitations.

Isobel was the second of the seven O'Sullivan children. Fiona had been born third in the birth order just eighteen months later. The two of them had been closer to each other than to any of their other siblings right up until Fiona had an affair with Felix while he was married to Isobel. Fiona had been twenty-three at the time. Heavens above, *twenty-three*. That much younger version of her had way more spunk than sense. Way more confidence than wisdom. When one was very green, it was dangerous to believe oneself to be mature and invincible, but that described twenty-three-year-old Fiona to a T. Filled with passion, she'd been willing to give up anyone and everyone for Felix. And more than willing for him to do the same. Sure enough, when the affair came to light, it ruptured both Felix's marriage to Isobel and Fiona's relationship with her sister.

These days, she looked back on their affair and her subsequent marriage to Felix with chagrin and regret. Especially because her poor decisions had become national news. They'd formed her persona. They'd sentenced her sons to notoriety. In the end, her poor decisions had broken not just Isobel's heart. But her own.

When it came to her sister and the eclipse, Fiona might have to do what ran contrary to her nature.

Accept defeat.

She'd already done everything she could do to entice Isobel to the Maine eclipse. Perhaps it was time to accustom herself to the idea that the hurt she'd caused was so deep that it could never be forgiven. In which case, she and Isobel would remain estranged for the rest of their lives and their parents, now in their eighties, would never have all of their children in the same room again.

That outcome was harsh.

Yet, in all fairness, no less than she deserved.

Max looked up from where he was kneeling in front of the galley fridge inside the *Camdenball* to see Jude descending the stairs.

"Bottled water?" Max asked his friend.

"Yes, please."

Max rose holding two bottled waters, passed one over, and

closed the fridge door with his toe. It was just the two of them below deck. Probably best, since space was tight.

"I'm glad I have you alone for a minute," Jude said.

"Yeah?"

"Months ago, I mentioned to you that Sloane told me she was coming back to Groomsport in early July. I haven't heard from her since. Do you know if she's back?"

"She's back."

"Staying with Ivy at Ivy's house?"

"Staying with Ivy in my garage apartment."

Jude's eyebrows shot up. "Excuse me?"

Max explained how he'd arranged that.

"How long have Sloane and Ivy been in your apartment?"

"Almost a week."

Jude scratched the skin under his ear. "What do you hope to achieve?"

"I want some type of ending between Sloane and me that I can understand." Max unscrewed his water and threw back a long swallow.

"Because the last ending, you did not understand."

"Right." He gestured with the water, a few drops sloshing over the side. "An ending I can understand, I can accept. That will let me close the book and move on."

"Mm-hmm," Jude said, very neutral.

"What does that mean?"

Jude shrugged. As usual, his clothes had not a single wrinkle. "How're things going between you and Sloane so far?"

"Very well."

"If so, how come you're gloomy despite the fact that it's a beautiful day *and* my birthday party?"

"I'm not gloomy."

"Are you gloomy because Sloane didn't agree to step into the iron maiden you had waiting for her?"

"Not gloomy."

"Has she refused to let you shut her in your dungeon?"

"Things with her are going very well," Max said again. "She's already explained a few things about why she left that I didn't know before." He wouldn't admit it to Jude but since his last conversation with Sloane, a dark cloud had been following him around. He *was* gloomy.

He'd made progress toward his goal of closure. He should be pleased.

Yet it turned out it didn't please him to know how broken-hearted and grief-stricken Sloane had been over the death of her sister. She should have told him about Harper's overdose and let him and others take over her responsibilities at work. When Titan came calling, she should have turned them down flat.

Those were her mistakes.

But for the first time in four years, he was starting to think that his mistakes were worse. Blowing up at her and then kicking her out of Libri? Remembering what he'd done gave him a sinking feeling because, objectively, that *was* worse.

Jude was eyeing him as if doing his best to read Max's mind. Which was uncomfortable, seeing as how Jude had known him so long that he'd gotten good at reading things in Max's mind that Max didn't want him to know.

"I have something to ask you about," Max said, purposely changing the subject.

"Sure."

"Do you remember a tiara that was part of Maple Lane's art collection when we were kids? It once belonged to Empress Eugenie of France." It made him feel like an idiot to say the words *Empress Eugenie* and *tiara* out loud. Those were words that belonged in a fairy tale for little girls.

"I have a vague memory of a tiara."

"It disappeared around the time that my mom and I left Maple Lane. Did you know that?"

"No."

"Felix is convinced that my mom stole it. He's asked me to get the tiara back."

"Hmm."

"I didn't take the tiara," Max went on. "I've discussed it with my mom, and she says she didn't take it, either."

"Okay." Jude gave every indication of accepting that without issue.

"Felix is convinced she has it. I don't want this taken public so, to my mind, the best way to resolve this is to figure out who does have it."

"Who do you think that might be?"

"Fiona's my best guess. Maybe Jeremiah?"

Jude had an impressive poker face. "How can I help?"

"Will you talk to them about the tiara and let me know what they say?"

"Yeah. You know I like a good mystery. Add in a jewel heist, and it's even more interesting."

"You solve these types of things for a living."

"For a living," Jude agreed.

"Just don't involve the FBI in this particular mystery. I'd rather not be thrown into federal prison."

Chapter Six

The following Wednesday morning, Ivy emerged from her bedroom with rumpled hair wearing the UMaine sweatshirt and pajama pants she'd slept in.

"Good morning," Sloane greeted her brightly. "I was thinking of making avocado toast for breakfast. How does that sound?"

"Sounds great. High five, Aunt Sloane."

Sloane didn't point out that a high five did not pass muster in terms of etiquette. Instead, she tapped her palm to her niece's upraised one—

Movement in her peripheral vision drew Sloane's face to the side in time to see a mouse run across the living room rug.

Ivy gasped. Sloane screamed.

"Run!" Sloane ordered, taking off toward the door. Nobly willing to sacrifice her life to protect Ivy, she waved for the girl to exit the apartment first, then dashed out after her. Sloane plunged down the stairs with her arms above her head as if she was on a roller coaster.

It was only when they'd sprinted several yards along the

driveway and were standing surrounded by nothing but space —no place for a mouse to hide—that Sloane stopped, heart racing.

Some of the places she'd lived as a girl had been seedy enough to have issues with rats, mice, cockroaches, spiders, flies, and more. Once, she'd opened the pantry door to reach for a box of cereal and a rat had leapt forward and bitten her on the shin. Her father hadn't taken her to the doctor, the wound had become infected, and it was only thanks to Sloane's third grade teacher and the school nurse that she'd received treatment. The physical scar of that bite had faded. The mental scar had not.

Shuddering, she shook out her arms and legs. While doing this jig, Sloane caught sight of Max, sitting at his outdoor table as he did every morning.

He stood and crossed to them. "What's the matter?" he called, still several yards away.

She started to reply, then realized she didn't have enough breath to do so. She gulped air. Pointed an accusing finger. "There is a mouse . . . in your house!"

His posture relaxed. "Are we speaking in rhyme? If so, Sloane . . . don't moan. You yelped. Now I'll help."

Ivy released a snort of amusement.

"Don't you dare patronize me! Ivy's parents are paying good money for us to live in that apartment and clearly the pest control is subpar. Which is an issue you need to rectify *immediately.*"

He had the gall to look as if he found this entertaining.

"We obviously," she said, "cannot go back in there until that terrible—"

"Fire-breathing creature?"

"Disease-carrying varmint has been removed. And since Ivy needs to change clothes and get ready for the day before I drop her off at the church in an hour, let me emphasize just how quickly the situation needs to be dealt with."

A smile spread across his lips, molasses slow. A glint in his eyes, he took in her outfit.

With a bolt of realization, she comprehended that she was standing before him in a pale-yellow silk pajama set and slippers. She hadn't yet pulled on the robe she always wore while having her coffee and devotional time outside. The cut of her pajama set was modest. Yet silk was not the most concealing of fabrics. Also, she hadn't brushed her hair and knew it must look like a tumbleweed.

"You were scared, I see. I will rescue thee," he said.

Ivy laughed.

Oh, she *hated* him in those joggers and that white T-shirt, with that black hair, which, unlike hers, looked fabulous when messy.

Sloane glared at him so venomously that it should have obliterated him to ash. "You seem to find this hilarious, but Ivy and I were scared out of our wits just now. Where is your sympathy?"

"Aww. Were you scared out of your wits?" he asked Ivy kindly.

"More surprised than anything."

"Sorry. Need a hug?"

"Yes, please." Max and Ivy shared a brief hug, then he opened his arms to Sloane. "Do you need a hug, too?"

"Not even if my life depended on it. What are you going to do about this?"

"I'm going to go up there and see if I can shoo the mouse away."

"There can't be any *seeing* if you can shoo the mouse away. There must be literal shooing away of the mouse."

"Where was the mouse?"

"Living room."

"I'll carefully search the living room. If I don't come out in ten minutes, call the fire department." He climbed the stairs and disappeared into the apartment.

"You okay?" Ivy asked Sloane.

"I'm fine." Though, truthfully, she still had a case of the heebie-jeebies. She made a cringy face and picked through strands of her hair to make sure the mouse wasn't hiding inside it.

They waited. Sloane greatly missed her robe. It wasn't as warm outside as it had been in the apartment.

She hoped to see their apartment door open and a mouse scramble out, followed by Max. But when he came out, he came out alone.

He returned to them. "I couldn't find the mouse. Which I believe means he's returned to wherever he lives."

"What if he lives in our sofa cushions?" Sloane asked.

"I was thinking more that he's returned to where he lives *in the forest.*"

"Ivy and I can't reenter that apartment without a clear-cut resolution to the mouse issue."

"What do you suggest?"

"An immediate visit by a professional."

"Fine. I'll get someone here today."

"And this person won't kill the mouse," Ivy said worriedly. "Right?"

"Um," Max said.

"I'm sure there are pest-control companies who've figured out how to remove mice alive and, you know, release them into the wild." Ivy looked at Max with entreaty. "I'm a rat mom."

"A what what?"

"I have two rats that I really, really love. I can't stand to think that anything bad would happen to the mouse. Because I'd never want anything bad to happen to Kevin and Ricky."

Personally, Sloane cared not at all whether the mouse found its happily ever after.

"I'll see if I can find a pest-control company that releases mice into the wild," Max said with a straight face.

"Thank you! It will really creep me out if I have to live in an apartment where a mouse was murdered."

"We will have a conversation about mouse mortality at a later time," Sloane told her. Then, to Max, "From the apartment, we'll need clothes, toiletries, our phones, my laptop, and my purse."

"You want me to go in for your clothes and toiletries?" he asked skeptically. "And paw through your drawers?"

"I'll go in with Max," Ivy volunteered. "He can be my mouse bodyguard while I grab our things."

Max made gun hands with his fingers. "No need to sob," he said to Sloane, "I'll do my landlord's job."

He was an ogre. A sad excuse for a person.

Max and Ivy entered the apartment together.

Sloane checked her watch repeatedly during the five minutes it took them.

"Did you see the mouse?" Sloane asked as they neared.

"Nope," Ivy answered.

Where is the mouse? It really might be in their sofa cushions.

"Ivy told me that you two were just about to have breakfast when the mouse invaded," Max said. "So I invited her to have breakfast at my place and she said yes. Will you join us?"

Sloane didn't want to share breakfast with him. Nor accept his charity. However, as their landlord, he did somewhat owe them food and coffee seeing as how they couldn't access the food and coffee in their apartment. "I'll join you."

Max held his back sliding door open for them. Like the last time she'd been inside, she noted that the air carried a subtle note of citrus—a smell Max had always liked.

Even as a college student short on money, he'd had great taste and kept his living quarters in good shape. His current house reflected those qualities as well as his net worth.

When she thought of the interiors of Victorian houses, she thought of very small rooms and spindly, feminine pieces of antique furniture. That stereotype was not this. Max had definitely enlarged the space from what it would have been originally by removing walls and increasing openings between rooms. The furniture was masculine and sophisticated. He'd gone more for a showplace than for a cozy home. Which was typical Max. He liked comfort but he liked the trappings of success more.

"Wow!" Ivy said. "Your house is so pretty."

"Thanks. How about I make you my specialty, raspberry waffles?"

"Awesome," Ivy answered.

"We'll help," Sloane said. Good manners demanded she and Ivy do their part. "I'll go change clothes and be right back. Excuse me." She carried one of the tote bags Ivy had removed from the apartment to a half bath under the stairway.

Oof, she thought when she looked in the mirror.

Clothing, shoes, makeup, hair, nail polish. All of it helped her feel confident and in-control. She'd been devoid of everything but the nail polish this morning. She regained composure with every item she put to rights.

Emerging a few minutes later dressed and presentable, she felt much more like herself as she entered a kitchen that boasted oak cabinetry and enough white quartz on the countertops and backsplash to have exhausted a quarry.

Ivy was chatting comfortably as she poured batter into a

waffle iron. Max turned bacon in a skillet. Sloane went to work brewing coffee, then poured waters and orange juice. When the meal was ready, they settled at the breakfast table positioned next to a bay window.

This felt . . . oddly intimate.

"Delicious," Ivy proclaimed. "I've never had a raspberry waffle before." She was shoveling far too much dazzled admiration Max's way for Sloane's comfort.

Sloane wanted to warn Ivy, *Don't trust him.* But she couldn't voice that while he was hosting them for breakfast. So she simply gave herself the admonishment.

Don't trust him, Sloane.

Napkin in her lap, she bolstered herself by consuming breakfast in the most elegant way known to man.

"Are you taking any summer school?" Max asked Ivy.

"Only a driver's ed course."

"Which class did you find most challenging your freshman year?" he asked.

"Algebra."

Sloane had to admit that Ivy was right about the deliciousness of the waffles. They were divine.

Max swallowed a bite of bacon. "My advice as a graduate of Penn's business school is to get really good at using a math calculator. You don't need to be able to do anything on paper or in your head. The calculator can do it faster and more accurately."

Sloane cleared her throat, setting down her utensils. "Well, *this* graduate of Penn's business school believes there's a great deal of merit in learning concepts using pencil, paper, and your brain."

His pale green gaze flicked to her. "I'm not surprised to hear that's your stance." His attention returned to Ivy. "Your aunt is old-fashioned about some things."

Frustration toward him heated to a simmer. "I'm every bit as technologically advanced as you are."

"Says the person teaching other people habits established hundreds of years ago to the person running a company that caters to the reading tastes of modern-day people."

"I'm the person," she immediately countered, "who came up with the inspiration for the company that caters to the reading tastes of modern-day people."

"Please pass the syrup?" Ivy interrupted with a mix of cheer and desperation. "Any other tips for me, Max?"

"Use AI as a tool."

"But never to do your work for you when your teachers are asking you to do the work," Sloane stated.

"Attend every tutoring session your teachers offer and win them over with your charm. That will often bump up your grade."

"Be kind because kindness is important not because you're trying to manipulate your way to a better grade."

"Avoid boys until you and they are twenty-four years old. Only then will they be mature enough to deserve you."

"I recommend avoiding all men under the age of thirty-five." Sloane gave him a pointed look. "They're astonishingly immature until that age."

"Success is the best revenge," he told Ivy.

"Worldly success is not everything in life. Chase it and you'll end up lonely and unfulfilled."

"Great wealth takes the edge off loneliness and unfulfillment."

"I could name many wealthy celebrities who prove that statement false."

"All I can say, Ivy, is that *I've* found it hard to be miserable while driving my Porsche and living here in my mansion."

Sloane set her lips together in order to maintain decorum.

For the rest of the meal, Max concentrated the full power of his attention on the girl, getting her talking about her great passions. One, rats. Two, watching other teenagers make crafts on YouTube. Not making those crafts herself, mind you, which stumped Sloane. But simply watching other teens make crafts.

The instant they'd all finished breakfast, Sloane rose and carried her tableware to the sink. "Ivy, can you be ready to leave in ten minutes?"

"Sure." The girl headed to the bathroom.

"You don't need to do that," Max said, referring to the fact that she was rinsing the dishes and sliding them into the dishwasher.

"Ivy and I clean up after ourselves."

He moved around the space, putting things away. "I'm not sure how long it'll take me to find an exterminator who believes in a catch-and-release system with mice. If I can't get someone to the garage apartment today, will you be comfortable sleeping there?"

"No."

"Then how do you feel about sleeping in one of the guest bedrooms here?"

"Similar to the way Princess Leia felt when held prisoner by Darth."

His grin had sharp, predatory edges. "I'm Darth Vader?"

She lifted her shoulders. "The two of you are honestly *so* similar."

"Would you prefer taking your chances with the mouse or being a prisoner of Darth?"

She considered. "Darth."

"In that case, I'll show you the bedroom options." She followed him up the stairs, wondering how a morning that had begun as normal and peaceful had come to this.

Max's bedroom, bathroom, and office dominated the

second story. He continued up the next flight of stairs. They reached the third level. "There are three bedrooms and two bathrooms on this floor. If you and Ivy need to stay here tonight, you can take your pick. All the sheets are clean. All the bathrooms are stocked with towels."

Like the rest of his house, everything on this level appeared to have been remodeled by an expert designer.

They backtracked downstairs, Sloane striving not to compare this gorgeous, historic house to her simple home in LA.

In the foyer, he opened a drawer. "Here's an extra house key." He dropped it into her palm, a smug sparkle in his eyes.

Chapter Seven

In an example of spectacularly poor timing, the mouse emergency occurred on the same day that Sloane had scheduled a meeting with her father.

If Sloane had been the type to cancel established plans at the last minute, she'd have cancelled the meeting. But alas, that was not good etiquette. Also, she couldn't let Ivy down. The teen had been counting the days until they could go through Harper's records, housed at Dad's condo, because Ivy had high hopes of pinpointing information in those records that would lead to her birth father.

After Sloane picked up Ivy from the church, the two of them grabbed chowder for lunch, then drove toward Sloane's hometown of Waldoboro.

As the scenery became more and more familiar, a sense of dread grew within Sloane. The dread had nothing to do with the town itself and everything to do with her childhood here.

When Sloane was one and Harper three, their mother had left their father. Her parents had never been married, so there'd been nothing to dissolve legally. Not a marriage and not custody, since their mother hadn't desired custody. Gone had been *gone*. After their mother departed, Harper and Sloane had never seen her again. Nor heard an update about her until midway through Sloane's high school years, when Dad had informed them that she'd died of complications of pneumonia.

Reading between the lines, Sloane had eventually concluded that Dean Madison had loved their mother but that his gambling addiction had driven her away. The loss of her had removed whatever stuffing he once may have possessed. Without stuffing, he'd acted like a doll missing its insides.

Her father hadn't yelled at her and Harper. He hadn't hit them. He was not an evil man.

Unfortunately, he wasn't a good one, either. He'd been unreliable when present and absent a lot of the time—bouncing from job to job. He'd worked as a forklift operator. He'd mowed lawns. He'd stocked shelves. He'd driven trucks. He'd served in Maine's National Guard.

When employed, he gambled away much of the money he made. When unemployed, their family of three survived on unemployment insurance.

Without a trustworthy adult in the house, she and Harper had been forced to teach themselves to bathe, brush their teeth, and comb their hair after being ridiculed by other kids for being dirty and unkempt. They'd almost never had clothes that fit. Their kitchen had rarely been stocked with enough food. They'd made it to school only because she and Harper had gotten themselves up and walked there. They'd depended on the free lunch program because Dad seldom provided meals at home.

It hadn't been until much later that Sloane realized what she'd endured as a child had a name.

Neglect.

Her father's struggles had plunged Sloane into a chronic state of stress. She now understood that some of the demons Harper had battled—anxiety, an eating disorder, substance abuse—were struggles shared by others who'd been neglected. Even Harper's decision to leave home at eighteen to escape her role of caregiver to Sloane was a behavior shared by many.

Though Sloane's demons were different, she had her share. She needed to be orderly. She struggled to delegate or let others in because she found it hard to trust people to take care of things. She didn't feel safe unless armed with etiquette, clothing, and grooming.

She reached her father's condo complex—a grouping of buildings that reminded Sloane of a woman who'd enjoyed a few glory days when young but was now well past her prime and had given up on maintenance. Together she and Ivy walked toward her father's unit.

Ivy had communicated her eagerness to dive headlong into her search for her birth father. Yet the teenager had shown neither excitement nor negativity regarding the prospect of seeing her biological grandfather. Which made sense because Dean Madison was a non-entity in Ivy's life.

Sloane's father answered their knock looking a decade older than his fifty-eight years. He was uncomfortably thin beneath his threadbare gray sweater and beige pants. His beard was grizzled, his loosely curling brown-gray hair untidy. Deep lines furrowed his hawkish face.

A panicked fear—that she'd be stuck here with him, depending on him—flashed through Sloane's mind. But no, she reminded herself. She was an adult. Free to leave this condo at any time. Secure in the income she made. Able to depend on herself.

"Hello, Dad."

"Hello. Welcome." He did not attempt to hug Sloane or Ivy. Tiredly, he motioned for them to enter.

He'd moved in here around the time Sloane graduated from college, so this condo had never been her home. Yet it shared similarities with the apartments they'd lived in when she was growing up. Worn-down furniture. Mess. Dust.

Coming face-to-face with him was like stirring sand that had been resting dormant in the bottom of a pail of water. Suddenly granules of resentment, pity, and guilt were spinning upward within her.

"How's your health?" Sloane asked.

"Not great. My emphysema isn't getting any better."

She nodded. Decades of smoking had caused the condition. Based on the smell of the condo—cigarettes and burned coffee—he was never going to quit. "What can I do to help you while I'm in Maine for the next few months?"

"Nothing."

"Do you have plenty of food?"

He lifted a bony shoulder. "Enough."

Many years ago, he'd sustained an injury on the job and been living on disability pay ever since. Sloane went to the kitchen adjoining the living room. He made a protesting sound, but she ignored it in order to take stock of the refrigerator and pantry. As expected—very little there.

She'd spent most of her life trapped in a cycle of hoping he'd come through for her and Harper, realizing he wasn't going to, and hoping anew. During her time at Penn, she'd finally brought an end to that cycle.

However, this kitchen empty of food—such a jarring throwback to her childhood—pricked her spirit. He hadn't come through for his daughters, but she would come through for him. At the very least, with groceries. Sloane could not allow her parent to starve while she herself was living in the lap of luxury down the road in Groomsport. "I'll be stopping by weekly. When I do, I'll clean for an hour and bring food."

"No need—"

"I'll be stopping by weekly," she insisted in her business-owner tone. "I'll text you to set up a time."

He didn't fight her on it. He was still a doll missing its insides. "Come sit down." He took an armchair.

Sloane and Ivy perched on the front edge of the sagging sofa.

"You said over the phone that you wanted Harper's records?" he asked.

"Yes."

"I pulled them out of the closet for you. They're there." He bobbed his chin toward two containers stacked in the hallway.

"Thank you. We'll take them with us when we go."

A pause. "What're you after?" he asked.

"Details on my biological father," Ivy answered.

He responded with a cough.

"Did Harper ever say anything to you about Ivy's biological father?" Sloane asked.

His hollow eyes seemed to peer back through time. "I know they were together for a short time when she lived in Boston. When you were born, Ivy, I told Harper to call your father and tell him he needed to support you financially."

"What did Harper say to that?" Ivy asked.

"She told me it was none of my business and that her relationship with him hadn't been a public thing. I remember that very well. Those were the words she used. *Not a public thing*. I asked her what she meant by that."

"And?" Sloane asked.

"She wouldn't say."

Sloane's phone chimed, alerting her to an incoming text. From an unknown number.

> There are very few pest-control companies in the northeastern United States of America who remove mice from homes alive.

Clearly, this was from Max. As landlord, he'd have access to her phone number thanks to the rental documents for the garage apartment.

MAX

> But my assistant looked high and low and finally found one who lives near Acadia National Park. I'm going to pay him a small fortune to come and remove your mouse, but he can't be in Groomsport until the day after tomorrow.

This Wednesday was becoming a real kick in the teeth.

Sloane stood. "Ivy and I will be on our way. If you remember anything else about Ivy's birth father, please let us know." She couldn't wait to leave.

Sloane carried a box out. Ivy carried a box out. And her father shut the door behind them.

On the way back to Groomsport in Brooke's big SUV, Ivy turned down the Bruno Mars song she was playing to ask, "Does it make you sad to see Dean?" Ivy didn't call Sloane's father "Grandpa" because they didn't have that type of relationship.

"To be honest, it does."

"Yeah. I thought so. How come you said you'd go by there every week?"

Sloane rubbed the side of her thumb against the steering wheel. "Do you agree that one of the most famous verses in the Bible is 'Do to others as you would have them do to you'?"

"Yep."

"In the devotional book I've been reading, the author suggested a way to rephrase that verse. It's this . . . Give to other people what you need. I've spent time pondering it as a question. *Am I giving to other people what I need?*"

Sloane had come to faith during her college years when her roommate had invited her to a Bible study. She'd been the daughter of an unloving and unfaithful father. Learning that she had a capital F Father who did and would love her unconditionally? Who was faithful by nature? That had changed her life, flooding the dark places inside her heart with sunlight.

Ivy had been raised in a family of faith and so it was a joy to have this bedrock part of both their lives in common.

"The second I saw that my dad barely has any food," Sloane went on, "I felt this internal nudge. I knew that I was meant to give him some of the things I needed when I was little. Groceries. A clean place to live."

It didn't matter whether he wanted or appreciated the groceries. The concept of giving others what you need didn't come with qualifiers like, "Only if the person is grateful." Or "Only if the person deserves it."

Sloane darted a glance at Ivy and saw that the girl was watching her with sympathy. "I'm sorry," Ivy said, "that you and Harper didn't have groceries and a clean place to live when you were kids."

"That's kind of you to say, sweetheart."

"And I'm glad that you're okay now."

"I'm definitely okay now," Sloane reassured her. It was true. Thanks mostly to God's grace, but also to therapy, distance, and the passage of years, she *was* okay now.

Pulling onto The Gables property, they didn't have the option of returning to their apartment, currently the dwelling place of two caged rats and one free-roaming mouse. Which meant they had no choice but to take Harper's containers into Max's mansion.

It was midafternoon, a time of day when Max was always at the office. Even so, they knocked on his front door, rang the bell, waited. No response, so Sloane used the key he'd given her. It felt a little as if they were breaking and entering as they eased into the silent foyer and then transported Harper's boxes up the stairs.

"This house is amazing," Ivy stage whispered as they deposited their boxes on the third-floor landing. "Like, I think this is the best house I've been in. Ever."

Yes, look at the splendid place where he lives thanks to the company I co-founded. "It's gorgeous," Sloane admitted. It was Max's house, so she'd have liked to resist its charm on principle. However, The Gables was such a brilliant mix of old-world character and modern comfort that the house was seducing her into loving it.

The tote bags with their belongings from the apartment were still downstairs so they brought those up, selected which rooms they'd be staying in, then plopped onto the floor of the third-floor hall beside Harper's containers.

Ivy opened her box immediately.

Sloane, needing a moment to prepare herself, took a deep breath. *You can do this, Sloane.*

She removed the lid and saw Harper's jewelry box resting on top. She lifted it out and opened it with a creak. Several necklaces, rings, bracelets, earrings. These were all worth pennies yet held great value for her because she could remember Harper wearing each of these items.

She *missed* her sister. The enormity of her loss pressed into her like a gale-force wind.

"Are you all right?" Ivy asked.

Sloane looked up. "Yes. I love Harper. So . . . going through these things is definitely good. But also hard."

"My siblings are super important to me. I can't imagine losing one of them."

Ivy's siblings were now twenty-five, twenty-two, and twenty. The oldest, Chelsea, was a nurse in Portland. Next oldest, Caleb, was finishing his college credits with a study-abroad program in Spain. Next oldest, Jordan, was working all summer in Canada. Ivy was rich in sisters and brothers—all of whom had always doted on her. Sloane wouldn't have had it any other way for her niece. But she would have had it a different way for herself. If she'd been able to choose, Harper would be with her still and that version of Harper would be whole and healthy.

Sloane set the jewelry box to the side. Next came high school yearbooks. A graduation cap Harper had personalized on the top to say, *One degree hotter*. A leather jacket.

Ivy was going through the loose papers in her box one by one. "I'm seeing bills and stuff."

Sloane had also reached paper at the bottom of her box. "Same here. We're after records that have to do with you. Your birth, your adoption."

They studied each page. Most were irrelevant and could be thrown away.

"Oh!" Ivy held up a yellow folder.

"That looks promising."

Ivy crawled across to sit next to Sloane and opened the folder on the carpet in front of them. "You can go through it, Aunt Sloane."

"No, it's all right. This is your search. I'm here as your ally and supporter."

The teen flicked past Harper's birth certificate and Social Security card. She gasped. "*Look*. Here's my birth certificate."

They both leaned forward to read it.

"The space for the name of my birth father is blank," Ivy said, disappointment clear in her tone.

"Let's keep going."

Ivy flipped over a few more documents.

"There," Sloane said. This paper was titled "Voluntary Adoption Surrender." Sloane tapped her finger on it. "Look, this is dated five months after your birth, right around the time when you were placed for adoption."

"*Wait!* I think you're right. Is this his name? Here? It says Seth Taylor."

Sloane rapidly scanned the text. "I believe that is his name, yes. Your biological father."

"Seth Taylor," Ivy said slowly, as if test-driving the syllables.

Ivy's profile was still bent over the paper, strands of strawberry-blond hair drifting forward. Her niece was one of the greatest gifts Sloane had received in her lifetime. It was hard to compute that anyone would have terminated their parental rights to her, but Seth Taylor had. Was Ivy feeling a sense of rejection in response to the black-and-white evidence of that?

But Ivy, so well-adjusted and cherished, didn't appear upset. Only enthusiastic. "Let's look him up!"

"Sure. Can you grab my computer from my room?"

Ivy was back with it in seconds, returning to her spot beside Sloane. "Should we start with Google?"

"Seth Taylor is a fairly common name, but we can certainly start with Google." Sloane ran a search.

The Seths that came up in response to Sloane's search all lived far away and none were the right age.

"I could try to find him on Facebook," Sloane suggested.

"Yes, please!"

Sloane ran a search there. Several Seth Taylors appeared. Again, none seemed like a match.

They did the same on their other social media apps. No viable hits.

"Bummer," Ivy whispered.

"We're just getting started," Sloane said. "We'll do more research on how to find people and then we'll keep trying. Remember that we actually had a very productive day."

"Right! Because now we know his name."

Max arrived home that evening feeling unusually pleased with himself.

A mouse was occupying Sloane's apartment. Which meant Sloane was occupying his house.

He found he liked, very much, the idea of having her under his roof.

He hadn't planted the mouse. But he would have if he'd understood that doing so would land Sloane at The Gables. The mouse had earned the right to live. Maybe Max should negotiate a mouse raise and mouse food for life.

He entered his house, set aside his keys, and listened. He couldn't hear Sloane or Ivy.

He climbed to the second story and stopped, looking up toward the third story. "Everyone doing okay?"

A distant "Yes!" from Ivy. The girl bounded into sight.

"Do you ladies need anything? Dinner, for example?"

"We ate an early dinner out."

"Help yourself to the pantry and refrigerator." Where was Sloane? He craned his head for a glimpse of her but couldn't see her.

"Thanks! And thank you for letting us stay here. Would

you mind helping me bring Kevin and Ricky over from the apartment? While we're there, I'll get clothes for me and Aunt Sloane for tomorrow."

Which was how Max ended up standing in his garage apartment with his hands on his hips, eyeballing Ivy's rats. "What horror movie did these two escape from?"

She giggled. "They're cute!"

"They're hideous."

"Look at their sweet little ears and noses."

"Look at their creepy tails."

"Want to cuddle one?"

He met her eyes. "If there's any detail of me that makes you think I'm the type of person to cuddle rats, tell me, so that I can change that detail."

Smiling, she rolled her eyes.

One rat was eating while the other one was doing its best to climb on its head.

"They're very intelligent," Ivy said.

"Yeah," he responded dryly. "It looks like it."

"And friendly and silly. You have to have at least two of them because they're social."

She covered the rat cage with a blanket. Then Max and Ivy began the journey to the main house, Ivy talking his ear off about the details of rat care.

Sloane did not emerge from her room all night.

Max would have much preferred it if he'd had a chance to see and talk with her. But he wouldn't complain. It was surprisingly satisfying simply to know she was sharing his space. The feel of his whole house was different. Better. Fuller.

More alive.

More complete.

The next night, Sloane and Ivy reclined side by side on the bed in Sloane's guest bedroom at The Gables. Sloane had propped her computer on a pillow between them. It was playing the scene from *The Princess Diaries* when Mia arrives in Genovia.

This was their fourth shared movie night since Sloane had arrived in Maine. She and Ivy were taking turns picking movies. So far, Sloane had gravitated toward selections like *The Princess Diaries* that introduced her niece to movies Sloane had enjoyed when she was a kid. So far, Ivy had found all of Sloane's selections weird, but Sloane pressed on, maintaining that it benefited the girl to receive a solid introduction to the early 2000s.

Far below, Sloane could vaguely make out the sound of the front door opening and shutting. The hum of conversations.

When they'd come downstairs this morning, Sloane had informed Max that they'd planned to get breakfast on the way to the church. But she'd floated that plan too late. He'd already been in the process of making them cheese omelets with a side of ham.

He'd fed them and sparred with Sloane in equal measure.

The garage apartment had provided Sloane with a modicum of separation from Max since arriving in Maine ten days ago. A sense of urgency to return to the privacy of that was mounting inside her.

Max did not appear to be experiencing the same urgency. On the contrary, he acted as if their presence at The Gables was a battle he'd won instead of what it actually was—a battle he'd lost when he'd allowed *a rodent* to invade *his property*.

After dropping Ivy off at the church, Sloane had taken her computer to Java Junkie and worked there. She'd updated My Fair Lady's social media accounts, answered emails about upcoming events, paid bills.

She'd removed herself from The Gables in order to put

space between herself and Max. Also, she worried that if she spent hours alone at Max's house, she might be tempted to snoop through his bedroom.

If anything was bad etiquette—that was it.

The Princess of Wales did not snoop.

"I think Max is having people over," Ivy whispered now.

"I think you're right."

After another fifteen minutes passed, Ivy paused the show. "I'm dying to go down there and see what's going on. Can I?"

"No."

Ivy scrambled off the bed. "How 'bout if I just peek over the stairs? They won't see me. 'Kay? Please?"

"Fine. But stay out of sight."

Ivy moved stealthily onto the third-floor landing. Sloane followed, hanging back as Ivy angled her body to try to get a look at Max's guests.

Trendy music overlaid with male and female laughter bubbled up to them. It sounded over-idealized, as if Sloane was listening to a canned party-scene track.

"I can't see anything." Ivy returned to Sloane and wrapped her hands comically around her neck. "I'm thirsty. There aren't any glasses up here. What are we supposed to do? Lean over and slurp water out of the sink faucet? Surely that's bad etiquette, right? I can't imagine you drinking water that way."

Sloane pursed her lips.

"The party might go on for hours and hours," Ivy went on. "We'll be parched."

The girl was obviously angling for a visit to the party. Nonetheless, she'd made a decent point. For the third time since they'd come to this estate, Sloane and Ivy were once again in need of water to drink. Max should have let them know that he was having people over so that she and Ivy could have prepared accordingly. But of course he hadn't.

"Let me go downstairs and get us some glasses of water. Please." Ivy made prayer hands.

Sloane was suggestible enough to be feeling a sudden pang of dry-mouthed thirst. She ran a cost-benefit analysis in her head. Inject herself into Max's party? Or slurp from sink? "Fine," she told Ivy. "I'm going with you."

She didn't think anything untoward was happening downstairs. It sounded jovial yet dignified. Even so, she refused to send a fifteen-year-old into an adult party solo. "We're going to be *very* unobtrusive and quick. We'll just get our water and come back upstairs. All right?"

"Yay!"

In wide-legged gray sweatpants and a matching cropped sweatshirt, Sloane was wearing the most casual garments she ever wore during waking hours. She wholeheartedly believed in dressing as the person you wanted to become and coached her students to do the same. That meant she selected clothing as formal or more formal than the people she came into contact with. It would be uncomfortable and unusual for her to be dressed less formally than the people at Max's party. But also not her fault since he'd given them no warning.

Ivy hurried down the stairs. Sloane followed at a more sedate pace.

Upon reaching the first floor, it became immediately apparent that Max was hosting a stylish and expensive gathering. Oh dear. There were more people down here than she'd realized. The women were in party dresses, the men in sport coats.

Sloane nodded to the knot of guests in the front hall. Turning into the formal dining room, she encountered more guests, as well as a meal served by a catering team. She met people's eyes, nodded, murmured polite hellos as they moved through. In the kitchen, they each speedily filled water glasses.

Any route back to the third floor had to be less crowded than the route they'd just taken, so once they had water, Sloane exited the kitchen in the direction of the living room. As she did, her attention intersected with Max on the far side of the space.

He was staring directly at her. Clearly, he'd spotted her before she'd spotted him.

Positioned near the fireplace, dressed in a suit, he was talking to three women. They were all his type. Bikini-model bodies, long hair, short dresses.

A shaft of displeasure iced through Sloane. What had she expected? He was a rake doing rakish things.

Sloane lifted her glass and mouthed, *"We just came down for water."*

Max mouthed back, *"Stay."* Though she couldn't hear him, she could read his lips, even after all this time, as effortlessly as he'd read hers.

She shook her head and was guiding Ivy toward the hallway when a man to her right said, "Sloane!"

She and Ivy halted to face the speaker. In a flash, Sloane recognized him.

Nate Whittaker. He'd been an employee at Libri during her last few years there. They'd dated for a couple of months around the time she'd been booted from the company. His light brown hair and ruddy complexion had always been appealing, as had his long-lashed hazel eyes and calm, friendly demeanor. He had a square face and the stout body of someone who'd played football in high school. He was more muscular than she remembered and, on the whole, looked to have improved with age.

"Nate. It's wonderful to see you again."

"You too." He came in for a hug, which she returned.

They stepped apart. Sloane gestured with a water glass

toward her teen sidekick. "Nate, may I please introduce my niece, Ivy."

"Hi, Ivy," he said amiably.

"Hi!"

"I didn't know you were back in the area," he said to Sloane.

"Ivy and I are renting Max's garage apartment this summer. There's a pest-control issue in the apartment tonight so we're staying in the guest bedrooms upstairs out of necessity."

"You're staying in Max's garage apartment?" His expression communicated, *I'm highly confused because I thought you two were enemies.*

"Yes." She didn't owe him an explanation so didn't provide one. "We crashed this party because we got thirsty."

"Ah, gotcha. Party crashing for a good cause." He grinned.

Sloane smiled back.

"Is this party celebrating something?" Ivy asked Nate.

"Excellent quarterly earnings," Nate told them. "Every time that happens, Max hosts his employees and several other people from the local business community here."

"Ah," Sloane said. "So you're still working at Libri?"

"I am. I moved to Maine when Max brought the headquarters here. I could've stayed in Philadelphia and worked remotely but I've always liked coming into the office. I'm pretty near the introvert line but I am, technically, an extrovert. It's good for me to be around people. *Wow.* I can't believe you're here. Will you . . . stay down here so we can talk more?" Nate gestured to the glasses. "I can set those aside for you ladies if that would help."

"Thank you for offering, but we're going to head back up."

Ivy slumped at that announcement.

"It's really so good to see you, Sloane," Nate said. "There

are at least five of us from the days when you were at Libri who are still around. Now and then we talk about how awesome you were."

Were. As if she was deceased.

"And I think about you often," he continued. "Always with fondness."

"I often think about the Libri team with fondness, too." Except for Max. "It would be wonderful to catch up with you some other time."

"Is your cell phone number still the same?" he asked.

"No, it's different."

"Would you mind sharing it with me?"

"Not at all."

He pulled out his phone and she rattled off her number.

Nate wasn't wearing a wedding band, which was surprising. He'd make a terrific husband and father. Maybe he was married and not wearing a wedding band? But if so, why was she getting chemistry vibes from him? It felt, despite that she was wearing sweatpants and holding enough water to replenish a fishtank, that he might be interested in revisiting the romantic relationship between them that she'd broken off.

"I'll be in touch." He pocketed his phone.

"Fabulous. Enjoy the party." She moved off.

"Nice to meet you, Ivy," Nate called.

"You too."

As they made their way down the hallway, Sloane's vision landed on Max's mother, who was coming in their direction.

The older woman halted, face lighting up with delighted surprise. "Sloane?"

"Nicole," Sloane said with warmth.

"Oh my goodness! Sloane!" The older woman embraced Sloane—a long, tight hug. "I missed you."

Sloane's personality had always endeared her to the parents

of her friends and occasional boyfriends. For the nine years that Max had been in her life, so had Nicole. Max's mother could be feisty. But, overall, she'd been wonderful to Sloane. Caring, encouraging, approving. When Nicole had visited Philadelphia, she'd made big meals for Sloane and Max. She'd sent Sloane birthday gifts. They'd had long talks during which Nicole had asked countless questions and shown genuine interest in Sloane's life.

Back when she'd lost Libri, she'd lost a lot of people other than Max. People like Nicole. People like Nate.

Sloane introduced Ivy.

"You were this tall the last time I saw you!" Nicole told Ivy, holding her hand near her waist.

"Was I?" Ivy asked.

"Yes. My, how you've grown." Nicole's focus lifted to Sloane. "I had no idea you were going to be here tonight. Have you and Max made up?" Shaking her head, she swished both hands forward like, *Never mind, don't answer that.* "I'll get the story from him later. And I'll give him a piece of my mind about the fact that he didn't tell me you were in Maine. Why is he so secretive? He should tell his mother the important things. I raised him to tell me the important things. But does he? No. He's as tight-lipped as a spy. Are you doing well?"

"Very well. I live in LA and run my own etiquette-teaching business."

"I did *not* approve when I heard you'd been forced out of Libri. I've told Max that several times over the years."

Sloane nodded. Silence could be her only reply because no way would she say anything negative about Max to his mother or any of his other guests.

"I'm extremely proud of my son," Nicole continued. "But he has his faults. And his strengths. Did you know that he bought me a house?"

"I didn't. Where?"

"In Montville. I love my house. Please, the two of you, come over for lunch one day soon and I'll show you where I live."

"We'd like that."

"Max has done so many things to support my family. He asked me not to tell people about this, but I'll tell you because you're you. He paid off my parents' home. He bought cars for all his cousins. He invested in my brother's business and paid for the foundation work my sister needed."

Sloane didn't know where to file the kindness and generosity Nicole was attributing to Max. It didn't seem to fit on the shelf next to "Man who coldly excluded me from my two-hundred-million-dollar share of Libri."

"That's very nice of him." Ivy stepped into the void to make the appropriate comment.

"I hope you can find it within yourself to forgive Max." The hope in Nicole's eyes was hard for Sloane to see.

When Sloane hesitated, Nicole once again swished her hands forward in a *Never mind, don't answer that* way. "Max would throttle me if he knew I'd said that." She laughed. "We girls need to have our secrets, don't we?" she asked Ivy with a wink.

"Yep," Ivy agreed.

"Nope," Sloane corrected Ivy with a smile. "You're not allowed to have secrets until the age of twenty-one."

"This has made my day," Nicole told them.

"We're staying on the third floor and came down for water glasses," Sloane explained. "We'll head back up there now and let you get back to enjoying the party."

"I'll be in touch about having you over for a meal," Nicole said in parting as Sloane and Ivy carried their water upstairs.

Once they were out of earshot, Ivy whispered, "*Oooh.*"

"*Oooh* what?"

"*Oooh*, that Nate guy likes you. And also *Oooh*, those people are all so fancy. Did you see the women with Max? I think one of them was Milla Smithson."

"Well, if Milla knows what's good for her, she will not allow herself to fall for Max."

"Why?"

"Because there's no more certain route to heartache."

Sloane shut them back into her room where they both guzzled water and resumed the spots they'd left on top of the bed's comforter. She tried to interest Ivy in returning to the movie, but Ivy was suddenly obsessed with locating pictures of Max online.

Ivy found one photo after another of him circulating through the social scene in Maine, New York, and Pennsylvania. Art galleries, philanthropic events, concerts, cocktail parties. In every picture, a different gorgeous woman stood beside him.

As many dates and girlfriends as Max had had back in the day, he'd never cared about a "social scene" per se. It seemed that had changed.

"I was right," Ivy crowed. "That woman downstairs is Milla Smithson. She's a socialite. Her father owns an aerospace company, and she has her own line of cosmetics."

"Shall we turn on the movie?"

"Can we wait just one more minute? This Instagram account is called Maine Social Scoop and this lady who calls herself Social Sophie reports on gossip and events and—look!—Max is a favorite of hers. He's in so many of these photos! Here's one of him in a tux with the brunette who was downstairs." Ivy held her phone screen so that Sloane could see. "She's an investment banker and she's wearing a gown by Marchesa."

Instinctively, defensively, Sloane tried to block the image from hitting her retinas but didn't succeed.

More scrolling. "And here's one of him with a model who was born in Amsterdam."

Sloane had attempted to shut Max and Libri completely out of her mind when she'd left them both behind. However, the "completely" part of that sentence had proven unattainable. More than once, she'd stumbled on articles about Libri in business publications. Posts about Max routinely invaded her social media feed. Several times, she'd sat next to people on airplanes who were reading on the Libri app in flight. A year ago, she'd turned on her TV to the sight of him giving an interview. Friends from her Philadelphia years brought him up in conversation.

So many reminders.

She'd tried to resist feeling envious. Had prayed against that countless times with mixed results.

Sloane had once loved Libri, dreamed big dreams of its success, and poured herself into the company. For her, all of that had ended in scorched pieces of wood. Which Max had gone on to build into a blazing bonfire without her.

It stung to be Blockbuster in the story of how Netflix offered to sell their company to Blockbuster for fifty million and Blockbuster turned them down. It stung to be Ronald Wayne in the story of how Apple's third co-founder had sold his ten-percent stake in the company for eight hundred dollars.

Some days it felt as if she was achieving peaceful acceptance of her past with Libri. Other days, like this particular day in Max's expensive house surrounded by a fortune in original art, doing so felt impossible.

So what are you going to do, Sloane? Give in to jealousy and bitterness?

No.

Acceptance seemed impossible at this moment, but that was a lie she couldn't let herself believe. It *was* possible to accept. It was.

Once the closing credits rolled on *The Princess Diaries*, Ivy padded to bed.

Just like earlier when Ivy had mentioned their lack of water and Sloane had instantly craved water, she was now craving food. They'd eaten an early dinner specifically so they'd have as little reason to interact with Max as possible. It was now 10:20. Five hours since dinner.

She thought covetously of the berries, crackers, cheese, and chocolate stored in the cupboards of the garage apartment. Was the mouse feasting on those items at this very moment?

She shuddered. No way was she braving a trip across the backyard to the apartment. And no way was she braving a trip downstairs if Max's guests were still present. She hadn't registered party noises for quite some time. Maybe they were all gone?

She tiptoed to the banister. She could still hear people below. Very few now. Just Max's low baritone and feminine voices purring back at him.

Yeesh!

Returning to her room, she got herself ready for bed, then switched off the light and tried to sleep.

Couldn't.

Her mind's eye replayed how Max had looked earlier this evening. In a suit without a tie, a trio of women admiring him.

She rolled from her back onto her side. From her side onto her back. She scrunched closed her eyes. Then opened them wide and stared at the moon-silvered window shade.

She was starving!

An hour crawled past.

She crept back out to the landing. This time, she registered only silence.

She waited, straining her ears. All clear. She could safely go downstairs and forage for snacks.

Mellow lighting had been left on in the kitchen, which she used as a beacon as she made her way across the first floor in her slippers. Just as she was gliding through the living room, a masculine voice from the darkness spoke.

"Parading around in front of me in your sleepwear again?"

Chapter Eight

S loane jerked to a stop, heart rate spiking.

Max sat in deep shadow in an opulent leather armchair. His strong fingers loosely held a crystal tumbler half-full of amber liquid—likely bourbon. He'd never been much of a drinker, but even back when he could seldom afford good-quality bourbon, he'd had an appreciation for it.

"If you're trying to seduce me," he went on, pale eyes gleaming, "it would be faster and more expedient for you to simply tell me you want me." He was giving the impression of being mostly in control of his faculties, but something about his demeanor—an underlying recklessness?—made her suspect he was feeling his liquor.

"I can assure you that the *only* thing I want," Sloane said, "and the *only* thing that brought me down here is food."

"Help yourself."

"If you'd bothered to inform Ivy and me that you were having a gathering, we could've planned accordingly and taken water and food upstairs. Had that been the case, we wouldn't have had to disturb your guests."

At some point since she'd seen him last, he'd freed the top few buttons on his business shirt. The glow from the kitchen slid over him lovingly, highlighting the hard planes of his face, nestling into his disheveled hair, gleaming against his diamond cufflinks. "You didn't disturb my guests."

"Well, if nothing else, it disturbed *me* to insert myself into a party to which I had not been invited."

"I'm giving you a standing invitation to every party I host here while you're living on my property."

"And I'm preemptively registering my RSVP to that as a no."

She crossed to the fridge. Bingo. Leftovers from the caterers. She found a plate and served herself roast beef, corn salad, and a popover.

From his chair, Max watched Sloane perch on a stool at the island and begin eating in her Miss Manners way.

He rose and came to a stop across the island from her, setting his bourbon down with a *clink*. This was a better viewing position. Much closer. He noted how a few caramel brown strands of hair curved to a stop near the base of her throat. How the pink silk of her pajama collar rested smoothly against her ivory skin.

He'd screwed up the really good thing he'd had with Sloane. It hadn't been until she'd gone that he'd understood just how good of a thing, how rare of a thing, it had been.

She popped a bite of bread in her mouth. "Oh," she murmured in response to the taste. Every now and then, he was lucky enough to hear Sloane make that soft *oh* sound unconsciously.

She gathered another bite of food on her fork. "I'm surprised to find you downstairs alone."

"Why's that?"

"Because I expected you to be spending quality time with one of those women from earlier."

He could have been doing just that. But he hadn't wanted to. "You sound annoyed. Are you jealous of those women?"

With everyone but him, her eyes communicated compassion and calm. At the moment, they communicated nothing but indignation. "Why would I be jealous of them? I pity them. And you. More than a decade has passed since we first met and you're still choosing women who are interested in you for your looks."

"Oh? You're acknowledging that I'm handsome enough to draw women with my looks?"

She regrouped almost instantly, dabbing her lips with her napkin. "You know very well that you draw women with your looks and have always used that to your advantage. Which is a big part of your problem."

"What problem? That of being desired by beautiful women?"

She cut a bite of beef into a precise rectangle. "You have no idea what type of woman would make you happy."

"And you have no idea what type of man would make you happy. I saw your reunion with Nate." Max had gotten along well with Nate for the past four years. But seeing Nate slobber over Sloane this evening had reminded Max why he'd been unable to stand the guy back when Nate and Sloane had been dating. The sight of them together had caused his mood to curl at the edges like burning paper. "He's dull and predictable."

"Unlike some people, he's friendly, kind, and respectful toward me."

"Enter into a relationship with him and you'll soon be bored out of your skull."

"I prefer bored out of my skull to what you'll be once those women are done with you. Which is emptied of your money."

"It's cute that you think my money could be emptied." He threw back the rest of the bourbon. "My bank accounts are bottomless."

She was striving to look unbothered by this exchange and doing a pretty good job of it. But small details were making it past her control. He watched her pull off another piece of popover with too much force, then chew it rapidly. "While we're on the topic of your women—"

"—Which you brought up—"

"—Do you think you can find it within yourself to behave well this summer while Ivy's staying at The Gables? I would much prefer it if she doesn't see you set an example of valuing women for nothing but their sex appeal."

He raised his eyebrows a fraction.

"I don't want her witnessing anything above a PG level," Sloane said. "Brooke and Jared and I would appreciate it very much if you could tone things down to a suitable level while she's here."

"Oh? Are Brooke and Jared spending a lot of time worrying about my dating life while over in the Middle East?"

"Can you tone things down to a suitable level?"

"That question implies that I'm not operating at a suitable level now. I've had one party since you moved in, and you came down and saw it. Completely suitable."

"Answer my question, please."

"I'll make sure that Ivy doesn't witness anything above a PG level. Are you going to permit me to conduct R-rated behavior in private? Or are you ruling that out as well?"

"What you do in private is none of my business."

"It could be your business, if you're the one in private with me." He'd spoken without thinking, his mouth getting ahead of his brain. But as he watched Sloane blush, he didn't regret his words.

He could make her blush. At the very least, he could do that.

During their friendship and business partnership, he hadn't said things like that to her. He'd thought them. A lot. He couldn't count the number of times he'd felt the tug of physical attraction toward her. But he'd never said anything suggestive because he'd been afraid of injuring their friendship. In the end, had that carefulness benefitted him? No. Their friendship had been injured anyway.

"Did this evening's cloud of perfume damage your short-term memory?" she asked. "I clearly stated a few minutes ago that the *only* thing I wanted, and the *only* thing that brought me down here, was food."

He smiled at her—his very best smile. This was the wide, flattering smile that had won him numerous hard-to-get women.

She blinked once, slowly, then gave her head a little shake. All of a sudden, she was a blur of motion. Standing and sweeping up her plate, cutlery, napkin. "I'll be taking my food upstairs."

He didn't want her to go. Yet she'd already vanished.

Leaving him lonely.

The following evening, Ivy parked herself on Max's front steps and waited for him to get home from work.

It took ages. She didn't mind because she could entertain herself on her phone. But man. She couldn't *imagine* working until eight o'clock at night. When she was in school, she was dying to leave by 3:30 p.m.

She heard his car first, then saw it. He usually drove his Porsche, but she'd seen inside his garage, so she knew he also owned a new Mercedes and the car he was driving today—a 1970s Chevy Blazer.

She waved.

Instead of continuing past the house to the garage, Max parked nearby on the drive and walked over. He'd stayed at the office so late that it was almost sunset. The cooling air had a gray-blue tinge. Fireflies hovered in the bushes.

"Did you escape your terrible Aunt Sloane," he asked, "in order to tell me that you'd like to take me up on my generous offer of a Gucci purse or Tiffany bracelet?"

Grinning, she pressed to her feet. "No. I'm here because your assistant called Aunt Sloane this afternoon to tell her that the mouse was rehomed. We moved out of your house back to ours."

"I liked having you both at my house. If it were up to me, I'd have let the mouse become the new tenant of the apartment and kept you guys here at The Gables." He looked like he was serious.

"Really?"

"Yeah."

"Aunt Sloane never would have gone for that."

"No. She's a spoilsport."

"She's a lot of fun!"

"Only if you enjoy discussing which glass to use for dessert wine."

Ivy giggled. She was standing on the lowest step, which brought her closer to his eye level. "First, I want to thank you *so much* for finding a way to let the mouse live. Kevin and Ricky and I are super happy about how it all turned out. The rat boys celebrated by eating grapes after we got back to the apartment. They're thrilled."

"Always glad to thrill a pair of rats."

She toyed with the hem of her neon pink T-shirt. "The second thing I wanted to talk to you about is kind of personal."

"That's a terrifying intro. It's like I've got a speed train full of cars labeled with all the personal issues of teenaged girls whizzing in front of my eyes."

"This issue isn't terrifying," she rushed to say. "It's about my birth father."

"Your birth father?"

"Yes. I'd like to meet him. Aunt Sloane and I learned that his name is Seth Taylor. We think he once lived in Boston, back when Harper lived in Boston. But that's about all we know."

"I see."

"We googled him and looked for him on social media. But we couldn't find him. I wondered if you could help us. You're smart and great with computers and you're the type of person who gets things done, right?"

"Right. I'll definitely help you."

"Great, because I feel kinda bad that I've dumped all of this on Aunt Sloane. It would be good if we had someone with your connections working with us, you know? To share the load." When she was young, Max had come with Aunt Sloane to her house lots of times. He'd played board games with her, made crafts with her, kicked a ball with her, joked with her. Twice, she'd visited the Libri office in Philadelphia with Aunt Sloane and both times he'd taken them out for ice cream. She'd always been a giant Max fan.

Ivy didn't understand everything that had gone wrong between Sloane and Max. But she, personally, couldn't be happier that they were living on his property. His property was gorgeous. And this was Sloane and Max's big chance to make up.

"Your aunt will oppose including me in the search for you birth father," he said.

"I know. Sunday afternoon, I'm going to my friend's house to spend the night. If you, um, wanted to talk with Aunt Sloane about it then, you could."

"Very cagey." He raised his fist.

She bumped it. "You think you can get Aunt Sloane to agree?"

"Unsure. I meant it when I said I'd do anything for you. That includes going toe-to-toe with your Aunt Sloane."

Across town, Fiona was also returning home from a long day at work. She emptied her mailbox near the stone wall outlining her property. Then flicked through the items on autopilot, going through mail in the same way she went through mail six days a week—

One of the letters caused her nerves to jolt.

Isobel had sent her a letter. *Isobel.*

Her older sister had handwritten the address. The penmanship was recognizable to Fiona, even after all this time. This was the first communication between them that Isobel had initiated in thirty-five years.

It could be bad news, she cautioned herself. Maybe a sentiment along the lines of, *I will hate you as long as I live. Never reach out to me again under any circumstances.*

It could also be good news, Fiona's stubborn streak countered.

Mind spinning, she drove her Aston Martin the rest of the way to her house. Once inside, she set everything else down and made a circuit of her kitchen, tapping the letter against the palm of her free hand.

She stopped and peered at the letter, suspense pinging inside her like a pinball. Finally, she went to her favorite chair in the living room, the one she used for reading. Instead of reclining back into it as if it were a hug like usual, she sat upright.

Gathering courage, she ripped open the envelope's flap and slid out an ivory notecard embossed at the top with her sister's monogram.

Fiona,

If you'd like for me to consider joining you for the eclipse, as you've expressed, then I have a stipulation. Restore communication between yourself and Nicole. Extend her forgiveness. Send me a photo of the two of you together.

This will show me that you understand how hard it is to do the thing you're asking me to do. But that you're willing, as you're asking me to be willing.

—Isobel

Diabolical. Fiona had never once anticipated this. And yet, Isobel's request made a terrible kind of sense. Fiona had done to Isobel what Nicole had done to Fiona. And so if Fiona wanted Isobel to forgive, then it wasn't completely shocking to think that Isobel would demand that Fiona forgive first.

Since the day she'd learned that Felix was Max's father, Fiona had seen Nicole from a distance a couple of times in Groomsport. That's it. That's as close as their paths had come to crossing. They'd never spoken because when Nicole slept with Fiona's husband, she'd betrayed their friendship in the worst way. Nicole had become someone Fiona loathed.

And these are, no doubt, an inner voice pointed out, *the feelings that Isobel has toward you.*

Nicole had cost Fiona and her sons immeasurable pain when she'd called that reporter and announced Max's paternity to everyone in the United States of America. Fiona had barely survived the scandal. Her sons had been scarred by it, Jude most of all because he'd been her caretaker when her mental health had tanked following the divorce. His high school years had mostly been consumed by Fiona's depression. And all of this had started with Nicole.

Fiona's conscience flared.

It wasn't fair to lay all the blame at Nicole's door. Felix bore half the responsibility. Her ex-husband's inability to resist sex outside of marriage had left a wake of relationship destruction behind him. Including the destruction she and Felix together had wrought on Isobel.

In the years since her divorce, Fiona had endured Felix because that's what was in the best interests of her sons. The same could not be said for Nicole. It had suited Fiona to cut Nicole out of her life and, as far as she knew, that had suited Nicole, too. Her former friend and housekeeper had never tried to reach out to her.

Fiona reread the short note two more times.

If one of them, she or Nicole, was going to make a move to mend fences then it should be Nicole because Nicole was the one who owed Fiona an apology. Nicole was the one who should express remorse.

Fiona, understanding this law of the universe, had done exactly that with Isobel. But now Isobel was asking Fiona to make contact. To forgive the person Fiona least wanted to forgive, a person who hadn't asked for forgiveness.

With a growl, she flicked the letter to the side, yanked off one high heel, and threw it hard. It landed with a *plunk,* skidding. She yanked off the other high heel and chucked it, too. Then she speed-dialed Burke.

"Fiona," he said with pleasure.

"I just received a letter from Isobel." She brought him up to speed on her sister's demands. He listened quietly as she railed. She knew him well enough to recognize that the silence was not full of judgment or criticism. She trusted that he wanted her best and was on her side.

The kindness in his voice confirmed it when he spoke. "What are you going to do?"

"I have no idea. My immediate plan is to stew on this for the next few days."

"Okay," he said without a trace of censure. "Want me to bring dinner over so we can talk through it more?"

"Yes, but only if the dinner you bring is very, very fattening."

He chuckled. "You'll never forgive me if I bring over a fattening dinner. I'll only remain in your good graces if I bring over lean meat and vegetables."

"Fine," she said irritably.

"You know, Fiona, that I'll bring you the most fattening dinner Groomsport has to offer if that's what you really want. Is that what you really want?"

It was very hard to sustain any level of annoyance with him, even for seconds at a time. "No, you read me right," she said, relenting. "Lean meat and vegetables it is."

Sloane, it's Nate. I'm so glad I ran into you at Max's house. I'd love to take you out for lunch or drinks sometime next week, if you're free.

SLOANE

That sounds lovely, thank you. How about lunch on Tuesday?

NATE

Perfect. I can't wait.

JUDE

I spoke with my mom and Jeremiah about the missing tiara. They both remember it, my mom especially. Neither of them realized it was missing and neither of them have any idea what happened to it.

MAX

Thanks for checking with them.

JUDE

Sure. What are our next steps?

MAX

How do you feel about snooping around in their houses?

JUDE

Strongly against.

MAX

K. I figured. Forget I said anything about that.

JUDE

Forget it because you're not going to snoop? Or forget it so that I can play dumb about it if you get caught snooping?

MAX

The latter.

JUDE

Look, it's not right that my dad's pressuring you to recover the tiara. And I definitely don't want any more media attention on your mom or you. I'll help you. But let's chase other avenues before you consider snooping.

MAX

Like?

JUDE

I'll talk with a colleague who has experience with jewelry thefts of this caliber and get back to you.

Nicole Cirillo was giving Sloane and Ivy an extraordinarily thorough tour of her home in Montville.

After Max's party, Nicole had followed up with Sloane to reiterate her lunch invitation. Sloane had accepted and, now that she was here, found she was glad she had. Not only was it polite etiquette to take Nicole up on her gracious offer. But it also felt good, after years of silence, to restore communication with Nicole, who'd been a mother figure to Sloane during a formative season of Sloane's life.

The older woman glowed with pride as she showed them every room, bathroom, and even every closet. Nicole went into raptures over the storage the house offered. They admired the kitchen cabinetry, the natural light, and the herbs growing in profusion in Nicole's backyard.

There could be no doubt that Nicole cherished her house.

As well she should. It was an adorable Tudor-style—a whimsical mix of original craftsmanship and excellent updating. Despite the merits of the house, Sloane understood that Nicole's verbal enthusiasm for it today was less about the building and more about convincing Sloane that Max, who'd purchased this house for his mother, was a decent human being.

That message was not lost on her. Whatever Max's faults, whatever the ways he'd wronged Sloane, he obviously loved his mother and had provided for her well.

A man who loved and provided for his mother could not be a completely irredeemable man. Though there were likely death row inmates who loved and provided for their mothers. So maybe that hypothesis wasn't correct.

Nicole served them lemonade on her back patio while grilling burgers for their lunch.

Sloane couldn't help but make an uncomfortable observation. Max was doing a better job taking care of his single parent than she was doing taking care of hers. That stemmed mostly, though, from the fact that Max was rich, and she was not. If she was still co-owner of Libri, she could've afforded to purchase a home for her father, too.

"My son was never happier than he was during those years when you and he were close friends," Nicole said, standing at the barbecue with a spatula in hand.

"That's interesting," Ivy said. "Because weren't you and Max pretty short on money in those days?"

"Not only did we have very little money, we also worked really long hours." It might be revisionist history on Nicole's part to think Max had never been happier than he had been then. However, Sloane couldn't discard Nicole's conclusion out of hand because she herself had been happy then, too. "There was something special about those years despite the struggles. When we were building Libri, we had the sense that we were onto something that had the potential to be big. Our efforts felt meaningful. Everyone on our staff shared our vision. It was exciting."

"Max and Sloane were the best team," Nicole told Ivy. "They both pursued excellence. They both wanted to make something of themselves and their opportunities. Both were charming. It was wonderful for me to see them together because they had the kind of relationship that I never did find for myself yet have always wanted for my son."

Nicole flipped the three burgers, then looked to Sloane. "What I valued most, though, is how you complemented each other. You stood up to him and disagreed with him when he needed that. He made you laugh when you needed that. Adding your intelligence to Max's intelligence was like one plus one equaling twenty."

"Thank you for saying that." It was gratifying to hear that Nicole had seen and appreciated Sloane's contributions.

"You're welcome. Libri never would have become what it became without you."

Except that, in the end, Libri *had* become what it became without her.

The next afternoon, Max cut off the water to the garage apartment.

This was one of the best signals ever invented. Mayday—the phonetic English pronunciation of the French *m'aidez*, which meant *help me*—signaled distress. The cutting off of water signaled to Sloane that a conversation with him was required.

An hour passed. Max watched golf in his living room while impatiently waiting for her to show. He'd rather argue with

Sloane than actually go and do some of his favorite things, things he paid to do—like playing golf or attending NFL games.

Another thirty minutes went by.

A notification came through on his phone alerting him to activity on the motion-sensor camera pointed at his driveway. Ideal. This meant she was heading his way.

He opened the video feed. Sure enough, his phone screen showed a live image of Sloane wearing a navy one-piece pantsuit. He anticipated her marching past the camera's field of view toward his front door. Instead, she leaned over and fit a long tool into the keyhole of the water valve's cover. She lifted the cover away, fitted the other end of the tool onto the valve, and confidently turned it ninety degrees.

Max stared open-mouthed at his screen, then threw back his head and laughed.

Sloane had gone to the hardware store, purchased the equipment needed, and learned how to use it in order to get water flowing back to her apartment.

Well played, Sloane.

He wouldn't have believed he could have more respect for her than he already did. But he'd been wrong.

He grabbed his keys and made for his car.

She was forcing him to change his tactics.

Chapter Nine

A knock sounded on Sloane's door.

She was sitting at her kitchen island, in the middle of a Zoom meeting, answering questions that had arisen from the women in LA teaching My Fair Lady classes.

Another knock, more authoritative this time. Which gave her a bad feeling about the identity of the knocker.

She ignored it. Any normal person would go away when their knock was met with inaction.

But Max kept knocking.

And knocking.

One of the women was explaining something to the other at the moment, so Sloane muted her mic and turned off her video feed. Still listening to their conversation, she hurried to the door. Opening it, she found Max filling up most of the portal. Thick scruff on his cheeks, soft lips, hard body dressed in jeans and a gray T-shirt. He wore a baseball cap on backward and held a sack in each hand. "I brought Greek food for dinner."

"I did not order dinner."

"But as a human being, you are likely to need dinner."

"No."

"No you're not a human being?"

"No to dinner. I'm in the middle of a Zoom meeting."

"On a Sunday evening?" He made a *tsking* sound. "Not an impressive way to spend your weekend."

She attempted to shut the door. He stuck his foot in the jamb and the door rebounded open.

"This"—he lifted the bags—"is called a generous gift."

"Step back and I'll show you a generous slamming of the door."

"One would think that, as an expert on manners, you'd be better at the art of accepting generous gifts." Max strode inside and set the bags in her fridge. He then made himself at home on a living room armchair. "Don't mind me." He motioned toward the laptop on the kitchen island. "Return to your meeting."

"I will once you go."

"This is my garage apartment on my property. I'm sure you've read the fine print of the lease agreement, so you'll be aware that, among other rights, I have the right to hang out here anytime." He angled his chin toward the laptop.

Sloane jerked earbuds from her purse and put them in, then resumed her position in front of her computer. After she turned on her video feed, she made sure the camera did not capture Max loitering in the background.

This was tricky because she was far more aware of the man she *wasn't* looking at than the faces on the screen she *was* looking at. She wrapped things up as quickly as possible. After logging off, she filled a glass with water to make a point. *Look, Max! I have access to as much water as I want.* She gracefully drank it.

He looked more entertained than perturbed as he pushed out of the armchair and straightened. "A few days ago, Ivy told me that she's searching for her birth father. She asked for my help. I agreed."

The news froze Sloane momentarily. Why would Ivy have gone to him for help without talking to her first? Sloane hadn't been rushing the search because she wanted to give Ivy time to adjust at every stage of the process. Maybe Ivy had gotten impatient?

As if he'd read her mind, he said, "She mentioned that she feels bad about dumping the whole birth father search on you. She thinks my connections would be helpful and she's right. They will be. I'll make sure of it."

"No thank you to your offer of assistance. We'll solve this without you."

"This is Ivy's search. Ivy gets to decide."

She bit the inside of her lip. Shoot. He had a point. "Wait here. I'll call her."

"Be my guest."

Sloane stepped into Ivy's room to turn on the girl's retro radio to mask the sound of the conversation she was about to have. Bruno Mars's "Just the Way You Are" filled the air. In response, the rats poked their heads over the side of their hammock.

"You look very handsome this evening," Sloane told them, continuing with her flattering tactics. Then she shut herself inside her room and dialed Ivy.

"Hello?" the girl answered. Sloane could hear kids' voices in the background.

"Having fun?"

"Yes! We're playing video games with Faith's two little brothers. They're so cute." She awkwardly added, "Really cute."

Ivy was likely realizing that while she'd been having a blast with her friend, Sloane had been dealing with the ambush attack by Max that Ivy had arranged.

"Max is here," Sloane said.

"Oh?"

"He mentioned that you invited him to help with the search for your biological dad."

"Um. Yes!"

"Is there a reason why you didn't talk to me about including him first?" she asked calmly.

"Well . . ."

"You can tell me."

"I was afraid you'd shoot down the idea."

"That was a likely outcome," Sloane acknowledged. "But being afraid of that outcome doesn't make it okay to go behind my back instead."

"You're right, you're right! It was just . . . Remember how Max said I should let him know if I needed anything? I thought about that and it kinda seemed like I should ask him to join us. I'm pretty sure he can help. Plus, then you won't have to be the only one working with me on this."

Ivy was spinning things to cast herself in the most altruistic light.

"Also," Ivy went on, "I think Max is lonely."

I don't believe Darth gets lonely, Sloane thought. "You yourself have been following his very busy social life online."

"Yes, but people with busy social lives can still be lonely. I think he needs us." Sloane heard a door close on Ivy's end. The background noise lessened abruptly. "Think about how excited he was to host us for breakfast when we were staying at his house."

Sloane said nothing.

"It might be good for him," Ivy went on, "to be a part of the search."

"Except, as you know, Ivy, Max and I aren't really on speaking terms."

"Aunt Sloane?" she ventured.

"Yes?"

"Friendships are like . . . one of the best things in my life. I remember you and Max when you were friends. You were really good ones to each other."

On that, Sloane could not disagree.

"I know he messed up and did things that hurt you. But maybe . . . Maybe it's time to forgive him?" Ivy suggested tentatively.

Sloane remained quiet.

"The other day," the girl went on, "you were talking about the idea of giving to other people what you need. What do you need from Max?"

"For him to move to a different continent."

Ivy laughed. "But since that's not possible?"

"I need politeness and respect from him." Which was convicting. Because that meant she should give politeness and respect to Max. The very idea of that sent defensiveness rushing upward inside her. "Look, Ivy. Forgiveness is hugely important. In the case of Max and me, maybe it's best to learn from what I say and not what I do?"

"Aunt Sloane, you're one of the most forgiving people I know. I look up to you. You're good to everyone. You have an amazing heart."

Ivy was telling her in the kindest way possible that Sloane's antagonism toward Max was beneath her. Her attention fell on the photo of Princess Kate. And then the quote. *With grace and elegance, anything is possible.*

Princess Kate's gaze, shining out of the picture, seemed to ask Sloane, *Are you going to take the high road like I do?*

Sloane's heart was set on making the most of these precious

months with Ivy. Absolutely set on that. Maybe more than at any other time in her relationship with her niece, it was imperative that she be an excellent role model. "You really want Max to join in the search for Seth Taylor?"

"I really do."

"Are you sure?"

"Very sure."

Sloane had a lot of abilities. But she *did not* have the ability to disappoint Ivy.

"Is that okay with you?" Ivy went on. "For him to join us?"

"Yes," Sloane made herself say.

"Aunt Sloane! Yay! Thank you a million times."

"Enjoy your sleep-over. I'll pick you up in the morning."

"'Kay! Love you."

"I love you, too."

Sloane ended the call and took a few calming breaths while she continued to consider Princess Kate. *You're asking a lot of me here*, Sloane silently told her. *Max is maddening beyond belief.*

Kate's confident smile did not waver.

Sloane walked into the living room. Max was still standing, hat on backward, where she'd left him.

"I spoke with Ivy," Sloane said, "and she confirmed that she would like you to have a role in her search for her birth father."

"Ah. So you couldn't talk her out of including me?"

"No, I couldn't. I'm going to respect her wishes and her parents' wishes every step of the way with this search. Which means you may be involved if you'd like to be involved."

"I'd definitely like to be involved. When should we meet with Ivy to discuss this?"

Sloane consulted her phone calendar. "Your back patio, Wednesday evening at seven?"

"Good."

"Listen, Max. If you do anything to disappoint Ivy . . ."

"You'll what?" Creases of humor formed around his pale green eyes.

"I'll train Kevin and Ricky to attack you and then you'll die by a thousand rat bites."

"You're a rat trainer now?"

"I'm willing to become one for this purpose."

"I'm not convinced a thousand rat bites would kill me."

"One can only hope." She walked to the door and held it open. "You may leave now."

He pushed his hands into the pockets of his jeans. "You're not going to invite me to stay for Greek food?"

"I'll be eating solo this evening. Feel free, though, to take your Greek food with you."

"Nah. The food's a generous gift, remember?" He passed by her. "I'm a prince among men."

FIONA

Max, I'd like to chat about something with you for a few minutes. May I come by your house Tuesday evening after work?

MAX

Certainly.

In an effort to keep her hands from showing her age, Fiona applied cream to them no less than six times a day. She'd just depressed the doorbell of Max's gorgeous old Victorian and used the moments following to squirt a dab of hand cream into her palm and rub it in. This particular hand cream was manu factured by her own business, Lavish. The scent she was currently obsessed with lifted to her nose. Almonds and vanilla. *Divine.*

Max appeared, dressed in athletic gear. His cheeks were flushed, and he wiped sweat from his face with a hand towel. "Hi." Clearly, he had a home gym tucked away in this big house somewhere. Fiona was a workout-with-a-personal-trainer person herself.

"Good evening," she said.

He motioned her forward. "Please come in."

She did so.

"May I offer you something to drink?" he asked.

"No, thank you." A very large glass of wine with her name on it was waiting for her when she reached home, but she'd wait for that until then.

She followed him down the hall. As always, she was dressed to the nines. Today in a plum-colored dress, hair in a chignon, high heels clicking against hardwood. In the living room, she arranged herself on an upholstered chair.

He took one of the smaller, simpler leather chairs opposite her.

"Thank you for seeing me," she began. "I asked to come by because I wanted to talk with you about your mother."

"My mother?"

"Yes." Fiona had never before raised the subject of Nicole with Max and would have been happy to go the rest of her life without doing so. However, no one had ever accused Fiona of lacking determination. If this was what it took to see and speak with Isobel again, then this was what she was willing to do. Gathering her gumption, she forged ahead. "I would like the opportunity to speak with her, in person. Not to argue. The opposite, in fact. A civil conversation is the goal."

"For what purpose?"

"I'm trying to reestablish communication between my sister Isobel and myself. Isobel has stipulated that I'll need to meet with Nicole, forgive her, and send Isobel a photo of the two of us, before she'll consider communicating with me."

"I see." His features remained neutral.

It was galling to admit all of this to Max. It felt too private to share with a person of the generation below hers who she wasn't particularly close to. But there was no way around it.

Nicole was a single mother of just this one son. When she and Nicole had been friends, it had been abundantly clear to Fiona that Max was the central light of Nicole's life. Nicole would be far more likely to agree to see Fiona if Max was the one asking his mother for the meeting.

Fiona kept her chin high. "Would you be willing to ask Nicole if she'll talk with me?"

"I'll ask her."

"Thank you. I appreciate it."

"I can't guarantee she'll say yes."

"I understand."

Fiona moved to rise—

"I have a question for you before you go," Max said.

Fiona stilled. "Certainly."

"Jude told me that he spoke with you about the missing tiara."

"He did, yes. It's a stunning piece of historical jewelry. An artifact. I was very surprised to hear that it's been missing."

"Who do you think has it?"

Fiona was too diplomatic to accuse his mother immediately after asking Max for a favor. "I have no idea." He was observing her intently. Max didn't miss much, and it occurred to Fiona that he suspected *her* of taking it. "If I knew, I'd happily share the information with you."

"Who had access to the case where the tiara was kept?"

"The keys to that case were stored in our safe. So really just Felix, me, and your mother whenever Felix handed the keys to her so she could clean the case."

"Are you talking about the safe in the master bedroom closet?"

It shouldn't surprise her that he knew that. Alongside her sons, he'd probably explored every inch of Maple Lane. "Right."

"I've seen inside that safe, thanks to Jude and Jeremiah. Were there times when it was left open?"

"Well. Yes." She felt like a suspect being questioned in an Agatha Christie novel. "If we'd opened the safe, for example so that I could wear a piece of jewelry for a dinner party, we might leave it open the duration of the dinner party. Then shut it before turning in for the night."

He appeared to think that over.

"Any other questions for me?" she asked.

"No."

"I won't keep you." They rose. Had the two of them had a more affectionate relationship, she'd have given him an air kiss or a hug before departing.

But they weren't air kiss or hug people, she and Max Cirillo.

Wednesday evening, Max leaned back in his patio chair, fingers interlaced on his abdomen, legs stretched out and crossed at the ankles as he listened to Sloane. They were meeting to discuss finding Ivy's birth father and Sloane was kicking things off by reading aloud from her laptop a Wiki article entitled "How to find a current address for someone."

Once, meetings that included Sloane and himself had been

an almost daily occurrence. So much so, he'd taken them for granted. He was definitely not taking this meeting, the first he'd had with her in four years, for granted. She could have been reading a grammar manual aloud and he'd have been riveted.

"One of the sites recommended in the article was called FamilyTreeNow.com," she said when she was done. "That jumped out as promising because the article mentioned that this site could search based on where a person had *once* lived."

"Which is good," Ivy said, "because we know Seth once lived in Boston."

Sloane's fingers flew over the keys. "Heading to that site now and filling in search fields. Okay, so it's provided a list of numerous Seths. Would you like to bring your chairs around?"

Both Max and Ivy moved their chairs next to hers so they could see the screen.

"We don't know how old our Seth is," Sloane said. "But I can make an educated guess."

"What's your guess?" Ivy asked.

"Harper's MO was to date guys around her age. So I'd guess that Seth's age is anywhere from a year younger than Harper to—at the outside—five years older. Harper would have been thirty-four now, so let's look first for Seths who are currently thirty-three to thirty-nine."

Max pointed to one of the listings. "There."

Sloane clicked it. They pored over the entries, eventually finding four Seths who seemed to be the right age and had lived in Boston at the time when Harper and Seth would have been together. Two of the Seths lived there still. One was now in Arizona. One in Tennessee. Using a gold pen, Sloane wrote each of their addresses in a small turquoise notebook.

When done, she closed the laptop and set aside the notebook and pen.

He and Ivy brought their chairs back around so that they

occupied three sides at the end of the table. Ivy had on her usual T-shirt and shorts combo. Sloane was wearing a pink headband and a white sundress. She'd acquired a slight tan since moving to Maine. She looked better rested and healthier now than she had that first day, which reassured him.

"I've been doing some research on the etiquette of contacting prospective birth parents," Sloane announced. "There are some things we need to talk through."

"'Kay." Ivy nodded.

"We'd all like to think that a birth parent will be warm and welcoming and pleased to get a chance to know you, but that might not be the case. Several other outcomes are possible."

"Like?"

"Like we might not be able to find your biological dad."

"I intend for us to find him," Max said. "I won't leave any stones unturned."

"It's also possible, Ivy, that Seth has passed away."

"Unlikely, though, right?" Max said. "If he's only in his thirties?"

"It's unlikely." Sloane met his eyes, and he felt the contact as if it had a physical component. "But it's still something we need to consider so that we're prepared."

"Got it," Ivy said. "What else?"

Sloane looked to her niece. "It could be that your biological dad and his situation won't be at all what you would want them to be. For example, he might be an alcoholic or have a terrible temper or be incarcerated."

"If he has a terrible temper," Max said to Ivy, "I'll beat him up."

Sloane continued in her business-like tone. "It's also possible that he won't want contact with you or that he'll deny fathering you."

"If he doesn't want contact with you or denies fathering you," Max said, "I'll beat him up."

The girl smiled at him. "Thank you, Max."

"I think it's important," Sloane said, "that you go into this understanding, Ivy, that people can be flawed and complicated."

"Take Sloane, for example," he whispered to Ivy. "She's both of those things."

"While you," Sloane shot back, "are too shallow to be complicated. Which means you're only flawed."

Max laughed.

Ivy clapped. "You two are *so fun*."

He was glad he could bring some levity to this. Geez, no wonder Ivy had invited him to take part. They'd needed him more than he'd realized because Sloane was making this whole thing as serious as a heart attack.

"As I was saying." Sloane regained her composure and addressed Ivy. "Seth might be flawed and complicated."

"But it's also possible," Ivy countered, "that he'll be a nice person who won't mind having a conversation with me."

"Exactly," Max said.

"If you move forward," Sloane told her, "you'll just need to go in with your eyes open, ready for any eventuality, guarding yourself against disappointment or rejection."

Ivy tilted her head thoughtfully. "I can handle some disappointment or rejection, Aunt Sloane. You don't have to keep me safe from every sad thing."

"Don't I?"

"No."

"I can't stop myself from wanting to."

Ivy reached across and patted her hand sympathetically. "I know."

Max pressed the heel of his hand against his heart to stop

the tenderness toward Sloane that was overtaking it. That, he could not—definitely not—allow.

"I've done some reading on how best to phrase a letter to a prospective birth parent," Sloane told them. "I was thinking we could work out a draft of a letter now from me to these four Seths. Once we have it how we want it, I'll hand-write it out and mail it to them. What do you think?"

"I think that would be awesome," Ivy answered.

Sloane reopened her computer. She was an extremely fast typist and spoke each word aloud as she went. "Dear Seth. My name is Sloane Madison and I'm writing on behalf of my niece, Ivy Ray. Ivy was born in Monarch Hospital in Boston on December ninth, fifteen and a half years ago. Her birth mother was Harper Madison, my sister, who passed away four years ago. At five months of age, Ivy was adopted by Jared and Brooke Ray, and has been raised as the youngest of four children in their wonderful family." Sloane's fingers stilled. "How am I doing so far?"

"Like, amazingly good. Can you write essays for me when school starts?"

"And emails for me," Max asked, "when I'm too bored to do so?"

"I will not," Sloane told him crisply. Then, to Ivy, "I won't write your essays, but I'll gladly proofread them if you need me to." She continued with the body of the letter. "Ivy is very well provided for and is a healthy, happy teenage girl—"

"Ugh." Ivy pulled a face. "Can you take that part out? I don't want you to list my good qualities as if I'm a puppy in need of a home."

Sloane's lips curved up and the sight of that warmed Max like bourbon.

What was happening to him?

"Fine, though it goes against my grain not to list your good qualities." Sloane cleared her throat. "Ivy would very much like the opportunity to meet and speak with her biological father. According to the research we've done, you are one of the men who might fill that role in Ivy's life. If you do fill that role, we'd be very grateful if you would let us know and also consider a brief meeting with the two of us."

"Three of us," Max said.

"You're intending to meet Seth?" Sloane asked.

"If Ivy says I can, then yes."

"You can," Ivy quickly said.

Sloane sniffed. "Consider a brief meeting with the two of us and a . . . family friend," she read, typing. "We would be happy to travel to your town and visit with you at a time that's convenient. Feel free to reach out to me in the following ways." Sloane glanced up. "This is where I'll provide my phone number, email address, and the mailing address here. Sincerely, Sloane Madison."

"It's perfect!" Ivy crowed.

"Really?" Sloane asked her. "Because I'm happy to edit any part of this."

"No, I like it just as it is. What do you think, Max?"

"I agree that it's perfect."

"In that case," Sloane said, "I'll go ahead and write out the letters."

"You could just print out copies," Ivy said, "and mail those."

Sloane's features communicated disbelief. "You're asking the etiquette expert to spit out letters on a printer? Ivy! I need to work on developing your appreciation for good stationery and handwritten notes."

Sheepishly, Ivy held up her palms. "Okay, okay. I was just trying to make things more convenient."

"Convenience has become hugely important to people—"

"Like me," Max said. "I love convenience."

"But I believe," Sloane soldiered on, "in *taking time*. I believe in things that are worthwhile even if they're not convenient. I'm not saying that one approach is better than the other. I'm simply inviting you to consider your own approach and not just go along with the sheep as if you're part of a herd."

"Mm-hmm," Ivy said. It was obvious to Max the teenager's attention had wandered. "Are we done with the Seth part tonight?"

"Yes."

"Should we set a time for our next meeting?"

"When and if we hear back from the Seths, we can schedule another meeting then."

"Except Max is really busy, so I want us to get on his schedule ahead of time. And now that you're going on dates with Nate, I want us to get on your schedule, too."

Sloane was going on dates with Nate? That news twisted, black and cold, right in the center of him.

"Ivy," Sloane said, "you are my priority while I'm here. I will always be available for things that are important to you."

"Cool. But Max works a bunch and goes out several nights a week. Right, Max?"

"Right. I'm very popular." The words felt hollow. He was dazed, like he'd been smacked in the face by a board.

"So can we plan to meet same time next week?" Ivy pressed.

"How about the same time in two weeks?" Sloane proposed. "I'll mail the letters tomorrow but then it might take five days or so for them to arrive at their destinations."

Sloane had gone out with Nate?

He didn't want it to be true, but he'd seen them interacting at his party with his own eyes.

"Two weeks will work," Ivy said.

Max's immediate thought was that two weeks was far too long. A lot could happen between Sloane and Nate in the space of two weeks.

They could fall for each other in that amount of time.

It occurred to Sloane shortly after entering her father's apartment that her new life was represented by the apartment she and Ivy were living in this summer. Bright, clean, comfortable, modern. But her father's place absolutely represented her childhood. Dirty, disorganized, squalid, dingy. It made her remember in a visceral way the desperate details of her earliest years.

"I've bought groceries," she announced, setting the sacks on his kitchen counter. "After we unpack them, I'm thinking you and I can do some cleaning."

He hovered in the mouth of the kitchen, shoulders slumped. "The house is fine, Sloane. I'm too tired to clean."

"The house will be more fine after we do some cleaning. And I'm sure that you have enough energy to do one hour's worth of work." She slotted groceries into the refrigerator and pantry shelves.

Sloane was naturally neat and orderly. Living by herself in California, she did not find it taxing to keep her home tidy. In fact, there was something cathartic about taking a bit of disorder and bringing order to it.

Even so, no part of her wanted to clean her dad's apartment, which had a gross, moldy component to it. In order to put boundaries on what could become the black hole of trying to help her father, she'd determined that she would stop by for one hour a week while she was living in Maine. "Today," she said, "let's vacuum, clean the kitchen, and get laundry going."

Her father released a heavy sigh.

Early that evening, Sloane was sipping tea in the living room and inputting business expenses into a spreadsheet when Ivy emerged from her room. "Is it all right if I bike over to Corrie's house?"

"Sure." Sloane tapped the envelopes sitting beside her. "I finished the Seth letters, but I recommend you wait as long as you'd like to send them. I want you to be sure of this next step."

"I'm sure." With the blasé approach toward destiny only a teenager could have, she scooped them up. "I'll drop them in the post office box on the way."

With that, she was gone. And Sloane, an adult who did not have a blasé approach toward destiny, was left to grapple with the weight of the potential ramifications of those letters.

Chapter Ten

The following Tuesday, Sloane glanced at the From column of her newly received emails and the name *Seth Taylor* jumped out.

She startled, then cautiously clicked on the email to read it. Was this hope she was feeling, or fear? Gravity—she was feeling that for sure.

Sloane, I got your letter and just wanted you to know that I'm not the father of your niece.

That was it. That was the whole email.

She had no idea which of the four Seth Taylors this was.

She replied.

Dear Seth,

Thank you for responding. I mailed four letters. Can you please let me know if you're the Seth who lives in Boston on Pierce Street, Boston on W. 5th Street,

**Arizona, or Tennessee? Once I know that, I'll make sure
that we don't follow up with you again.
Sincerely, Sloane**

He had the grace to reply with four words.

I live in Arizona.

Communicating with these strangers about a subject as
weighty as paternity was intense. Thank God all of this interaction was going through her. This way, Sloane could serve as a
buffer. No matter how hard the information, at least it would
be delivered gently by someone who loved Ivy.

Sloane updated Ivy as soon as she picked her up.

Ivy took the news in stride. "I'll text Mom to let her know.
Then I'll text Max to let him know, too."

FELIX

Checking to see if you've made any headway
in locating Eugenie's tiara.

MAX

I'm still working on it.

The following morning, Sloane received a text from an
unknown number.

> I received the letter you sent and wanted to
> tell you that I am the father of your niece. But
> I'm not open to a meeting at this time. Sorry. -
> Seth Taylor

Sloane, who was in the kitchen, preparing to take a cup of coffee outside, peered at the words. Her reactions bolted in two directions. Pleased surprise—because it seemed, amazingly, *they'd actually found the correct Seth Taylor*. Disappointment—because Seth wasn't open to the meeting Sloane knew Ivy wanted.

Earlier, she'd heard her niece moving around in her room. "Ivy?" she called.

"Yes?" came the response.

"Can you come out here for a minute?"

Ivy emerged.

"I just received another reply," Sloane said, "to the letters we mailed to the Seths."

"Really?"

Sloane showed her the text message.

"Oh my gosh, oh my gosh," Ivy murmured. "We found my biological father?"

"I think so, yes."

"*Oh. My. Gosh.* I can't believe it." She bent her head over the phone for long seconds before raising her attention to Sloane. "He's not open to a meeting."

"No."

"He says he's not open to a meeting *at this time*. Do you think that means he might be open to it later?"

"Perhaps. Yes."

"Anything we can do to change his mind?"

"No, sweetheart. We have to be respectful of his decision. The best I can do is text him back to thank him and encourage him to reach out if he changes his mind."

She'd been worried about the sadness this search might cost Ivy. And she did see sadness in Ivy's face. Yet her niece had said, *"I can handle some disappointment or rejection."* And Sloane could see that was true, too . . . in the way Ivy squared her shoulders and in her small, brave smile.

Sloane hugged her, pride welling high.

Her sister's daughter was everything Harper could have dreamed she'd be. And more.

Ivy had called this morning and told Max that her biological father had texted Sloane but wasn't willing to meet with her. Ivy had also told him that Sloane had said they had to respect Seth's decision.

It didn't surprise Max to hear that Sloane was advocating for respect and patience. With almost everyone in the world except him she was the poster child for respect and patience.

Given that, Sloane could do nothing more regarding Seth.

However, the same could not be said of him.

Max had plenty of experience dealing with men who did not fulfill their paternal rights. Also, if he'd waited around for people to change their mind because he was concerned about giving them respect and exercising patience, Libri would have been dead in the water years ago.

He refused to let Seth keep Ivy and Sloane in a holding pattern.

Max lingered at home until Sloane drove off the property with Ivy. Then he crossed to the garage apartment and let himself in with his key. Sloane's perfume greeted him when he reached her bedroom. He paused, breathing in the light, flowery, classy scent.

Right away, he spotted what he'd come for—her turquoise

notebook—on her desk. He opened to the page where she'd written information about the Seths. As expected, she'd updated the information. The Seth in Arizona had been crossed out and she'd added a phone number at the bottom of the page that she'd circled and starred.

Bingo.

Max typed the digits into his phone. Let himself out of the apartment. Dialed as he walked the dirt path that led away from his house through the forest toward the stream at the far end of his property.

His call went to voice mail.

"Seth, this is Max Cirillo. I'm the CEO of Libri. I know we haven't met, but we have a mutual friend, and I have a question for you. I'd appreciate it if you could give me a call at this number. Or feel free to call Libri's office, extension 210. My executive assistant will put you through. I look forward to hearing from you soon. Thanks."

Max was betting Seth would look Max up. And, when he did, almost certainly call him back.

Sure enough, barely an hour passed before Seth called Max on his cell. By then, Max was sitting in his ocean-view corner office at Libri's headquarters.

Max cut right to the point. "I know that you received a letter recently from my friend Sloane Madison about her niece Ivy Ray. I'm the family friend Sloane mentioned in her letter."

"Oh—I . . ."

"I know that you're Ivy's biological father. And I know you said you weren't open to meeting with us at this time. Look, I realize your time is valuable. If you'll meet with Ivy for thirty minutes, I'll pay you five thousand dollars."

"That's . . . *You will?*"

"I will."

"That's very generous."

"We'll enter into an agreement in writing, of course. My assistant can get a document to you today. Following your conversation with Ivy, you'll receive the money. I have two stipulations. The first is that you meet with Ivy, Sloane, and me *this* weekend. I'd like to get things moving and I don't see any reason to delay. Do you?"

"Uh . . . no?"

"My second stipulation is that you not mention this to Sloane and Ivy. I don't want them knowing about the five grand, so you'll need to act like we're speaking for the first time when we meet. Got it?"

"Yes. I—I don't know what to say."

"Say you'll meet with us this weekend." Seth did not immediately respond, so Max applied pressure. "This is important to me. We have a deal, right?"

"We have a deal."

"Very good. Please text Sloane back today and set up a meeting."

SETH

Sloane, I think I was too quick earlier to say that I wasn't ready for a meeting. I've reconsidered. I can visit with Ivy for thirty minutes this weekend.

SLOANE

Ivy will be delighted to hear that! Thank you. Where do you live?

SETH

Boston.

The messages had arrived while Sloane was waiting in the parking lot of Ivy's driving school. As soon as the girl bounded into the car, Sloane, beaming, showed them to her.

Ivy squealed. "We waited and he changed his mind!"

"Yes. Politeness for the win!"

"I was praying that he'd change his mind. God worked faster this time than I dreamed." She grinned. "Can you text him back, please? To set up a time to meet?"

"At the risk of sounding like a broken record, I want to reiterate that we do not have to rush. We could propose meeting with him a few weeks from now to give you both time to process."

Ivy gave her a look like, *Are you crazy?* "No, the sooner, the better."

"Sure?"

"Yes!"

SLOANE

We can meet you either Saturday or Sunday in Boston.

Right away, dots appeared. Sloane and Ivy, heads close together, watched the screen with humming expectation.

Harper had always chosen football-player types. She'd been a teenager completely lacking in protection, so thinking back on it, it made sense to Sloane that her sister had gone for boyfriends who were, at least, physically strong. Some of her football-player-type boyfriends had been decent guys, but Harper herself had never been healthy enough to sustain a long-term relationship with any of them.

For Ivy's sake, Sloane hoped that Seth fell into the decent-guy category.

A text from him arrived with a *ping*.

SETH

How about Sunday afternoon at three at Coffee and Chocolate Haus?

Ivy threw back her head with a whoop and thrust both fists into the air.

"I take it that's a yes?" Sloane asked.

"Yes!"

SLOANE

Wonderful. We'll see you then.

"Do you think Max can go with us this weekend?"

"I'll ask him but it's likely he already has something scheduled for this weekend." At least one could hope *very, very* hard that was the case.

"I'm going to celebrate back at the house by putting Kevin and Ricky in their exercise balls."

Every few days, Ivy placed the rats in specially made, vented balls. They walked and ran inside the balls, causing them to roll around their apartment. Sloane feared they'd roll a ball against something, and the ball would spring open. At which time Kevin (or Ricky) would vault loose and make a run for Sloane's jugular.

"In that case," Sloane said, "I'll make a point to spend some time outside at the café table."

"Still afraid of my rat boys?"

"Terrified."

SLOANE

Ivy's birth father, Seth, texted me just now.
He's willing to meet with us Sunday afternoon
in Boston.

MAX

I'll join you.

SLOANE

That's definitely not necessary.

MAX

It is to me. When are we leaving for Boston
and when are we returning?

SLOANE

Ivy and I are thinking about leaving Friday
afternoon and returning Sunday night. We're
planning to go on a "Walking Tour of the
Freedom Trail, Women's History Edition" on
Saturday.

MAX

I'll have my assistant make all of the travel
arrangements.

SLOANE

If you could join us only for the meeting with
Seth, that would be best.

MAX

If I'm picking up the tab, I'm going on the
entire trip.

SLOANE

No one asked you to pick up the tab. We
wouldn't dream of it.

MAX

I'm going on the entire trip. I'll take care of the
transportation to and from Boston. And the
hotel. And dinner out—bring nice clothes for
that. In return, can you do one thing for me?

SLOANE

What's that?

MAX

Buy me a ticket for the Walking Tour.

SLOANE

I don't believe men are permitted.

MAX

Nice try but 1) That would be discrimination and 2) Think how much satisfaction you'll get from watching the tour guide torture me—I mean lecture me—about women's history.

In the past, breakfast out had been a twice weekly treat that Fiona enjoyed alone. But nowadays, Burke often joined her at Java Junkie, a coffee shop in downtown Groomsport located just a few blocks from Fiona's office. She and Burke had rekindled their friendship ten months ago and, in that time, he'd become her closest friend.

Before Burke, she'd viewed her solo breakfasts as a luxury. (One of the many she indulged in since what was the point of living if one wasn't frequently indulging in luxuries?) But her breakfasts with Burke were an even richer luxury because Burke was the type of person whose companionship both lowered her blood pressure and lifted her spirits.

There was probably a saying, written on decorative signs and hung up in houses, that emphasized this general concept. Something along the lines of, *Joy is multiplied when shared with a friend.* Fiona was not a decorative-sign type of person. Not at all. Yet her friendship with Burke had convinced her that joy really was multiplied when shared with a friend.

This morning, he'd brought along his three-year-old granddaughter, Lottie Rose. This was his daughter's daughter, and she looked exactly like Fiona remembered her brown-haired mother looking back when Lottie Rose's mother and Jeremiah had been in kindergarten together.

The little girl clearly idolized Burke, and with good reason. Fiona was biased, but he seemed to her to be the world's best grandpa. Calm, kind, supportive. Burke always regarded Lottie Rose with so much approval and tenderness that there was no way this little girl was going to grow up not trusting in her own worth.

This display of grandparent/grandchild happiness emphasized to Fiona how *beyond ready* she was for grandchildren of her own. She had a lot of love to give, and she wanted the chance to view her own little grandbabies with approval and tenderness.

The three of them were sitting at a table together, Lottie Rose perched on Burke's knee. Fiona had selected a sugar-free blackberry lemonade muffin and a skinny cappuccino. Burke— a Danish and black coffee. Lottie Rose—a small cinnamon roll and milk.

Currently, the child was ignoring her breakfast because she was appropriately preoccupied with Fiona. Lottie Rose's little hands twirled Fiona's rings and feathered over her gleaming manicure.

"Can I have nail polish?" she asked Fiona.

"Absolutely. A lady is never too young to look her best. In fact, I think I have some clear polish in my handbag here. If so, I'd be glad to apply it for you."

Her round face lit up.

Sure enough, Fiona did have polish, as well as several other things she viewed as female necessities. Hand cream. Powder compact. Seven lipsticks for different occasions and lighting. Roll-on perfume. A hairbrush.

"Place your hands on the table," Fiona instructed.

Lottie Rose did so, keeping her fingers very still as Fiona applied the polish to her minuscule nails. "When I'm done with this, I can also update your hairstyle, if you'd like. How do you feel about two French braids?"

"What are French braids?"

"Oh, my young protégé, you have much to learn." She eyed Burke teasingly. "What are you teaching this child?"

"Things that have nothing to do with French braids," he admitted.

Lottie Rose's outfit and hair had obviously been overseen by Burke this morning. Like many men, he hadn't the faintest idea how to handle a three-year-old girl's outfit and hair.

"What's protégé?" Lottie Rose asked.

"It's kind of like an apprentice."

"What's apprentice?"

"It's kind of like a student."

"Oh." She smiled up at Fiona.

With his big, weathered hand, Burke gently smoothed Lottie Rose's bangs out of her face.

It did not take Fiona long to finish the nail polish. "Come sit with me, darling."

The girl's slight, warm weight settled on Fiona's lap. Fiona swiftly went to work on French braids. When finished, she handed over her open compact, so the child could admire her hairstyle in the mirror.

Lottie Rose's lips formed a delighted oval. "Thank you."

"You're welcome. Come to me for manicure, clothing, and hair advice anytime. I love discussing those topics."

Burke went to get more coffee.

By the time he'd returned, Fiona had coaxed the girl to eat most of her cinnamon roll and consume all of her milk.

Burke lowered into his seat and grinned at the sight of Fiona and Lottie Rose. "My two favorite girls."

"As well we should be," Fiona returned. "Right, Lottie Rose?"

"Right!"

"Want me to take her?" Burke asked.

"By no means. I deserve more snuggle time."

He sipped his coffee. "You still haven't heard from Max as to whether Nicole is willing to talk with you?" Burke asked.

"Still haven't. Do you think I should pester him about it? It's in my nature to pester."

"No. Good things come to those who wait."

"Good things come faster to those who pester."

He chuckled. "In this case, I think waiting will pay off."

JUDE

I had a conversation with an agent who's active in the FBI's Jewelry and Gem Theft Program. He suggested I check out a jewelry database for transactions that show where the tiara might have been sold or purchased. I went through it carefully, Max. I don't see any transactions indicating that the tiara's been sold.

Max had booked a private plane for their trip to Boston.

A private plane.

In retrospect, Sloane reflected, this should not be taking her aback as much as it was. Yet, she absolutely felt taken aback as she and Ivy followed a beautiful employee across the tarmac toward a rolling staircase situated beneath a jet. Max waited for them there, wearing sunglasses and a smug expression.

He really was *so* frustratingly good-looking. The secret bolts of attraction she'd harbored toward him back in the day were beginning to make a comeback. The more she tried to block them, the more they made themselves known with a vengeance.

Back when a limo had arrived with a chauffeur but without Max to pick them up at the garage apartment, Sloane had concluded that Max had booked airline tickets. It was only when the limo carried them to the airstrip in Rockland (a place she'd never used in her life) that she'd comprehended they were not flying commercial.

This was how Max Cirillo could afford to travel these days. By private plane.

A gulf existed between this and how she remembered them traveling in Libri's early days when they'd taken trips to New York to meet with publishers and several other states to meet with potential investors. Then, their budget had been tight. They'd driven long distances to save money, or they'd rooted out the cheapest possible fares on planes and trains. Yet now, with a snap of his fingers, he'd booked a private plane for something that wasn't even related to business.

"I feel like I'm in the movies right now," Ivy said to Max when they were still several yards away. "Is this real?"

"This is real." Max was obviously enjoying the role of benevolent Daddy Warbucks.

"I've never flown anything except economy," Ivy said. "Not first-class and definitely not this."

"I'm glad I could introduce you to something new."

Ivy scampered ahead up the stairs and out of sight.

"This wasn't necessary," Sloane told him. "Ivy and I don't need luxury."

"I know. But I do." His eyes were masked behind the gray lenses of his sunglasses. "This is just the beginning. Wait until you see the hotel I've booked and the restaurant where we're eating dinner tonight."

She studied him for a long moment. He'd mastered the mocking, hard, sophisticated image he presented. Since coming to The Gables, it had been easy for her to believe that's who he was now. She hadn't looked closely for evidence to the contrary.

But now she was looking. She, who'd known him tremendously well. And she could see in the details—the worried aspect of his forehead, the way he curled his fingers in with a vulnerable flick—that there was still more to Max than he was letting on.

Felix hadn't acknowledged Max as his son until he'd been forced to do so. Sloane knew that rejection had dealt a huge blow to Max's pride and that, ever since, Max had been striving to prove his worth independent of the Camdens.

He still was. The mansion. The expensive cars. The private plane. The colossal success with Libri.

Would enough ever be enough for Max Cirillo? Would he reach a place of contentment? Or would he spend his life accumulating more and more in order to prove to the world that the illegitimate son had made good? Whether Max realized it or not, the world *already* believed he'd made good. Quite possibly the only person remaining who didn't believe that was Max himself.

Max checked them into the most extravagant hotel in Boston. He snorted with approval when he saw his room. An Eastern European princess would have found this place too opulent.

That night, they ate at a restaurant so fancy that their server wore a tuxedo. Most of the menu was incomprehensible. He'd chosen this place because he knew Sloane adored fine dining.

"Aunt Sloane, can you teach us the etiquette of how to eat here?" Ivy asked as soon as they settled at their table.

Sloane brightened. "You'd truly like to know?"

"Yes, please. You'd like to know, too, right, Max?"

"Absolutely." Honestly, he wasn't interested in etiquette. Never had been. But he definitely did want the chance to sit back and watch Sloane talk about . . . anything. Even this.

"We start by placing our napkins in our laps, like so." With one subtle movement, her napkin disappeared.

Max and Ivy mimicked her.

"We won't set any of our personal items on the table," Sloane instructed. "No cell phones. No eyeglasses."

Max, who'd already placed his phone on the table, picked it back up. "What if I'm expecting an important call?"

"Make sure your phone's on vibrate, stick it in your pocket or partially under your leg. If an important call comes in during the meal, excuse yourself and leave the table. We never keep our ringer on when dining and we never answer a call while sitting at the table with others."

"Huh." He stuck his phone partially under his leg, which wasn't all that comfortable.

Their server delivered menus.

"This is very expensive," Ivy whispered. "Should I just order one small thing?"

"I'm paying," Max told her. "Order whatever you want."

"Here's my recommendation." Sloane tipped her menu down so she could see Ivy over the top of it. "If you're a guest of someone—and tonight you're a guest of Max—do not order the most expensive thing on the menu because that's not in good taste—"

"You can order the most expensive thing if that's what you'd like, Ivy."

"It's wise," Sloane continued, "to casually ask the host what he's thinking about ordering. If Max is only getting one course, then follow suit and order one course. If he's ordering two or three courses, feel free to order two or three."

"I'm ordering three courses," he told Ivy. "Maybe four because I'm afraid the portion size here is going to be small enough to fit in a matchbox."

They navigated ordering, three courses for each of them, then their server moved off.

"We refrain from grooming at the table," Sloane instructed Ivy. "No messing with your hair, no toothpicks, no applying lipstick."

"I can't apply lipstick?" Max asked.

"If there's a need to pass anything around the table, we pass to the right with our right hand. If we're passing salt and pepper, those two always remain together. When the food comes, we'll wait for everyone to be served before anyone begins. I suggest taking—at most—four bites of food before setting down your cutlery and pausing. Oh, and don't cut anything on your plate except the bite you're about to take. Cutting a dish into small pieces in advance is only for children." Sloane was sitting very straight, gesturing gracefully. He could easily picture her as a duchess from long ago.

"What do I do with all these forks and knives and spoons?" Ivy asked.

"When the food arrives, we'll start from the outside and work our way in."

"Is it okay to lean forward?" Ivy rested her elbows on the table.

"We never place our elbows on the table. Throughout Western culture, that's considered rude. Not to mention, it causes us to slouch our posture."

"Oh. So where should I put my hands?" Ivy held them up like stop signs.

"Under the table," Sloane answered, "except to eat, drink, or motion with them when speaking."

Soon their first course arrived, and Sloane demonstrated to Ivy which pieces of cutlery to pick up. She held her fork in her left hand and her knife in her right in a position she called the "continental" style.

Sloane took a bite of food, and he caught himself staring at her mouth.

"Will you teach me more etiquette when we get back to Maine?" Ivy asked her aunt.

"Of course. I'll teach you all the etiquette you'd like to know."

Max tried his appetizer—a prosciutto and fig dish. "Mmmm," he moaned loudly in a bid to amuse Ivy.

The girl broke into a huge smile.

Sloane blinked at him.

"Is moaning good etiquette?" he asked Sloane.

"The best etiquette is about being considerate of everyone. So I decline to scold you for moaning."

"Declining to scold me must be hard for you." He took another bite and moaned again.

"It's requiring herculean effort," she admitted.

Ivy had oohed and aahed her way through every new reveal of the day. Their hotel room. The Mercedes (piloted by another chauffeur) that cruised them to dinner. The restaurant's decor.

Ordinarily, Sloane loved seeing Ivy happy. Yet her niece's bubbling began to grate on Sloane by the time they returned to their hotel that night.

For one thing, the girl was shoveling an outsized portion of fangirling in Max's direction. For another, Sloane didn't want Ivy placing gigantic value on expensive items that didn't actually matter in the grand scheme of life and death.

Sloane, for one, had taken in as much splendor and watched as many females flirt with Max as she could stand for one day.

Sloane locked herself inside the bathroom, stepped into the marble shower, and stood under its spray. She'd been constrained by her own good manners all day, speaking nothing but crushingly polite words to him since the tarmac. But now, with the water pounding her shoulders, and the sound providing cover, she indulged herself by calling Max every bad name in the book. She lambasted him. Railed. Chided. All in a whisper that went no farther than her ears.

The following morning, Max dressed in a gray T-shirt, joggers, and a pair of Adidas in advance of their walking tour. The three of them shared a quick, early lunch at the hotel, then their driver dropped them off at Bunker Hill. It wasn't hard to recognize their tour guide because she was the only person wearing historical clothing. She had on a big, old-fashioned, blue and white dress and shoes with buckles.

Max wasn't a costume guy and so regarded people who willingly dressed in costume with suspicion.

The woman beckoned the three of them forward to join the group already assembled around her. "Welcome, one and all. I am Abigail Adams."

"*The* Abigail Adams?" Sloane asked. "Married to John Adams?"

"One and the same." She was a very circular person. Circular face that made him think she was around forty-five. Circular waist. Circular wig of gray curls. "I don't believe we've been formally introduced. Will you grace me with the honor of your surnames?"

"My surname is Madison," Sloane supplied.

"Ah!" Abigail smiled with recognition. "Are you a relation of James Madison, the statesman who helped to organize the Constitutional Convention?"

"Yes, that's right," Sloane answered, playing along. "I'm his granddaughter."

"He's a patriot indeed."

"And the fourth president of the United States."

"My dear, this is the year of our Lord 1800. My husband is president." A plane flew overhead and teens staring at their iPhones walked past.

Everyone else supplied their surnames. The other tour participants included two fifty-something women who were eyeing Max so venomously that he had to wonder if they hated men in general. In contrast, four women around his age, who might be on a girls' weekend, were eyeing him with deep appreciation. A few friendly-looking grandmotherly types rounded out their group. He was, of course, the only male since no ordinary man would ever sign up for this.

"A few years ago," Abigail announced in a loud voice, "I wrote a letter to Mr. Adams, and I don't mind sharing with you what I said. I wrote, '*I desire you would Remember the Ladies, and be more generous and favorable to them than your ancestors. Do not put such unlimited power into the hands of the Husbands. Remember all Men would be tyrants if they could. If perticuliar care and attention is not paid to the Laidies we are determined to foment a Rebelion, and will not hold ourselves bound by any Laws in which we have no voice, or Representation.'"*

The two women with the venomous gazes clapped enthusiastically.

Abigail inclined her wig. "Because of my affinity for the ladies, it is a particular joy to have been tasked today with the honor of guiding you on this walk and sharing with you tales of the valiant women of the American Revolution. Huzza!" She pronounced the last word strangely. "I see your confusion," she went on. "Our most common cheer is huzza, spelled H-U-Z-Z-A and pronounced *huzz-ay* so that it rhymes with day. Let's practice. Huzza!"

"Huzza!" everyone but Max returned. He was already sacrificing as much of his dignity as he was willing to part with.

"The president and I were deeply involved in the Revolutionary War and the earliest years of our good nation. Mr. Adams was the first vice president of the United States, making me the first vice presidential wife. Currently he is serving as the second president of our United States, making me the second presidential wife."

"Congratulations," Ivy told her kindly.

"Why isn't the president here with us today?" Max asked Abigail.

"The president is currently attending to matters of state."

"Or lying six feet under for the past two hundred years," he whispered to Sloane.

A smile transformed her face.

The sight of that smile gave him an instant dopamine hit.

"'*I am fearfull of the small pox.*'" Abigail was quoting again from her letters.

He tuned her out.

When, where, and how had Sloane become so beautiful?

He'd classified her as plain when they'd first met but there was nothing even remotely plain about her now. The sunlight slanted across her gentle features, emphasizing her porcelain skin. Everyone but Sloane and Abigail were wearing athletic clothes or shorts for the walk. Sloane had chosen a cream V-neck top. Her wide black skirt was drifting in the breeze. Her slip-on shoes were spotless.

Abigail droned about the Battle of Bunker Hill. Had Max been married to this Abigail at the time of the battle, he'd have thrown himself into the line of musket fire.

"Brave Deborah Sampson was so committed to our cause," Abigail informed them, "that she disguised herself as a man and enlisted in the Fourth Massachusetts Regiment. She served for a year and a half, scouting territory and reporting on British troop movements. She helped lead expeditions and participated in a raid that captured fifteen men. At one point, she received a cut in her forehead from a sword. Upon being shot in the thigh, she retrieved the pistol ball herself and continued. When it was eventually discovered that she was female, she was honorably discharged and received a military pension."

Abigail led them downhill, and they wound past well-preserved New England buildings, their flower boxes dripping with color. They crossed a bridge over the Charles River to Copp's Hill Burial Ground, then on to the Old North Church.

"*'I have sometimes been ready to think,'*"—Abigail raised an arm dramatically as she stood before the church—"*'that the passion for Liberty cannot be Eaquelly Strong in the Breasts of those who have been accustomed to deprive their fellow Creatures of theirs.'*" Max's mind wandered, coming back in time to hear her say, "*'that generous and christian principal of doing to others as we would that others should do unto us.'*"

As time passed, it became clear that in Abigail, Sloane had

found a kindred spirit. They were both passionate about old-fashioned manners.

When they reached the Paul Revere House, Abigail relayed Paul's story, then continued. "Are you familiar with the girl known as the female Paul Revere? Sybil Ludington was sixteen years of age when her father, Colonel Henry Ludington, learned that the British were on the move. He needed to stay with his men, so Sybil volunteered to warn local militia and rode forty miles through the night to do so, outsmarting bandits and the British on the way."

Near Faneuil Hall, Abigail mentioned something about *abhorrent spies* and Max felt like one of those, sent to this tour by the percentage of the population that had one X and one Y chromosome.

The closer they got to downtown, the more old construction gave way to skyscrapers.

"Margaret Corbin followed her husband to war, assisting as so many women did, as a camp follower. In that role, she cooked, cleaned, nursed wounded men, and brought water to the front line. When her husband was struck down while manning a cannon, she stepped into his place at once and continued to fire the cannon upon the Redcoats. Fellow soldiers noted her steady aim and sure shot."

They came to a stop on a street corner, waiting for the crosswalk light to signal green. Abigail was talking about relying on horses as their transportation. "In fact, Mr. Adams and I departed our wedding ceremony on a single horse to begin our lives together."

"Have you ever thought about taking a Tesla from point A to point B?" Max asked.

Abigail responded the same way she'd responded to every such question on this tour. "I do not know this Tesla of which you speak."

"Might be worth checking into," Max said. "A lot less poop involved with Teslas than horses."

Sloane was pointing her phone upward to take a photo and stepped back, bringing her closer to the curb. Instinctively, Max braced an arm against her lower back to keep her from accidentally falling into the street.

Sloane gave a small gasp and looked at him, their profiles inches apart. He could feel the contours of her spine and ribs through her shirt. Blood rushed desire through his veins—

"Mr. Cirillo," Abigail said, "I will not allow that type of forward advance in my presence."

"Excuse me." Ensuring that Sloane was safe, he removed his arm from her. "I was trying to save James Madison's granddaughter here from being squished by a Tesla."

The tour concluded at a place named Abigail's Tea Room in honor of the real and dead Abigail Adams, not this circular Abigail.

"My tearoom overlooks one of Boston Harbor's inlets." Her wig was starting to sag in the heat, one curl trembling sadly near her jaw. "The Boston Tea Party took place in December of 1773. Our people protested taxation without representation by throwing bales of tea into the water. '*Surely the very Fiends feel a Reverential awe for Virtue and patriotism,*' I wrote in a letter. Huzza!"

"Huzza." It was clear to Max, if not to Abigail, that even the most gung-ho in this group were getting sick of saying *huzza.*

"I can't help but think that this Abigail might be more comfortable in a mental health facility," Max said to Sloane. "She seems to be living in a very deep and extended delusion."

Sloane peeked at him out of the corners of her sparkling eyes. "The same could be said of you."

Ivy frequently felt nervous. Like when she had to speak to a group of people. Or take an important test. Or dance with her friends in the school gym in front of people.

But it was unusual for her to feel nervous for this long.

It was Sunday, the day of her meeting with Seth. And as soon as she'd woken up in the hotel, nervousness had jumped on top of her like a cat with sharp claws. The hours of this day had gone on forever. But it was finally almost time to meet Seth.

Max held the door of Chocolate Haus open for her. She entered the coffee shop, which smelled like coffee beans and liquid chocolate.

Aunt Sloane had insisted they arrive fifteen minutes early. Seth wouldn't be here this early, probably. Or would he? Ivy looked around, stomach jittery.

She didn't see any men alone inside.

"Would you like something to drink?" Max asked her.

She shook her head.

He turned to Sloane. "Would you like something?"

"An English breakfast tea would be lovely."

Max nodded and moved toward the line as Sloane took Ivy's elbow and steered them to a square table surrounded by four chairs. Ivy took the seat that had the best view of the door. To her side, a large window showed people walking past on the sidewalk.

"How are you holding up?" Sloane asked.

"Nervous."

"That's understandable." Ivy could tell by the tightness of Sloane's mouth that she was on edge, too. "Is there anything I can do to help?"

Ivy shook her head. She hoped Seth wasn't disappointed

when he saw her. She'd washed her hair and blown it dry and done her makeup. She'd put on her favorite dress—the white one with the little blue flowers on it.

When Max reached their table, he set Sloane's tea before her. He'd purchased one of those tiny mugs of strong coffee for himself. Espresso? He didn't try to draw Ivy out, and she was thankful. But when her eyes met his, he looked back with an extremely steady expression. She and her aunt might be shaky in this moment, but he was not. She saw nothing but confidence in Max right now and some of his calm slid into her, helping a little.

Earlier, she and Sloane and Max had gone to the fine art museum. If she hadn't been so stressed today, she'd have been able to enjoy spending time with them the way she had yesterday and Friday. Being near Sloane and Max was like living inside a romantic movie because it felt at any second like one of their arguments might lead to kissing.

Ivy didn't want Sloane to fall for a player and it seemed like Max was a player. But Ivy believed he'd straighten up if he had the chance to be with Sloane. He looked at her all the time like he was crazy about her.

Ivy reached for her phone, deciding to play a game on it to distract herself.

Every time the front door opened, Ivy caught her breath and glanced up. Each time, the person who entered wasn't Seth. Still nine minutes to go until three. She played the game as if her life depended on it.

At two minutes before three, she raised her face at the sound of the door and saw immediately that the man walking through it must be her biological father.

This is him, she thought dumbly.

This is him.

Chapter Eleven

The man who'd just arrived had red hair. His hair was a darker, more brownish shade than Ivy's, but definitely red. He also had Ivy's light skin color and freckles. His face was handsome. His height, tall. He looked to be the right age.

He'd spotted her and was walking toward their table dressed in jeans and a white Nike golf shirt. She could feel Sloane and Max coming to their feet beside her as she stood.

Seth's focus touched on the adults before returning to her face. "Ivy?"

She nodded, finding it hard to speak over the emotion swirling inside her. This man was the only biological parent she had left.

"I'm Seth. It's nice to meet you." He stuck out his hand.

She shook it.

Those familiar words—*nice to meet you*—and shaking hands with him helped this feel more normal, more like meeting any adult for the first time. "Nice to meet you, too."

He exchanged introductions with Sloane and Max, which gave her a chance to pull in some deep breaths. Her hands were shaking so she interlaced her fingers in front of her as they all sat.

"Thank you very much for meeting with us," Sloane was saying to Seth, "I know this means a lot to Ivy."

"You're welcome." He glanced at Max. Then at Ivy. She had the sense he was absorbing the details of her just like she was doing with him.

It was fascinating to see him in person.

"This is interesting, isn't it?" Seth said.

Nodding, she felt more of her anxiety melt. "Yeah."

Silence followed. Her mind blanked. She didn't know what to say.

Seth cleared his throat and adjusted his position. "How are things for you, Ivy? With your family, school?"

"Good! I have a great family. An older sister and two older brothers. They're all out of the house now, so it's just me left with my mom and dad, who are geologists. On assignment overseas. Which is why I'm spending the summer with my Aunt Sloane." She pointed at Sloane, then thought, *That was dumb. He knows who Sloane is, so I didn't need to point to her.*

To Sloane, Seth said, "You're Harper's sister."

"Yes."

"She told me about you."

Sloane smiled.

"You resemble her," he said.

"That's a lovely compliment."

He glanced at Max. "Did you know Harper?"

"I did."

"When you reached out to me," he told Sloane, "I was sorry to hear that she'd passed away. What happened to her?"

"She died of a drug overdose."

"I see. That's really sad. She was . . . wonderful."

"She's greatly missed," Sloane said simply.

A memory of the last time she'd seen Harper flashed through Ivy's mind. Harper's long brown hair. Gorgeous face. She'd worn lots of necklaces, a leather vest with nothing on under it, and bell-bottom jeans.

"What kinds of things are you into?" Seth asked Ivy. "Sports? Video games? Student government? That kind of thing?"

"I'm into rats. In fact, I own two." She pulled up a photo on her phone and aimed it at Seth.

"Wow."

"I play lacrosse, but I'm not very good. I like to hang out with my friends, watch YouTube videos, and read."

"What are your favorite subjects in school?"

"English and history."

He nodded.

"Ivy," Sloane said gently. "Do you have some questions for Seth?"

"Um. Yes!" She'd planned her questions and, thankfully, they finally dropped back into her head. "Can you, um, tell me about how you knew Harper?" That hadn't come out exactly right but good enough?

"She and I met at a party when I was a senior in high school. She'd recently moved here to Boston and was living in an apartment with a bunch of other girls. She was a year older than me and working at Union Oyster House, which is the same place where a buddy of mine was working. My buddy invited her to the party and she and I hit it off. I . . . She was amazing. My first love."

"My dad," Sloane said to Seth, "mentioned to me that Harper told him her relationship with you was not public."

His face fell a little. "I'm the oldest of three kids. My parents were more relaxed with my younger siblings, but they were all over me during my high school years. I didn't tell them about Harper when we started going out because I knew they wouldn't approve. I snuck Harper up to my room one night and my mom caught us in a pretty . . . intimate situation. They told me I couldn't see her anymore. Which of course made me want to see her more. From then on, we kept our relationship secret."

"How long did your relationship last?" Ivy asked.

"Three months or so. I thought things were going well. But then, one day in the spring of that year, she just . . . broke up with me out of the blue. She said she'd had fun and thought I was a good guy. But just"—he shrugged—"didn't feel *that way* toward me anymore." He seemed to lose himself in the past for a second, frowning. "After that, she cut off communication. I had a really hard time getting over her."

It was weird, to have been conceived by teenagers who hadn't wanted a baby. Ivy had always known that was how her life had begun. Yet that had never felt like it belonged to her because her parents had made it so clear that she *was* wanted, that she *was* planned for—by them. Her mom liked to say that Ivy was the one who'd made their family complete.

She'd been conceived accidentally. But the bigger part of her identity was that she'd been *adopted purposefully*.

"When did Harper let you know that she was pregnant?" Sloane asked.

"After we broke up, I worked all summer, then went to Michigan that fall. I'd been going to classes for a couple of months when she called from the labor and delivery floor of the hospital after giving birth to tell me I was a father."

Ivy winced. He'd been eighteen and Harper had been nineteen when Harper had gotten pregnant. That wasn't a lot older than Ivy was now.

It would be *terrible* to get pregnant at nineteen.

Like really, really terrible.

It kind of blew Ivy's mind to imagine being Harper back

then. It especially blew her mind to imagine having a baby the way Harper had—alone. She hadn't told Seth, and she hadn't told Sloane or their dad.

Before Harper passed away, Ivy had seen Sloane way more often than she'd seen Harper even though Harper was her biological mother. Sloane never cancelled their plans, but Harper cancelled their plans often. The times when Harper had come by, she'd always brought a gift, which was really sweet of her. She was a dazzling type of person yet there'd been something sort of . . . hectic inside of Harper. It was hard to explain. It had felt like Harper couldn't just relax and be peaceful. Which had made Ivy uneasy when she was around her.

Never had Ivy thought, *I wish I'd been raised by Harper.* Instead, Harper always caused Ivy to think, *I'm so glad for my mom and dad.*

"I was totally shocked to find out I was a father," Seth continued. "I told her that I would leave school. That we could marry and be parents together. She didn't want that. She had her mind absolutely made up about the babies."

"Baby," Sloane corrected.

Seth's forehead lined.

The longer Seth stared at them in confusion, the more it felt like a cold wind was blowing across Ivy's heart.

"*Babies,*" Seth emphasized. "Twins."

Shocked quiet answered.

Twins? The word bounced around inside Ivy's skull. Instinctively, she glanced at Max, who once again gave her that unshakable *I am here, and everything is going to be fine* expression.

"Harper only had one baby," Sloane said. "Ivy."

"You didn't know about the other one?" Seth looked between them. "I'm sorry. I thought you knew. When did Harper tell you about Ivy?"

"Five days after Ivy was born," Sloane answered.

"And she never mentioned the other baby?"

"No. Never."

"I'm surprised." Seth scratched the side of his head, then dropped his hand. "During her phone call with me she said she'd decided, soon after learning she was going to have twins, that two babies would be too much for her. Months before she delivered, she'd made a choice to place one with an adoptive family."

Ivy was speechless. It appeared that Sloane was, too.

"Was the other baby a boy or a girl?" Max asked.

"A girl. Harper called that baby Baby A and said something about how she was the bigger of the two twins. Which made her feel like Baby B was the one who needed her a little more . . . . Or something along those lines. Sorry, I don't remember all of this perfectly. It's been a long time."

"Baby B was me?" Ivy asked.

"Correct. She told me that she was going to name you Ivy and that you were healthy. Then she asked me to sign a document giving up my rights for Baby A. She emailed instructions to me."

"What was Baby A named?" Sloane asked.

"No idea. By that point, the day of the twins' birth, an adoptive family had already been lined up for Baby A and they were the ones who were going to name her."

"Have you learned any other information about that baby over time?" Max asked.

"No. That adoption was a closed adoption."

"You don't know where she was raised?" Max asked.

"No."

"Do you remember the name of the adoption agency that handled that adoption?" Sloane asked.

Seth chewed the inside of his lip thoughtfully. "Unfortunately, I don't. I was a college kid at the time. All I remember is that, in the email, Harper explained that we had to wait four days and then I'd need to sign the document in front of a notary public and witnesses. Which was what I did."

Ivy's brain was still stuck on the news that she had a twin sister. *I am one half of a set of twins?*

"I regret to say that I was very immature back then," Seth added. "I didn't follow up with Harper. I just . . . went on with my life. After that, I heard from Harper just one other time, when she asked me to sign the same document, releasing my parental rights to you, Ivy. I can't remember how many months later that was."

"Harper placed me for adoption when I was five months old."

"Okay, so it must have been five months later. That time, she said she was going to do an open adoption. But again, she assured me that her decisions didn't include me. All she wanted was a signature on a paper. So, that's what I did."

"And has your life gone well?" Ivy asked. "Since college?"

"It has. I moved back to Boston after graduation. I got married five years ago and my wife and I have a two-year-old little boy and a daughter on the way. She's due in November."

"Oh, that sounds really nice."

Seth's expression turned more serious. "My wife, my parents and siblings . . . I never told any of them about you and your sister, Ivy. There just didn't seem to be a point. I never had a role in Harper's life after she broke up with me. And no role in Baby A's life or your life."

It sounded like Seth had kept a big secret from the people closest to him. His wife would probably be *very* mad if she found out that he'd had children he'd never mentioned.

"That's why, this"—Seth motioned between himself and the rest of them—"is sensitive for me. When I got your letter, I wanted to help. But I'd hate to hurt my wife or family. And they *would* be hurt if they learned that I'd kept this from them. I . . . I didn't keep this from them because of anything to do with you, Ivy. I kept this from them because of some of the decisions I made along the way. I didn't want to let them down. And I don't want to injure them now. Can you understand?"

"I understand completely." Ivy jumped in to extend grace. She'd never want to injure Seth or the people who loved him.

She'd been an open part of Harper and Sloane's life. But because Seth had never told anyone about her, she couldn't be an open part of his life. It still meant a lot to her to fill in the blank space of her biological father with an actual person. Maybe this—meeting him today—was enough?

Yeah, it was enough.

Max leaned forward. "Did you keep copies of the release forms you signed for Ivy and her sister?"

"No, I didn't. I was scared someone would see the forms and find out about the babies."

"Do you use the same email address you had fifteen years ago?" Max asked.

"It's one of the ones I still use, yes."

"Would you be willing to look back in your email inboxes for emails to or from Harper about the babies? It's possible Baby A's adoption agency would be included in the body of the email or the attached forms."

"Ah . . ."

"We'd really appreciate it," Max said firmly.

"I don't think the emails are still there, but when I get home, I'll check. Just in case."

Max thanked him.

"Any other questions for me?" Seth asked.

"Is there anything we should know about your family's

medical history?" Sloane asked. "Any risk factors, for example, that run in your family?"

He appeared to think that over. "No. Not really. We're a healthy group. All four of my grandparents are still living."

"If you remember anything else concerning Baby A or Ivy," Max said, "you'll let us know?"

"Yes. How about I give you my work email? If you guys have any other questions, you can reach me there."

"Sure." Sloane put his contact details into her phone.

Seth hadn't *had* to show up here today. He could have ignored her letter and ghosted her. "Thank you for speaking with us."

"You're welcome. You seem great, Ivy. I'm glad everything is going well for you."

"Same to you."

He rose. "Take care, okay?" he said to Ivy.

"I will. Goodbye. Thanks again."

He weaved his way to the door. Then was gone. The sights and sounds around Ivy seemed to heighten, as if they'd been muted while Seth was sitting across from her and had now returned to their regular level. She was buzzing inside. From meeting him. From the revelation that she had a biological sister.

"Excellent job, Ivy," Sloane said. "You comported yourself beautifully."

"You think it went well?"

"You handled that pressure cooker *so well*," Max said, "that you're now going to have to take a job with Libri as CEO."

"You're CEO."

"You can have the job. You'd be better at it."

"Mark down his words," Sloane told Ivy. "That's the first and last time you'll ever hear him say that someone is better at something than he is."

Ivy grinned. "You guys"—she fisted her hands and pounded them softly on the tabletop—"I have a twin sister."

"I'm stunned," Sloane admitted. "I couldn't believe it when he said that. Not once did Harper tell me that she'd carried twins, that you had a sister."

"I've had this nagging feeling for a while now that I needed to know more about my start in life. I thought that feeling was about meeting my biological dad. And maybe some of it *was* that. But now I think that nagging feeling was mostly because of her. My sister. Maybe intuition or . . . I don't know? . . . the part of me that remembers that far back? Something was pushing me to find her."

"I'd love to meet her myself," Sloane said. "*I have another niece.*"

"You have another niece! And I have a twin. How are we going to find her?"

"I've no idea."

"Max?" Ivy looked at him hopefully.

"No clue."

"It sounds like getting information on her might be difficult," Sloane pointed out, "since that adoption was closed."

"But we will try?" Ivy asked.

"Yes," Sloane agreed with conviction. "And if it's possible to succeed, we will succeed at finding her."

Chapter Twelve

When they'd entered the private plane for their return trip to Maine, Sloane had taken the seat next to Ivy. It faced toward a table, the two chairs on the far side of the table, and beyond that, the plane's nose. Max had opted for the chair directly across from Sloane's. Which she hadn't thought much of at the time.

But now that they were thousands of feet up and coasting smoothly through the sky, Ivy had accepted the pilots' invitation to visit the flight deck. Based on the excited snippets of conversation floating back to Sloane, Ivy was asking a thousand questions, and the pilots were giving Ivy answers so in-depth that the girl would soon be prepared to teach a physics course.

Which was great and all. *Except* that it meant Sloane was stuck in a seat that faced Max squarely. And the two of them were alone back here.

As if her life depended on it, she was trying to focus on reading and replying to email on her phone. It was just that, like when she had her morning devotional time at the café table, she could *feel* Max's attention. And that didn't permit space in her head for anything else.

"Ivy seems okay to me," he said, voice pitched so their conversation would remain private. "Do you think she is okay?"

Lifting her face, she set her phone on her thigh. "I do. I talked with her once we were back at the hotel packing our things."

He waited for her to elaborate.

"I was afraid," she continued, "that the fact that Seth didn't express interest in building a relationship with Ivy might have hurt her."

"And?"

"I think that was just me, projecting the hurt I felt from my father's disinterest in me onto her. She seems fine. We have to remember that Ivy was raised in a wonderful, close-knit family. She's already as treasured as a daughter can be, which means she's much more well-adjusted than I was at that age."

His face held understanding. So much so, the unexpected pressure of tears suddenly pushed against the backs of her eyes.

"It sounds like our investigative team of three now has a twin sister to find," he said.

"It sounds that way."

Things had shifted between her and Max on this trip. He'd chipped away a bit of her animosity toward him. How? It wasn't just one thing, but the sum of all the things. His outstanding treatment of Ivy. And her. He'd been helpful and kind and funny. He'd taken on the travel arrangements and the expense of the trip—which would have fallen on Sloane's shoulders if not for him. Yesterday, he'd protected her when she'd come close to stepping into the street. He'd arranged meals for them. He'd asked Seth smart questions.

In general, Max had been an asset this weekend, just the way he'd been during their years of friendship. Which meant the old dynamic between them—the Sloane and Max rapport—was rising to the surface after years underground.

She didn't know what to do with that.

Ignore it? Make peace with it? Resist it?

So much time had passed. She'd be returning to California in early November, so what good was reestablishing a rapport with him now? Also, a rapport might lead to more time with him. And she couldn't afford more time with him. Because just the few days she'd spent with him this weekend had turned up the dial on his physical appeal.

Like right now, for instance. She was wearing a travel pantsuit and a knotted headband made of floral fabric. She was dressier and more presentable than he was. So why did he look so wholly, painfully desirable to her? He had on basketball shorts, a black T-shirt, and a black baseball hat that read *Porsche* across the front. Dark hair curled against his neck at the base of the cap.

She couldn't let his desirability sway her.

This was Max. The one who'd come at her with so much anger the day of her panic attack, when she didn't show to give her presentation. Max, the one who'd forced her out of Libri. Max, forever desired by women, but never captured by them. Elusive, conniving, ungettable, self-centered Max.

"There are times when something happens in life," he said, "and you have no idea while it's happening how important it will be."

"Are we still talking about Ivy?"

"No. We're talking about us."

"There is—"

"Don't say *there is no us*," he interrupted, reading her mind.

For once, she didn't argue. It felt disingenuous to claim there wasn't an *us* when she'd just been pondering the undeniable existence of that very link.

"There are times when something happens in life," he repeated, "and you have no idea while it's happening how important it will be. Or how much it will change everything that comes after. The day we had our last argument, the day of the annual general meeting, was like that for me. I had no clue how much damage our fight would do. I definitely didn't plan at that time on running Libri alone. Or that I wouldn't talk to you again for four years."

She nodded.

He angled forward, forearms on the table. "I should have realized that you were overwhelmed. I'm sorry that I was so hard on you. And I'm sorry that I pushed you out of Libri. I wish I'd been understanding . . . and more of what you needed."

She couldn't have been more surprised had a unicorn cantered down the center of the plane. Max had just said he was sorry. He'd coldly informed her when she'd moved to The Gables that he wanted an apology from her. But now he'd been the one to give that very thing to her.

Those words were powerful.

His *I'm sorry* began to soften something that had been jagged in her for a long time. "Thank you for saying that."

He held her eye contact.

It was too difficult to be locked with him in such a raw moment, so she looked out the plane's window at the sea of white cloud below.

Several seconds passed before he spoke. "If you could go back in time and change what went wrong between us, would you?"

Slowly, she turned her chin back to him. "That's a complicated question. So complicated, that I don't know the answer. On the one hand, I'm grateful for my life in California and for my new business. On the other hand, I mourn Libri and the life

I had. It's been hard to live with the mistakes I made because they ended up costing me so much."

"If I could go back, I'd change the mistakes I made."

"How so?"

"I'd change my behavior in all the ways needed to make you stay." His eyes were pale jade pools beneath the shade of his hat's brim. "We built Libri together. Only the two of us know what that took."

"True." Her memory sped through a reel of images. Their late-night planning sessions in college. All the coding they'd done in the earliest stages. Meticulously putting together their business plan and presenting it to investors. "The fact is, my time at Libri ended the way that it ended. Imagining it happening differently changes nothing."

Ivy returned and began passing on her newfound knowledge of flying to Max.

Sloane resumed her attempt to catch up on email.

What was the status of her relationship with Max now? She didn't know the answer to that.

She could no longer stick him in a box labeled "enemy."

Yet placing him in a box labeled "friend" felt like too big a risk.

On Tuesday, Max's entrance into his grandparents' home set off the usual commotion. Everyone hurried over, some of them flapping their hands, most of them talking. He had cousins on his mom's side of the family both older and younger than he, but he'd always seemed to be the cousin who generated the most attention. Maybe because his other cousins had siblings, but he was his mother's only son. Maybe because of his notoriety due to the scandal and later, success.

"You're here!" His stout grandmother embraced him. His grandparents had been raised in Greece before emigrating to America and having their children here. They were bilingual but still spoke English with a thick accent.

"Hi, Giagia."

"Let me at him," his grandfather demanded, giving Max a hug that finished with back slaps.

"Good to see you, Pappous."

Max greeted his mother, aunts, uncles, and cousins. They all remained crowded into the small living room.

"Have you been presenting the Cirillo name in a good light?" His grandfather asked Max this question every time Max saw him.

"I have."

"We are *proud* of the Cirillo name," Pappous said, like a coach giving a pep talk to the team before the final game of the season. "We are a close family. We have dignity. We have integrity. And so many accomplishments." He went around, pointing at each person and listing their achievements. When he got to Max, he said, "You own a company and employ many, many people." Which, in Max's opinion, was a mile above the accomplishments of the others, which included things such as "a bachelor's degree!" and "good at giving manicures!"

"Max," Giagia said, "Groomsport's Pumpkin Festival is coming up in October and the Greek Heritage Society will take part in the parade. You should—"

"Yes!" Pappous interrupted her, as he had a habit of doing. "You should be in the parade with us."

"Sounds interesting," Max lied, because he'd been taught to respect his grandparents and not to disagree with them outright. "What is the Greek Heritage Society doing in the parade?"

"Dressing in traditional clothing—" Giagia began.

"And marching in the parade, waving Greek flags," Pappous finished.

There was *no way* that Max would ever dress in a pirate-style white shirt, vest, sash, white skirt, and white tights. "Hmm," he said.

"I'll call you with the information." Giagia patted his cheek.

"Are you seeing anyone?" Pappous asked.

"That reminds me!" Max's mom crowed. "I forgot to tell you all that Sloane Madison has come back to Maine."

"Sloane!" his grandparents, aunts, and uncles said in unison.

The Cirillos had treasured Sloane and had never been shy about telling him so. After his mom ran into Sloane at the party the other night, she'd scolded him for not notifying her that Sloane had returned and was living at The Gables.

"She's staying in Max's garage apartment this summer with her niece." Mom seemed to be enjoying delivering this information without a care for how many questions about Sloane he'd now have to field from this group.

Giagia bounced up and down, clapping. "Living on your property?!"

"I've *always* thought Sloane was the one for Max," Mom stated. "Now they can marry."

"*Yes,*" Pappous agreed wholeheartedly.

"She can march in the parade with you," Giagia suggested. "I'll tell Sloane she can borrow my costume—"

"You should marry that girl. Don't waste this chance." Pappous thumped him on the shoulder.

Then everyone was talking at once about how he should propose to Sloane.

Until just a few days ago, Sloane hadn't even been able to look at him without glaring, but there was no point wasting his breath trying to explain that to them. When they got like this, they had zero interest in reality.

"Mom?" he cut in. His visit today had a goal: fulfill the favor Fiona Camden had asked of him. "May I speak with you outside for a minute?"

Her expression turned inquisitive. "Okay."

He led her away from the chaos.

His mother had been hired by Fiona Camden a few months before Jeremiah's birth. Which meant that, at the point in time when everything blew up, Mom had been working for the Camdens for sixteen years.

Many of Fiona's wide circle of friends had been shallow women as wealthy as she was. Fiona, who'd come from humble beginnings, had relied on Mom not just as her maid and grocery shopper and cook, but as Fiona's favorite confidante.

As a kid, he hadn't fully clued in to the touchiness of Nicole's friendship with Fiona. For one thing, their friendship hadn't been all bad. He remembered his mom and Fiona sharing laughter and after-hours glasses of wine on Maple Lane's back porch. For another thing, his mother had never bad-mouthed Fiona to him.

Looking back now, he was better able to understand why a friendship between two women so unequal in power had not been an easy thing. Especially for Mom, the one with no power. She'd probably been dealing with undercurrents of hostility for years.

In return for the job and the friendship Fiona extended to Nicole, Fiona had expected the utmost in loyalty and effort. When he was fourteen, his mother had overheard Fiona telling her friend that she was worried Nicole's work was slipping because Nicole was becoming complacent.

Perhaps Mom had been exhausted that day, in a terrible mood, dealing with a splitting headache, overwhelmed, overworked. The specifics of the reason had been lost to time. What was certain—the undercurrents of hostility had boiled over and washed away all the things about her work that she was usually grateful for. An excellent, rent-free house. Fair pay. Steady employment. A flexible schedule.

Nicole had confronted Fiona, telling her that she'd overheard the conversation and demanding to know why Fiona hadn't come to her and talked about these things with her to her face. Fiona, who could be fiery herself, had stood by the criticisms she'd articulated. At that point, his mother had voiced all her criticisms of Fiona. Long and loud.

Then his mother had stormed back to their house, called the town newspaper, and informed a reporter that her son, Max, had been fathered by Felix Camden.

It had been an act of mutiny toward Fiona. Only after Nicole calmed down did she realize there would be no recovering from her rebellion. That she had, in many ways, sabotaged herself.

Now, Max and his mom stepped into his grandparents' backyard. Quiet met them. The garden was tall this time of year with neat rows of vegetables and fruit. He came to a stop on a patch of grass lined by ripe tomato plants.

"What do you need to talk to me about?" Mom asked.

"Fiona Camden."

Her eyes flared, then narrowed.

"She came by the other day to say that she'd like to have a conversation with you."

Mom crossed her arms. "Why would she want to have a conversation with me?"

He explained that Fiona was seeking to resume communication with Isobel, who'd informed Fiona that she'd need to mend fences with Nicole first.

"Mend fences!" Mom scowled. "What does that involve?"

"Fiona is asking for one brief, civil conversation. She'd like to tell you that she forgives you and snap one picture of the two of you together that she can send to Isobel as proof of the meeting."

"I've never asked for her forgiveness."

"Even so, it might be nice for you to hear her say that she forgives everything that happened, right?"

"Fiona herself had an affair with Felix when he was married to Isobel, *her own sister*. Now she wants to forgive me like a queen on high for doing the very same thing she did?"

"In short, yes. You're the one who had an affair with Felix when *Fiona* was married to him."

She screwed up her face. "Why would I want to help her have a relationship with her sister again? Why would I want to help her in any way?"

"You could help her as a nod to the fact that you and Fiona were friends once. I remember that there were good times between you."

"She was the person who wrote my checks. If I'd been choosing a regular friend, I wouldn't have chosen someone so pampered."

"She has flaws just like the rest of us. But she also has strengths. She's supportive of her sons. She's generous. She runs a successful business."

"Are you, my son, singing *Fiona Camden's* praises to me?"

"Your son is encouraging you to talk with her for a few minutes. That's it."

"I planned on never seeing her again."

"I get it. But here's what I know about you. You are strong enough to handle uncomfortable things."

She kept stubbornly quiet.

"Because of Jude and Jeremiah, I'm around Fiona from

time to time," he said. "It would be helpful to me if you could find it in your heart to honor this request of Fiona's."

Still, she did not agree.

"Just think on it," he said. "All right?"

She gave a grudging nod. "Did you find the tiara you were asking about a few weeks ago?"

"Not yet."

"You can bet Fiona has it."

"She says she doesn't have it, but she might. I haven't ruled out that possibility."

She moved to the back door. "You coming in?"

"I'll be there in a second."

He remained outside alone, trying to relax, trying to find a sense of contentment inside himself.

In Boston, he'd been part of things with Sloane and Ivy. He'd enjoyed every minute of his time with them. Technically, he belonged here with the other Cirillos. It's just that he could only take them in small doses and didn't find it as simple to enjoy himself in this setting as he had with Sloane.

Since they'd returned to Groomsport, Sloane and Ivy had continued living life as a pair and he'd resumed his familiar role as an outsider. He didn't fit with them the way they fit together, just like he hadn't fit with Jeremiah and Jude after he'd left Maple Lane.

He'd taken to spending a stupid amount of time looking from his giant house toward Sloane's much smaller apartment. Doing so made him feel, irrationally, as if he'd gotten the shorter end of the stick.

In the town of Waldoboro, Sloane was dealing with a parent of her own. "I'm here to pick you up and take you to your doctor's appointment," she reminded her father on the threshold of his apartment. "Remember?"

"I wish you hadn't scheduled that appointment." He fussed with the hem of his old sweater. "I hate going to the doctor. And I don't need to go. I'm feeling okay."

"This is a regularly scheduled appointment with the doctor who's treating your emphysema. Going to these appointments is an important part of maintaining your health."

"It's a waste of money. I don't have health insurance, and I can't afford to pay for it out-of-pocket."

"I will pay for it out-of-pocket, so you don't have to worry about the financial piece. Now, come with me so we're not late." It took a fair amount of cajoling before she had him in the SUV and they were on their way.

"It seems like it's easy for you to pay medical bills," he commented as neighborhoods blurred by. "You're flush with cash these days, huh?"

"My income is stable."

"It must be nice to be flush with cash."

It's certainly nicer, Sloane thought to herself, *than the way Harper and I spent our childhood.*

"I got a hot tip on a horse," he said, "but I need to pay off fifty grand before I can make that wager. Would you front me fifty grand?"

The resignation she experienced whenever she interacted with her father settled over her like a suffocating blanket. "No. I don't think it would be wise to front you money for gambling."

"It's a sure thing."

"You can count on me to continue to help you out weekly the way that I've been doing."

She was here to give to him the things she'd once needed because this was what she heard the Lord asking her to do.

Nowhere did it say that giving to others would always be easy or rewarding.

Hoping for that—that this would be rewarding to her—revealed that she was somehow still putting herself at the center of this. Yet her efforts on her dad's behalf weren't about her at all. They weren't for her. Giving others what you need was about *them*.

Her involvement with her father didn't feel good in this moment.

But this absolutely was, nevertheless, grace.

On Wednesday morning Max received a text from Seth Taylor.

As he sat reading it in his office, he was glad for two reasons. One, glad for Ivy because this might provide her with the next step in her search for her twin sister. Two, glad for himself because this meant he wasn't going to show up empty-handed for their second planning session—the one he, Sloane, and Ivy had scheduled for tonight two weeks ago.

The board meeting he had to attend that afternoon ran long. Which ratcheted up his stress as he glanced repeatedly at the time. The second the meeting ended, he jogged to the elevator. If he floored it on the way to his house, he could get to Sloane and Ivy on time. As the elevator carried him down, he checked his phone, immediately stalling on messages from Sloane that had come in while he'd had his phone off during the meeting.

SLOANE

Ivy's friend is performing in a musical tonight and so she's hoping to reschedule our planning session so she can go support her friend. Will that work for you?

SLOANE

You haven't texted back, which likely means
you're busy at work. Totally understandable.
The musical is starting soon, and I've told Ivy
she can attend. So we won't be meeting
tonight.

Max's energy left him like water down a sink drain. The
elevator doors opened. He passed through the lobby and
outside. Ground fog had moved in, blotting out the sun. Once
inside the Porsche, he typed a message back.

MAX

I just got out of a board meeting. I was going
to tell you and Ivy tonight about the message
I received from Seth today. The information in
it is useful.

He waited, drumming his fingers against the gear stick.

SLOANE

What information?

His lips hitched into a half smile.

MAX

It's too classified to share over the phone. In
person only. Meet after the musical on my
patio?

SLOANE

Ivy's going to a campfire to have s'mores
after the musical. I can meet you to discuss. It
might be best if I hear the information first
anyway, so I can think on it, then pass it on to
Ivy in a digestible way.

Digestible way. He'd always liked the way Sloane talked.
She wore vocabulary the way soldiers wore medals.

MAX

Good. See you in fifteen minutes?

SLOANE

I'm out at the moment myself. I can be back
at 9.

MAX

Are you also at the musical?

SLOANE

No.

No? Where was she? Probably at the gym, he assured himself. Out with a friend. At the library.

MAX

See you at 9.

A knocking sound caused him to flinch. One of the board members had rapped on the hood of his car and was now smiling through the window. "Have time to grab dinner?" the older man asked.

"Turns out I do," Max answered.

By the time he reached The Gables, it was 8:50 and fully dark. His headlights illuminated the Suburban Sloane drove, parked in its usual spot to the side of the garage. Her apartment was dark, which likely meant she wasn't back yet. But her car was? Strange.

He left his Porsche in the garage, the mechanical door whirring downward as he crossed to his back door.

When Sloane had been co-owner of Libri, she'd put her fancy stamp on the culture by insisting everyone wear business casual. After she left, he'd done away with that requirement. Rarely these days did he dress in suits. Today, though, he'd changed into a suit before the board meeting. It wasn't as comfortable as he liked, yet he resented the time it would cost him to change, so he simply whipped the tie free and unfastened the top button of his shirt.

He paused in his kitchen long enough to dump his keys, wallet, and tie. Flicking on the backyard landscape lighting and string lights, he let himself out through the sliders, then leaned against his outdoor table and waited for Sloane to show.

He didn't have to wait long. Within minutes, he registered the sound of a car engine. A Jeep Grand Cherokee came into view. Sloane exited the passenger side and spoke to the driver. He was too far away to make out their words, but he did recognize the car.

It was Nate's.

He could actually *feel* jealousy multiplying inside him like a deadly virus.

The Cherokee drove off and Sloane made her way in his direction, wearing a strapless, pink sundress. It was fitted to her waist, then expanded into a flowy skirt that almost skimmed the grass.

She stepped onto the patio stones and came to a stop. "Good evening."

"Good evening. Out on a date with Nate?"

"I was, yes."

"On the night of our planned meeting?"

She tilted her head like, *That's a nosy question*. "Not that I'm obligated to explain myself, but grabbing dinner with Nate was a spur-of-the-moment thing after I cancelled our meeting."

"What's going on between you two?"

"That's none of your business," she said in a cheerful, polite tone.

"Are you a couple?" *Answer me*, he wanted to insist in the torturous seconds that followed.

"No, we're not a couple. We're just . . . getting to know each other again."

Max would bet anything that Nate wanted them to be a couple.

"You said that you received a message from Seth?" she prompted.

"I did."

"Which seems strange since I'm the only one who gave him my number."

What was she talking about? It was hard for him to move his mind off Sloane's date to anything else.

She was talking about Seth.

"Seth had my number, too," he said. At this point, he was fine with telling her about his role in setting up the meeting between Ivy and Seth in Boston. It was too late for her to intervene or try to stop him. Also, the steps he'd taken had worked, which reflected well on him.

"How did he have your number?" she asked.

"From when I called him."

"You called him? But . . . how did *you* have his number?" Her pretty eyebrows shot up. "Oh my goodness! You got it from my notebook, didn't you?"

"Yep."

"Max!"

"What? I own that apartment. You know I have a key."

"What did you discuss when you called Seth?"

"That I'd pay him five thousand dollars to speak with you, me, and Ivy in Boston."

"*Excuse me?*"

"He said yes, as he should have, since five thousand for thirty minutes was a sweet deal for him."

Her mouth formed an O. "You *paid* Seth five thousand dollars to meet us at the coffee shop?"

"I did. And I'd do it again. In case you didn't notice, that guy's pretty selfish. He was never going to help Ivy without incentive."

"You had no right to butt in on Ivy's search."

"I had every right. Ivy asked me to help. So I helped. You should be thanking me because the approach you were taking with Seth was doomed to fail."

"You're such a—such a . . ."

"Yes?" He gave her a slow smile.

"Schemer."

"That's accurate. Now, are you going to be grateful about the information I received from Seth today or testy about the fact that I was the one who received it?"

"Both? May I see Seth's message?" She extended a pale palm.

He brought up the text and passed his phone over.

As she read, he studied her bent profile.

SETH

Max, I looked way back in my email to see if I still had anything from Harper and this is what I found. She sent it to me for Baby A. I hope it's helpful to you. Thanks for the payment you sent.

Sloane tapped the attachment that had come in after the text. That opened a document titled "Voluntary and Unconditional Surrender." Many of the blanks hadn't yet been filled out when Seth had received this form. But in the blank labeled "agency or person receiving custody" someone had written *Dawson Adoption Agency.*

"Oh." He'd bet she didn't realize she'd just made that breathy sound. It was one of his favorite quirks of hers. "The name of the adoption agency that placed Baby A."

"Exactly."

Into a web-browsing app on his phone, she typed the

agency's name. He'd already done this but didn't interrupt. An outdated-looking website appeared. Text filled the homepage. *Thank you to all of our wonderful families for your support the past 28 years. Rod and I have retired and so we've closed the agency. If you need to reach someone, contact our son Mark.* A phone number followed.

"I'll call Mark in the morning." Sloane swiftly captured a screenshot and texted it to herself. She passed back his phone.

"You can call Mark in the morning, but I'm going to go ahead and call him now."

"In the morning."

"I've already waited hours since Seth texted this to me. I don't want to keep waiting."

"It's not good etiquette to call after business hours—"

"And yet we have Mark's number thanks to the fact that his parents posted it for all to see on this 2010 website." He punched in the digits—

"No," she hissed as if Mark could already overhear.

Max hit the speaker button, and the call began to ring. Sloane made a swipe for his cell, but he held it high above his head.

"This is Mark" came a voice from the phone.

Max thrust the phone in front of Sloane's face and though she shot him a murderous look, she took it from him. "Hello. Please pardon the lateness of my call." She spoke in her most mannerly voice. "I've just realized that I have a niece whose adoption was handled by the Dawson Adoption Agency fifteen years ago. I saw on their website that they're now closed but your number was listed."

"Glad you called," Mark said happily.

Told you so, Max mouthed.

"What can I do for you?" Mark asked.

Sloane whirled and paced a few steps away. "We're hoping

to contact my niece but have been told by her biological father that it was a closed adoption. Is there any way to gain access to records?"

"I recommend that family members start by checking the Massachusetts Adoption Reunion Registry. It's a mutual consent registry. Lots of people have gone on that site and indicated that they're willing to communicate with their biological children or parents or relatives. If she's open to talking to you, then you might find your niece there. In that case, you'd be off to the races."

"And if my niece isn't listed there?"

"There's the Registry of Vital Records and Statistics. Get in touch with them and they'll talk you through their options. If all else fails, you can try petitioning the court for the records."

"Got it. Thank you so much."

"You're welcome. All my best to you!"

Sloane disconnected the call and shoved his phone against his chest. It *clinked* against a button. "Max! I do not approve of you making phone calls against my will."

"Sloane." He slid his phone inside his suit jacket. "Are you going to be grateful about the information we received or testy about the fact that I was the one who placed the call?"

"*You. Are. Maddening.*"

"I am determined."

"You are every bit as stubborn as you used to be."

He drew nearer to her.

She stood her ground.

"Come back to work at Libri," he said.

"What?"

"I dare you," he said distinctly, "to come back to work at Libri."

"You're not serious."

"Try me."

"I will absolutely not be coming back to work at Libri."

"I pay well."

"You imagine I'd come back there as an employee after being a co-owner?"

"It would be a promotion over the work you're doing at My Fair Lady. You're far too smart for that job."

"You're complimenting and insulting me simultaneously."

"My specialty."

They were standing just inches apart now, which forced her to tilt up her face to match him stare-for-stare.

Fierce desire swamped him.

Sloane's thoughts and emotions tangled together in confusion.

Max in a suit, the shadow of his stubble, his long eyelashes. He was troubling her and confronting her and discomforting her and making her feel . . .

Very swoony.

Her libido had snoozed through her time with Nate this evening. She hadn't given Nate the signals that would have led to hand-holding or kissing or any other type of physical closeness.

But those hormones that had been absent earlier were now flowing liquid in her veins, heating her from the inside out, turning her breath shallow.

Max moved even nearer. "Come back to work at Libri."

"No."

"I insist."

"I resist. Where is this invitation to work at Libri coming from? It seems totally out of left field."

"I told you on the plane if I could go back, I'd change the mistakes I made. Since I can't go back, I want to fix my mistakes."

"It's too late."

"Is it?" He stepped into her personal space.

What was he doing? Was he going to kiss her? His expression, position, and body language all told her he wanted to. But she and Max didn't kiss each other. They never had. Neither of them had even made an attempt at that.

She could smell his soap that made her think of Greece—sun and ocean. They contemplated each other with gravity, with tension. She swore she could hear his heartbeat. No, that might be her heartbeat.

He wasn't moving back. She should move back but didn't want to because heady thrills of sensation swirled against the backs of her knees, soles of her feet, fingertips.

This type of intimacy between them was a terrible idea. Also the best idea. Also the thing she suddenly wanted more than anything in the world in this night-dark, spinning moment in time.

He lowered his head.

And then his lips were on hers, firm and soft.

This could not be happening. And yet it was. The details of the kiss circled Sloane like sparkling constellations. His hands came up to support her jaw on both sides. Her palms met the fabric covering his chest. The kiss turned more intense.

This was revelation, glory, worry. Years and years of history were in the kiss. So were deep feelings—friendship, loyalty, hurt, trust. She was kissing *Max*. This was the first time she'd kissed a man she knew as well as she knew him. He was, in fact, the only man she knew this well. And that made kissing him lightyears different than the prior first kisses of her life. Kissing Max was unimaginably good.

Guardrails were thrusting up and crashing down inside her. Hard to pay them any mind because she was inundated with her own drugging, wonderful responses.

He made a masculine sound of approval.

He was an excellent kisser. Of course he was an excellent kisser. He'd kissed one million people. He no doubt kissed brilliantly even when kissing someone he didn't care about at all. He could kiss just for the fun of it. Or to manipulate. Or to persuade. He might have instigated this kiss for one of those reasons.

If so, this has the potential to be hugely destructive, Sloane.

She ignored that voice. This was too addictive to stop.

She was not ordinarily a self-indulgent person, but she dearly wanted to indulge in this. She would deal with consequences later—

Sloane, her intuition whispered with dire warning. *Sloane, you must stop this. Sloane!*

She jerked away from him, taking a few steps back. She didn't embarrass herself by gawking or gasping for breath. On the contrary, she channeled everything she had into communicating cool poise that she did not feel.

He remained silent, his face oddly expressionless. Illumination from the string lights pooled on his wide shoulders. The only thing that gave away any hint of turbulence? His eyes. They were smoky green and dazed.

She armed herself for his reaction. Was he going to laugh? Remark on how obviously she'd enjoyed that? Say something about how unaffected it had left him?

He said and did nothing.

"Well," she finally said. Then faltered, having no idea how to go on. "I guess we should probably talk about this?"

"If you want to."

"I don't, actually."

It almost looked as though his strong frame was braced against injury. Was she imagining that?

"Let's just"—she flicked her hands as if clearing water droplets from them—"let it go and move on. Okay?"

A long beat passed. "Okay."

"Good night." Etiquette demanded a closing salutation. Now that she'd given it, she hurried toward the apartment as if Kevin and Ricky were chasing her. Once she'd shut herself inside, she collapsed onto the nearest chair and bent her head into her hands.

Chapter Thirteen

What in the world? What in the world?

Sloane was quaking inside. Not in an altogether bad way. In an "I've been whisked to heaven and now returned to earth" way. The best-ever case of kiss jet lag.

She'd been close friends with Max for a long time before things had unraveled between them. Had she had any idea how amazing it would be to kiss him, maybe she'd have attempted it sooner—

Sloane. That's ridiculous.

They'd been smart not to kiss back then. They'd been wrong tonight, to cross that line and let it happen. At least, her head knew they'd been wrong. Her body, soul, and heart were all going rogue and fixating on how right and good it had felt.

You'll realize how wrong it was soon enough, she scolded her body, soul, and heart. *It's going to be wildly awkward to be around him now.* She didn't think awkwardness was something Max allowed himself. He'd likely sail ahead without giving it much thought. For her, though, since she was a normal person with a decent EQ, interaction with him was going to prove highly uncomfortable. It must have been obvious to him how much she'd loved that kiss.

Just like it's obvious to you that he loved it, a voice within her pointed out. Max was experienced at hiding his true emotions. But he hadn't been able to hide his passion during that kiss. Maybe it had only been a physical thing for him, though? It was impossible for her to know.

She was going to have to proceed like an adult who had not been rocked by that kiss.

When she'd been totally, completely . . . What in the world? . . . *rocked* by that kiss.

Max hadn't moved. He'd remained where Sloane had left him on the patio, his vision taking in data but his brain registering none of it.

He felt changed.

There had always been an unwritten rule between him and Sloane that they wouldn't make a move on the other. They'd started out as friends and as friends and business partners they'd continued. He'd—they'd—broken that rule just now.

He'd recklessly done the thing he'd wanted to do. Their friendship had already cracked so who cared about the risk anymore? But it occurred to him all of a sudden that he *had* been risking some things that he wasn't willing to give up.

His sanity. Self-control. Dignity.

Sloane had ended the kiss and though that had felt like the worst thing that could happen to him in the moment, it may have been a mercy. That kiss had shaken him far too much, right down to his foundation. He should avoid letting himself be shaken to that degree again, otherwise the whole structure of him might come crashing down.

He was a selfish creature. He'd always put his success first. What he'd experienced with her just now—the possessiveness, the tenderness, the need . . . Those feelings had the potential to make a fool of him. He'd spent most of his life protecting himself but if he let her, Sloane could strip him of that protection.

He moved to the doors. Sliding one to the side, he noted that his hand was trembling. Furiously, he climbed the stairs to the master bathroom and cranked hot water in his shower.

With any luck, that kiss had gotten Sloane out of his system—

No. He was only telling himself that to run from the fact that the opposite thing might be true. That she'd gotten way down deep into his system now.

He'd been proud of himself when he'd orchestrated Sloane's residency for the summer here at The Gables. He'd wanted to make her regret her actions toward Libri, to show her how well he'd done without her. He'd wanted closure. An apology. All of that had come back to bite him.

Worse, he sensed she'd somehow taken the upper hand.

He yanked off his shirt with a growl.

Two nights later, Sloane and Ivy settled into what had become their customary side-by-side spots on the sofa when watching TV or looking at the same computer, like they were doing now.

After Sloane had passed along the name of Baby A's adoption agency and the recommendation she'd received to try the voluntary registry first, Ivy had immediately agreed that they should start there. With the free-spiritedness of youth, Ivy kept pulling forward on this birth family search like an overexcited dalmatian on a leash.

Sloane finished inputting the requested information into the registry on Ivy's behalf. Once that went through, they were free to begin hunting for a match.

"Let's start," Ivy said excitedly, "like we talked about, by running a search for my birthday, since Baby A will have the same birthday as me."

Sloane input that date. Amazingly, two matches came back. One of which was for a female.

Ivy gasped. "Do you think this is her?"

"I don't know. Maybe?"

The rumble of Max's car reached Sloane. He must be returning home from work. The sound increased in volume as he pulled into the garage beneath them, then abruptly cut away.

Her attention flicked to the time displayed at the top of her computer. 7:42 p.m. Was he working late? Was that what was putting him home after seven every night? Or was he going out with women for drinks or dinner following work? Or a combination of both?

Surely he was just working late, as was usual for him. She'd go with that because the idea of him having drinks or dinner with conventionally-pretty-and-thin women was hard to stomach.

She listened but couldn't hear anything else. Not his footsteps or car door or his side of a conversation on his cell phone.

She'd been acutely aware of his comings and goings for the past forty-eight hours since their kiss. She was trying to overcome that. In fact, she was trying very hard *not* to spend all her time thinking about Max and overanalyzing the change in their relationship.

She'd do well to remember that, truly, there was no real change in their relationship. She'd said she didn't want to talk about the kiss, and he'd been fine with that and so nothing had altered.

Yet everything had altered.

She'd continued to go to her café table in the mornings for quiet times. The last two mornings, he hadn't appeared at his outdoor table. Consequently, she hadn't seen him since the kiss. She didn't know whether it was better not to see him or better to get the first meeting post-kiss out of the way—

"Aunt Sloane?"

She startled. "Hmm?"

"Everything all right?"

"Yep!"

"You're holding the edges of your computer really tight."

She looked down and saw that she was gripping the two front corners of her laptop like a drowning person would a life preserver. "So I am." She returned her fingertips to the ready typing position on the keyboard. "Where were we?"

"We were wondering if this person could be Baby A." Ivy pointed to the screen.

Sloane hit a button that revealed the information volunteered by the female born the same day as Ivy.

"It looks like . . ." Ivy leaned closer, chewing on the edge of her lip. "This girl's name is Anna Thomas. That's a really pretty name."

"I agree."

"There's no phone number or address provided."

"Which is what we did for you, too. Anna's a minor so it makes sense that she and her parents wouldn't be comfortable making their phone number and address public."

"This says she was born at Monarch Hospital in Boston. Right? Isn't that what it says?"

"Yes." Sloane turned her chin toward her niece and met the girl's gaze. "Same as you."

Ivy's brown eyes widened.

"Given that you and Anna were born on the same day at the same hospital and both of you were adopted, which is why you're both part of this registry . . ."

Ivy peered at Sloane, waiting.

"I think this girl," Sloane continued, "is most likely Baby A."

"We found my twin sister?"

"It looks that way to me. We're fortunate that she put her information into this database."

"I wish I'd known about this database sooner! I'd have put my information in and found her sooner. I wonder how long she's been waiting?" Ivy regarded the screen again, with wonder. "There's an email listed for her. Is that our only way to contact her?"

"Yes. It looks like the email belongs to someone named Stephanie. Anna's mom, I'm guessing."

"Let's email her now!"

"I'll gladly transcribe an email now but then let's sleep on it."

"Why?"

"Because contacting a twin sister is a big deal. She may not know that Harper passed away or that Seth isn't open to publicly acknowledging his daughters. She may not know she has a sister. She may not know that sister's a twin." She tugged on the end of Ivy's strawberry-blond braid. "When possible, it's always best to sleep on important things before taking action. We'll only get one chance to make a first impression, so we need to do this right."

It was mid-August. For Fiona that meant many things. At this time of year, she liked to get fresh champagne-blond highlights. Fresh Botox. A fresh spray tan. Then treat her sisters—the sisters she still spoke with, anyway—to a trip somewhere. This year they'd soon be going to Spain. She'd been pulling weeds in her garden and glorying in the beautiful, big blooms she'd cultivated. She ate outside every chance she got. Wore sleeveless tops and dresses.

Also at this time of year, she immersed herself in an undertaking both utterly for fun and extraordinarily competitive. The fantasy football draft. She'd been a Patriots fan since birth but had picked up fantasy football later when Felix had gotten the boys interested in it. She'd realized back then that she could either learn how to participate in fantasy football with them or she'd be left out of it completely. She'd joined in and, to her surprise, become the family member most fanatical about it.

Today, she was hosting a summer outdoor picnic. She and her tribe would consume luxurious food while exhibiting friendliness and love toward one another. After which, they'd congregate in her media room to draft their fantasy teams and exhibit a great deal of snark and self-interest. Hard to say which part of the day she'd love best.

Guests would be arriving shortly, so Fiona cast an exacting eye over the tables arranged in her backyard. A picnic basket had been placed on its side on the food table, giving the impression that it was spilling bounty like a cornucopia. Through a combination of her own cooking efforts and those of a caterer, her menu included lobster rolls, watermelon and tomato salad, kettle chips, fruit, blueberry pie, apple pie, lemonade, and iced tea. Two female caterers were on hand, both wearing floral aprons and both watching her nervously, as if worried that she would find fault.

"Excellent work," Fiona announced. Everything was up to her standards, including the butcher-paper runners down the middle of the eating tables. Every foot and a half or so down the length of butcher paper, vases sprouted arrangements of yellow black-eyed Susans, pink and purple summer flowers, and pale greenery.

At the sound of a car approaching, she adjusted the tie at the waist of her striped shirtdress and made her way to the top of the drive to greet her guests.

First to arrive? Her parents. Her father was constantly hungry, her mother constantly confused. They'd arrived eighteen minutes early because Mom had mistaken the start time. In their eighties now, they were two of the nicest people in Maine. Which was saying something because most people in Maine were intrinsically friendly. Felix's family were the exception that proved the rule.

Second to arrive? Jude, who arrived at every destination fifteen minutes ahead of schedule. He'd brought his girlfriend, Gemma, with him, which doubled Fiona's pleasure.

Next came her sisters Margaret and Alice and brother Mike.

Then Jeremiah and Remy, who brought with them Remy's elderly friends Wendell and Marisol. Having married in an outdoor ceremony two months ago, Wendell and Marisol were newlyweds who indulged in frequent PDA.

Burke got there next, thank God. He was both handsome and willing to jump in and assist when necessary.

Then her remaining siblings arrived, Jack and Elizabeth.

Jeremiah sidled up to her. "Did I mention to you earlier that I invited Dad?"

"What's that you say?" she said with false mildness.

"He and I were smack-talking about fantasy football this

season. I *need* the chance to go head-to-head with him." His vision snagged on something behind her shoulder. "Here he comes now."

Chapter Fourteen

She turned to see a Rolls-Royce slide to a stop.

This was happening very fast. She hadn't girded herself for a party that included Felix. But her sons, especially Jeremiah, threw this type of curveball at her from time to time. She had to be equal to this challenge because she refused to let Felix dim one bit of her enjoyment in this gathering.

Her ex-husband approached dressed in clothing that made him look as though he was exiting the back nine at Pebble Beach. Most men's faces turned puffy and began to look as if they were melting as they got older. Not so with Felix or Burke. Time was etching character, ruggedness, and masculinity into their already-great bone structure.

"Hey, Dad." Jeremiah extended a fist toward Felix.

Felix bumped it. "Son."

"Mom was just saying how pleased she is that you were able to join us."

"*So* pleased," Fiona said.

"I can see that Jeremiah just sprung me on you." Felix

grinned. "Being as popular as I am, it's rare that I have the opportunity to be uninvited company."

"You might not often be uninvited company," Fiona said with a beatific expression, "but I'd hazard a guess that you're unpopular company more than you realize."

Jeremiah laughed. Felix inclined his head in a show of respect. He exchanged air kisses with her. "You look beautiful, Fiona. Now. Who's here?" He lifted his regal head and scanned the guests. He was wearing his gray-blond hair slicked back today, Gordon Gekko style. "Ah, good. Your family. They'll be pleasingly offended by my presence. Jude and Gemma. And my future daughter-in-law, Remy. Outstanding. Lots to keep me busy here, apart from humiliating Jeremiah in the fantasy draft."

"Help yourselves to food." Fiona shooed them toward the buffet table, then made a circuit, checking on the rest of her guests.

Assured that everyone was having a lovely time, she filled a plate for herself. Burke came through the line behind her because he'd been busy pouring drinks and refilling the ice bucket. They sat next to each other near Fiona's parents, Wendell and Marisol, and Jude and Gemma.

Fiona remained partially aware of her ex-husband, who was currently standing near a tree, holding his plate nonchalantly, and applying himself to the task of putting Remy under his spell. If Felix ever tried to corner the market on Fiona's future grandchildren, it would be war. She'd have to obliterate him the way Napoleon had done the poor Austrians.

As if her gaze had summoned Felix, he looked over. She instantly diverted her attention to Burke, who watched her with a concerned expression.

Felix crossed to Fiona's table and lowered into the chair at the head. Obviously, he'd concluded that sitting near Fiona would be the most fiendish of all his choices.

Both Burke and Fiona's dad stiffened.

"Felix," Fiona said calmly, "this is Burke Ainsley. You'll remember that we were friends with him and his wife, Kay, when Jeremiah was at The Kellan School with their daughter."

"That's right," Felix said smoothly as he and Burke shook hands. "Good to see you again."

"You too." Fiona knew Burke must actually feel that it was anything *but* good to see Felix again. Burke was Team Fiona, which meant by law he must not be Team Felix.

"Is Kay with you today?" Felix asked.

"Kay passed away a few years ago," Burke answered. "I moved back to Groomsport more than a year ago to be near my kids and grandkids."

"Sorry to hear about Kay," Felix said. "I liked her."

"She was wonderful," Fiona said nobly. In truth, she didn't dwell on thoughts of Burke and Kay together because they made her feel at odds with herself. In the here and now, Burke was very much *her* person.

"Are you two dating?" Felix asked Fiona, gesturing between her and Burke.

"No. We're good friends."

"You and Burke would make the cutest couple," Marisol proclaimed, as earnest as ever.

"Burke's the only man I know good enough for her," Wendell said.

"I was good enough for her," Felix pointed out.

"Until you weren't," Fiona quipped, keeping an upward tilt to her lips.

"Felix and Fiona had the most memorable wedding," Mom piped up with a dreamy smile that spoke of old memories. "There were six hundred guests in attendance and what felt like acres of flowers. Even cameras, because it was televised live."

Dad was too busy chewing to correct his wife.

"I believe you're referring to Dad's marriage to your daughter Isobel, Grandma." Jude reached out and took hold of his grandmother's hand.

Fiona's mom continued as if Jude hadn't spoken. "I'm delighted that you and Felix are still so happy together, all these years later."

"As God is my witness," Felix said, "Fiona and I are as happy as any divorced couple can be."

"Here we are," Mom went on, "celebrating your anniversary with this beautiful party."

"Or," Jude proposed mildly, "celebrating the opportunity we're about to have to become cutthroat over fantasy football."

"You, cutthroat?" Gemma met Jude's eyes flirtatiously.

Fiona considered herself savvy at the art of flirtation, but Gemma was equally skilled.

"I'm very cutthroat when it comes to fantasy football," Jude said. "And I'm not going to make an exception with you as my opponent."

"I should hope not. That would take all the fun out of it when I best you at this."

"Gemma, I will bet you five gallons of rocky road ice cream that you will lose to me in fantasy football this season."

"Accepted. Now seal it with a kiss because this cutthroat side of you has me in a tizzy." They were both smiling as they exchanged a kiss.

Jude and Gemma's kiss inspired Wendell to give Marisol a peck. "Did you know, Felix," Wendell asked, "that Marisol and I were recently wed?"

"No," Felix said, then under his breath so only Fiona and Burke could hear, "having never seen you before in my life."

"My bride has transformed my life with her love." He placed a shaky hand at the back of Marisol's head and brought her gently forward for another long smooch.

"We should kiss like that more," Fiona's mom said to her father.

"Darling, we've been married for sixty-four years. They've been married for two months."

"That shouldn't make any difference. We should still kiss like that more."

"Fine. Happy to oblige when I finish eating this delicious lobster roll."

Wendell and Marisol's kiss ended with a smacking sound.

"All this love on display is making me think that you and I should give it another go, Fiona." Felix shot her a wicked smile. "If you follow your mom's suggestion, we can make this an anniversary lunch going forward."

Gemma's eyes widened.

"I would sooner wear Birkenstocks," Fiona stated, "than give a relationship with you another go."

"Your loss." Felix shrugged. "Listen, this is as good a time as any to mention that I'm trying to recover Empress Eugenie's tiara. You remember that piece of jewelry, yes?" He looked to Fiona, then Jude.

They both nodded.

"I don't think it was fair of you, Dad," Jude said, "to ask Max to find it."

"I asked him to find it because I'm ninety percent sure Nicole or Max has it."

"It's possible someone else took it," Jude said.

"Do you have any evidence of that?"

"Not yet."

"Any theories about who the mystery thief could be?"

"No."

"Do either of you remember anything that might help me find it?" Felix asked.

Fiona and Jude shook their heads.

"If either of you remember something that might help, or if you come up with a theory about the identity of the mystery thief, I'm all ears."

The fantasy draft of players went swimmingly, if Fiona did say so herself. She'd been as strategic and vicious as she knew how to be and harbored high hopes for the season.

When the draft ended, Felix had thankfully left the premises. Her parents and most of her siblings had remained. They'd stayed so long that the sky had turned dark, and they'd dug into leftovers once the dinner hour rolled around.

Now everyone was gone with the exception of Burke, who'd remained to help her clean the kitchen. Her storybook house—decorated in shades of white, cream, and muted pastels—had a replete atmosphere at present. Fiona loved the productive feeling of a party well hosted. The only fly in her ointment was her awareness that Burke was not himself.

He'd spent time talking with everyone, listening in his stellar-listener type of way. He had the demeanor of a popular psychotherapist because he made you feel that your experience mattered and that he cared deeply to hear about it. Outwardly, he'd been mostly normal this afternoon. Yet she knew him well enough to detect the subtle signals that indicated he was upset.

The silence between them that usually felt companionable was feeling spiky. So even though many dishes still waited to be loaded in the dishwasher, Fiona turned off the sink faucet.

Setting down a tray containing empty wine glasses, Burke gave her a questioning look.

"I can tell that something's bothering you," she said. "What's the matter?"

He didn't reply right away, and she understood he was taking time to formulate his answer. He was not a man who spoke rashly or in anger.

"I'm worried that you're still in love with Felix."

It took Fiona several seconds to metabolize that. "What gave you the impression that I'm still in love with Felix?"

He positioned strong hands on the hips of the jeans he'd paired with a maroon shirt. "You kept Felix in your peripheral vision the whole time he was here. You seemed completely distracted by him. You . . . bantered with him. You became this very polished version of yourself. Even more polished than usual. As if you were trying to impress him."

For the first time she could remember, Burke had said something that made her defensive. "It's true that when he's around I keep an eye on him and am distracted by him. That's because I'm wary of him. As far as acting more polished . . . He's always very polished, so I respond in kind. He's not someone I can be casual with because I have to keep my guard up with him."

"He joked about the two of you giving a relationship another go. You know that he could, at any time, apply himself to the task of winning you back."

"He won't. He only goes for women half my age or younger."

"Fiona, he doesn't lack intelligence. Even someone with very little intelligence would recognize that you are gorgeous and smart and successful bend funny. Women like you are very rare."

"Felix doesn't see me that way. I was irresistible to him once but that was forever ago. Back before he started having an affair with Nicole."

"I won't be surprised if he decides he wants you back."

"I hope that he does decide that."

Burke looked as if she'd slapped him.

"It's only in *my wildest dreams* that he'd want me back," she continued. "If he did, then I could turn him down and recover some of the pride he trampled on. I would never resume a romance with that man."

He didn't appear to believe her.

Irritated, she dashed a fallen lock of blond hair out of her eyes. "You don't think I'm telling the truth?"

His forehead knotted. "It's just . . . after what I saw today, I'm troubled."

"Because?"

He looked directly at her and spoke slowly and emphatically. "Because I love you. It would devastate me if you went back with him."

Goosebumps swirled down her shoulder blades.

Once, nine months ago, he'd told her he was interested in dating her. She'd gently told him she wanted only friendship and that had been that. Until now. The power of his words reverberated through her.

"I'm a grown man," he continued. "Not a child, like Felix. You would always be able to count on me. I would be faithful to you. I would share with you everything I have."

She couldn't recall how to breathe. "I'm . . . surprised. I was planning on us continuing as we have been."

"I'm sixty-five years old. I don't want to beat around the bush. I don't have time to waste. I want to spend my life with you, starting yesterday."

"The type of commitment you're describing . . ." Her words trailed off.

"It's marriage that I'm describing. Not a fling. Not living together. I want to marry you and be your husband."

"I never intend to marry again."

"Because of Felix," he said.

She didn't verbally confirm it.

Burke didn't seem to need verbal confirmation. "You're still letting him have a hold on you. You're still letting him dictate your life."

"The choice to marry or not to marry is mine to make. And I made the choice not to marry a long time ago."

"Things change. You could make a new choice now because of me."

"I could," she acknowledged. The last part of that thought —*but I won't*—went unspoken yet was loud between them.

Hurt showed plainly on his face. She didn't want to hurt him. He was fabulous, her dearest friend. Yet she didn't regret what she'd said because she'd meant every word.

He turned and walked out of her house.

IVY

We haven't seen you in several days. All OK?

MAX

All OK. It's been crazy at work. We just launched a new update to the app. Please let me know when I can help with the next step of your search for your sister. If I need to break the arms of some federal judges in order to gain access to Baby A's sealed adoption records, I'm willing to do it.

IVY

LOL!

MAX

It's cute that you think I'm joking.

IVY

Aunt Sloane and I are going out to eat tonight
but I'll come by your house to say hi soon.
Cool?

MAX

Cool.

IVY

I don't want you to feel lonely.

MAX

I'm never lonely.

IVY

LOL!

MAX

It's cute that you think I'm joking.

Max set his phone down on the surface of his desk in his office at Libri. He'd lied a few times in that exchange with Ivy. He'd said he was okay. And he'd said he was never lonely.

He hunched forward onto his elbows, planting his fingers against his temples.

For the past week, he'd avoided Sloane. He'd hoped her absence would bring calm. Instead, he'd become increasingly rattled and panicky as the days had gone by. He was conflicted all the time—wanting her but telling himself wanting her wasn't good for him. A portion of his mind remained dedicated to Sloane while the other portion of his mind dealt with meetings and email and decisions and the rest of his larger life.

He hated feeling this way.

He coexisted well with stress concerning his business. He confronted risk head-on. He thrived under pressure. He dealt with the responsibility of running Libri like he'd been born to it, which he had been. His ancestors on Felix's side had been business moguls for centuries. The ability to take decisive, confident action was in his blood.

But this? What he'd been experiencing since kissing Sloane? It wasn't about business. This made him feel a bunch of ways he didn't want to feel. Vulnerable and unsure and miserable.

So far, he'd told no one about any of this. Secrecy came more naturally to him than transparency. At this point, though, he was willing to do just about anything to regain his footing. And since the coping mechanisms he'd been using weren't working, he should change something. He should tell someone.

He picked up his phone.

MAX

Any chance you're free for lunch?

JUDE

You in Bangor for work?

Bangor, where Jude lived, was over an hour away.

MAX

No, but I'm willing to drive there.

JUDE

In that case, I'll clear my schedule.

Chapter Fifteen

Max and Jude placed their orders at the walk-up window of their usual lobster pound in Bangor. Then chose an outdoor table overlooking the Penobscot River. The setting—sun, breeze, trees lazy with leaves—communicated relaxation. Even Jude looked relaxed. Since he'd fallen in love with Gemma, there was an ease about him that hadn't been there before. Loving Gemma had made Jude less uptight and significantly happier.

In principle, Max was glad for Jude and glad for the good weather. But in practice, the contentment around him was serving as a contrast to his own discontent. Which underscored how out of step he was with the rest of the world. Out of step with himself, even. And that, in turn, underscored his sense of aloneness.

Whenever he and Jude came here, they ate the same meal —whole lobster with coleslaw, corn, and a bread roll. Max argued with himself about how to bring up the topic he'd come to discuss as they dug into the food. They chatted about Jude's work. Gemma. Sports. About the missing tiara—no progress to report there.

Eventually, Jude gave him a considering look. "It feels like you're stalling."

Max pulled lobster meat out of the shell, dunked it in melted butter, chewed.

"How are things going with Sloane?" Jude asked with pretend innocence.

Wiping his fingers, Max sat back in his chair. "She's driving me crazy. I've had no peace in days."

Jude gave a sympathetic nod and a *go on gesture*.

"When she moved in, I thought that would make me happy and her unhappy. Instead, she's happy and I'm worse than unhappy. I wish she'd never come to Maine."

"Any specific reason why you're unhappy?"

"We had a . . . moment a week ago."

"A moment?"

Max shoved a hand through his hair. "A few kisses. That's all it was." He shrugged because he himself didn't understand why a stimulus as small as a few kisses should have had this seismic effect. "I've been on a downward spiral ever since."

"I see."

Jude was incredibly familiar to Max. Someone he'd known all his life, respected, trusted. "What's your advice?"

Jude lifted his brows. "You never ask for my advice."

"You know me and you know Sloane. You just went through a roller coaster with Gemma and survived. This time, I'm asking."

"How to fix your downward spiral?"

"Exactly."

"Sure you're ready to hear my take on this?"

Jude was offering Max a chance to turn back.

Truthfully, Max wasn't ready to hear Jude's take. But nor

did he want to have lousy sleep and a mood set permanently on irritable and pain in his ribs every time he looked in the direction of the garage apartment. He'd come to Jude because he needed to fix this. "Yeah. I'm ready to hear your take."

Though they were both only halfway through their meals, Jude followed Max's lead, paused his eating, set aside his fork. "You became friends with Sloane at the end of your freshman year." Jude regarded him levelly. "By the end of your sophomore year, you were in love with her."

The statement wound around Max like thick nautical rope, tightening.

Jude winced as if to say, *Sorry, buddy*. But he kept going, relentless and calm. "The opposite of love is not hate, it's . . ." Jude motioned for Max to complete the sentence.

"Indifference."

"And you've never been indifferent to Sloane. Never. Not these past four years. Not now. That's because you've kept on loving her all this time. She was dating that Nate guy, remember, when you had your big fight? You weren't thinking straight. If she hadn't been dating him then, you wouldn't have been so on edge and maybe wouldn't have overreacted the way you did."

Max's heart beat fast and hard. His instincts were urging him to disagree. But something stronger, fed by the misery of this past week, kept him sitting in silence.

"Then you heard that Sloane was contemplating selling her shares," Jude went on. "That news wouldn't have had the power to crush you the way it did if you didn't love her. She broke your heart, though I don't think you've ever admitted that to yourself. Afterward, you became more cynical and more ambitious than you were already. Now you have everything and yet you have nothing because you don't have her. To fix your downward spiral, you'll need to win Sloane over."

The nautical rope cinched tighter.

"Start by telling her how you feel," Jude said.

Nothing Max had ever encountered in his life had the ability to scare him as much as that did.

"Then work to earn her trust," Jude added. "It's not going to be easy. She's leery of you after everything that went down and everything you took from her. She lives in California. She thinks, with good reason, that you're not husband material."

Max registered birds singing. Another note of contentment that conflicted with his state of mind.

"If you're going to be worthy of her," Jude said, "it won't work for you to party, or chase models, or spend as many hours at the office as you always have. The good news is this—I don't think you actually get much satisfaction out of the parties and the models. Libri is trickier. You've spent a lot of time making that your everything."

It was true. Libri was his everything. His source of worth, his life's work.

So how come not even Libri had been able to save him this past week?

"I have hope that Sloane might give you a shot," Jude said.

"Wha—" Max's voice was rusty. He cleared his throat and tried again. "What makes you think that?"

"Before she moved to California, I watched you two finish each other's sentences, or communicate without any words at all, or laugh at the same things. You'd banter and joke and disagree. You'd come through for each other when it mattered."

"None of that means she'd be willing to give me a shot."

"Occasionally, I'd catch her looking at you with deep affection and I'd think that maybe she cared or could come to care about you the way you cared about her. Again, I think you should start by telling her how you feel."

"Definitely not."

"To what?"

"To all of it. I don't even agree with this theory of yours. I don't love Sloane."

Jude regarded him with knowing patience. "Don't you?"

"And I'm not willing to change anything about my life."

"Max—"

"I'm through talking about this," he said raggedly. Looking to the side, he scowled at the river.

"It's going to be all right," Jude said.

It didn't feel like it was going to be all right.

Sloane didn't love him. She wouldn't have him. He'd never be able to convince her. When he imagined her turning him down, panic tightened his throat at the thought of the humiliation he'd feel.

That night, Max flicked through his photo roll from the last couple of months in search of the women he'd hung out with before Sloane moved in.

He stopped on the face of a blonde. Academically speaking, she was hotter than Sloane. Younger than Sloane. She certainly dressed sexier than Sloane. She was even nicer than Sloane. He pulled her up in his contacts and placed a call.

She answered right away. "Max!"

"Hello, beautiful. I've missed you," he lied.

"I've missed you. It's been too long."

"I agree. Any chance you're free to go to a club tomorrow?"

"I'd love to."

The next evening around ten, Sloane was tucked under the duvet in her silk PJs reading a cozy mystery when Ivy's voice drifted through her closed bedroom door.

"Max is out clubbing tonight with an actress!" the girl called.

Tension overtook Sloane's body with the speed of a light switching on.

"Can I come in?" Ivy asked.

"Yes, you may." Sloane *did not* want to see or hear about Max's romantic escapades. But she couldn't very well forbid that because then Ivy would ask why talking about Max's escapades was forbidden. And Sloane would have no explanation to give.

Ivy hurried over, sitting on the edge of the bed to show Sloane the image on her phone. "I've been following Social Sophie and she's been quiet about Max for weeks. Until now. She reposted this picture of him taken tonight with some woman who was on a Netflix series. Social Sophie says she's wearing Tom Ford."

The photo, of Max and the actress entering a night club, had captured his handsomeness well. The lines of his body were elegant. His face blatant in its symmetry. He gave the impression of debonair composure.

"I don't think," Sloane said carefully, "we should place too much value on things like designer clothes."

"I know, I know! I don't. It's just cool to see *our* Max on social media. He's a little bit famous!"

"He's . . . something."

Ivy was already madly texting, probably updating her friends on this Max sighting, as she darted out of Sloane's room and closed the door behind her.

A pit formed in Sloane's stomach.

She'd been having a delightful evening. She'd taken a long bath and applied pale pink polish to her fingernails and toes.

That picture of Max and his date shouldn't have the ability to take all that had been good and rip it in half. She'd known his dating playbook.

It was good, great even, that he was reverting to his usual ways and taking any fleeting interest he'd had away from her. So why had that photo left her feeling deflated and angry?

You have no reason to feel either of those ways, she told herself.

He's not worth tanking your mood, Sloane.

That sentiment fell flat. In all fairness, Max Cirillo was actually worth quite a lot. More than he knew, even.

She remembered him painting her first apartment. She remembered him rushing Advil to her on more than one occasion when she was immobilized by a headache. She remembered him leading meetings, his cheeks flushed because their company meant so much to him.

She'd long understood that Max was a heartbreaker and not cut out for long-term romantic commitment.

She'd kissed him one time. They didn't owe each other anything. It wasn't sane to hope for more with him.

All these commonsensical things, Sloane articulated to herself.

However, the pit in her stomach remained.

For the next six nights straight, Ivy showed Sloane Social Sophie's pictures of Max.

Every night.

A new, glamorous location. Nantucket. Bar Harbor. Manhattan. The Hamptons.

A new, glamorous woman.

A new, glamorous set of clothes for him and her.

Max was consuming hedonism the way competitive eaters consumed hot dogs on the Fourth of July. After she'd expressly asked him to model propriety in this area while Ivy was living on his property. Given, he hadn't brought a single woman home as far as she could tell. But still.

She and Ivy went back-to-school shopping for supplies. The first day of school arrived and Sloane made breakfast, oversaw the packing of Ivy's lunch, and proudly took pictures of her niece holding a handmade sign that read, *10th grade*. After a FaceTime call to mark the big occasion with Brooke and Jared, Sloane dropped the girl off at the high school. She got teary-eyed because here was yet another special moment in Ivy's life that Harper was not around to experience. Yet God, in His mercy, *had* granted Sloane the ability to experience it. Which was bittersweet.

Above all of it—every one of those late-August days— hovered the dark, quiet shadow of Max's mansion. Two weeks had gone by with no contact or conversation between them. Maybe this was their new thing? Not seeing and not speaking to each other?

If so, it made her blue. And the swath he was cutting through socialites made her seethe.

She began concocting revenge fantasies.

She'd steal all his cutlery except his dessert spoons, so he'd never be able to lay a place setting with good etiquette ever, ever again.

She'd hide Kevin and Ricky in his bed. Except that would mean handling Kevin and Ricky, so never mind that plan.

She'd figure out how to turn off *his* water. Take that, Max!

IVY

I just heard you park your car in the garage.
Can I come by and say hi tonight?

MAX

Sure. I was planning on eating a ham
sandwich for dinner in about an hour. You
want one?

IVY

Yes, please! What can I bring?

MAX

Nothing.

IVY

Aunt Sloane has started giving me etiquette
lessons. She'll kill me if she finds out I invited
myself over AND brought nothing.

MAX

Then I guess she'll have to kill you.

IVY

How bout if I bring the rat boys in their
exercise balls?

MAX

YES.

IVY

The cuteness of the rat boys is the best gift I
can give you.

MAX

My thought exactly.

An hour later, Ivy knocked on Max's back sliding door.
He walked into view and eased the glass panel to the side.
Ivy held up the rats in their exercise balls. "Here's my gift!"

"Just what I wanted."

Ivy gently set them down. Right away the boys started running inside the balls, sending them in crazy directions.

"Are the rat boys drunk?" Max asked.

Ivy laughed.

"Ready for a sandwich?"

"Ready." She followed him into his kitchen, where he already had an assembly line of sandwich stuff set up on his counter.

"There's something you should know about me."

"Okay."

"I love sandwiches. And take them seriously. You're fifteen, right?"

"Yep, fifteen."

"Tonight's sandwich is made with Iberico ham and I'm not sure you're old enough to fully appreciate Iberico ham. But I'm going to give you the benefit of the doubt because you seem like a discerning fifteen-year-old."

"I *am* discerning. For sure."

"In addition to ham, these sandwiches are made with French bread, arugula, goat cheese, and spicy pepper jam. I'm no sandwich rookie, so I'm not playing around with this."

"I see that."

"Ready?"

"Ready!" They built their sandwiches. If she'd been alone, she'd have skipped the arugula, goat cheese, and spicy pepper jam. But she didn't because she wanted to prove to Max how "discerning" she was.

They carried their plates to the kitchen table, where they'd had breakfast the mornings she and Aunt Sloane had stayed here. The sky was still bright, the wind gently thumping the purple hydrangeas planted outside against the bottom of the window.

He motioned for her to take a bite.

"Your verdict?" he asked when she finished chewing and swallowing.

"Delicious." It surprised her but this sandwich was super, *super* good.

"Yeah?"

"Yeah."

Ricky rolled his ball between the island and the stove.

"Tell me what's up with your search for your sister," he said as they ate.

"Aunt Sloane and I checked into that Adoption Reunion Registry thing."

"And?"

"And we found a girl born on the same day at the same hospital as me. In other words, we're pretty sure we've found my sister."

He looked impressed. "Wow."

"Her name's Anna Thomas. Sloane sent an email—'cause that was the only contact information listed for Anna—to who we think is Anna's mom. But we haven't heard anything back yet."

"Great progress, though."

"This search is taking *forever*."

"You learned the name of your birth father just over a month ago. And now look at you. You've already met Seth and know the name of your sister."

"It's taking *for-ev-er*." Which it was.

"Is there a reason for us to continue to meet to discuss how to help you?"

"Not right now, because we're sort of stuck. But if anything happens, I'll be sure to tell you right away, 'kay?"

"Yep."

For some reason, Max looked kind of . . . lost.

His eyes were tired, and his hair was messy. He was saying normal things but underneath his words, she sensed sadness. "I'm sorry we cancelled our last meeting so I could see my friend's musical."

"Not a problem."

She'd texted him last week and asked if everything was okay and he'd said it was. After that, he'd been out every night, so she'd thought he was good. But now she was pretty sure that he wasn't good.

She'd said to Aunt Sloane that Max was lonely. Sloane hadn't agreed and even Max had told her he was never lonely. But Ivy could tell that she was right. *Max was lonely*. Maybe he was partying a lot because he was lonely?

Guilt poured over her. She'd let a whole week go by since she'd texted saying she'd stop over. Why hadn't she come by sooner? "So even though we don't have a reason to meet to talk about my birth family search right now, I think Sloane and I should come over here for sandwiches a few nights a week for dinner. Like we're doing now, but with Sloane. You can teach us about making sandwiches and Sloane can teach you and me about etiquette. She's given me a few lessons since our dinner in Boston and it's been *so* fun."

"I do not find etiquette to be fun."

"But you adore me and Sloane." She interlaced the tips of her fingers beneath her chin and lifted her elbows high, giving him the big "please" smile her dad had a hard time saying no to.

"Whatever you're doing with your face and arms is not going to make me change my mind about etiquette."

She slapped her palms down on the table. "When we moved in, you said that you'd do anything I asked."

He threw his head back and groaned.

"This is what I'm asking for," she pressed.

"Your aunt will probably refuse to share sandwiches with me."

"We'll come over two nights a week," Ivy went on. "Like Tuesday and Thursday? We won't stay long. Just long enough to eat and have a lesson. We're going to have such a great time!"

Ivy left right after they'd cleaned up the remains of dinner.

Had he agreed to A) feeding Sloane and a fifteen-year-old sandwiches and B) receiving lessons in etiquette?

Not to worry. Sloane would never agree to Ivy's plan.

But maybe she would. He hoped she would—

No, he didn't. He hoped she wouldn't agree.

He'd gone out for a lot of nights in a row. He could go out again tonight because that would be better than sitting here in his house in a black mood.

He picked up his phone and opened his contacts.

His gaze lost focus.

What was he doing?

He'd been searching for distractions, hunting for a woman who could make him feel . . . anything.

He hadn't succeeded.

One woman had a laugh that set his teeth on edge.

Another only ate lettuce.

And on and on. They were the cream of the crop of the dating pool, and he didn't like any of them. He'd bought them food and drinks; he'd flirted. But he hadn't kissed a single one because the thought of doing so turned his stomach.

The more nights he'd gone out, the harder he'd searched for oblivion, the emptier it all felt and the more entrenched his anxiety had become.

He was doing much worse now than he had been immediately after kissing Sloane.

For two weeks, he'd been running. And now he was exhausted.

Jude's words came back to him for the thousandth time. *"By the end of your sophomore year, you were in love with her."*

Max walked straight to his home office. He immersed himself in work until the clock read 1:00 a.m. Surely now, he was tired enough to fall asleep.

He showered. Brushed his teeth. Got in bed.

"By the end of your sophomore year, you were in love with her."

Apparently, he wasn't tired enough to fall asleep. With a growl, he rose from the tangled covers and went to stand at his bedroom window that provided a view of Sloane's bedroom window.

"By the end of your sophomore year, you were in love with her."

Was there any chance that Jude was right?

Max was accustomed to making things happen in accordance with his will. He'd set a goal, work toward it, achieve it. If something ran counter to his will, he squashed it.

Falling in love ran counter to his will. It wasn't something he'd wanted. Never in his life had he thought to himself, *I'm in love*. It hadn't occurred to him that he might fall in love *despite* the fact that it was against his will and regardless of whether he'd labeled his feelings as "love" or not.

This situation was yanking him back in time to when he'd discovered that Felix was his father. He'd had no control then to stop or change it. He hadn't given his mother and Felix permission to have an affair or to conceive him. By the time he'd found out about Felix's paternity, he'd been a teenager, his parentage fixed long before.

In many ways, the possibility that he might love Sloane felt similar. Again, he'd had no control to stop or change it. He hadn't given himself permission to love her. In fact, he'd consciously chosen to remain her friend and then her business partner. Many years had passed since they'd met. If his fate was set, it had been fixed long before.

He'd hated finding himself, powerless, in the center of the scandal his mother and Felix had caused. He couldn't say he was enjoying the powerlessness of this current predicament either.

It was true that by the end of his sophomore year, Sloane had become one of the most important people in his life, one of the people closest to him, someone he was intensely—secretly—attracted to.

But was that love? And if it was, how was it possible that he'd never recognized it as that?

Had he been too proud to admit it?

Too scared?

Too dishonest with himself?

Too young and immature?

One thing was certain. He wasn't going to figure out his emotions toward Sloane standing *here* and staring at her apartment over *there*.

He'd been a coward.

He'd go to her tomorrow. Face her. And tell her as much of the truth as he could bear to say.

Chapter Sixteen

Mid-morning the next day, while working at her desk in the bedroom, movement beyond the window drew Sloane's attention.

It was Max, walking purposefully through the drizzly weather toward the staircase to the garage apartment. That jolted her with what felt like an instant caffeine rush.

Clearly, he was coming to see her.

Darth wanted an audience.

Frustration muscled to the front of her emotions. Also self-consciousness because she hadn't forgotten one millisecond of their kiss. Also grim determination. After two weeks, it was past time to rip the Band-Aid off.

Sloane made her way to the door with resolute strides, her sandals visible beneath the hem of her blue sundress. It was highly unusual for Max to be at home at this time of day, and she certainly hadn't predicted he'd initiate a conversation with her on this ordinary Friday morning at the end of August. Thankfully, though, she prioritized dressing and doing her hair and makeup before driving Ivy to school each morning. Which meant she was not at the disadvantage of having to speak with him, once again, in pajamas. Earlier, she'd knotted a strip of blue floral cloth into a headband and now adjusted the knot's jaunty tips.

Remain cool and calm. Hold your own. Don't let him ruffle your feathers. Do not, under any circumstances, mention that you noticed the parade of women he's been romancing.

After sucking in an energizing breath, she opened the door. He wasn't yet visible on the landing, for which she was glad. The sight of Max, close-up, was going to be an onslaught.

He mounted the final stair, turned toward the door, and came to a sudden stop, his expression showing surprise to find her already standing there.

Good. Let him feel off-balance.

Their gazes locked and held.

Behind him, a storm shifted across the sky, gray and rumbling. Max's thick, black hair was damp with rain. His fingers had left tracks as he'd combed the strands up and back on the sides. Tiny droplets clung lovingly to the tops of his shoulders.

She stepped back and, wordlessly, he walked inside. She shut them in, which muffled the sound of the weather yet exaggerated the lightning that existed between them.

He'd dressed slightly more formally than usual today, as if taking extra care with his appearance. His sweater appeared to have been made on a loom by the hands of cherubs. If not, it was certainly as expensive as if it had been made that way. The beautiful, simple crewneck was a shade of green somewhere between jade and gray and brought out the matching color of his eyes. He had on dark jeans and retro Adidas with flat soles and three black stripes on the sides.

Her hormones had become more and more enamored of him as the summer had gone on—as evidenced by her behavior the last time they'd interacted. Sadly, the last two weeks hadn't obliterated those hormones, but they *had* succeeded in reminding her why she couldn't put her faith in him.

His face was closely shaven. His features set in serious lines. "Hello, Sloane."

"Hello, Max."

"How have you been?" he asked as if he genuinely wanted to know.

"Very well," she replied, crisp. "How have you been?"

"Not great."

Now she was knocked off-balance. She'd expected smooth, sardonic Max. "Not great," she repeated. "Why?"

"Because of what happened between us. I'm here to talk to you about it."

"Ah."

"Real talk?" he asked.

She'd forgotten that the phrase "real talk?" had once been their prelude to discussions about sensitive or uncomfortable issues regarding Libri.

"Real talk," she agreed.

He took a moment to gather himself while looking right at her. "I really, *really* liked kissing you."

Goosebumps eddied over her skin. All indications had been, during their kiss, that he liked it. But hearing him say it was another thing entirely. Validating. Also confounding. "You liked kissing me—"

"—I really, *really* liked it—"

"—Yet have a strange way of showing it because you followed up kissing me with two weeks of silence."

"And you followed up kissing me with two weeks of silence," he pointed out calmly.

He wasn't wrong. "I was trying to sort out my thoughts."

"Same here."

"Though only one of us has spent the last week on a dating bender." Why had she said that? She'd expressly decided not to mention it.

He cocked his head. "How did you know about that?"

"Ivy follows your adventures on social media and shows me all her findings."

"Okay. I admit that my dating bender was not a good look." He raked a hand through his hair, dropped his arm. "Our kiss rattled me."

"Why?"

"I'm not used to being that affected or . . . caring for the other person as much as I care about you. I ran from it. I was trying to distract myself—with all those nights out. It didn't work. In fact, it made me feel lousier."

Her brain spun. She had not anticipated statements like these and didn't know what to do with them.

"Just so you're aware," he went on, "I didn't . . . do anything, physically, with those women. I didn't so much as kiss any of them."

She narrowed her eyes skeptically.

"I didn't, Sloane."

He looked earnest but it seemed foolish to believe him wholesale.

"Where is your head at regarding our kiss?" he asked.

"I also really, *really* liked it," she acknowledged, rewarding his truthfulness with some of her own.

A masculine grin flashed across his lips.

"I was also rattled by it," she continued. "I've categorized it as fleeting lunacy. We argued for a month after I arrived in Maine. Kissed. Then avoided each other for two weeks. This is not rational behavior."

"*We sparred in a flirtatious way* for a month after you arrived in Maine," he corrected.

She scoffed. "Turning off my water was flirtatious sparring?"

"I found it highly flirtatious when I watched you march out to the valve and turn the water back on yourself. And our kisses were *world class*, so who cares if they were rational?"

"Me. I care. Obviously, we shouldn't do that again."

"I disagree."

She raised her brows.

"I want more," he said.

"More?"

"More."

Desire curved in her abdomen, urging her to answer with an undignified *YES, MORE!* but she was much too self-controlled for that. "What do you mean by more?"

His eyes glittered. "I want you to be with me."

What was going on here? What alternate dimension was this? "Be with you?"

"Yes. Be in a relationship with me. Give dating me a try."

"Why?"

"For the same reason that any two people get together. Enjoyment."

Her mouth went dry because he had this new, wild power over her that she didn't understand. "That would not be wise."

"Because?"

"Because I had a front-row seat to your romances for years. Women enter your life for the sake of enjoyment but then exit through a revolving door that's probably not very enjoyable for them at all. I have no desire to be one of them."

"With you, it would be different. *I* would be different."

"Different how?"

Before her eyes, he switched into business-tycoon mode.

She knew why. He'd perceived her question as the opening salvo in a negotiation and Max excelled at negotiation. She'd seen that calculating glint enter his expression numerous times in the boardroom. She'd never fathomed that he'd direct it toward the goal of winning *her*. Never imagined he'd state so frankly that he wanted to be with her—

"Here's how I'll be different," he said. "I'll give up going out, except to events you're interested in attending with me. I'll cut down my work hours as much as I can to spend time with you. I'll only travel for business when necessary. I'll show you how well I can treat you and how much you can count on me."

This was *Max* talking. It was astonishing and worrisome and a tiny bit thrilling and she really needed to keep her head. "I'm not asking you to make those changes for me."

"I know. I'm making them for myself because I know those things are prerequisites to you giving me a chance."

"The fact is . . . I'm nowhere near ready to give you a chance, romantically. You're still the man who kicked me out of Libri. You're still the man who's spent his adult life idolizing success, money, and power. I can't snap my fingers and suddenly forgive you and trust you."

"Tell me what else I can do to earn your forgiveness and trust."

"I think . . . I mean, it's just going to take time. Time hanging out with each other. Time to be certain we can be civil to each other and, more than that, genuinely good for each other."

"Done. How much time do you think you'll need?"

"I can't guarantee I'll *ever* be up for a romantic relationship with you." She broke etiquette by placing her hands on her hips. "Honestly, I don't understand what's going on here. Where did your interest in me come from?"

"From our history. From you coming back to Maine."

"Your interest will likely leave as suddenly as it came."

"It didn't come suddenly, Sloane. It's been thirteen years."

Wait. Was he saying he'd been romantically interested in her since they met?

"I'm being honest with myself and you. I admit, that's unusual for me. But now that I'm being honest, I can see clearly what I want." Max moved in closer the way he'd done that night on the patio before they'd kissed. "And I'm going to put my single-minded focus into getting what I want," he said in a velvet tone.

"Oh no you don't." She stopped him with a hand on his chest. Then took a healthy step backward.

His gaze twinkled. "Don't what?"

"Don't scramble my head by getting close to me."

His mouth tipped up. "I have the ability to scramble your head?"

She didn't answer that. "Stay where you are. Two yards of distance between us feels about right."

He chuckled. "Shall we agree to terms? I won't go out with anyone else while we're figuring this out. Will you do the same?"

She hesitated.

An indent formed between his brows. "You and Nate haven't gotten together, have you?"

"Nate expressed an interest in taking our relationship to the next level, but I told him I'd prefer for us to remain friends for now."

"For as long as you keep me in the friend zone, will you keep Nate in the friend zone, too?"

"No, I won't agree to that. It's not logical for me to refuse dates with other people on the off chance you and I might one day start dating each other. It's not logical for you to refuse dates for that reason either."

"I won't go out with anyone else while we're figuring this out," he reiterated. "I'll be too busy showing you why I'm *miles* more desirable than Nate."

"And miles more difficult."

"Will you say yes to Ivy's idea of sandwiches and etiquette lessons?"

When Ivy had come home from Max's house last night, the girl's sandwiches-and-etiquette plan hadn't seemed feasible. Sloane had bought time by telling Ivy she'd think on it. This exchange with Max had shifted the landscape. "I'll say yes."

He made his way to the door. "See you tomorrow morning during your devotional time."

"See you then."

Lightning flashed between them again. The moments spun outward, heavy with awareness. She had just enough time to register her libido yelling, *YES MORE!* before he walked out and left her in the quiet.

NICOLE

Because I love you, and only because I love you . . . I will talk with Fiona.

MAX

Thank you.

NICOLE

You're welcome, Yios. Tell her to meet me at the playground at Lake St. George Park at 10 a.m. on Monday.

Days had passed since Ivy and Sloane had written an email to Anna Thomas's mother, Stephanie—which was driving Ivy crazy. So many days! And, still, no response. Aunt Sloane did not seem bothered by this. She was totally content to wait around, which Ivy did not understand *at all*.

It was 10:00 p.m. and Ivy was in her room, cuddling Ricky while Kevin chewed on an applewood stick.

Ricky looked up from her cradled palms, whiskers twitching.

"I'm too impatient to wait forever to find my sister," Ivy told him.

I understand completely, his tiny face seemed to say.

"I feel like I should do something."

You should.

She rubbed a fingertip on his forehead, then gently placed him back in his cage and handed him an applewood stick of his own. "You boys are the cutest things ever," she whispered, her heart filled with love.

She leaned into the stack of pillows on her bed, opened Instagram on her phone, and typed "Anna Thomas" into the search bar. Dozens of accounts matching that name appeared and she began making her way through each one.

It was easy to rule out most of them. These Annas were all too old to be her Anna. Near the bottom of the list, she clicked on an account that took her to the profile page of a pretty, brown-haired teenager.

Anna's bio read, *Washington High School. Class of—*

"Oh my gosh!" She sat bolt upright.

This Anna was graduating from high school the same year as she was. Her bio went on to say that she lived in Newbury-port, Massachusetts. A Google search for Newburyport revealed that it was located north of Boston near the Maine border. Very believable to think that a baby who'd been born in Boston would be living there with her adopted family now.

Ivy tapped on the most recent picture Anna had posted, two weeks ago. It showed her and a friend with their arms around each other on a city street. Ivy resembled her biological father, Seth. But Anna looked a lot like how Ivy remembered Harper looking. Anna and Harper had the same shade of brown hair. The same sharp, beautiful features.

Ivy rushed to her feet and began walking a track from one side of her room to the other. The rats watched, heads going from side to side like spectators at a tennis match.

She clicked through photo after photo that Anna had posted. Read the captions. It seemed Anna was the middle child of three kids. She had an older sister, a younger brother, and really friendly-looking parents. She went on trips to places like Mexico and Ireland and didn't seem to be hurting for money. She had lots of friends and had even had a boyfriend for a while last year. She was on the drill team at her school and sang in the choir.

I have found my sister myself! And it hadn't even been hard.

If she told Aunt Sloane and her mom about this, she knew what they'd say. They'd say to go through the proper channels, to wait until they received an email back from Anna's mom, Stephanie.

She peered again at Anna's profile. Then hit the Message button and started writing a DM to her.

IVY

Hi! I think you're my twin sister.

No. Geez. That was too much. When they'd communicated with Seth and Stephanie, they hadn't come right out with the truth like that.

Delete, delete, delete.

Hi! I think we might be related. I'm Ivy. I live in Groomsport, Maine. I'm the youngest of four kids and am adopted. This summer, I've been looking for some of my biological relatives. I know I have a relative with your name who is your age. So, yeah! I think we might be related.

She read it out loud, which sometimes helped her spot typos.

Was this fine?

She said a prayer. Read it again. Hit send.

Nervousness and excitement were tugging upward in her midsection like helium-filled balloons. Some people had their notifications set so that they got an alert every time someone left a DM. If Anna had her notifications set like that, Ivy might hear back soon.

She went to the kitchen to pop microwave popcorn. Standing at the counter, she ate it obsessively while staring at her phone. When she'd almost reached the end of the popcorn, a reply arrived.

No way! That's so cool. How can we find out if we're related?

I could come by your hometown one weekend to meet you. Do you like frozen yogurt?

I do.

> IVY
>
> Let's get yogurt!

ANNA

Yay. When?

> IVY
>
> When are you free?

ANNA

Next Saturday afternoon?

Ivy went to the monthly calendar that Sloane kept filled with her schedule and Ivy's. Her aunt would be giving an online etiquette class that day so it had already been arranged that Ivy would spend the day with her friend Corrie, then sleep over at her house.

> IVY
>
> You'll never believe this, but I think I found my twin sister.

CORRIE

WHAT?!

> IVY
>
> Do you think you can drive me to meet her next Saturday in Newburyport, Massachusetts?

Corrie was already sixteen and had gotten her license two months ago.

CORRIE

How far away is that?

Ivy searched it up.

> IVY
>
> Two hours and forty minutes.

CORRIE

> My parents will never let me drive that far.

Ivy's spirits dipped.

Corrie was the bravest girl in their friend group. She was always up for anything and loved a dare. Corrie had screamed, then practically danced a solo when "We Are Never Ever Getting Back Together" by Taylor Swift had come on at the school dance in the spring. She was the one who'd jumped, spinning in the air, off the diving board at the Groomsport pool last weekend. Usually Ivy was the one keeping Corrie in line. But she *had* to meet up with Anna, and Aunt Sloane would never be willing to take her.

IVY

> What if we don't tell your parents or Aunt Sloane that we're going? I'll send Sloane some pictures of us doing things in town. You'll send your parents pictures of us doing things in town.

CORRIE

> I like the way you think, but my parents can track my location.

IVY

> We'd have to turn our locations off. So long as we keep in touch with them and send them pictures of what we're "doing," they might not check our locations. But if they do, we'll play dumb and say we don't know why our phone disconnected from tracking.

CORRIE

> Ingenious. Girl, you know I'm up for anything.

IVY

> You'll drive me to Newburyport? We won't stay long. We can be back before dark.

CORRIE

YES! I'm excited to meet your sister.

Ivy returned to her conversation with Anna.

IVY

Next Saturday is perfect. Can't wait to meet you!

Chapter Seventeen

Moments after they'd taken their seats at church prior to the worship service, a whisper from Ivy interrupted Sloane's reading of the bulletin.

"There's Max!"

It was absurd, the sparkle of delight this instantaneously set off within Sloane. "Surely not." Max didn't come to church.

Ivy, sitting on the end of the pew, was twisted in her seat, waving. "Max." More waving.

Sloane turned and, sure enough, Max was walking down the center aisle. He'd spotted them and gave a nod in recognition of Ivy's efforts.

"You came to our church!" Ivy said.

"I did." He moved past Ivy and sat next to Sloane.

"It's good to see you here," Ivy told him. "Welcome."

"Thanks."

One of Ivy's friends skipped toward them, and the two girls started chatting. Which left Sloane sitting in very close proximity to Max while a wave of interest in his arrival eddied through the females in the congregation. He had on a beauti-fully tailored navy suit with a white business shirt. He smelled like paradise.

"What brings you here?" She directed the question forward because if she looked fully toward him, they'd be nose-to-nose.

"I think you know."

"A sudden desire to worship prompted by the Holy Spirit?"

"Not to diss the Holy Spirit, but no. You're familiar with the phrase 'the way to a man's heart is through his stomach'?"

"I am."

"Well, I think one of the ways to your heart is through the doors of this church." His eyes crinkled when he smiled. And those dimples! "That's what brings me here. It's a genius move on my part, you have to admit."

"I admit no such thing," she responded. "If you come to church, you should come for a genuine reason."

"Oh, my reason is very genuine, I assure you." He looked around approvingly. "I went to church with my mom every Sunday when I was growing up. The Cirillos, including me, are Christians, don't forget. We have been for generations."

"I did somehow forget this information. I wonder why? Hmm . . ." She tapped her chin. "Oh! I think I know. *All* your behavior in *all* the days since I met you," she teased.

His smile widened even more. In his contrary way, Max adored bickering. "I admit that my heart could use some redeeming. So here I am."

The musicians took the stage, which meant they had just seconds before the first song started.

"There's grace even for me, right?" The smug set of his chin informed her that he knew he had her there, because she couldn't very well answer that question with anything but the truth.

"Right."

"Good. I'll take all the grace I can get. From Him." He glanced upward, then back to her. "And from you."

The music began and they stood to sing.

He leaned near her ear. "When we sit back down, can I put my arm on the pew behind you?" The rumble of his words sent heat feathering along the shell of her ear, jaw, neck.

"No."

"Okay. We'll work up to that on a future Sunday."

Fiona did not use the word *butt.*

It was crude and beneath her. Thus, the thought in her head as she arrived at Lake St. George Park for her meeting with Nicole Cirillo was this. *Nicole is a pain in my derriere.*

Max had told Fiona that Nicole had agreed to see her, which was the outcome she'd wanted in order to meet Isobel's demand and thus achieve her goal of seeing her sister in the long term. However, she dreaded interacting with Nicole in the short term.

Nicole, of course, had asserted control when she'd dictated the time and place of this conversation. By choosing a park, Nicole was telling Fiona that she didn't want Fiona anywhere near her home. By choosing a weekday at this time, Nicole had forced Fiona to clear her work schedule and drive more than thirty minutes to Nicole's turf.

Though Fiona typically ran late, she'd made an effort to arrive here at the scheduled meeting time. She positioned herself near the playground, where Nicole couldn't fail to spot her.

A few preschoolers clambered over the equipment. Their

squeals and chatter merged with the more modulated tones of their caregivers. A man jogged past. He was shirtless. Fiona was all for shirtlessness on joggers with chiseled torsos, but this particular man did not fall into that rarefied category.

Nicole was nowhere to be seen, another control move. She was making Fiona wait.

Fiona adjusted her short-sleeved, pink and white Hermes sweater. She'd wrapped herself in style and wealth for this unwelcome reunion. Her heels were high. Her gray pants, tailored. Her hair and nails, impeccable.

When one heel began to sink into the gravel, she carefully adjusted her footing so both feet were firmly set. Now that she was in her late fifties, she frequently sensed just how easy it would be, at any moment, to fall and break a bone—

She spotted a woman walking in her direction. Recognition instantly slotted into place. Nicole. The sight of her former friend spurred a kaleidoscope of memories.

The first time she'd met Nicole—to interview her for the housekeeping position. Laughing together in the kitchen at Maple Lane. Max's birth, and the giant floral bouquet Fiona had brought to the hospital for mother and baby. She and Nicole sitting on the back deck, watching the three little boys playing. Her two sons so fair-haired; Max with his dark hair and olive skin. And, finally, she recalled their last exchange when Fiona had fired Nicole and ordered her to move off the property immediately.

It had been twenty years since she and Nicole had been face-to-face. As the other woman neared, Fiona noted that her former housekeeper bore the evidence of the passage of time. Nicole had always looked like she could've been Andie MacDowell's slightly-less-attractive cousin. Still did. Her hair was gray. Her squarish face more lined than before. Her body curvier than it had been. Nicole had dressed with almost aggressive casualness in jeans, sneakers, and a T-shirt. All of which communicated, *I feel no need to dress up for you.*

Nicole came to a stop a few feet away.

They eyed each other. Nicole's expression gave away little. Had they both arrived barefoot, Nicole would have been an inch or two shorter than Fiona. But Fiona's heels amplified her greater height, so that she was looking down to meet the eyes of the woman who'd slept with and then had a baby with Fiona's then-husband.

This was shockingly painful. This was bringing back the glowing red coals of betrayal and the bitterness that Fiona had thought she'd banked long ago. Which gave her a glaring glimpse into how Isobel likely felt about her.

"Hello, Nicole," she made herself say.

"Hello, Fiona."

Fiona had selected the opening remark she was about to deliver. Selecting it hadn't been hard, seeing as how there was really only one compliment she could give to Nicole. "Max is wonderful. He's turned out very well." That was extraordinarily gracious of her to say.

"Thank you," Nicole said stiffly. "Jeremiah and Jude have also turned out very well."

Anger snapped like a crocodile at Fiona. The words *No thanks to you* rushed to her tongue, unspoken. The scandal with Nicole and Max had been awful for Jeremiah and Jude. Fiona's sons had prospered, yes. But they'd been forced to overcome the scars Nicole had given them in order to do so. "I assume Max relayed to you the motivation for my requesting this meeting?"

"He did." Nicole waited like, *Go ahead and say you're sorry so we can get this over with.*

When Fiona had learned of Felix's affair with Nicole, she'd

racked her brain to fathom what Felix had seen in the other woman. Fiona had been more beautiful than Nicole. She was five years younger than Nicole. She'd been in love with Felix. Felix had left his supermodel wife for her, and Fiona had paid him back for that by being very good to him. They'd shared two children. Fiona had thought their marriage was strong. And still—Felix had betrayed her.

In the end, there'd been no explanation for it other than the fact that Nicole had offered an available body. Fresh adulation. And the excitement of infidelity.

"I want you to know that I forgive you," Fiona lied. She'd spoken the words only to fulfill Isobel's demand.

"Fine. Max said we need to take a photo?"

"Yes." Fiona slid her phone from her purse.

"World's Most Uncomfortable Selfie?" Nicole murmured, revealing a flash of the humor Fiona had once associated with her.

"Indeed it is," Fiona admitted, holding up the phone. "We should call the Guinness Book of World Records."

They stepped just close enough to one another to appear in the same frame.

Fiona gave the camera a small smile because, thank God, this meeting from hell was almost over. Nicole did not smile but she also wasn't glowering or looking pained. Figuring this was as good as she was going to get, Fiona captured the shot.

"Will that do?" Nicole asked, backing away.

"That will do."

"Goodbye, then." Nicole turned, presenting Fiona with her back and striding off in her robust way.

Fiona watched Nicole depart through narrowed eyes.

Felix Camden was an utterly faithless man. He'd proven that to Isobel, Fiona, and Nicole. But only the two of them, herself and Nicole, had given birth to his children. Theirs was a small and vicious club.

Once Nicole had driven away, Fiona placed a palm over her heart. She forced air into tight lungs.

Why had that exchange been so hard on her? For ages, she'd viewed herself as a woman who'd recovered from the end of her marriage and the ensuing grief. Perhaps there were still tiny corners of her that hadn't recovered?

She walked toward her Aston Martin.

"I'm worried that you're still in love with Felix," Burke had said to her the day of her picnic.

She'd insisted that was not the case. While she did occasionally experience flashes of physical attraction toward Felix, he had burned all her love for him out of her heart with his treatment of her.

Then Burke had said, *"You're still letting him dictate your life."*

In the wake of her meeting with Nicole, maybe she needed to give that more thought.

Was she letting Felix dictate her life? At least when it came to dating, love, and marriage?

In a way, yes. She'd gone so far downhill after Felix broke her heart that she'd promised herself she'd never fall in love or marry again. That decision had served her well for twenty years. But was it still serving her well?

Burke had told her point-blank that he loved her and wanted to marry her. Nineteen days had passed since the picnic, and she hadn't seen or communicated with him.

She *missed* him.

There could be no doubt that in all the ways Felix was undeserving of a woman's love, Burke was deserving of it. He'd been a wonderful husband to his wife—remaining at her side during the grueling final months of her life. He was an excellent father to his two children and incredibly involved in his grandchildren's lives. He'd been *amazing* to Fiona. Encouraging, filled with common sense, gentle.

It was horrible, frankly, to live with the knowledge that her close friendship with Burke had ruptured. For the first several days after their argument, she'd hugged defensiveness to her chest, telling herself that she was the injured party, and waiting for him to relent and apologize. But soon all of that had proven hollow. *He* might be the injured party here. And he might never relent and apologize.

She was no stranger to animosity in relationships. Her spunky determination and high standards had led to plenty of conflict in her female friendships. She'd learned to weather that. She knew how to prevent the fact that a friend was upset with her from tanking her day or her week. She knew how to have difficult conversations that resolved issues. She knew how to let go of the friendships that couldn't recover from an argument. She knew how to tell herself she was better off without that particular friend and the drama she brought.

But none of that applied to this situation with Burke.

She couldn't weather this. The fact that he was upset with her *had* tanked her days. She'd yet to figure out how to tackle a difficult conversation with him that would resolve their issue. And he was far too important to her to let go.

Max wasn't getting enough Sloane in his life.

Not even close to enough.

Since their talk at her apartment on Friday, he'd spoken with her when she came outside each morning and at church on Sunday. That was it. He was striving to show her how agreeable he could be. But restraint did not come naturally to him. He was, at his core, a demanding person.

It was Tuesday night, and he was finally going to get more time with her because he could hear Sloane and Ivy coming through his sliding door for sandwiches and an etiquette lesson.

He should relax and enjoy this. He *was* going to enjoy this. But relaxing was harder because his brain was already gnawing on how to stretch this dinner out. From his spot at the kitchen counter, he lifted his gaze alertly and watched as Sloane came into view, wearing her white sundress, hair wound into a loose bun thing at the back of her neck.

"Thank you for having us over for dinner." She handed him an object, which turned out to be a lemon-scented candle.

"For me?"

"Yes. It's a gift."

"You didn't have to give me a gift."

"Is part of the goal of these dinners to teach Ivy etiquette?"

"Yep!" Ivy piped up.

"Then we did have to give you a gift," Sloane said kindly. "It's good etiquette to bring a gift to the host."

"In that case, thank you."

"You're welcome."

"I like the smell of lemon."

She gave a knowing nod, and he realized she'd chosen this scent because she already understood that he liked the smell of lemon. This candle might be small, but it was a symbol of something big—Sloane's knowledge of him.

"What's the polite thing to do here?" he asked. "Am I supposed to light this right now or set it aside?"

"Feel free to set it aside. I never give gifts that require immediate action from the host or hostess."

He set it in a place of honor next to the sink faucet. "Tonight, we're having a classic. Pastrami on rye." He'd already buttered the bread, toasted it on the griddle, and placed slices of Swiss on top. The pastrami and sauerkraut were warm and ready.

Max talked them through assembling their sandwiches and adding mayo pickle relish.

"I'm impressed to see you trying new foods, Ivy," Sloane commented.

"I'm impressed with myself. This is my first time to eat a pastrami sandwich. But I'm willing to give it a try for you, Max."

While Ivy was looking down, Max caught Sloane's eye over the top of the girl's head. "I'm honored when I can convince people to try new things," he said directly to Sloane.

She smiled and he felt like he'd won the lottery.

They added chips and a pickle to their plates and were soon sitting around his kitchen table.

No one made a move to start eating.

"Did I do the napkins and silverware right?" he asked.

"Yes," Sloane assured him. "Ivy, you've already learned that we place our napkins on our lap as soon as we sit at a restaurant table. But in a private home like this one, it's good etiquette to wait for the host to place his or her napkin in their lap. Then we follow suit."

He placed his napkin in his lap. They did the same.

"Our goal with the napkin," Sloane continued, "is to display only the clean side. We fold it in half. Then, during the meal when we dab our mouths, we bring the inside of that fold up to our lips without hunching over. Dab. Return the folded napkin to your lap with the clean side still showing." Sloane demonstrated.

He was having a hard time not staring at the tiny daisy charm on Sloane's necklace as it slid then rested then slid against the skin of her upper chest. Turned out, he was going to love etiquette class. Etiquette class meant he got to watch Sloane while she was teaching.

Ivy mimicked her aunt, dabbing her lips with her napkin.

"Well done," Sloane told her.

"Should I wait for Max to take a bite before I do?"

"The main thing is that you wait until everyone has their food before you start eating. That said, it's especially nice if the host gives the table the go-ahead to begin by saying something like 'please enjoy.'"

"Please enjoy," he said.

Sloane sent him an appreciative glance. "You two will have the manners of Princess Kate in no time."

"Can I have the manners of someone more manly?" he asked.

"Certainly. You, Max, will have the manners of James Bond in no time."

He took a bite of his sandwich. Delicious.

"When did your Princess Kate fandom begin?" Ivy asked Sloane.

"Prince William and Kate announced their engagement when I was seventeen," Sloane told Ivy. "I was *fascinated*. A prince had fallen in love with a commoner. Like me. Like you. Imagine."

"A real-life fairy tale," Ivy said.

"*Yes*. Kate married William and became a princess. In the years since, her beautiful etiquette has allowed her to glide through the highest levels of society. I thought, if Kate Middleton can become Princess Kate, then what's stopping me from rising above my start in life? Etiquette as beautiful as Kate's is available to us all." She was gesturing with her delicate hands and color was blooming on her cheeks as she talked about this thing she loved.

And sitting there at his kitchen table on a summertime

Tuesday night, Max comprehended that *she* was the thing he loved.

Jude had been right.

He loved her.

The realization was so terrifying that it froze him.

"At its heart," Sloane was saying, "etiquette is about showing respect to everyone."

"What do you mean?" Ivy asked.

"Etiquette teaches us tangible ways to give consideration to others. We learn how to interact with people kindly and thoughtfully. What could be more respectful?"

Surreal to have normal conversation continue around him after the epiphany he'd just had.

"Princess Kate is an inspiration because she's a living example of kindness and thoughtfulness. She's grace personified."

"You're grace personified." Max's voice came out rough-edged. "To me."

Sloane's face and Ivy's face swung toward him.

Sloane recovered first. "That's a lovely thing to say."

"It's true."

Ivy's eyeballs were practically popping out of her head.

"Let's talk more about the continental way of holding our cutlery," Sloane suggested to Ivy, rescuing the conversation.

Jude had recommended that Max tell Sloane how he felt. But there was no way he could tell her he loved her at this point. She'd laugh him out of the building.

For now he was committed to following through on the things they'd discussed Friday. They'd hang out. He'd stop partying, curtail travel, work fewer hours. He would do everything he could to convince her to be with him.

Nothing would stop him from executing that plan. It was similar to a compulsion—he *had* to give this his best. Here was the kicker, though. He *had* to give this his best even though he was fairly sure the endgame would be his own destruction. He was acting like a person who knew they had a weakness for alcohol yet had decided to drink like crazy for the next several months.

He loved Sloane. He needed this opportunity with her.

No matter what it cost him.

Chapter Eighteen

"What's going on between you and Max?" Ivy asked Sloane as soon as they were out of hearing range of Max's house on the way back to their apartment after pastrami sandwiches.

Should Sloane dodge Ivy's question? Or tell the truth?

She supposed she should go with the truth since as a matter of principle and policy, Sloane really did try to set an example of honesty for Ivy. "Max has informed me that he'd like for us to date one another."

"You're kidding!" Ivy screamed, going straight to the hysteria level Sloane would have expected had Ivy spotted Bruno Mars in the flesh.

"No, not kidding."

"Did you tell him yes? That you'd date him?"

"I did not."

"Why?!"

Two hundred million reasons, Sloane thought. "I'm not convinced that we're suited for each other."

"He's so great, though! He's funny and nice and smart and rich. And he's your friend from way back."

"I challenge the assertion that he's nice." *Nice* was way too weak an adjective for Max.

"Most of all, you two are spark-y! You always were. I *knew* he liked you and I *knew* you liked him, and I *knew* this would happen! He'll settle down for you, I bet. And then you're going to be so happy together!"

They mounted the stairs to the apartment.

"He said you were grace personified," Ivy gushed.

"I didn't hate that compliment," Sloane admitted.

"Remember how I said back when we moved in that he looks at you like a panther who wants to eat you? Well, he still looks at you like that. But now I know it's not because he hates you and wants to kill you."

The day of Ivy and Corrie's secret road trip to Massachusetts had finally arrived, and today Ivy would meet her twin, Anna Thomas.

Corrie's Subaru zoomed along the highway below a sky marked here and there with giant, bright clouds that reminded Ivy of scoops of whipped cream. They sang along to Bruno Mars and Taylor Swift, Corrie's messy blond top knot bobbing to the beat.

Corrie seemed really relaxed. As far as Ivy could tell, her friend didn't mind deceiving her parents. Ivy was only pretending relaxation because she kind of hated deceiving Aunt Sloane. All morning, she'd been feeling nervous and excited and guilty. A few times, she'd been tempted to tell Aunt Sloane but then the excited part of her convinced her not to worry about the nervous and guilty part and simply to go ahead with the plan. Everything was set up! Anna would be waiting for them.

It was a shame that parents underestimated what teenagers could do. If Corrie's parents and Aunt Sloane would have been open to letting them make this trip, they would have asked them. They wouldn't have had to hide it. After all, Corrie had gotten her driver's license two whole months ago. Other than the one time when Corrie had almost changed into a lane at the same time as another car almost changed into the same lane, and the other time when Corrie had realized she was going ninety-two miles per hour—she'd been super good on the highway.

They reached downtown Newburyport five minutes before their meeting with Anna. Right on schedule! But then neither of them could figure out where to park. Ivy ran searches on her phone and Corrie circled around blocks, looking. It was a Saturday. *Everyone* was downtown. Adults handled parking. Ivy had never had to think about it before and didn't know what to do.

Anxiously, Ivy watched the clock tick past their meeting time. "There, there!" A car was exiting a spot on the side of the street.

Corrie wasn't the best parallel parker. She kept squealing and Ivy had to get out to direct her. Working together, they finally got the Subaru into the spot. But then the parking meter did its best to confuse them. Who carried coins these days? They did not. They finally figured out how to pay on an app using Ivy's debit card, then rushed to the frozen yogurt shop they'd driven by twice already.

"You did so well," Ivy said. "Thank you for driving me here."

"You're welcome. Sorry we're a little late."

"It's okay." In truth, she didn't like being eight minutes late.

She was not irresponsible and the idea that Anna might think she was made her jumpy.

"Eee! I'm so excited." Corrie's wide face beamed. "Can you believe this is really happening?"

"No, I can't."

"Ready to meet your twin sister?"

"So ready."

"She's going to love you."

"I hope so."

Corrie swept the shop door open. Ivy hurried inside and spotted Anna right away, waiting to one side. Her sister wore jean shorts and a cute, striped, scoop-neck tee. She'd parted her long brown hair down the middle.

"Are you Anna?" Ivy asked.

"Yes." She smiled. "Hi."

"Hi! I'm sorry we're late. We drove from Maine."

"That's okay."

Ivy introduced herself and Corrie.

Corrie beamed back and forth between them. "I'll go get us yogurt."

"I'm buying it for everybody," Ivy hurried to say. "As a thank-you." She pulled a twenty-dollar bill from her pocket and handed it to Corrie, who asked for their orders and moved off.

Anna was very pretty, confident, and surely more popular than Ivy was in school. It had seemed like that on Anna's Instagram. A cute ex-boyfriend. Lots of friends. Drill team. And it definitely seemed like that now that they were meeting in person.

Into an awkward silence, Ivy blurted, "Want to sit outside?"

"Sure."

Outdoors, a patch of stones supported a rusting metal table and three chairs. Motion surrounded them. Cars moving past.

Shoppers. Parents pushing baby strollers past The Black Dog General Store across the street.

Anna set her phone on the table, keeping her French-manicured fingers clasped around it. "So you still think we're related?"

"I do."

"Cool! How?"

"Um. So." Ivy bit her bottom lip. Now that Anna was looking at her and waiting for her to explain, she was having trouble remembering exactly how she'd decided to say this. "I was adopted when I was five months old. I have a great family—a mom, dad, and three older siblings. But lately, really just this summer, I've been, um, wanting to learn more about my biological family. I got to meet my biological dad."

"Oh my gosh. What was that like?"

"Good. I mean, kind of strange *and* good. He never told his family about me and doesn't want them to know. So that part was a little weird. But it's his right not to tell them, if he doesn't want to. I understand that. So, yeah. Mostly, I was thankful I got to meet him. His name's Seth. He seems like a nice person."

"Have you met your biological mom?"

"Yes, I knew her from the start because my adoption was an . . . open adoption? Her name was Harper Madison. Unfortunately, she died four years ago."

Anna's face fell. "I'm sorry."

"It was an overdose. I still have my Aunt Sloane, though. That's Harper's sister. Aunt Sloane and I are close. In fact, I'm staying with her this summer."

Corrie came out of the shop, holding a tray with three frozen yogurts.

"Thank you so much," Anna said.

"You're welcome!"

They all went to work on the food.

Ivy's was vanilla-flavored with crushed Oreo topping. Self-consciously, she licked her teeth because she knew Oreos often left behind tiny black crumbs. She wasn't sure if she was glad or not that Corrie had come outside right when she was about to hit Anna with her big news. But then Corrie gave Ivy an encouraging nod and she realized that she *was* glad to have Corrie at her side for this. "I was just about to tell Anna how I think we might be related," she said to Corrie.

"'Kay." Corrie swirled a big bite of creamy yogurt onto her spoon, then popped it into her mouth.

Glancing down, Ivy noticed that she and Anna both wore flip-flops and had painted their toenails yellow. A sister similarity? "When I met with Seth, I learned that I have a twin sister." She swallowed. "And so Aunt Sloane and I checked this thing called the Adoption Reunion Registry and found out my twin sister is named Anna Thomas."

Anna went still, except for her eyes, which turned big and round.

"Anna and I would both be fifteen and sophomores this school year. I think . . . I'm pretty sure you're her. My sister."

Anna set both palms on the table, face smooth with shock. "You're saying you think *I'm* your twin sister?"

"Yes."

"That would mean I'm adopted, too?"

"Right."

Anna's mouth hung open. "No one's ever told me that I'm adopted."

"Oh." Ivy didn't know what to say to that. Why did adults like Seth and Anna's parents keep such huge secrets?

"You think," Anna said, "that this Harper and this Seth you've been talking about are my biological parents, too?"

"Right. And we're fraternal twins."

Anna seemed more astonished than upset. Ivy had had

days to think about all of this, but this was new for Anna, and it must be *way* weird for her. Especially because, unlike Ivy, she hadn't known she was adopted.

Of the three of them, Corrie was the only one still eating.

"*Oh my gosh!*" Anna pressed to her feet. "Come with me. My house is a ten-minute walk from here. Let's go talk to my mom about this."

"What about our yogurt?" Corrie asked.

"We can eat it on the way," Anna answered.

Uneasiness settled over Ivy like a rain cloud. "You want us to talk to your mom with you?"

"Yeah. Come on." Holding her yogurt, Anna stepped onto the sidewalk and motioned for them to follow.

Ivy wasn't sure about this plan, but she couldn't tell Anna no at this point, right? It would be rude to announce that they were sisters and then refuse to go to Anna's house and talk with her mom.

The three of them set off.

"I honestly can't believe this." As they walked, Anna talked about her older sister and her younger brother, wondering aloud if she was the only one who was adopted. She remembered her parents bringing her brother home from the hospital but maybe they'd really been bringing him home from an adoption center.

She said that her parents could be crafty. Like the time they planned a trip to Disney World but didn't say a thing about it until they surprised their kids thirty minutes before they needed to leave for the airport. Or the time they'd said they were going to a PTA meeting but had come home sort of drunk and Anna had later found out they decided to get margaritas and Mexican food with friends instead. "This, though, is *by far* the craftiest thing they've ever done, and I am going to kill them if they did not tell me that I'm adopted."

Discomfort mounted higher inside Ivy. She'd just met Anna. She didn't know Anna's parents. If this turned into a family battle, it was going to be terrible to stand there in the middle of it. Her stomach squeezed and she wasn't capable of eating any more yogurt. She and the others tossed their bowls in a trash can they passed.

They entered an old neighborhood full of beautiful trees and houses. And too soon, before Ivy was ready *at all*, they reached the Thomas home. It looked like it had cost a fortune. Four stories tall, huge front porch, painted white with black shutters.

"Come in." Anna held the door for them politely. Then she yelled, "Mom!" in a very impolite voice.

"Yes?" came the answer from somewhere on the same level. Anna's mom did not sound at all concerned by her daughter's tone.

"Come out here, please," Anna called. "I have someone for you to meet."

Ivy stood with the other girls in the foyer, wringing her hands. The inside of Anna's house was a mix of new furniture and antiques. Tidy, with a little bit of family clutter.

A woman came out from the hallway, dressed in a Lululemon shirt and leggings. Her long brown hair formed a ponytail through the hole at the back of a pink ball cap. She took in the sight of Ivy and Corrie with a welcoming expression. "Hello."

Before Ivy could respond, Anna spoke. "Mom, I'd like for you to meet Ivy and Corrie. Ivy is *my twin sister*." She followed that up with an accusing frown and urgent gesture toward Ivy.

Ivy *dreaded* Mrs. Thomas's reaction.

But Mrs. Thomas only gave them an amused smile. "I'm surprised to learn that you have a twin sister, Anna, seeing as how I don't remember having had twins."

"Ivy's adopted. She's saying that I'm adopted, too. So if you failed to tell me that, *now is the time* to tell me. Because this girl, right here, is proof."

Mrs. Thomas laughed. "Now is the time?"

"Yes." Anna crossed her arms.

"Brace yourself," Mrs. Thomas said to her daughter.

"I'm braced!"

"You are not a twin. And you are not adopted . . . though I do myself wonder where you came from whenever you sing in the choir because the rest of us aren't musical. Even so, I assure you that your dad and I are your biological parents. And the story I've always told you about your birth is the truth. My water broke on the stroke of midnight. Your father ignored all traffic laws driving me to the hospital because I was screaming at him to get there faster so that I could be given an epidural. A few hours later they handed you to me, all red-faced and mad at being dragged into the world. And your dad and I fell in love at first sight."

Anna's body language didn't relax. "Ivy's twin sister is fifteen and named Anna Thomas."

"I see. Ivy, is your birthday October eighteenth?"

"Oh," Ivy whispered, as the air left her lungs. "No, my birthday is December ninth." *Why* hadn't she thought to ask Anna what her birthday was? She'd been so sure that she'd found her twin, that she hadn't even thought to ask her birthday. "Is your first name Stephanie?"

"No, it's Erin."

"And I guess you didn't put information about Anna into an Adoption Reunion Registry?"

"No," she said gently.

Ivy's shoulders sagged. She'd gotten it all wrong. This Anna Thomas was not her sister.

"Please come in and tell me about yourself and what's been

going on." Mrs. Thomas guided them to a small den that opened to the kitchen. "Sit down, sit down." She waved them to the sofa.

The three girls sat.

From inside a closet, Mrs. Thomas pulled out a tub that had the name *Anna* on the front of it. She lifted out a book. "This is Anna's baby book. I feel like everyone might need a little extra reassurance, plus it's a joy for me to look at pictures from my kids' baby books." She flipped a few sheets. "Here's a picture of me right before Anna was born. My feet and ankles were huge, so I made sure Brian only took this picture from the belly up. At this stage, every time I bent down to pick up something off of the floor, I'd have to stay down there for quite a while because it was really hard to get back up again." She turned the book around, showing them the photo.

"You really were big," Anna commented.

"Right. And it was all your fault," she said with dry humor. She paged through more of the book before sliding a piece of paper from a plastic sleeve. She handed it to Anna. "Your birth certificate. As you'll see, your dad and I are your parents. You're stuck with us, kid." She lowered into a chair across from the girls.

Anna passed the birth certificate to Ivy.

This Anna Thomas had indeed been born on October eighteenth and at a hospital here in Newburyport. Not Boston.

Ivy was mortified. If only she could rewind time and undo her actions. "I am *so* sorry."

"It's okay," Anna said lightly, wrapping an arm around Ivy's shoulders and giving her a squeeze. Anna's earlier flare of temper was gone, likely because she'd learned that her life was the way she'd always believed it to be. "I get why you thought I was your sister. She and I have the same name."

"Yeah, but it was really dumb of me not to have asked more questions before meeting you."

"Don't worry about it for a second," Mrs. Thomas assured her. "I was having a somewhat boring day. You've made it a lot more interesting."

Corrie, too, wrapped an arm around Ivy, who found herself at the center of a three-girl group hug.

When they released her, Mrs. Thomas asked, "Do you have adults helping you find your twin sister?"

"Yes, I do." She definitely should've told Sloane when she'd found this Anna Thomas on Instagram. But she didn't want to tell Mrs. Thomas that she hadn't included her adult helpers in this because Anna's mom might insist on calling Aunt Sloane and Corrie's parents. Then Corrie would get in trouble and so would Ivy and that would make everything worse.

Mrs. Thomas crossed her legs. "I'd love to hear more about you, and your story, and your search for your Anna Thomas."

Ivy told them the basics.

At the end of it, Anna announced, "I'll help you find your twin sister."

"Yes," Mrs. Thomas said at once. "I think that would be fitting. Ivy, Anna is a surprisingly good little sleuth. She can be very crafty."

Anna laughed. "That's exactly what I said about you and Dad on the walk over here. Crafty."

"Craftiness can become a superpower when used for good." To Ivy Mrs. Thomas said, "Stay as long as you'd like. You could head up to Anna's room or play video games down here or chill out on the porch."

"We have to go pretty soon," Ivy told her. Corrie hated driving in the dark. When they'd planned this trip, they'd agreed to start driving back to Groomsport right around now, so they'd arrive home way before dark.

But Corrie said, "We've got time."

Then Anna said, "Awesome!"

And before Ivy knew it, two hours had passed.

That meant that Ivy and Corrie were only halfway back to Groomsport when the sun set. After that, night came shockingly fast. Which scared Corrie. Which scared Ivy.

Ivy kept saying things like, "Just drive slowly and carefully. No hurry." But her words didn't seem to be helping.

Corrie's knee jiggled. She was biting her lip.

It was completely black out and they were in the middle of nowhere when the car sputtered and began to slow.

"What's going on?" Corrie shrieked.

"I don't know."

Corrie steered the car onto the bumpy shoulder. It continued to lose speed, then came to a stop.

Ivy's heart was galloping. She'd been sure she and Corrie were old enough to make this trip without an adult. She didn't think that anymore.

The engine died.

"Ivy! Oh my gosh. What happened?"

"I have no idea." She wanted to cry.

Corrie tried to turn the key. Nothing. Staring with alarm at the dashboard, she gasped. "*Oh no*. We ran out of gas."

Chapter Nineteen

"I—I can't call my parents," Corrie said. "They'll be mad."

"I know who to call." Ivy dialed Max.

"Hello?"

"Max, it's Ivy." Her words came out small and shaky.

"Is something wrong?"

"I'm with my friend Corrie in her car and we ran out of gas."

"Where are you?"

Ivy punched the speaker button. "On the side of the road. GPS on my phone says we're forty minutes away from Corrie's house."

"Which road are you on?"

"Route 1," Corrie said. "Going north."

"Have you passed Damariscotta yet?"

"Yes," Ivy answered, "but we're not in any town right now."

"Did you pull over to the side?"

"We did."

"Did you turn on your hazard lights?"

"No," Corrie answered. "How do I do that?"

He explained to look for a button with a red triangle. After some searching, Corrie located and pressed it.

"I'm already in my car on the way there," Max told them. "I keep ten gallons of gas in my garage in a portable tank, so I have that with me. We can either give your car gas to get it going again or you can climb into my car, and we can leave Corrie's car on the side of the road."

Corrie cleared her throat. "Can we, um, please get my car going again? If I leave it on the side of the road, I'll have to explain that to my parents."

"I see," Max said without judgment. Ivy had known he'd react that way, which was why she'd called him. "In that case, we'll get your car going once I arrive. Stay on the phone with me until then. It definitely won't take me forty minutes to get there. I have a very fast car."

"Thank you for coming to get us."

"Sure. I'm glad you called me."

Even if he got here in thirty minutes, that still felt like a *long* time to wait. Light came from the headlights of cars roaring toward them from in front and behind. Ivy had five-percent battery left on her cell.

"If anybody pulls over and approaches you," Max said, "and they're not the police, keep the windows up and the doors locked. Thank them through the window for stopping and tell them that you've already called an adult who is almost at your location."

"Okay," Corrie said. Her skin had turned ghostly white.

Regret washed over Ivy. She was *never* going to break another rule or do anything behind Aunt Sloane's back or her parents' backs again.

"It'll be just fine, girls," Max said. "I like getting to play the part of the rescuing hero." Max's certainty had meant a lot to Ivy in Boston, and it was calming her again now. She wouldn't feel totally better until he got here. But while they waited for him, it made a big difference to have him on the phone.

"How about you take this opportunity to explain to me, in full," he suggested, "how you ended up forty minutes outside of Groomsport in a car that ran out of gas?"

While Ivy and Corrie were tag-teaming the explanation, one stranger stopped. Then, later, another. Both men, both seemed friendly. Nevertheless, Ivy and Corrie panicked each time, followed Max's advice, and sent the men away.

Max made it clear when he was pulling up so that they wouldn't panic a third time. He parked behind them and approached the passenger side of the car—a dark figure against the headlights of his Porsche. Ivy rolled down her window.

"How's your evening going?" he asked nonchalantly.

They both giggled.

"Perfect," Ivy answered.

"So fun," Corrie agreed.

A giant surge of relief brought tears to Ivy's eyes. Max had reached them. They were going to be all right.

"Your gas attendant will now pour fuel into your tank." He disappeared from sight.

Ivy rolled her window back up.

"You didn't tell me he was so good-looking," Corrie whispered. "He's like a movie star or something."

"I know," Ivy said with pride. "I think he has a crush on my Aunt Sloane. Isn't she lucky?"

"*Very* lucky."

Once he'd transferred gas into her tank, Corrie started her car. Max pulled in front, and they followed him. He might have driven fast to get to them, but now he was going exactly the speed limit. They stopped at the nearest gas station to fill Corrie's tank the rest of the way.

Max and Ivy stood next to the Subaru as Corrie darted inside to the restroom.

"I can't thank you enough for doing this for us," Ivy said.

"You're welcome. I'm more than willing to do this kind of thing for you anytime."

"I'm really sorry to have disturbed your evening."

"Like I said, *anytime*."

"How can I pay you back for helping us?"

"Just one way."

Ivy waited.

"Come clean with your Aunt Sloane about this."

Ivy gritted her teeth.

"Please," he added.

It would be really nice if Ivy could bury this whole thing the way the rat boys sometimes buried food beneath their bedding. However, there was no way that she could turn down Max's one request. Also, she was feeling so guilty about everything that it was giving her a stomachache. It would probably be better to confess than live with this stomachache. "I'm going to Corrie's now to spend the night, but I promise I'll tell Aunt Sloane about this tomorrow, when I get back to our apartment. Will that work?"

"That will work."

Corrie came back and the girls followed Max's car all the way to Corrie's house. He did a U-turn on Corrie's street but didn't drive off until he saw them enter safely through the front door.

The following day, Sloane waited inside the parked SUV, watching as Ivy exited Corrie's house and approached down the walkway. The teenager had twisted her hair into a claw clip, the top tail of which swung as she walked. Her sweatshirt that read *Most Likely to Bring Home a Rat* was wrinkled after having been crammed into her overnight bag.

Her sister's child. Goofy, sweet, wonderful Ivy. Emotion clutched within Sloane's chest because this girl, raised by Brooke and Jared, had transcended the mire of poverty and neglect that had sucked at the ankles of Harper and Sloane.

Ivy climbed into the passenger seat. "Thanks for coming to get me."

"You're welcome. Did you have a good time?"

"Yep."

Quiet settled while Sloane steered them toward The Gables. Ordinarily, silences between them rested easy. But she clocked Ivy shifting self-consciously. "So . . . I have something to tell you," Ivy said.

"Oh?"

"Corrie and I drove to Massachusetts yesterday."

Sloane blinked, trying to compute her words.

"We met with an Anna Thomas that I found on Instagram. I thought she was my sister. But it turned out that she wasn't. Then, on the way home from Massachusetts, we ran out of gas. And Max came to rescue us."

Sloane had literally *just* been complimenting Ivy in her head. And now Ivy was saying *she'd taken an unauthorized trip to Massachusetts?* "Please explain."

Ivy did so. Blotchy color appeared on her cheeks as she poured out the story.

Sloane was Ivy's temporary guardian. That was a huge, *huge* responsibility. Ivy's parents were counting on Sloane to keep their daughter safe. *Sloane* was counting on herself to keep Ivy safe. She'd been too gullible, which had resulted in Ivy going on a road trip with a sixteen-year-old driver and getting stranded.

What if they'd been in a car wreck? What if the person they'd found online, the one they'd believed to be Anna Thomas, had actually been a predator or child trafficker? What if another car had slammed into Corrie's car while the girls had been stuck on the side of the road?

Thank God. Thank God the girls were all right.

"Max was great," Ivy was saying. "He drove toward us right away and never got off the phone with us the whole time. He brought gas and had us follow him to a gas station and then all the way to Corrie's house."

Ivy's wellbeing was one of the most important things in Sloane's life. There was nothing Max could have done that she'd value more than the actions he'd taken to protect Ivy.

"Why didn't you tell me you'd found an Anna Thomas on Instagram?"

"Because I knew you wouldn't want me to contact her, that you'd want to wait to hear back from the email to Stephanie."

"True. That's because your parents and I agree that it's important to go about this search for your biological relatives the proper way. With a lot of care for all concerned."

"I know. You're right. I messed up."

"How come you didn't call me when you ran out of gas?" She was shaken but somehow sounded just the way she was trying to sound—rational and composed.

"Because at that moment Corrie and I weren't planning on telling you or her parents what we'd done. But then Max made me promise I'd tell you."

Sloane parked at the garage apartment and turned to face Ivy.

"I'm very sorry, Aunt Sloane. Can you forgive me?"

"Yes, sweetheart. I forgive you."

"Hug?" Ivy stretched her arms across the center console, and they embraced.

"You know," Sloane said against her niece's head, "that we have to call your parents and confess this to them, too?"

They straightened apart. Ivy nodded dejectedly.

They remained in the car to FaceTime Brooke and Jared. Ivy relayed the story again to them. Brooke and Jared didn't lose their tempers but did ground Ivy for the next two weeks. The girl accepted her punishment and Sloane remained on the call as Ivy exited and preceded her into the apartment.

"I'm sorry," Sloane told Ivy's parents. "I take responsibility for my oversight."

"I'm not going to let you feel badly over this," Brooke replied. "If I'd dropped Ivy off for a sleepover at Corrie's, I would've trusted that she and Corrie had remained at Corrie's house just like you did."

"It sounds like Max was a huge help to the girls," Jared said.

"Absolutely," Brooke agreed. "Will you thank him for us?"

"I will."

An hour later, Max answered Sloane's knock on his front door, wearing a hoodie and track pants. His hair was in even more disarray than usual, endearingly so. He truly did have the most thick and beautiful head of hair. Women the world over would kill for that hair.

"May I come inside for a moment?" she asked.

"I hope you'll come inside and stay for many moments. Millions of them." There was undiluted affection for her in his eyes. So much so, it rendered Sloane slightly dazzled and unsure of herself.

She entered, hands in the pockets of her wide skirt. The door remained open, letting in air scented of the sea. "I'm here to thank you for helping Ivy and Corrie last night."

"You're welcome."

"I'm grateful. Brooke and Jared asked me to pass along their gratitude, too."

"It wasn't a problem. I'd do anything for you and, by extension, Ivy."

Her heart skipped a beat. "It's . . ." She cleared her throat. "It's terrifying to think about the danger the girls put themselves in. I didn't realize Ivy was capable of hiding something like that from me, of making that caliber of mistake."

"As you know, I haven't always been a stickler for doing things the responsible way. That was always more your territory and Jude's territory. So, as someone who was once a rule-breaker—"

"Once?"

"I'm reformed."

"Mm-hmm." She couldn't deny how great it felt to have her old, friendly rapport with Max back. It was like slipping into a dress you'd had for a long time and realizing that you'd forgotten how much you loved it, how comfortable it was, and how well it suited you.

"I think there's a silver lining to the fact that Ivy snuck out on her own and did something gutsy."

"Which is?"

"Until yesterday, I would've said that Ivy was so timid that she'd get eaten alive in the jungle of the real world. I'm not as worried about that now."

She nodded. It was true that a certain amount of gutsiness was required in the real world. Sloane had needed to develop truckloads of that in order to survive. "Well." She stepped toward the doorway. "I won't keep you."

"Stay, please. May I get you something to eat or drink?"

She tilted her head, considering.

"You can't remove my ability to spend time with other

women from my life," he said, "then let me sit here alone all weekend every weekend."

Her lips parted. "I didn't remove your ability to spend time with other women from your life!"

"You kind of did. It's *because* of you that I'm not spending time with them, so now you owe me your company."

"That's preposterous. Also preposterous for you to pretend you've been sitting here alone all weekend when you've been gone most of the day. I had to wait for the sound of your car to know you were home."

"You listen for the sound of my car?" he asked in a sexy undertone.

"Anyway! I'm off. Thanks again for helping Ivy—"

"I have something to talk to you about before you go."

She looked at him with prim expectancy, as if she was a governess and he was her most adorable yet trouble-making charge.

"Felix is missing a priceless, one-of-a-kind tiara," he stated, apropos of nothing.

She squinted at him. He might as well have said, *My mother is standing on the Great Wall of China*. Or *Jude just caught a fish*. "Felix," she repeated slowly, "is missing a priceless, one-of-a-kind tiara."

"Correct. It belonged to the last empress of France."

A huff escaped her. "Excuse me?"

"He thinks my mother stole it because it went missing around the time my mom and I left Maple Lane after it came out that he was my father."

The last thing Max would want? For his mother to have taken something that belonged to Felix Camden. Max had spent decades proving that he neither needed nor expected anything from his biological father.

"I have to return the tiara to Felix," he said, "before he sics investigators on my mom, but I don't know where to look next."

"Are you telling me about this because of my extensive background in detective work?"

He grinned wolfishly. "I'm telling you about this because I'm stuck. You're smart. And you have a fondness for tiaras because you follow Princess Kate. I could use a fresh viewpoint."

"What steps have you taken to find it so far?"

He listed them.

It would be much easier to remain immune to Max if A) his mouth didn't bring back visceral memories of their kiss and B) he hadn't lowered her defenses by becoming Ivy's hero yesterday. "What does the tiara look like?"

"I have a picture of it on my phone." He pulled up the image and passed her his cell.

She released a whistling breath. "Oh my goodness. That's stunning."

"Three hundred and twenty carats of square-cut diamonds."

"I'm officially intrigued. Give me time to research this tiara and think on it." She handed his phone back. "If anything comes to me, I'll let you know." She moved to go—

"Sure you don't want to stay to eat or drink something?"

It surprised her, how much she longed to say yes. She'd love more time one-on-one with him, more minutes to simply look at him, more echoes of the old partnership that had existed between them once and accomplished so much. "I'm sure," she lied as she departed.

She was leaving because her heart was softening toward Max in a way that scared her to the core.

These days, Fiona rarely turned photos into prints. But she'd done exactly that with the photo of herself and Nicole so that she could tuck the photo inside an envelope and send it to Isobel.

She sat back in her desk chair at work and read over what she'd written.

> Isobel,
>
> I'll admit that it threw me for a loop when I received your letter asking me to forgive Nicole. I understood why you made the request. It's just that I was reluctant to reinstate communication with someone who'd hurt me so badly long ago. Which made it extremely clear to me, how difficult it is, this thing I asked you to do when I requested that you come to Maine and experience the total solar eclipse with me.
>
> I want you to know that ending our estrangement is of the utmost importance to me, so I met with Nicole, talked with her, and told her that I forgive her . . . even though she did not appear to desire or enjoy my forgiveness. I've included the photo of myself and Nicole.
>
> I am still a woman of faith, though I admit that I haven't always lived out my faith well. I've tended to put myself first. It couldn't have been easy to be my sister even before my affair with Felix. Not just because I was selfish, but because I was also demanding and emotional, and always seeking our family's attention.

You managed me with more grace than any older sister could have been expected to show. The younger version of me took your love for granted. That version of me was jealous of your success and beauty and wanted Felix for myself.

I'm very sorry for what I did.

I don't expect you to forgive me, but it would mean the world to me and the rest of our family if you and I could be civil to one another at family gatherings. I still want, very much, for you to come to Maine for the eclipse-watching party in early October. I'd truly love to see you there.

A lump formed in Fiona's throat. What a stupid and recklessly destructive twenty-something she'd been.

Picking up her pen, Fiona signed the letter.

Sniffling, she sealed it, addressed it, then placed her palms on top of it. She closed her eyes and prayed that God would speak to Isobel through this letter and that His will would be done.

Other people no doubt deserved their spot at the foot of the cross more than Fiona did. But she was abundantly thankful that God had made space for her there, even so.

She walked the letter to the end of the block and inserted it into the post office box herself.

Chapter Twenty

During the first week of September in Midcoast Maine, Sloane, Ivy, and Max gathered twice at The Gables. They ate muffaletta sandwiches and discussed the etiquette of sitting. Then reuben sandwiches and the etiquette of standing.

The second week of September, they enjoyed club sandwiches and banh mi sandwiches and etiquette lessons on shaking hands and air kisses.

The third week of September, they paired chicken salad sandwiches with clothing etiquette and Cuban sandwiches with the etiquette involved in performing introductions.

The fourth week of September, they enjoyed French dip sandwiches and hoagie sandwiches while Sloane tackled the topics of cocktail party and networking etiquette.

For Sloane, September gradually revealed itself to be a gilded month. She would remain here in Maine with the niece she loved until early November, and had the deep sense that she was right where she ought to be.

Now that she and Max had buried the hatchet, the stress he'd elicited in her during her first two months on his property had lifted. Which meant The Gables was free to become the fairy-tale place to live that it had always had the potential to be. Beauty winked at her from every plant, tree, and blossom on his acres. From the lines of his Victorian house. From each string light that glowed at night. From every cheerful inch of their apartment.

Near the end of the month, the daily high temperatures dipped into the sixties and Sloane pushed her short-sleeve tops and sundresses to the back of her closet in favor of sweaters and lightweight jackets and closed-toed shoes. The leaves began to change color—a taste of the lavish fall foliage that would arrive in October. This year, Sloane would be present to see it.

Sloane was set on making the most of her stint Down East and, to that end, became more proactive about planning things for herself and Ivy on the weekends. They loved eating breakfast out at a bakery named Savory—Sloane favored the scones, Ivy the donuts. They went to the beach or hiking or shopping. Both Ivy and Max accompanied her on a whale-watching excursion that left them all awed, and to an oyster extravaganza featuring a shucking contest, local bands, and oysters priced at two dollars.

Max had told her, *"I'll show you how well I can treat you and how much you can count on me."* And for five straight weeks he'd dedicated himself to doing exactly that. Which reminded Sloane why he'd become her friend in the first place. He was quick-witted, generous, and charming. Strong-willed, yes, but also reliable. He was Sloane's champion, as well as Ivy's. He showed Sloane in dozens of ways that she was his top priority. Social Sophie stopped posting photos of Max because he stayed home. He scoured Groomsport for ingredients for their sandwich dinners. He drove Ivy's carpool when the water pump in Brooke's car broke and the Suburban had to be towed to a repair shop. Sloane chatted with him outdoors at her café table every morning. Their twice-weekly dinners at his house simmered with laughter. He sat next to Sloane on Sundays at church.

Sloane relaxed around Max more and more. Liked him more and more. Thought about him more and more when they were apart. The bitterness toward him that had been lodged like a stone between Sloane's ribs began to shrink. He didn't pressure her to date him. However, she knew he hadn't changed his mind on that because she saw banked fire in his eyes when he looked at her. Max was simply doing the thing she'd asked him to do. He was giving her time.

If September had held any disappointments, it had been these.

One, their search for Ivy's twin sister had stalled. Or maybe failed altogether? Definitely, it had stalled. Anna's mother, Stephanie, had never responded to Sloane's initial email. After two weeks, Sloane had sent a gentle follow-up email. That, too, had gone unanswered. It could be that Stephanie was no longer reachable via that email address. Or it could be that she had received the emails but decided against communication with her daughter's biological family.

Sloane and Max had both done additional research into the other channels available to Ivy. Because Anna had been placed through a closed adoption, their next options for finding her lay with the Central Adoption Agency and petitioning the courts. But both of those avenues would need to wait until Brooke and Jared returned.

Two, Max's search for Empress Eugenie's tiara had likewise hit a wall. Sloane had spent many happy hours reading about the tiara and its fabled history. As an experienced British royal watcher, she'd relished her deep dive into French nobility. However, her newfound knowledge of Eugenie and her Greek-inspired meander tiara had furnished zero ideas regarding how to find the missing artifact.

Three, Sloane's weekly visits with her father always left her grappling with a fresh wave of loss. Even though the loss of a good relationship with him wasn't fresh. On the contrary, it was one of the earliest and deepest losses of her life.

"Remember that we have a few things coming up," Sloane said to Ivy and Max on the night of Tuesday, October first. They'd just finished straightening up after their dinner of Monte Cristo sandwiches. She and Ivy would be returning to their apartment soon and before they left Max's kitchen, she wanted to make sure everyone was on the same page regarding their schedules.

She consulted her phone to ensure she was relaying the correct information. "Are we on for Thursday dinner?" she asked Max.

"Definitely."

"Then on Saturday, the three of us are going to the Pumpkin Festival and Regatta at eleven."

"Oof!" Ivy slapped a palm to her forehead. "I think I'm volunteering with the youth group Saturday. Here, I'll check. They texted me . . . Yep. I told them I'd volunteer that day so I can't go to the pumpkin thing."

"Oh, what a shame," Max said.

Ivy was still looking down at her phone so couldn't see that the expression he directed to Sloane indicated that he viewed Ivy's inability to attend as *the opposite* of a shame.

"I know." Ivy tutted sympathetically. "Sorry."

He lifted an eyebrow at Sloane like, *I dare you to go to the festival and regatta alone with me.*

Ivy's presence during their dinners and outings had been like training wheels on a bike. Was Sloane ready to take the training wheels off? "You don't have to come with me," Sloane told Max. "I don't mind attending by myself."

"I can assure you I *do* have to come. I must."

"Why?" Ivy raised her face, confused. "Do you love pumpkins or something?"

"Yes, that's it," he said. "I love pumpkins. I'll drive us, Sloane. And I'll be ready to go at eleven."

"Very well," she said in a businesslike tone. "Finally, the total solar eclipse of the sun is happening a week from Thursday. Ivy, you'll be at school during the eclipse, and I've already confirmed that they'll provide protective eyewear."

"Jude invited me to watch it with him and Jeremiah and their girlfriends," Max said. "Will you join us, Sloane?"

"Thank you, but I wouldn't want to intrude."

"You wouldn't be intruding. You'd be making it an even group of six. Three guys, three girls."

"I think you should go with them, Aunt Sloane. I mean, Jeremiah Camden! He's so famous and he and his brother are really handsome."

"They're actually not that handsome in real life," Max told the girl. "They only look that way in pictures because of their heavy use of photographic filters."

Sloane chuckled.

"Look," Max said to Sloane, "if you don't want to watch the eclipse with Jude and Jeremiah, I'll tell them no and you and I can watch the eclipse here or on the beach." He shrugged.

"I don't want you to miss out on time with them on my account."

"Good, then come with me."

She weighed whether or not she should agree. She'd like to see Jude and Jeremiah again. On the other hand, she couldn't be sure if she really was a welcome addition to their eclipse-watching group or if Max was overstepping by inviting her.

"Come with me." Max focused on her so intently that butterflies circled upward euphorically inside her stomach. "I will supply protective eyewear."

"All right," she relented, "but only because, mark my words, Ivy."

"Yes?"

"Jude and Jeremiah actually *are* that handsome in real life."

Max was not the sort of man who ordinarily spent his Saturdays at pumpkin festivals.

In fact, he'd been living in Groomsport for the past four years and had never once attended the annual event. Yet, he'd spent the past three hours of this cool, cloudy day looking at a bunch of pumpkin art. Also eating lunch at the festival's food court followed by pumpkin cheesecake. Also watching a parade celebrating the pumpkin that had won the weigh-off—a piece of produce that was the pumpkin equivalent of Jabba the Hutt. His grandparents had marched in the parade with other members of the Greek Heritage Society. When they'd spotted him and Sloane, they'd rushed over to pat Sloane's cheeks, thank her repeatedly for returning to Maine, and assure her she had their undying devotion.

Currently, he and Sloane were standing on the edge of the harbor with spectators on every side, observing the regatta. Several people had hollowed out huge pumpkins, turning them into makeshift boat hulls. Those people had then plopped their pumpkins in the water and climbed inside. A woman dressed as a mermaid was rowing her pumpkin boat. Two men—one dressed as a Viking and one dressed as a gnome—had fitted outboard motors to the backs of their pumpkin boats and putted by.

This was a far cry from what he'd called entertainment before Sloane came back into his life. In the past month, he hadn't been to any clubs. Nor fancy restaurants. Nor sporting events. He hadn't traveled except for one necessary two-night business trip to New York. He'd insisted his assistant cancel every other trip, preferring to stay home. Needing to be near Sloane.

He was aware that some of his high-level managers worried about his sanity and his priorities. But his sanity had never been better nor his priorities more certain.

He'd had a lot of years to put himself first. He'd achieved a great deal with his career. He'd amassed money. He'd lived as wildly as he'd wanted. He'd indulged himself.

And none of that had made him half as content as he was right now at this small-town festival with Sloane. The restlessness that had hounded him most of his life had been quieting over these last weeks. His driving need to succeed, to win, was receding. He no longer felt desperate to prove himself. Why would he? He'd earned back Sloane's acceptance of him. And her acceptance was better than the admiration of a thousand strangers.

These realizations were life-altering, seeing as how he'd never planned to love someone. Never, even, viewed himself as capable of that. These past weeks had given him time to wrap his head around his feelings. And from this vantage point, looking back at his whole life, his destiny was clear.

Of course he loved Sloane.

Of course he did.

He'd loved her since he was a boy halfway through his college years. He was now a thirty-two-year-old man, and his love for her was the one constant since college.

As tremendous as the last four years had been for him work wise, they'd been pale and lonely without her in them. So grim, in fact, that he'd lured Sloane into his garage apartment. He felt sheepish now about his tactics. The end had justified the means, but he could admit that the means he'd used to land her on his property were more than a little underhanded.

He'd said none of this to Sloane.

It might scare her if he told her he loved her. A possibility that, in turn, scared him.

A raindrop plopped against his cheek. Simultaneously, Sloane looked upward and held out a palm.

Rain in Groomsport typically moved from west to east and so Max glanced over his shoulder to the west at the ominous clouds racing toward them. "It's about to start pounding rain. Should we make a run for the car?" He offered his hand.

"Yep." She interlaced her fingers with his.

They zigzagged fast through the crowd. Max was trying to focus on getting them to their parking spot, but it was hard to think beyond the fact that Sloane had let him hold her hand. Her touch was warm, intimate.

The rain intensified. No point asking if she had an umbrella because she'd brought nothing but the debit card and ChapStick he was carrying for her in his pocket. His jacket was waterproof, but she had on a patterned skirt and a gray turtleneck sweater that definitely weren't waterproof. Her knee-high boots were flat but slick—not made for running. He let go of her hand just long enough to whip off his jacket. "Here, hold this over your head." He didn't wait for her to comply, just took back her hand and drew her forward as quickly as he dared.

They were rushing past businesses toward Main Street when the downpour hit. If they kept forward through this, they'd both get soaked. To the side, cobblestones lined an alley between red-brick buildings. He drew her along the alley and into an alcove dotted with moss that housed two metal doors held together with a padlock and chain. The rain pelted the cobblestones, nature creating a temporary fourth wall for the alcove.

"Making it to the car seemed like a lost cause," he explained, not letting go of her hand.

"Sheltering here until this passes seems like the best call."

"You okay?"

"Totally fine."

"Cold?"

"No. Here's your jacket back."

"You keep it." He used his free hand to settle the jacket over her shoulders. She looked beautiful with her dark eyes and luminous skin. For once, he had her to himself, which was setting off all kinds of predatory instincts.

"If you don't take your jacket back," she pointed out, "*you're* going to be cold."

"Which is why I suggest we stay alive by sharing body heat."

She laughed. "I don't think we're quite at the level of urgency that would mandate sharing body heat to survive."

"Fine. Then I suggest we share body heat just for the fun of it." He tugged her forward.

She landed with both palms against his chest and released that breathy "*Oh*" that he loved.

He shook out his hair, sending droplets flying.

Sloane shrieked.

He smiled crookedly down at her.

"What're you doing?"

"Reminding you that you're the one who put me in the friend zone. And I'm the one who wants more. Every single day, I've grown more certain of that." His hands settled against her lower back. "Sloane?"

"Yes?"

"Please stay in Maine. Be my girlfriend. And come back to work at Libri."

She peeked toward the rain as if needing a second to compose herself, then slowly returned her gaze to him. "I'm not willing to commit to any of those things at this time."

"The fact that you said 'at this time' makes me think you might be willing another time."

Her pink lips bowed upward, and need swamped him. He adored her. Yearned to show her and tell her how much. "What's the etiquette around kissing?" he asked.

"This posture of ours is a bit too personal for a lesson on etiquette, don't you think?"

"If you were giving me an etiquette lesson on which knife to use for steak, then yes. But for an etiquette lesson on kissing, I happen to think this posture is perfect."

"You are experienced at kissing. I can't imagine why you'd need a lesson."

"Because I have very little experience at kissing you. Have pity on me, Sloane. I don't want to be a good-looking heartthrob—"

"No worries there since you're neither of those things—"

"—who doesn't know how to kiss you properly. Spell out the etiquette for me. Please."

Clearing her throat, she lifted her arms and twined her hands behind his neck.

The sensation of that shot his body heat upward.

"Well," she began, "consent is of the utmost importance. Some would say asking if you may kiss the other person kills the mood, but I contend that asking is the height of good manners."

"Makes sense. You should feel free, Sloane, to ask me if I'm open to letting you kiss me."

Her jaw dropped. "I'm not the one who initiated this posture or broached the subject of kissing!"

"But you want to kiss me."

"You have no idea if I do or if I don't because you haven't asked."

He unstuck a tendril of hair from her temple and smoothed it back, then used his thumb to trace the edge of her jaw. He heard the cadence of her breath quicken. "Can I kiss you?"

"I think you mean 'May I kiss you?'"

He growled. "May I kiss you?"

"Before or after I conclude this lesson?"

"Depends on how much longer this lesson will last."

"Not long."

"Good." He spoke in a low timbre. "I'm a fast learner." Their profiles were close. He could smell her shampoo. See the water droplet caught on her eyelashes.

"Telegraphing your intentions before a kiss through eye contact is important," she said.

"Check."

"Body language is important for the same reason."

"Not sure how my body language could be any clearer," he whispered.

"Most of all, it's key in this, as in every aspect of etiquette, to show respect toward the other person."

"I have all the respect in the world for you. I care about you more than I care about myself."

She pulled in air that wobbled.

"Why are you nervous?" he asked.

"Because it worries me to think where this might lead."

"Me too. But that's not going to hold me back."

"Let's just . . . No commitments. This is just for fun. Okay?"

"Okay," he agreed, though he was definitely going to want a commitment. For him, this was not just for fun. All in good time, though. "Now. May I kiss you—"

She shocked him by pressing her lips to his.

His heart knocked against his ribs. She splayed her fingers into his hair, then a rushing river of joy and physical bliss swept him away.

Tectonic plates shifted inside him in the best way. As if those plates were shifting into the places they'd always been meant to fill. He was hers in a way even he didn't fully understand. "The one" was a phrase he would have scoffed at before. Yet Sloane was simply, mysteriously that for him. She just . . . was. The one.

His person. His favorite. His other half.

He drew her body against his and the rain cascaded down, whitish gray when everything inside of him was shades of orange and red. Minutes spun out. One became ten. Maybe more? He didn't know or care because nothing mattered to him beyond this alcove.

"I think," she eventually said against his lips, "the rain is over."

"No," he said, not because she was wrong but because he didn't want this to end.

"Yes," she said, humor in the word.

"Stay with me longer."

"All right." She gave him a reassuring, sun-coming-out-from-behind-the-clouds type of grin and it was so sweet that he almost couldn't stand it.

Max hugged her and Sloane placed the side of her face against his throat, and he could feel her pulse on his skin.

He kissed the top of her head.

They stayed there, holding each other while the rain turned from drips to silent puddles. "Will you hang out with me back at my house?" he asked.

When she didn't answer right away, he died three deaths.

"Sure. Until Ivy comes home."

It was hilarious, how commonplace things befuddled Sloane in the wake of those alcove kisses.

For example, on the car ride back to The Gables . . . What was she supposed to do with her hands? Should she make conversation? No, thankfully Max was doing a good job of that. When they reached his house . . . Where was she supposed to sit? Ah, the sofa with feet on the cushioned ottoman. He got her ice water and handed her a throw blanket and lit a fire. Max took the spot next to her and they angled onto their sides toward each other, arms bent beneath their heads to form pillows as they smiled at each other, whispered, talked. They toyed with one another's fingers. They kissed.

Sloane heard Corrie's mom's car on the drive when she dropped Ivy off at the garage apartment. But *och*. Ivy was fifteen years old. She could certainly spend an hour or two alone at the garage apartment.

Sloane was as giddy as if she'd guzzled a bottle of champagne. She and Max had crossed over the boundary between one land and the next. Though they'd known each other for years, this next land was one they'd never seen or explored until now and yet this whole place was abounding with wildflowers and beauty and excitement.

She'd felt very alone almost all her life. But for this golden afternoon and evening, she wasn't alone. Max was with her. She understood his flaws, his strengths, his personality, the twists and the turns of his history. Neither one of them had enjoyed an easy, comfortable, or traditional family life growing up. Both had been raised by single parents. Both had known hardship and shame. He had wounded her. She had made serious mistakes.

It would be wildly dangerous to assume that this new land

would lead to something long-term. So she didn't assume that. He'd assured her this could be for fun and so why not? Why not embrace the enjoyment of this for now?

She leaned forward an inch, halting with a sliver of air and sizzling heat between them. He met her halfway, his lips against hers.

He was Max. The college student she'd met long ago. Her friend. Business partner. Enemy. Friend again.

And now . . . this.

Chapter Twenty-One

Max barely slept that night because his thoughts wouldn't quit churning happily over Sloane. He was out on his patio at 6:30 a.m. in fifty-six-degree weather waiting for her to appear. She stepped outside much later, at the regular time. When her chin turned in his direction to look for him, he was already striding to the base of her stairs.

"Good morning," she said, bundled up in long silk pajamas and a winter robe, holding her coffee.

"Good morning."

They smiled at each other and the memories of yesterday flowed between them like the sea.

"Will you spend the day with me?" he asked. "After church, I mean?"

"While Ivy's working on homework, yes."

At church, they exchanged secret looks each time Ivy's attention was elsewhere. Twice, he linked one of his fingers with Sloane's without the girl noticing.

God bless her, Ivy worked on homework most of Sunday afternoon, which meant Sloane returned to his house for hours.

On Monday, he was useless at work. By two o'clock, his ineffectiveness had become ridiculous, so he left, picked up two bags of Greek food, and delivered them to his grandparents' house.

He was feeling like the redeemed version of Scrooge and grandly told them that he'd come to family gatherings more frequently. He'd often viewed his relatives as suffocating but in his current optimistic headspace, he saw how fortunate he was to be suffocated by them.

He glanced at the clock repeatedly during the conversation with Giagia and Pappous. The minutes were dragging like a fishing line that had snagged seaweed. Finally, he excused himself and headed home earlier than needed because he wanted to ensure he'd be available when Sloane finished her workday.

Ivy and a friend were attending a rat parent meet-up at the local veterinarian's practice. He once again had Sloane alone for a few hours.

The same could not be said on Tuesday, when Sloane and Ivy arrived for their regularly scheduled dinner. On the menu, pulled pork sandwiches. Sloane arrived carrying a bowl of coleslaw. Her attention found him right away.

Ivy followed on Sloane's heels with bottles of Topo Chico. "Hi, Max."

"Hi."

"I'll set the table." Ivy disappeared into the pantry, where he kept napkins.

Max kissed Sloane's cheek. "I missed you."

"I missed you, too."

They stepped apart as Ivy emerged.

After filling their plates, they took their places around his table. In the middle of a story about a boy in her math class who'd been sent to the vice principal's office, Ivy broke off. She peered back and forth between the adults. "What's up?"

"What do you mean?" Max asked.

"I mean you two are, like . . . giving each other heavy, swoony looks. Is something going on?"

Sloane dabbed her lips with the inside of her folded napkin. "You could say that."

"*Something's going on?*"

"Yes."

"What? What's going on?"

"Undefined," Sloane said. "It's impolite to kiss and tell."

"So you're *kissing*?!" Ivy clapped her hands on the sides of her face.

"It's impolite to kiss and tell," Sloane insisted.

"We're kissing," Max confirmed to Ivy.

"Max!" Sloane scolded.

He laughed.

"Finally!" Ivy exclaimed. "Are you happy?" she asked Sloane.

"Why aren't you asking me if I'm happy?" Max wondered.

"Because of course you're happy," Ivy replied. "Aunt Sloane is the prettiest, wisest, kindest, best woman in the world."

"Thank you, Ivy." Sloane beamed. "And yes, I'm happy."

Later, when Sloane was loading the dishwasher, Ivy pulled Max into his home office and closed the door. "What are your relationship plans with Aunt Sloane?"

"Wait. Am I having the 'What are your intentions, young man?' talk with a fifteen-year-old girl?"

"Um . . . yes?"

"This relationship is just seventy-two hours old."

"That's not true, though, is it? Your relationship with Aunt

Sloane has been going on for years and you've been trying to win her over all summer."

"Okay, fine."

"So! What are your intentions, young man?"

He smiled at their role reversal. "I think it's only fair that I share my intentions with Sloane before I share them with you."

"I'm protective of my aunt."

"You should be protective of me. I'm the one who's likeliest to get decimated."

"Really? No offense, but you've dated a lot of women for like two weeks each. You *can't* be that way with Aunt Sloane. She deserves a lot better than that."

"I agree." He crossed his arms. "I can be who she deserves."

Ivy appeared to take his measure. "She said 'undefined' when I asked her what was going on. Does that mean you haven't gotten her to agree to be your girlfriend?"

"Not yet."

She chewed on her lip. "Is she still dating Nate?"

His stomach fell like a box that had been dropped. "No. I think she's only dating me." But Sloane's words came back to haunt him. "*No commitments. This is just for fun.*"

It would only be over his dead body that Sloane ended up with Nate.

"This is a first," Max said approvingly on Thursday.

Sloane came to a stop in the driveway, where they were meeting to ride together to the solar eclipse. "Are you referring to my athletic outfit?"

"I am. You look gorgeous."

"Thank you."

It was a powerful thing, to realize that ungettable Max

Cirillo found *her* irresistible. She almost never interacted with him or anyone wearing clothing this casual but today she'd selected a white sweatshirt, gray yoga pants, and a spotless pair of Nikes. "I teach my students to dress aspirationally, as if they've already achieved the goal they're striving toward. But you said we're meeting Jude and Jeremiah at Mount Battie, then hiking to an eclipse viewing spot. Yes?"

"Yes."

"So I'm dressing aspirationally as someone who's already achieved the goal of completing a hike."

"I see." He glanced down at himself. "Is my clothing on point?" He had on track pants, a long-sleeved navy T-shirt with the NASA logo on it, and a ball cap.

"You're already aware that everything looks great on you. It would've done wonders for your character had you been born half as attractive as you are."

"But then I'd only be one-tenth as attractive as you." His hands framed her jaw as he gave her a light kiss. "And that would have made it even harder to convince you to be with me."

Her senses heightened with pleasure when she was close to him. That effect could tempt her to forget the larger universe.

He kissed a spot below her ear.

"They're expecting us soon, right?" she asked unsteadily.

"Hmm?" He was clearly playing dumb, trailing kisses toward her shoulder.

"Jude and Jeremiah and their girlfriends. They're expecting us soon."

"It can wait."

"A celestial event that won't happen in Maine again for fifty-four years cannot and will not wait."

"Spoilsport." He winked at her.

They climbed into his Porsche and zoomed north out of town.

Excitement over the eclipse had been building collectively across Maine for weeks. It was the subject of news stories on TV, radio DJ conversations, social media posts. It wasn't uncommon lately when checking out at a store or waiting in line for a stranger to ask, *"Are you looking forward to the eclipse?"*

Kindness was the foundation of her etiquette classes, and it had been heartening to watch the eclipse prompt the exchange of so much kindness between acquaintances and outsiders alike.

She'd seen lots of partial solar eclipses in her life. Almost always through that pinhole paper-camera thing. She'd found them underwhelming. But this time her expectations were high. It had been hard to concentrate on work this morning because thoughts of the eclipse kept distracting her. Would clouds block the eclipse from view? Would their spot be ideal? Should she bring sunblock? Were the eclipse glasses that Max had purchased actually protective enough not to burn her eyes?

They slowed as they reached their destination's parking lot. "There they are." Max motioned his chin toward two men and two women standing beside a shiny BMW.

Max parked and they approached the others.

Jeremiah had been in his early twenties when Sloane had first been introduced to him, yet at that young age he'd already become a famous F1 driver. Which had left her starstruck.

Jude she knew much better than Jeremiah, and she'd always thought the world of him. He was humble and intelligent, the unicorn type of man who was dazzling in appearance and also genuinely cared about other people above himself.

Back in the day, the Camdens had aroused in Sloane a sense of protectiveness toward Max. That same protectiveness bubbled up in her now. It had never been a stretch for her to imagine how brutal it must have been for Max to learn that his father was from an American dynasty, was one of the wealthiest men in the state, yet had chosen not to acknowledge the biological link between himself and Max. Though he had openly acknowledged his two legitimate sons. Jude and Jeremiah had been given every advantage. Max, far fewer. To their credit, Jude and Jeremiah had used their advantages to make a positive impact.

Jude reached Sloane first. "It's great to see you again." They exchanged a hug.

"You too," she said, meaning it. Jude was so fair-minded that he'd kept in touch with her after she'd split from Max and Libri. He was Max's best male friend and so during the years when she'd been Jude's equivalent—Max's best female friend—there'd been an unspoken connection between herself and Jude.

"Thank you for giving Max a second chance," Jude told her now that Max was greeting the others several steps away, out of earshot. "He's always been head over heels about you. He just didn't know how to show it."

"He's definitely been finding ways to show it lately."

"He was getting so jaded that I was worried. I've been waiting a long time for someone to show him that he still has a heart. I couldn't be happier that the someone is you."

"I couldn't be happier that you're both his friend *and* his family."

Jude escorted her to the others. "You remember Jeremiah?"

"I do."

"Nobody ever forgets me, brother."

"Don't mind him," the blonde said to Sloane. "He's delusional."

Jeremiah gave Sloane a friendly hug.

It was as if these three sons of Felix Camden had been sprinkled with fairy dust. There truly was something extraordinary about them.

"Sloane," Max said, "may I please introduce Remy Reed and Gemma Clare." Max had phrased that introduction flawlessly, honoring Sloane by mentioning her name first.

Sloane shook hands with the blonde, Jeremiah's pretty fiancée, Remy. Then shook hands with Jude's curvy redheaded girlfriend, Gemma.

"We're going to need to be on our A game," Jeremiah said. "Sloane is an etiquette expert with a company dedicated to teaching people about manners."

"Yes, but it would be very bad etiquette of me to judge anyone else negatively for *their* etiquette." Sloane smiled. "So you can all relax."

The guys each strapped two lawn chairs onto their backs. Sloane, Remy, and Gemma distributed the food and drinks among their backpacks, and they set off.

"Max told me that you have a perfume shop and create your own fragrances," Sloane said to Gemma. "That's fascinating."

"My shop is in my hometown of Bayview. Next time you're over that way, please stop in and bring your niece. We'll find a perfume for each of you. It'll be my gift to you guys."

"I'd love that and so would Ivy."

"Just steer clear of the perfume of hers called Hope and Spice," Jude warned.

"Why's that?" Sloane asked.

"Jude thinks that one is a love potion," Gemma explained. "He's not the only person who's made that claim. But if Hope and Spice turns out to be the fragrance that's meant for you, Sloane, then so be it. The men of the world will have to deal with the consequences."

"If Sloane starts wearing a love potion," Max said, "my heart ventricles will explode."

"Remy is also a creative," Jude told Sloane.

"She's a brilliant sculpture artist," Jeremiah added.

"The part about me being a sculpture artist? That part, at least, is true." Remy had on loose overalls with a waffle-knit shirt beneath.

"We'll invite you and Max to Appleton soon," Jeremiah said. "I'll show you the wood sculpture Remy gave me for Christmas. Second to my ego, it's my most prized possession."

Their conversation, spread evenly between all six, kept Sloane highly entertained during the forty-five-minute walk. It was a treat to see Jude with Gemma and Jeremiah with Remy. They were similar to the men she'd known years ago. Yet different because of their relationships. More mature and at ease.

They arrived at the viewing spot, a lovely meadow that sloped downhill, dotted with just a few other people who'd hiked here for the eclipse. The expansive view was ideal, providing miles of visibility.

The partial eclipse would begin in about thirty minutes. It would then take more than an hour for the moon to move completely in front of the sun. When that happened, for three minutes, they'd experience a total solar eclipse.

Each couple had agreed to bring a themed food board to this gathering. It didn't take long to set up chairs and begin assembling food on the boards.

"Jeremiah and I volunteered to do an appetizer board," Remy said, "because he always keeps his refrigerator stocked with the yummiest appetizers."

"She fell for me because of my appetizers."

"Don't be silly," Remy returned. "I fell for you because of your boat."

"For our meat board," Gemma said, "Jude barbecued four different kinds of sausage this morning. They all have this phenomenal, smoky flavor. I sampled them liberally, so I know of what I speak."

"For our dessert board," Max said, "we brought enough tiny, rectangular cakes to feed twenty people."

"Ah! Petit fours," Gemma said with enthusiasm when she saw the cakes.

"What are petit fours?" Jeremiah asked.

"They're the height of elegance," Gemma answered. "That's what."

It was a luxury, a thrill, to be part of this group with Max. For one thing, he looked adorable in his NASA shirt. For another, she could feel his magnetism tugging at her no matter where she looked or with whom she spoke. More than once, she caught him watching her from beneath the brim of his ball cap.

Sloane was overtaken by gratitude. She wouldn't want to view this eclipse anywhere but here. With *him*.

Fiona had journeyed to her brother Jack's seaside cottage to view the eclipse with her family.

Never could she remember enjoying a family event less.

So far, she'd spent her time at Jack's waiting with anxious misery to see if, by some miracle, Isobel would join them. Twenty minutes ago, the moon had started its slow journey over the sun. Isobel still hadn't shown. Which almost certainly meant she wasn't coming. Which almost certainly meant that this eclipse was going to become a giant disappointment for Fiona, in stark contrast to her first total eclipse of the sun at the age of eight.

Her parents had also invited Isobel to join them here today, so Fiona knew for sure that her invitation hadn't been the only one Isobel had received. After the recent letter and photo she'd sent to Isobel had failed to generate a response, she'd toyed with the idea of sending another letter or attempting a phone call. In the end, she hadn't taken further action. She'd felt the time had come to, one, accept that she'd done all that was reasonable to do. And, two, surrender the outcome to God.

Except for Isobel, everyone in Fiona's family who'd traveled to Suriname for that other eclipse was reassembled in Jack's backyard. Mom and Dad, their amateur astronomer. Jack, Elizabeth, Margaret, Alice, Mike. In addition to that original group, a few of the wives and husbands who could get away from work on this weekday were present. As were Wendell and Marisol, who'd become fast friends of her parents following the Fantasy Football picnic.

Missing were Fiona's sons. If they couldn't be here with her, then second best was knowing that they were, at least, together. Jeremiah and Jude would live through a total eclipse side by side today—history repeating what she and Isobel had experienced side by side so long ago.

Her boys were close. She liked to congratulate herself for raising them to be that way. In truth, though, Jude deserved a lot of the credit. He'd been their glue, caring for them all, supporting her and Jeremiah when they'd gone through difficult seasons.

Fiona carried her plastic tumbler to the food and drink table for a refill of blueberry iced tea. On one side of her, the Atlantic sparkled. On the other side of her, stood Jack's house. That was the direction from which Isobel would appear. Or would *not* appear, as the case may be.

No sign yet of her willowy older sister.

"Have you tried these pigs in a blanket that Alice brought?" her father asked Fiona. "They're excellent."

"No, I don't tend to consume tiny, mass-produced hot dogs surrounded by fattening bread dough."

"Then now's the time to start!" Dad handed her one on a toothpick.

She took it because she was susceptible to calories when battling a low mood. Her pig in a blanket tasted rich, crispy, and meaty. A straight shot of comfort right to her stomach.

"Why are these paper plates so small?" Dad lamented. "How am I supposed to eat a meal on something the size of a saucer?"

"I suspect the small plates are Jack's attempt to slow down everyone's intake. The O'Sullivans can mow through food faster than a Biblical plague."

"I'm starving," he announced balefully.

Mom drifted over with a concerned frown. "Your father hasn't eaten in days."

"I'm positive that he ate breakfast a few hours ago. Didn't you, Dad?"

"I did. I had pancakes but I've burned through those already."

"He's been losing weight since we divorced," Mom said to Fiona.

"Mom, you two are not divorced and he's actually been gaining weight the last ten years. He's getting plenty of food." She peeked at the house. No sign of Isobel.

"Fiona," Elizabeth said from the other side of the table, "I was just telling Alice that the dream she had the other night of herself naked at her office signifies that she might feel like a fraud at her job."

"Huh," Fiona said without enthusiasm, having been subjected to Elizabeth's frequent dream interpretations for years.

"I think she's right," Alice admitted. "I try so hard to please everyone there. I think I've got a bad case of imposter syndrome."

"Speaking of work," Mike, the baby of their family, piped up. "I have a promising lead for a new job. I'm thinking about becoming a beekeeper."

Lord, Fiona prayed, *please never let anything go awry with Mike's marriage or his wife's teaching job*. If either of those two things fell through, Fiona was quite sure she'd end up supporting her youngest sibling.

She slipped on her eclipse glasses to check the sky. She could see absolutely nothing through the glasses *except* the sun. The dark moon had moved farther in front since the last time she'd checked, turning the sun into a Pac-Man shape.

The sight was interesting but not so interesting that Fiona desired to keep the glasses on, watching, for the full amount of time leading up to totality. Sitting a short ways away, it appeared that Wendell and Marisol, however, were doing just that.

Fiona crossed to them.

Wendell's patterned sweater featured a smiling moon surrounded by plump, yellow stars. He and Marisol were holding hands and seated in the type of collapsible outdoor armchairs that always reminded Fiona of attending her sons' preschool soccer games. The older couple couldn't see her thanks to their squarish eclipse glasses, which made them look a little like background dancers in a 1980s music video. But Fiona could see them well enough to note that they'd liberally slathered on sunblock. It was still partially opaque white over their faces.

"May I get you something to eat or drink?" Fiona asked loudly.

They reacted right away, sliding down their glasses, then blinking in the sunlight comically like moles.

"No, thank you, Fiona," Wendell said.

"We're doing great," Marisol assured her.

"I'm as content right now as any person can ever be," Wendell proclaimed.

"You look lovely today," Marisol said to her admiringly.

"Thank you." Fiona had dressed with exceptional care in an outfit that hit just the right note of eclipse chic. Wide-leg pants, white collared shirt open at the throat, statement necklaces, and two precious spritzes of Rhapsodie perfume.

"Is that handsome Burke here with you today?" Marisol asked.

"No, not today."

"That's a shame. He's such a wonderful man."

Fiona's heart contracted painfully. "Yes, he is wonderful."

Her gossipy sister Margaret sidled up. "Did something happen between you and Burke? He hasn't come to your house for football games so far this season."

"He's watching the eclipse with his children and grandchildren." It wasn't technically a lie because she was positive that Burke *was* watching with his children and grandchildren.

"Isn't God good," Wendell asked, "to let Marisol and me see a total eclipse together here in our very own part of Maine? You know the path of totality is only about one hundred miles wide? How phenomenal that the hundred-mile stretch would cover Groomsport."

"Yes." Marisol never missed a chance to insert additional positivity. "And the design of the sun and moon! The moon is four hundred times smaller but will look to us as if it's covering the entire sun because the sun is four hundred times farther away. Imagine."

"I've seen a few other celestial shows in my time," Wendell said. "The Northern lights. Falling stars. Halley's Comet when it came by last in 1986. Do you ladies remember that?"

"Oh, I do," Marisol confirmed.

Margaret and Fiona nodded. Fiona had been at her own personal zenith in '86, loving that decade, loving her youth. She would not be seeing Halley's Comet on its next trip near earth.

"I've seen harvest moons and blood moons and, a few times, planets through telescopes," Marisol added. "But I saved a total solar eclipse for you, Wendell, my dear. This is a first."

"I also saved a total solar eclipse for you, Marisol."

Marisol went googly-eyed. "How romantic."

Wendell sealed that with a kiss.

"Well, I'll leave you to it, then," Fiona said.

The air was losing its brightness, the ocean turning a dreamy silvery color. Jack's Labrador looked around at the party goers uncomfortably, as if to say, *Are you guys noticing that something is very wrong with the world?*

Out of the corner of her eye, Fiona noted the outdoor lights flicking on in response to the sensors that detected dusk. She swung her chin in that direction just as a female figure rounded the side of the house.

Fiona gasped, then brought her hands up to cover her mouth.

Her long-lost sister Isobel was here.

Shocking. Mind-boggling. True.

Isobel's appearance could only be attributed to grace because Fiona did not deserve it. She had asked for something —her sister's presence—that she could never earn through good works or apologies.

Grace. It was *the* most beautiful thing.

The others had clearly spotted Isobel because a hush swept over the group (except for Wendell and Marisol, who were oblivious to the magnitude of the moment). For the past three and a half decades, the O'Sullivan family had never had Fiona and Isobel in the same place at the same time.

Isobel, full of poise, came forward with excellent posture and a small smile. She was still taller and thinner and prettier than Fiona. Yet, unlike when Fiona had been young, that observation didn't sting. In fact, it brought with it a *some things never change* type of nostalgia.

En masse, the family released delighted exclamations. Everyone talked at once and hurried toward Isobel.

Fiona followed at a slower pace, hovering on the outskirts, understanding that she didn't have the right to crowd in when the rest of them had remained in contact with Isobel and she had not. When the others finished greeting Isobel, the family parted down the middle, so the two estranged sisters were facing each other.

Fiona had no way of hiding the tears that filled her eyes.

"Hello, Fiona," Isobel said.

"Hello, Isobel. I'm very glad that you came."

"I like your outfit."

With a bolt of recognition, Fiona computed that the two of them were dressed very similarly. Clearly, Isobel also had the good taste to understand eclipse chic. "I like *your* outfit."

"It's sweet to see that you two planned to dress alike today." Mom clasped her hands under her chin. "I used to dress you alike all the time when you were girls."

Isobel closed the distance and resolutely reached out to take Fiona's hand. "How about we watch the eclipse together, little sister?"

Emotion clogged Fiona's throat to such a degree that she had a hard time getting her reply out. "I'd love that."

The rest of the family prepared an outdoor chair for Isobel and set Fiona's chair next to it. She and Isobel dropped hands as they sat next to each other. The rest arranged themselves in haphazard lines of chairs behind them.

As the clock ticked toward totality, she and Isobel did not

dredge up painful things from the past. They did not grill one another on the big life events that had occurred in the years since their sisterhood fractured. They did not ask after each other's immediate families.

Instead, they dedicated themselves to drinking in every increasingly amazing detail of their surroundings. They pointed things out to one another. Like a star that had appeared in the sky. How the wind had stilled. How the birds had fallen silent. How the temperature had cooled.

"One minute until totality," Jack called.

"Frugality?" Mom asked. "That's always been an issue for your father, but I try not to hold it against him."

"Can I take my glasses off yet?" Wendell wanted to know.

"Not yet," Jack answered.

Then, through her glasses, Fiona viewed the instant in time when the moon moved fully in front of the sun. It. Was. Magical.

Jack gave the go-ahead to remove glasses. Fiona and Isobel did so, gaping at one another just as they'd done when they were children.

The family cheered. Some clapped.

"It's so dark," Fiona said. "As though it's forty-five minutes after sunset even though it's two thirty in the afternoon."

"And quiet," Isobel said. "Like the world is holding its breath."

"Precisely like that."

Isobel extended her phone and positioned the two of them inside its screen. She hit record on a video. "My sister Fiona and I and the rest of our family are here experiencing a total eclipse of the sun, and it is *absolutely incredible*. Don't you agree, Fiona?"

"I couldn't agree more."

She ended the video and the two of them marveled—splitting their attention between the sky, each other, and their surroundings. This would last such a short time. Fiona did her best to imprint these seconds on her heart because they were rare and spilling through her fingers much too fast.

"This is the most astonishing thing I've ever seen in my life," Wendell declared. He frequently made grandiose statements. For the first time, Fiona found his grandiose statement right on the money. God was giving them an extraordinary glimpse into His galaxy. After living a lot of life and seeing a lot of things, Fiona found this eclipse even *more* jaw-dropping than the first one.

Total eclipses were nothing like partial eclipses. Just like estrangement from a sister was nothing like closeness with one. This was a pinky-promise made in girlhood—fulfilled.

Jack instructed them to put their glasses back on. They did so, staring heavenward as totality ended and the day brightened significantly.

The eclipse was a representation of life. You couldn't keep it forever. You had to make the most of it while you still had the chance. Which drove home a truth for Fiona. She had to make the most of things with Burke while she still had the chance.

"I'm hungry," Dad said.

"Me, too," Isobel responded. "Is there food?" she asked Fiona.

"The pigs in a blanket are delicious."

Chapter Twenty-Two

The following day after work, Fiona steered toward Burke's house. Her mind was split between the unscheduled conversation she was about to spring on Burke and memories of the eclipse with Isobel.

Yesterday had turned into one of the best days in recent memory. Following the eclipse, light and normality and sound and wind had returned to Maine as if a celestial miracle had not just occurred. The O'Sullivan family, too, reset to normal. They'd enjoyed the view and the fresh air for quite a while before eventually moving indoors for heat and food. They hadn't originally planned on staying for dinner but the rest of them seemed to be feeling the same reluctance to end the gathering that Fiona had been feeling. Jack and his wife whipped up an impromptu meal of taco salad. They'd talked and laughed, then played cards in the usual way, except better because they were now *all* back together. No one absent. Isobel had stayed the night with their parents, then flown home to Manhattan today.

Isobel's willingness to let Fiona back into her life . . . even in the simplest way as she had done . . . had altered something within Fiona.

She could admit to herself that she was stubborn to a fault. She'd stubbornly resisted reaching out to mend fences with Isobel for decades. It was possible that Isobel wouldn't have allowed fence-mending between them had Fiona made an effort toward that fifteen or ten or five years ago. But maybe Isobel *would* have allowed fence-mending back then. If so, she could have had her sister back in her life for years.

In textbook fashion, Fiona had also stubbornly resisted having a conversation with Burke for two months now. She was *not* going to make the mistake of letting years go by without attempting to mend fences with Burke.

She parked outside his house. She'd missed his companionship. And other things as well. The way her heart pulled like a sail into the wind when they laughed together. His white beard. The way he made her feel—steadier, calmer, valued. His muscular forearms. Even *the lines of his house*, for Pete's sake, were welcome to her eyes.

She made her way up the walk, wearing a hunter green sheath dress, hose, and heels. Before she'd reached the path's halfway point, Burke opened the door . . . almost as if he'd been waiting for her.

He came forward and they drew to a stop facing each other.

His features and frame were rugged and angular. Burke had a presence about him that was just as composed as she remembered. However, she'd forgotten how *powerful* that presence could be.

"I came by," she said, "to tell you how much I regret that our disagreement has resulted in so many weeks of silence."

"I regret that, too."

Their familiarity was still in place, but so was a slight strangeness due to their time apart. It would take effort—effort she was definitely willing to make—to find the groove of their easy camaraderie again.

She interlaced her manicured hands at her waist. "The last time we spoke, you said that I was still letting Felix dictate aspects of my life. I wasn't open to hearing that then. But now that I've had time—a lot of time—to sit with it, I can admit that when it comes to love, my history with Felix is right at the root of my decision to avoid it."

He nodded. She saw no animosity in his face. Only understanding.

"I sank very low when Felix betrayed me," she explained. "So low it frightened me. The choice not to remarry was a shield. It allowed me to take back some control at a point in time when it felt like I had none. It brought me a sense of safety."

"That makes sense."

"It *did* make sense then. It's just . . . I no longer think I need a shield to protect me." Instinctively, she touched a hand to her updo to make sure it was in place. It was. A good chignon could provide a woman with a surprising amount of strength. "It feels like the right time to give myself permission to move *all the way* past my marriage to Felix and the heartbreak of my divorce from him. In every aspect of my life. Including my love life."

He smiled—a full, open smile that gave her butterflies.

She smiled back.

"I'm sorry we argued," he said.

"Me too."

"And I'm sorry I stayed away as long as I have. I've been really unhappy. But it turns out you're not the only one who can put up a shield in order to stay safe."

His truthfulness made her feel less like she was standing at the end of a high diving board alone and more like he was standing out there with her.

"I'd really like it if we can be friends again," Fiona said. "Maybe more than friends one day soon. But for now, friends?"

"Yes. No matter what else we might become to one another, I hope to always be your friend, Fiona."

"I hope to always be your friend, too."

"Do you have time to come inside for a glass of wine?" he asked.

"I do." They set off toward the house. "Especially if it's a twelve-ounce pour."

"I wouldn't insult you with anything less."

ANNA

I haven't forgotten about you, Ivy! Sorry, I got really busy with school and drill team and my new boyfriend. (He's so cute!) My mom reminded me that I told you I'd help you find YOUR Anna Thomas and she's low-key right. I've been using my socials. I have a pretty big following on TikTok, Snapchat, and Instagram, and I asked everyone to help me find an Anna Thomas who will be sixteen in December and who was born at Monarch Hospital in Boston.

IVY

Oh, wow!

ANNA

Nothing happened at first. But then word started to spread. And spread. And I think I found her.

IVY

You did?!?!?!?!?!

ANNA

We talked a little over DM and I told her I
spent time with you and that you're super
sweet and that you're hoping to meet her.
And I said I thought she'd have a lot of fun
with you and that she should talk to her
parents about it.

IVY

I'm screaming with excitement!

ANNA

Be ready, because her parents might contact
you. I hope they do!

IVY

I hope they do, too. Thank you so much!

ANNA

I told her she and I should form a little club
called The Anna Thomases. Even though
you're an Ivy, you'd be welcome since you
brought The Anna Thomases together.

"Aunt Sloane?" Ivy called.

"In the kitchen." Sloane thought but didn't verbalize the last part of that—*Daydreaming about Max while putting away groceries.* This Friday afternoon marked day twenty since the Pumpkin Festival and the rain and those kisses and the enormous change in her relationship with Max.

For twenty days, she'd been walking on air and it turned out walking on air was a fabulous way to live one's life. In fact, these twenty days had been the happiest stretch of time she could remember in her whole life. Past Sloane, who'd arrived at The Gables and been horrified to learn Max was her landlord, could never, *never* have imagined Present Sloane's state of mind.

Ivy came to a stop nearby. "The Anna Thomas I met in Newburyport texted me to say she thinks she found *my* Anna Thomas."

"She did?"

"Here!" Ivy passed over her phone.

A mantle of seriousness settled over Sloane as she read through the text message exchange. These girls were well meaning. Yet teenagers sometimes had the patience and sensitivity of the proverbial bull in a china shop.

Ivy bobbed on her toes as she accepted the phone back from Sloane. "When I was in Newburyport, she said she'd help me search for my Anna, but I didn't know she was going to use social media to find her. She did that on her own. Do you think it's okay? That this Anna DM'd the girl who might be my Anna?"

"I'm not sure. For starters, we have no way of knowing if this new Anna is actually your twin. If she is, her parents might not love that Newburyport Anna went around them to talk to their daughter directly instead of using the contact methods they set up on the registry."

Ivy winced. "Yeah. But . . . it could be all right. Don't you think?"

"It could be."

Longing showed on Ivy's pretty features. "Maybe this new girl is my twin? And this will be the thing that, you know, encourages her to communicate with us?"

"I hope so," Sloane said honestly. With just two weeks left in Maine, she was running out of time. She wanted closure on the issue of Ivy's twin for both Ivy's sake and hers.

"Want to come pet Kevin and Ricky?" Ivy made a *come here* motion as she walked backward toward her room.

"No, thank you." Sloane's fear of rodents had dissipated some over the months of living with Ivy's rats, due largely to the fact that she'd endured no middle-of-the-night attacks. But did she want to *pet* a rat? No, she did not.

"Want to feed them a treat through their cage?" More of the *come here* motion. "They're affectionate and I think they like you a lot."

Ivy's expression was so sweetly hopeful that Sloane found she couldn't say no. "I think I might be brave enough to give that a try?"

"Way to go, Aunt Sloane!"

Sloane went to stand next to Ivy at the rat condominium. Kevin and Ricky scampered toward them and a flash of memory—a rat lunging at her from the pantry when she was a girl—cut into her consciousness. She willed the memory away. This was not that. These rats were well-behaved. And Sloane was no longer that girl.

"Here's a hazelnut for each of them." Ivy placed two nuts, still in their shells, in Sloane's palm.

Not wanting to create a rat war over providing two rats with just one nut, she took a deep breath for courage, then stuck both nuts through the openings in the cage simultaneously several inches apart. Kevin and Ricky accepted the nuts from her like little, furry gentlemen with excellent etiquette.

Instead of feeding her own childhood fears, she'd fed rats hazelnuts. Which felt empowering.

"They're good emotional support animals," Ivy said. "You can stay here and watch them if you'd like."

"Thanks, but I think I'll go look at pictures of Kate, since she's my emotional support princess."

Back in the kitchen, Sloane consulted her phone for recent Royal Family pics. A shot came up showing William and Kate speaking with a clergyman wearing a robe. The clergyman's garment reminded her of the robes professors wore for graduation ceremonies here in the States—

Something niggled at the back of her mind.

Graduation.

Raising her face, she scoured her brain. There was something to connect here. But what?

She gasped because, all at once, she knew.

She dialed Max.

"It's been way too long since I've seen you," he said in lieu of hello. "When are you coming to my house?"

"I'll be over after I take Ivy shoe shopping. Listen, do you remember the gift your mom gave you for college graduation?"

"Cufflinks?"

"Right. You were wearing them the night of the party you had when Ivy and I were houseguests."

"Correct."

"As I recall, those cufflinks were squares of gold inset with square diamonds."

"Yes. They were. They are."

"The diamonds on Eugenie's tiara are square."

A gap of quiet followed. She could practically *feel* him absorbing the import of that even though he was across town at the Libri building. "You're suggesting that my mom has the tiara and that she removed two diamonds from it to have graduation cufflinks made for me."

"I'm suggesting that's a possibility worth investigating."

"I hope that's not what happened."

"I get that." Sloane remembered Max's surprise, back when he'd received the cufflinks. He'd thought maybe the diamonds were fake, but Sloane had looked closely at them. Unlike cubic zirconia, the diamonds in his cufflinks had imperfections. She and Max had decided they were real, which meant that Nicole had likely saved a long time to purchase them. Which still might be exactly what had occurred. "Where are the cufflinks?" Sloane asked.

"My bathroom drawer." He groaned. "What if I've been storing diamonds from *Empress Eugenie's* tiara in my bathroom drawer?"

"So long as you still have both cufflinks, I don't think Eugenie will mind."

"Sloane, my mom told me to my face that she didn't take the tiara. I can't accuse her of lying without proof."

"Agreed."

"If I take the cufflinks to a jeweler, do you think they'd be able to tell me if the diamonds were cut hundreds of years ago?"

"I would think so, but I don't know. Is there a jeweler in town that you use?"

"No. It's only been the last three weeks that I've had someone to buy jewelry for."

Her heart melted.

"I'll call Jeremiah," Max said. "I'm sure he has a local jeweler he can recommend."

The next day, Max waited in the private back office of a jeweler named Stan. Sitting across the desk from the older man, Max eyed Stan as Stan eyed Max's cufflinks. The jeweler had a round, friendly face and thinning gray hair. He was utilizing a magnifying eyepiece and holding one of the cufflinks with a tweezer-type tool.

There had been a lot of occasions over the years when Max had worn those cufflinks with a suit or tux. Was it possible that his mother had extracted a pair of diamonds from the tiara and had them mounted on gold to make the cufflinks for him? Had she let him wear, without him knowing it, diamonds stolen from Felix Camden's dynasty?

No. Let that not be it.

Stan set aside his equipment. "These diamonds are old, Mr. Cirillo."

Max's breath left him as if he'd been punched.

"These were cut using techniques we haven't used for more than a hundred years."

Stan said other things, but their conversation had become a blur of Max responding, nodding in the right places, thanking the jeweler. Then he was driving toward Montville. His blood boiling. His head a war zone.

At this time of day on a Saturday, his mother did a group workout at the gym. He hoped she wouldn't be at home when he reached her place and, sure enough, she wasn't. He let himself in using his key.

Where should he begin his hunt for the tiara?

He pulled down the trap door in the hallway ceiling. A staircase unfolded. In the attic, he saw only the ten or so storage containers he expected to see. He'd moved his mother into this house three years ago and so, thankfully, this place didn't contain decades of items. He snapped open each lid and looked inside, but found no tiara once worn by the last empress of France.

He retraced his steps to the main level and went through the closets. No sign of a tiara. He looked under the beds, in the dressers. As he completed his search of the kitchen, his vision intersected with the wooden side table stationed next to the sofa in the living room.

The sight of it caused a dim memory to stir. He went to the side table, standing before it with his hands on his hips. His mother had owned this piece of furniture for as long as he could remember. It was basically a rectangular box made of oak. It had a small, matching oak vase on top filled with dried flowers. When he was a kid, there'd been a trick having to do with this vase and side table. He hadn't thought about it in ages, but yeah. He vaguely recalled his mom kneeling next to this piece of furniture, showing him what it could do.

He lifted the side table a few inches and jiggled it. Something rattled.

Foreboding slithered down the back of his neck.

The vase was octagonal—a shape echoed in the indented, octagonal detail on the front center of the piece. Max yanked the flowers from the vase, then held the bottom of the vase to the indented detail. The exact same size. Recollection poured into his mind. The vase was a key. He slotted it into the indent. Nothing happened. He turned the vase clockwise—

Click. The front panel swung open, revealing a door that had been cleverly concealed with trim. A shelf divided the interior of the box in half.

He saw a stack of cash, documents, and Mom's passport resting in the lower compartment next to a bowl holding a few pieces of heirloom jewelry. The space above the shelf looked empty. Nothing but darkness. But as his knees hit the floor and he leaned forward, he saw that the darkness masked a black velvet drawstring bag.

Heart thudding sickly, he set the bag on the coffee table and loosened its drawstring. He needed to know what this bag contained and, at the same time, no part of him wanted to know what this bag contained.

He made himself reach into the velvet. The object felt cold, solid, spiky. He eased it into the light and immediately the diamonds on Eugenie's tiara came to life with a thousand white sparks.

A sinking, quicksand sensation opened in his stomach.

This piece of jewelry glimmered with historical significance and value. It had graced the head of Empress Eugenie more than a hundred and fifty years ago. It had been bought at auction by Charles Lewis Tiffany from the French government and sold to a Camden ancestor. It had been passed down from one member of the Camden family to the next for generations.

Max turned it, spotting two empty spaces on the far edge where his mother had removed diamonds in order to have cufflinks made for him. Anger shot upward with jarring force, like that carnival game where you hit the target with a hammer and send the puck streaking high.

Moving to the nearest chair, he sat holding the tiara between his knees, wrestling with his emotions and temper.

Minutes later, he heard his mom's car. It would have been better if he'd had more time. He hadn't calmed down. Hadn't decided what to say.

Her key sounded in the back door. "Yios?"

"Yes."

He lifted his face as she came into view wearing a gray sweatsuit, her hair in a ponytail.

In reaction to the sight of him holding the tiara, she came to a hard stop. Her features went sharp and defensive.

He straightened to standing, grasping the tiara in one hand. The living room of this house had been a restful space. Everything about it was the same—the comfortable furniture, the clean smell, the bright artwork. Yet it had suddenly become the opposite of restful. Conflict was churning the silence.

"You told me," he said as levelly as he could manage, "that you did not have the tiara."

"Were you searching my house when I wasn't here?"

"I was."

"*Max.* How could you—"

"I took the cufflinks you gave me for college graduation to a jeweler. They told me they'd been cut long ago. So I knew you'd lied when you said you didn't have the tiara. I came here to find it. Which I did."

"You had *no right* to search my house."

"Are you really going to lecture me about rights when you had no right to steal this from Felix?"

"I deserve that tiara, Max. I earned it."

"How do you figure?"

"After my affair with Felix ended, I raised *his child* without help. Did he change one, single thing about his life when you were a baby? A boy? A teenager? No. He did nothing." She pressed a palm to her chest. "I did everything. Including work for him and Fiona. I cleaned their house and bought their groceries and made their dinners *for sixteen years*. And then, when I had the audacity to finally tell a reporter about Felix's paternity, they expected me to leave Maple Lane, which had been our home all that time, with nothing? No. Absolutely not."

Max set his teeth so hard that pain flicked along his jawline.

"I have pride," she stated slowly, emphatically. "That tiara is mine. For all my years of work for Felix and Fiona. For back child support. For playing nice for as long as I did. For the pain and suffering they caused me. For the hatred I've had to put up with from the public."

Swallowing the idea that his mother had stolen this was like drinking acid. He was not a thief. And he was no one's charity case. Max hadn't taken a single dollar from Felix since Felix had written the last check for Max's college expenses. His financial independence from Felix was a huge part of his identity.

"Consider the damage Felix did to you," she continued, gaining steam and indignation. "It messed with your head to find out you had a father who hadn't claimed you, who treated you like you were his sons' playmate instead of his own son."

"Is Felix most at fault for the damage done to me?" he asked tightly. "Or are you?"

"What do you mean?"

"You're the one who broke the story about my biological link to Felix. Before that, we were living in a great house, on a great piece of land, and I was going to a great school. After that, everything was worse for me."

"Because of Felix and Fiona!"

"And you."

"They are the ones at fault," she insisted.

He saw then that she was not going to accept responsibility. Many years had passed and still, she was primed only to fight and defend herself and blame. Her bitterness had hardened around this issue.

His mother's life could have played out so differently. After Felix, she could have found another relationship, and with that, love and companionship. Maybe marriage, maybe other children. Instead, she was living alone with her resentments and a tiara for company.

Several elements of her life were positive. She was comfortable in retirement, had parents and siblings who loved her, friends, meaningful ways to spend her days. Yet she'd allowed and would continue to allow what had happened with Felix to harm her like cancer.

Max would not make her mistake.

He had as much pride as she had, if not more. He had his share of bitterness, too. But all the Sundays he'd spent at church had begun to reshape his thinking and his heart. The injured parts of him were healing.

For Sloane . . . for the chance at a life with Sloane, he'd crush his pride and bitterness to dust. He'd never wanted anything—not power, not money, not even Libri's success—half as much as he wanted Sloane. If he was willing to give up kingdoms and countries and fortunes for her, then the least he could do was give up pride and bitterness.

He'd known for quite a while now that he loved Sloane, but had he told her that even once? No.

His mother extended a hand. "Give me my tiara back."

"No," he said flatly. "I'm going to return it to Felix—"

"You can't."

"I can. Returning it will protect you from investigators and both of us from another scandal."

Her hand remained out. "*Give it back, Max.* Felix will have me arrested for theft if you return that to him."

"He told me he simply wants it back. Once this is in his possession, there will be no more loose ends to what went down between you and Felix. It will all, finally, be over."

She lowered her arm. Both her hands curled into fists. "It will never be over for me."

Max felt very old then. Exhausted. It was a huge shame, the path in life she'd taken. "I have to go, but I'm going to call Aunt Melissa and ask her to be here with you."

She didn't say no to that. In his mother's worst moments, her sister had always been a comfort to her.

"I love you, Mom."

He could tell by her body language that she was in no mood to reply with an *I love you*. It didn't matter. He knew she loved him. The main thing today was that she know *he* loved *her*.

As he drove toward Groomsport with the tiara riding on the passenger seat, he used voice controls to dial Sloane. He had no specific plan for the call. Dialing her was survival instinct, the actions of a man who understood who it was he could trust, who it was that could bring peace.

"Hey," she said and just that, just the sound of her saying that one syllable, eased something inside him.

"I found the tiara inside my mother's house," Max told her. "She took it from Felix. She's had it all these years."

"I'm sorry to hear that. Are you okay?"

"Yes. No."

"Where are you?"

"I'm driving back from Montville."

"Meet me at the stream?"

She was referring to the stream that cut through the back corner of his acres. "I'll be there in thirty-five minutes."

Sloane set out from the garage apartment through the woods to Max's stream.

She adored this walk. It felt charmed, like something out of a storybook, because the forest was so unbelievably, achingly beautiful in late October. The colors of the foliage! Greens, oranges, yellows, shades of rust. Rich, dark soil. Every hue was shimmering in the golden afternoon light.

Eventually, the path ended at black boulders that gave way to clear, cold water sweeping past. People paid for audio tracks that captured these sounds. A burbling stream, birds, wind in the branches.

She'd arrived here before Max as expected, given the ETA he'd provided. Much of her Saturday had been spent indoors. It was a treat to finally get out into nature. Before leaving the apartment, she'd put on a tweed coat over the camel-colored sweater and denim trousers she'd had on all day. Tucking her hands into her pockets, she admired the view.

She heard Max coming and turned in time to see him appear around a bend in the trail. As good as the view had been before, it had just improved a hundredfold. He had on a charcoal suede overshirt that functioned as a jacket. Cotton under-shirt. Jeans.

His voice over the phone had telegraphed how troubled he was, but now the solemn lines of his expression confirmed it. A gust of sympathy had Sloane opening her arms. And then he was holding her tight against him. Her hands snaked under the overshirt and around his lean ribs. She registered the warmth and vitality of his body. Breathed in his sun-and-ocean cologne.

They stood like that for a long stretch.

"Want to tell me about it?" she asked.

Never breaking their hug, he did so, bringing her up to speed on the conversations he'd had with the jeweler and his mother. He mostly spoke against the top of her head, but she heard him perfectly fine.

Only when he finished did she lean back so they could observe one another. She kept her hands interlaced behind his waist. His fingers gently massaged the back of her neck.

"I have something to say to you," he told her, "but I'm concerned."

"Why concerned?"

"I'm not used to being as honest with you as I'm about to be."

Apprehension flickered within Sloane. Was she going to like what he had to say? She was ferociously protective of the relationship they had going. This was ideal, just like it was. She didn't want him to alter it.

"It sounds like you've had enough stress for one day." She'd failed to make that come out as lighthearted as intended. "Maybe there's no need to say anything that will cause you more stress right now?"

"No, I need to get this out."

"Max—"

"I love you."

For several seconds, she was too stunned to speak.

"I think I've loved you since Penn," he said.

Her equilibrium was tilting. "Since . . . Penn?"

"Yes." His gaze remained unflinching. Max was the CEO of a billion-dollar company. He knew how to stand straight and maintain eye contact.

Joy tried to sprout within her. But that joy was coming from a part of her heart that was, Sloane had learned repeatedly during her childhood, destructively hopeful. Painfully naïve.

"I want you to be with me and only me," he said. "To live in Maine. To be my girlfriend and then one day my fiancée and then one day my wife. I want nothing more than to spend all the rest of my days with you. Every single one of them."

She could not believe the words coming out of his mouth. They weren't landing. She was much too afraid to trust these words. Cold rushed upward from the soles of her feet, forcing her to step back a few paces and break the physical connection between them.

His hands dropped to his sides.

"There's . . . no way you realized at Penn that you loved me." She couldn't balance that with what she knew of their backstory.

"You're right. I loved you then, but I didn't recognize what I was feeling as love until two months ago."

Two months ago? Her thoughts were swimming in a whirlpool. "You look like you're at a funeral. This is not the look of a man in love." Those sentences had come out of nowhere, unsanctioned by her brain.

"I look like I'm at a funeral because this feels like it might be *my* funeral."

"Then why tell me this?"

"Because I need for you to know."

"I . . ." Her breathing turned shallow. "I'm sorry. I'm . . . not reacting well. I'm freaking out, to be honest." She hadn't forgotten all the brokenhearted, discarded girlfriends he'd left in his wake. How could she? So many women. Max was too handsome for her to keep. Too hazardous for her to love. A committed, long-term relationship between them? Marriage? *That could never work*, a voice within her was warning.

She watched sadness lower over him. She was furious at herself for hurting him but also angry at him for rocking their boat.

Why couldn't she get enough air? Hooking a finger in the neck of her sweater, she tugged in a futile attempt to find more breath. "I need some time to myself to think."

His gaze communicated raw pain. "Take all the time you need."

She whirled and hurried down the path, wind skating against her cheeks.

Since the early days of their friendship, she'd known she was special to him, but she'd never dared to imagine that he loved her. She hadn't even thought he was capable of true love.

If she added up all the time she'd spent with Max, he was, by far, the man she'd been closest to for the longest period of time in her life. During those years with Max, unlike her years with her father, Max had been reliable. Max had cared about her. Until he suddenly wasn't and didn't.

She hated the idea of losing what they'd gained. But . . . she couldn't trust Max enough to hand over her heart.

Could she?

This felt like a panic attack.

Max had detonated a bomb just now.

And she was running terrified in the aftermath.

Chapter Twenty-Three

Max was not doing well.

Yesterday, he'd told Sloane he loved her, and she'd reacted as badly as his worst fears had told him she would.

He'd returned to his empty, silent house. Sleep had been like a small, frayed piece of fabric. He'd woken this morning with a raging headache, his stomach an iron ball.

He wasn't sure what was going on with Sloane because she hadn't told him. Based on what he knew of her, though, he guessed that it could be a few things. After her jacked-up childhood, singlehood might feel safer to her. His track record with women was likely still a problem for her. She had a home and career in California. Her feelings for him probably didn't match his for her.

Pulling the Porsche to a stop at a red light, he scrubbed both hands into his hair. He was on his way to Maple Lane to finish his unfinished business with Felix Camden, which did nothing to improve his mood.

The way Sloane had been with him these past weeks had made Max hope that she might love him. He wasn't an idiot.

He wasn't inexperienced. He knew when women were into him, and Sloane had been into him.

This relationship with Sloane, though, was lightyears different from any other because in the past when he'd seen that a woman held deep affection for him, he'd prayed that it wasn't love. If it turned out that the woman did profess to love him, he ended things soon after. But with Sloane, he'd seen that she held deep affection for him, and he'd prayed to the sky and back that it *was* love.

The light turned green. He accelerated.

Three things might be true of Sloane. She might love him but have valid concerns. She might love him but be stuffing that down and unaware of it. Or she might not love him.

Please let it be one of the first two options. He'd have something to work with if it was either of those two. She hadn't broken things off with him, after all. She'd asked for time. He'd been telling himself repeatedly that her asking for time didn't have to spell the end. If he could make himself believe that, then he could keep the boat of his life upright and moving forward.

He reached Felix's long driveway and saw that the famous maple trees of Maple Lane were dark red at this time of year.

He'd texted the older man to let him know he was coming. So, when Max knocked on the front door, it opened quickly.

"Good morning," Felix said.

For Max it was not, in any way, a good morning. "Hello." He'd left the velvet bag that his mom had used to store the tiara at her place. Max had the tiara in a backpack. That felt wrong but he didn't know the protocol on how to transport priceless jewels.

Felix gestured for Max to follow him into his home office—which tripped a sense of déjà vu. His arrival here today overlapped in his brain with his arrival for their first meeting about the tiara months ago.

"Have a seat," Felix said.

"No, thank you. This won't take long."

"Oh?" Felix, too, remained standing on the far side of his desk.

"If I've succeeded," Max said, "and have something to return to you, I want your word that this will be the end of it, that no further action will be taken." The marriage vows Felix had spoken were about as trustworthy as a bucket with a hole in it. But in other areas, like his career, Felix had shown himself capable of following through on things he'd said he'd do. Felix's word wasn't infallible, but it was better than nothing.

"No further action will be taken," Felix said. "You have my word."

Max reached into the backpack and handed over the tiara.

Felix's eyes lit up. He accepted it the way kings accept tribute paid to them by lesser nobles. For several seconds, he admired the tiara, then set it on the desk. "Thank you."

From a smaller pocket of the backpack, Max pulled free the cufflinks. He set them beside the tiara. "You'll find that the diamonds in the cufflinks fill the two empty spaces on the side."

Felix didn't blink. "Very well."

"Are we square?"

"We're square." Felix extended his hand. They shook on it.

They would never have a father/son relationship. And that was fine. In fact, that was how Max preferred it. But Max had, at least, made this right.

His mother had said, "*It will never be over for me*" in reference to everything that had gone on before with Felix. But with the return of the tiara, it *was* over for Max. All of it. The past. The scandal. Max's resentments. The money and power grab he'd been on for years.

Over.

"I have just one favor to ask of you before I go," Max said.

"Shoot," Felix responded.

Ordinarily, Sloane endeavored to bring more grace to her life by constraining work to work hours and enjoying rest all the other hours of her week. But on this Tuesday evening, she found herself sitting on the apartment's sofa, compulsively checking email on her phone at seven thirty, in a bid to distract herself from thoughts of Max.

One of the names in her inbox jumped out at her.

Stephanie Thomas. Anna Thomas's mother.

Sloane went still. This email might bring good news or bad news regarding Ivy's quest to meet her sister. Gathering herself to deal with either possibility, Sloane opened the email and read.

Sloane,

I appreciated the sweet email you sent when you reached out to me weeks ago to say that Ivy was interested in meeting Anna. In the end, your email required quite a bit of thought on my part and my husband's part. And then, eventually, it took discussion between my husband and me and Anna.

Anna hasn't yet met any biological relatives. Learning that she has not only a biological relative, but one that is her twin . . . That was a surprise. A good surprise, I hope. Yet a surprise that merited some processing.

Anna would like to meet Ivy, as would I and my husband, Raj.

We live in Auburn, Maine. We're frequent visitors to the

"Harvest Days" hosted at one of the farms outside of town. From their barn they sell vegetables, flowers, honey, fried donuts, hot chocolate, and more. They have a Harvest Day coming up this Saturday and, given the beautiful weather we're having, we thought that might be a nice place to let Anna and Ivy introduce themselves to one another.

I look forward to hearing your thoughts.

Sincerely, Stephanie

"Ivy!" Sloane called.

Her niece emerged from her room dressed in flannel pajama pants and a *My rat thinks I'm cool* T-shirt.

"An email arrived from Stephanie Thomas," Sloane said.

"Oh my gosh!" Ivy ran the rest of the way.

"Here." Sloane handed the girl her phone.

After several seconds of reading, Ivy took a cheerleader-style leap into the air. "How far away is Auburn?"

"An hour and a half."

"Can I meet my sister this weekend?!"

"Are you ready to meet your sister?"

"I've been ready for a long time, Aunt Sloane. This feels *so* right. Like God is telling me this is exactly the door to walk through."

"In that case, would you like me to email Stephanie back and let her know that you and I will be there on Saturday?"

"Yes, but please tell her that you and I *and Max* will be there."

"Um . . ."

Ivy waited with a quizzical expression.

"Max and I are taking a break at the moment."

"What does that mean?"

"Just that I need time to think through some things. Nothing to worry about," she lied.

"Did Max do something wrong?"

"No," Sloane was quick to say. "He did nothing wrong. It's more that he . . . would like for us to become more serious. And I'm not sure."

Ivy sat beside her on the sofa, their knees angling together. "I'm not surprised he wants to get more serious. It's pretty obvious that he's crazy about you. He's been good to you, right? Since you two got together?"

"Yes."

"And you've been happy. The happiest I can ever remember." Ivy gave her words time to sink in. "Which makes *me* happy. I've always secretly hoped that, like . . . you'd meet a wonderful guy and maybe have a family of your own." The compassion in Ivy's eyes conveyed that she understood the "family of her own" Sloane had been given at birth had been a trainwreck and that Ivy wanted Sloane to experience the type of family Ivy herself had known. "Would you want a husband and kids? One day?"

"Yes, with the right man."

"Could Max be the right man?"

The panic that had been riding close to the surface since her talk with Max pricked her chest. "I don't know."

"Well. You're an awesome aunt and I think you'd be an awesome mom."

"Thank you."

Ivy popped to her feet. "I'd like Max to be there when I finally meet my sister. Is that cool with you?"

Sloane nodded.

Ivy scampered back to her bedroom.

Sloane had made it through the past three days by hiding from Max.

She acknowledged that as cowardly and beneath her. Especially so considering that he'd been brave when he'd told her how he felt. He'd made himself vulnerable and she'd responded by protecting herself from vulnerability at all costs.

It was just that she still had no idea what to do or think about the things he'd said. Not only had he told her that he loved her. He'd also asked her to move to Maine. He'd floated the idea of her returning to Libri, even. These things would demand more change from her than they would from him. Did she trust Max enough to upend her life once again?

Her head was like fireworks—her fears going a hundred different directions at once.

Across town, Fiona and Burke were cooking dinner at Fiona's house. Well, Burke was doing most of the cooking. Fiona was looking decorative and assisting slightly.

Two and a half weeks had passed since they'd resumed communication. It had taken effort to bring their closeness meter back to a ten out of ten. But then, good things in life required tending. Like her relationships with her sons, both of whom she'd called today. Like her skin—smooth, thank you very much, due to recent Botox. Like her dress size. She planned to hang onto this dress size with both manicured hands as hard as she could for as long as she lived. Was that easy at this age? No, ma'am. It was not.

Entertained, she watched Burke chop vegetables at her kitchen island. He was making her a low-carb, low-calorie vegetable beef stew because he knew all about her mindset toward her dress size.

She'd come to treasure having this very masculine man in

her very feminine house. He was the best-ever counterpoint to her years of doing life alone here.

Jeremiah and Jude, her boys. Her sons. The babies they'd been and the little boys they'd been would live in her heart *always*. They'd needed her when they were small. They'd clung to her. They'd relied on her. She'd poured all the love she had into mothering them. But the passage of time was both a giver of gifts and a thief. Jeremiah and Jude had done what they were absolutely supposed to do—they'd grown. They'd left her home long ago and become independent men. They were wonderful to her, but they didn't need, cling to, or rely on her these days. Which was good, just as it should be. Yet also bittersweet.

Every time she saw a sentimental commercial featuring a mother and a son, she teared up. And she occasionally played "Slipping Through My Fingers" by ABBA when she needed an outright cry over it.

In the years since her sons had moved out, she'd filled her life with worthwhile things like running her company and an abundance of fun, frivolous things like golf and spa days. This last year with Burke, however, she'd come to understand that those worthwhile and frivolous things were no substitute for the daily, tangible presence of someone you cared about deeply.

It was joy and solace, to have Burke in her days. She was even more grateful for him now than she'd been before their temporary separation.

Prior to arriving here this evening, she and Burke had spent hours with the O'Sullivans because Isobel and her husband were stopping over in Maine for a few nights before heading out on a trip to Portugal. Today's family reunion had been on everyone else's calendar for months. It hadn't been on Fiona's calendar because Fiona couldn't take part in O'Sullivan events that Isobel attended. But then, after the eclipse, Isobel herself had texted Fiona to invite her and Burke to today's gathering.

It had felt like heaven to be included.

She and Burke had been discussing the O'Sullivans while he cooked. Over the past year, Burke could have earned a doctorate in her large family. He'd dedicated himself to memorizing data about each relative and knew which nieces and nephews belonged to which siblings. Today he'd had his first opportunity to meet Isobel. He'd been duly impressed by her, noting her calm personality and composure.

He wasn't wrong. "She's also fashionable," Fiona was saying now.

"You are fashionable, too." *Chop, chop, chop.*

"I'm Maine fashionable. Isobel is Manhattan fashionable."

"I happen to prefer Maine fashionable."

"Seriously?"

He set down his knife and faced her. "Isobel is a lot of things, but she is not you. In my eyes, no one held a candle to you today. No one could be as desirable or spirited."

"Is spirited code for challenging?"

"Yes." He winked. "And I wouldn't have it any other way. I adore everything about you."

Fiona had not, for a single minute of the time she'd spent with Burke, pretended to be anybody other than who she authentically was. He'd met her when their kids were small, when she and the other moms had referred to him as Nice Dad. She'd been herself then. Since he'd moved back to Maine, she'd been herself the whole time. He'd spoken those words while *accurately knowing who she was.*

Carried by a wave of fondness, she closed the distance between them, took his face in her hands, and kissed him. Just a peck, but quite a definitive one.

She wasn't willing to invest her emotions in just any old

man. But if that man was *this man?* If that man was Burke, so honorable and loyal? Could she be ready to give romance a try?

She could.

Leaning back, she settled her hands on his shoulders.

An astonished, lopsided smile moved across his face. "Does that kiss mean what I think it means?"

"It does."

"Fiona. That is very, very good news."

"Burke. It truly, truly is."

He drew her against him, kissing her with the assurance of a man who'd lived life well and earned true confidence.

Desire rushed warm through her bloodstream. She hadn't understood that such a low-key man could pack such a knee-tingling kiss. Hadn't known that she still had the capacity to experience this type of response. But here it was.

"Wow," she whispered, breathless.

"Wow," he agreed, hugging her against his sturdy chest.

This embrace felt like coming home after a lengthy journey that had been at times splendid and at times brutally hard.

There was a great deal of comfort in *home*.

Max accepted Ivy's invitation to go with them to Auburn.

Sloane did not attend the Tuesday and Thursday sandwich dinners. But when Saturday arrived, it was time to pay the piper. They'd agreed to depart for their trip to Auburn at 1:00 p.m. Which meant Sloane and Ivy were ready to go, waiting at the base of the garage stairs at 12:50.

For several miserable, conflicted days, Sloane had been giving herself pep talks to prepare herself to be near Max again. Yet the instant she saw him, all of that preparation went *poof*, and the breeze carried it away like ash.

He'd let himself out his back door and was walking toward them in a casual gray sweater, quilted vest, black joggers. He looked *irresistibly* good.

Were he to take her in his arms, she knew what he'd smell like. She knew how his arms would feel around her. She knew the sensations of kissing him. A week ago, she'd had access to all of that. Which seemed impossible now.

"Max!" Ivy extended a fist.

Max bumped it with his own fist, then his gaze came to rest on Sloane. He gave a strong, overall impression of fitness and health. Yet she could see in his eyes that he hadn't been sleeping well. Also, he seemed slightly thinner, as if he'd been undergoing too much stress.

"Hi, Sloane."

"Hi, Max."

He continued staring at her. With heat and awareness and grief.

"Which car are we taking?" Ivy asked, breaking the moment.

"My Blazer." He proceeded to reverse a classic SUV from the garage. It had been restored well on the outside and—when she climbed into the passenger seat—Sloane saw that the interior had been restored equally as well.

Ivy filled the drive to Auburn with words. It was as if the teen was carrying on a conversation with both Max and Sloane, but Max and Sloane weren't having a conversation with each other. The air between the occupants of the front seat was thick with things unsaid. They were handling that, and Ivy's presence in the car, by resorting to polite distance. Back when she was thinking of him as Darth Vader, she'd have been delighted with polite distance. Now it came as a severe disappointment.

She greedily cataloged tiny details of him. Like how his watch caught the light. The brand logo sewn into the side of his joggers near his hip. The angle of his fingers, one hand steering and one hand relaxed on the arm rest. His profile.

Sloane forced herself to look out the side window.

"I want you to be with me and only me." She pulled the well-worn memory of him saying that to the front of her mind. *"To live in Maine. To be my girlfriend and then one day my fiancée and then one day my wife."*

Had he truly said all that? Did he truly feel all that? Even if he did feel all that, could he keep that level of commitment going for a lifetime? The neglect she'd experienced firsthand made her doubt that he could.

Sloane had been the one to ask for time, yet she felt wrecked because of it.

Ivy had been nervous before meeting Seth.

Before meeting the first Anna Thomas, she'd been half nervous and half excited.

For this meeting with the second Anna Thomas, she was mostly excited and just a tiny bit nervous.

She'd gotten close with Sloane and Max over the last four months and so having them here today gave her a bunch of confidence. There was just one thing that would have made the drive to meet Anna better: if the two of them had still been the Sloane and Max from October. Today was November second and this Sloane and Max were super strange. Stiff, with not much to say to each other even though their spark-y vibe was as strong as ever.

Adults were weird sometimes! Sloane and Max were clearly meant for each other. But they were taking their sweet time about it. If Mateo, a boy in the grade above her at school, ever asked her to be his girlfriend, she'd say yes to that *right away*.

After Sloane had emailed Stephanie to say they'd meet them today, Stephanie had sent them the farm's address. They found it without difficulty, parked, and were now walking toward a red barn that had big, wide-open doors. The day was cool but sunny. The nice weather was probably part of why lots of other people had shown up for Harvest Day.

Ivy scanned the tables and chairs. No one sitting there was near her age. As far as she could tell, they'd arrived before Anna.

Ivy chose a table, and they sat.

Thanks to Sloane, she'd learned it was poor etiquette to show up too late and that it was also poor etiquette to show up at a host's house too early. But it was fine etiquette to show up eleven minutes early, as they had, at a public place like this one.

"Do you have any last-minute etiquette lessons for me?" Ivy asked her aunt.

"No." Sloane smiled at her. "Your etiquette's excellent. You're going to do great."

Ivy watched a bumblebee fly around and around before landing on one of the shrubs nearby. Then she looked toward the parking lot, and a *clang* went through her.

A family of three was coming from that direction. A plain, conservatively dressed mother with medium-length blond hair. A thin, tall, friendly-looking father with brown skin and dark hair. And their daughter . . .

Their daughter.

Ivy's mouth dropped open. Goosebumps pebbled her arms. Not taking her eyes from the family, she rose to her feet. The girl had clearly seen her, too, because her face mimicked the amazement Ivy felt.

This girl . . . this Anna . . . had pale skin and long, strawberry-blond hair.

"I can't believe it," Sloane whispered.

Anna Thomas was not just Ivy's twin. Anna was her *identical twin.*

It had occurred to her, of course, that Anna might be her identical twin. But only one-third of twins were identical. It had been hard to imagine that she had a twin sister, let alone an identical twin sister.

But the girl walking in her direction was living proof. This was like something out of the multiverse. Ivy was looking at *herself* and, at the same time, looking at a completely separate person. It gave her the sensation of being disembodied, observing herself from another point of view.

Anna's hair was almost the same length as Ivy's and they'd both worn it down today. They'd both dressed in sweatshirts, leggings, and tennis shoes. As Anna approached, more similarities came into focus. They had the same freckles everywhere. And had chosen the same shade of sheer rose lip gloss.

They'd grown up apart, she and Anna, but they shared big things. The same DNA. The same two biological parents. The same birthday.

Anna came to a stop.

It's you, Ivy thought.

You are the reason I was inspired to find my birth family. So that I could meet you and know you. So that we could be in each other's lives.

Ivy laid a hand on her chest and felt her heart sprinting. "I'm Ivy."

"I'm Anna." Even their voices were the same. "Would it be all right if we . . . hug?"

"I'd love that!" Then they were hugging, shoulder to shoulder, red hair to red hair.

Distantly, Ivy heard the adults exchanging names. Maybe her etiquette wasn't excellent after all, because she'd completely forgotten to introduce them.

"I'm so excited to meet you," Ivy said when she stepped away, her hands in a clapping position.

"Me too. I can't believe we're"—Anna made a small motion toward Ivy from head to toe—"identical twins."

"Me neither. You're so pretty!" Wait, had that been conceited, since she was calling someone pretty who looked just like her? The words had burst out because she genuinely meant them.

"You're so pretty, too!" Anna said, laughing. "I love your hair."

"I love *your* hair! Now that I'm seeing you, I think I even like my freckles."

"Same!"

Ivy held out her arms and they hugged again, this time squealing a little and jumping up and down.

Joy overran Ivy's heart like the bubbles of a Sprite, rising up and spilling over the sides of a glass.

"This is extraordinary," Raj said.

"We had no idea Anna had an identical twin," Stephanie murmured.

Ending the hug, the girls turned toward the adults.

Sloane, Ivy was surprised to see, was wiping away tears. At some point, Max had moved next to Sloane, not touching her, but standing nearby in a show of support.

"Anna," Ivy said, pleased to get to make a few introductions after all, "may I please introduce you to my—*our* Aunt Sloane. Her older sister, Harper Madison, was our biological mother. Harper died four years ago, and Sloane loved her a lot. Anyway, Sloane is fabulous."

"I'm honored to have this chance to meet you, Anna." Sloane extended her hand.

"I'm honored to meet you," Anna said as they shook.

"And may I please," Ivy continued, "introduce you to Max Cirillo, our friend."

"I am also fabulous," he said to Anna as they shook hands.

Sloane addressed Anna's parents. "Thank you both for making this possible. It's incredibly gracious of you."

"You're welcome," Stephanie returned. "Thank you for the very same thing."

"Identical twins," Raj said, "separated at birth, raised apart, then reunited. This must be a very rare thing."

"It feels miraculous," Sloane said.

The adults beamed at the girls.

She and Anna turned their heads in unison to smile at one another.

"You know," Anna said, "I always wanted a sister. Didn't I, Mom?"

"Yes. Anna's an only child. But starting when she was a preschooler, she asked repeatedly for a sister. Not a brother. A sister. Now I wonder if some part of her remembered you, Ivy."

They ended up spending the next two hours together. They drank hot chocolate, ate donuts, FaceTimed Ivy's mom and dad, and admired the shaggy cows in a nearby field.

Never had Ivy been as interested in anything, even rats, as she was in Anna. It seemed like Anna felt the same way because she asked Ivy lots of questions about her life, about Harper and Seth, about Sloane. Ivy asked Anna lots of questions, too.

Turned out, they both had strong faith in God. English and history were their best subjects. They enjoyed sports but weren't very athletic and so spent most of their time at games on the bench. They liked the same Netflix shows. They were both fans of Bruno Mars. They followed some of the same YouTubers.

She and Anna were essentially the same person, split into two bodies. Now they were back together. *And they fit.*

Aunt Sloane, of course, ensured that Ivy's group did not overstay their welcome. She and Anna had exchanged numbers, so when they said goodbye, Ivy wasn't sad. This didn't seem like an ending. This seemed like the beginning of something that would be an important part of her whole life.

In the back seat of Max's car on their way to Groomsport, Ivy smiled dreamily, replaying her favorite moments of the day. She had so many! If each memory was a seashell, then she had a whole beach of them.

She hadn't known she had a biological sister. But God had known. He'd seen Ivy growing up. He'd seen Anna growing up. He'd loved them both. He'd given them great families.

Right around the time Ivy began wanting to learn more about her biological relatives, God sent Aunt Sloane (the only biological relative she'd known all her life) here to help her. And now look what had happened.

God had given her and Anna to each other.

Sisters.

Chapter Twenty-Four

I t was Tuesday, November fifth, Sloane's final full day in Maine. Tomorrow, Brooke and Jared would return. She was looking forward to seeing them, but that was the only thing about tomorrow that promised sweetness. Several things promised sorrow.

Tomorrow, she would relinquish her role as Ivy's guardian.

Tomorrow, she'd move out of the garage apartment and The Gables.

Tomorrow, she'd depart her home state of Maine.

And the thing that twisted her heart most of all . . . Tomorrow, she'd leave Max behind.

She felt no peace about any of it. No *this is sad but it's for the best* assurance.

She'd dropped Ivy off at school this morning, then worked at her desk in the bedroom. Then taken herself out to lunch in town, observing the activity of Groomsport's harbor through the window situated next to her table for one.

And now she was finishing the final item on her to-do list

before returning to the apartment to pack. She knocked on her dad's door.

He answered looking scruffy. "Hi."

"Hi. How are you?"

"Fine. You?"

I'm struggling, she thought, but verbalized, "I'm okay." She walked in and scanned the scene. His living conditions still weren't great, in large part because he seemed unable to keep up with daily maintenance. But his conditions *had* improved since her first visit back in July. She had no choice but to try to find contentment in improvement instead of success. "Let's get a load of sheets and towels in the wash, straighten up, then sweep and vacuum everything."

"If you say so."

She moved in the direction of the hallway—

"Sloane?"

Stopping, she turned toward him.

"Sure you're okay?" He fidgeted with his hands before sliding them into his pockets. "You seem sad."

"Actually, you're right." It was highly unusual for him to notice or comment on her mental state. "I am sad."

"Why?"

"I'm not sure whether a relationship that I care about a lot is going to continue."

"Ah." His craggy features showed sympathy. "Look. I know I wasn't—I haven't been a good father to you. I'm sorry I failed at that."

His admission dumbfounded her. It was the first of its kind.

"I've never liked to see you sad," he went on. "You might not believe that, but it's true. What I want for you . . . What I hope you get? Is contentment."

"Thank you for saying that." Her voice broke. She'd been coming here for months to give him the things she'd once needed. But he'd just unexpectedly given her something *she* needed. Kindness.

"I've never been too good at contentment," he confessed. "But that doesn't mean you have to be the same."

Lips trembling, she nodded.

"You've spent a lot of time helping out your old dad. You didn't need to do that, but you did. I know I haven't told you that I appreciate it. But I do." He shifted awkwardly. Speaking about feelings was exceptionally uncomfortable for the two of them because they had *no* practice at it. "So. Thank you."

"You're welcome."

For the next hour they cleaned his apartment. A cyclone of emotion spun inside Sloane the entire time. After she put away the supplies, he trailed her to the door.

"I'm returning to California tomorrow," she said at the threshold.

"Oh? That's too bad. I'd never ask you to stay on my account. But is this . . . relationship of yours here?"

"Yes."

"So maybe there's a reason to change your mind and live in Maine?"

"Maybe. But if I return to California, I want you to know I'll hire a cleaning service to come by here a few times a month and I'll have groceries delivered."

"All right."

"Bye, Dad."

"Bye, Sloane." He retreated into the apartment, closing the door.

The emotion cyclone intensified as she walked toward her car. So much so that she decided not to get behind the wheel and instead took a detour to sit on a bench overlooking the complex's pool. At this time of year, the gates to the pool were locked, the cover over the pool blanketed with autumn leaves.

Even so, this spot reminded her of the photo of herself and Harper that she kept on her desk, the one of them side by side with their feet in the water.

You didn't have to be raised in the best facilities if you were raised with love and care, your needs met. Sadly, in the case of herself and Harper, the dilapidated pools of their childhood were an accurate depiction of the parenting they'd received. They hadn't been raised with love and care. Their needs hadn't been met. And Harper hadn't made it past the age of thirty.

A few days had passed since Sloane and Ivy had met Anna Thomas. At that charming farm on the outskirts of Auburn, Harper's two daughters had been reunited and Sloane had been present to witness it.

Yes, the reunion had been thrilling. But it had also been very sobering for Sloane—the realization that identical twins had been separated. It felt wrong that the girls had missed out on growing up with one another. More than that, they'd nearly missed out on even knowing the other one existed.

Harper had orchestrated Ivy and Anna's separation. She could have tried to keep them together. She could have informed the two sets of adoptive parents about their child's twin. The fact that Harper had done none of that pointed to Harper's own woundedness.

Ivy and Anna were shining examples of what a stable upbringing could do. It would have broken Sloane's heart to watch either of those girls repeat history by enduring a childhood similar to the one she and Harper had endured. Thank you, God—that's not how it had gone for Ivy and Anna. But that didn't undo the fact that Sloane and Harper *had* endured it. And just like she didn't want that for her nieces, she didn't want that for the girls she and her sister had been, either.

"I love you," she whispered to Harper, her heart tender toward her magnificent but troubled sister. She could and did forgive Harper all her mistakes. "Your daughters are well. Full of promise. Poised to live wonderful lives."

And you? The question came to her, clear yet without sound.

You are full of promise. Will you live a wonderful life?

On this final day of four months of weekly visits to her father, Sloane needed to face her own woundedness. All the etiquette in the world, the fashionable clothes, the abundance of food, the security she'd enjoyed for years hadn't fixed it. A portion of her still believed the lesson she'd learned early. Namely, that she was unlovable.

I'm unlovable had sent down roots when she was small. It had grown like a weed through her adolescence. *I'm unlovable.* And it remained still. She'd been a Christian for a long time and so *she knew*, intellectually, that she was loved. Her years of trust in God had removed the leaves and stems of the weed. However, the poisonous roots continued to cling to the deepest, darkest places of her soul. *I'm unlovable.*

That's why the prospect of happiness with Max seemed impossible and filled her with fear. That's why she kept telling herself that a man with his romantic track record would never work. If he hadn't loved any of those lovable women, how could he love unlovable her?

It's a lie.

The belief that she was unlovable was an absolute lie. The worst of lies. Evil. If she let it, this lie would gladly sabotage her future.

"I've never been too good at contentment," her father had said. *"But that doesn't mean you have to be the same."*

These poisonous roots *had to go.* She could no longer let this lie live and fester. She was finished with tolerating it. Finished with letting it influence her.

Inwardly, her faith swelled.

Outwardly, she rose to her feet.

IVY

It's Aunt Sloane's last full day in Maine and she seemed a little bummed this morning before school. Now she's at her dad's house and you know how hard that is on her. I was wondering if you could check on her when she gets back to The Gables.

MAX

I'm on it.

Max drove home from Libri at breakneck speed, worried that Sloane would reach The Gables before him.

When he neared his garage and saw that Brooke's SUV wasn't there, he blew out a relieved breath. Instead of parking his Porsche nose-first in the garage as usual, he parked it crosswise in front of two of the garage doors. Then ran into his house to retrieve something and ran back out to his car.

Ten minutes passed. He'd dressed casually for work today and wore a black puffer jacket over his clothes. However, he hadn't remembered to grab a hat or gloves when he was inside. The tips of his ears ached with cold, yet he refused to go back in because he didn't want to miss Sloane when she drove up.

Finally, the sound of the SUV's engine reached him, then Sloane's car came into view. She pulled to a stop a short distance away—closer to his house than her apartment. For a few seconds, nothing happened. Then she turned off the engine and climbed down. She'd been cleaning at her dad's house and was dressed for that the way only Sloane would dress for that. A long, navy wool coat buttoned from her neck to the hem. Boots. A navy floral headband, knotted at the top.

Hands in her coat pockets, she walked toward him.

His heart beat with painful hope because he desperately wanted her to open up and let him in. These last ten days since their talk at the stream had been horrible. The whole time, his courage had been fighting with despair.

Now he'd run out of time. She was leaving tomorrow.

Sloane drank in the sight of Max as she approached. He was leaning against his Porsche, feet crossed at the ankles, hands behind his back. The pose brought back a series of memories she hadn't thought about in ages.

Several times during the early years of their friendship, she'd found him waiting for her just this way when she'd left a visit with her father. Each time, he'd known how crummy she'd be feeling. Each time, he'd been leaning against his car, holding something behind his back intended to lift her spirits. A cup of coffee. A bar of French soap. Once, a framed glamour shot of him hilariously impersonating a male model.

The past telescoped forward, merging with the sight of him now. Max, waiting for her once again.

She loved him.

That's what this was—the deep devotion, the fire in her heart, the commitment in her veins.

She halted before him and took in the distinctive pale green eyes, the olive skin, the familiar and balanced planes of his face, the inky hair. Max. The illegitimate son. Max the Proud. The Brilliant. The Good. Max who'd pushed her away once. But who'd shown up for her many more times than that. Again and again. Even in this moment.

"Ivy told me you were with your dad," he said.

"I was."

"How are you doing?"

She made a *so-so* motion with her hand.

He nodded in understanding. "I have something that I thought might brighten your day."

"That would be really, really nice right about now."

From behind his back, he brought forward Empress Eugenie's tiara, unmistakable to Sloane after the hours she'd spent reading about it. *Never* had she viewed a piece of jewelry of this magnitude except behind glass at a museum. It was filled with a mind-boggling number of diamonds, and they were all sparkling wildly.

"It's way more beautiful in real life," she whispered, awed.

"I knew you'd like it."

"How do you have this?" She looked up at him.

He grinned. "I wanted to show it to you, so when I returned it to Felix, I asked him if I could borrow it once he had the diamonds from the cufflinks returned to their correct spots. He dropped it off yesterday."

"Thank you for showing it to me. I'm amazed by it."

"I'm amazed by you," he said simply. "Want to put it on?"

"*Oof.* I don't know."

"Why not?"

"I'm a little intimidated by it, seeing as how it's a priceless artifact."

"You won't hurt it."

"I mean . . . aren't tiaras meant for princesses?"

"You don't have to be born royal to be a princess, Sloane." And she could see that he was talking about a lot more than this tiara.

In a rush, she recalled that she and Harper had named The

Gables "The Prince's House" when they were kids. Now here he was, giving her a chance to wear a crown.

"May I?" he asked.

Moisture fuzzed her vision. If she was going to stop believing lies about her worth, this was as good a place as any to begin. She inclined her chin.

Max carefully removed her headband and set it aside, tucked her hair behind her ears, then placed the tiara on her head.

It was heavy but comfortable. Honestly, *wonderful*. It fit as if it had been fashioned for her. She reached up, marveling, running her fingertips over the ridges of the diamonds.

With grace and elegance, anything is possible.

"You look stunning," he said.

"Thank you."

"Let me get a picture, so you can see yourself." He pulled out his phone.

She posed. He snapped a shot and showed it to her.

Sloane blinked at the image. She looked . . . Well, she looked quite a bit like Kate herself.

Max pocketed the phone. "Need a hug, princess?"

"Yes, please."

He opened his arms.

Stepping forward, Sloane rested her tiara-topped head against his broad chest. She used the moments to gather the bravery she was going to need in order to say what she had to say.

When she straightened, he braced his palms on his car.

She set her hands on the chest of his jacket. "The day at the stream, when you said you loved me, my first response was joy. But I quickly squashed that because there were so many, many times when I hoped for the best with my family growing up.

And those hopes never came to fruition. At some point, it became too costly to keep on hoping."

"I understand."

"As soon as I squashed the joy that came up at the idea of you loving me, fear took its place." Her fingers moved up to interlace behind his neck. "Real talk?"

"Real talk."

"Given my past, if we're going to do this, I need you to assure me that I can trust you."

He looked her dead in the eye. "You can."

She took his measure while searching inside herself to determine if she had the strength to move forward.

"Sloane, you are the person I treasure most in this world. I'll sacrifice anything I need to for you. Follow you anywhere. Just don't make me live the rest of my life without you in it—"

"I love you." The joy she'd smothered standing beside the stream was back. It scared her still. Yet this time she gave it free rein to expand and expand.

He came to his full height in a fast motion, taking her face in his hands. "You love me?"

"I do."

"You do?"

"I do."

"Thank God," he whispered. "I love you so much, Sloane."

"I love you so much, too." Speaking words this honest was unfamiliar yet *electrifying*.

"Will you stay in Groomsport?" he asked.

"I will."

"Will you come back to work at Libri?"

"I won't. Libri is my past and My Fair Lady is my present. But I might consent to sit on the board of directors one day, so that I can still advocate for the success of the company we founded." She smiled. "You, Max, are both my past and my present."

"And your future."

"And my future," she confirmed.

"I love you."

Hearing him say those words to her was a *miracle*. Believing those words in her soul was a miracle, too.

He kissed her, which sent a heady torrent of rightness rushing through Sloane.

An audience of trees watched.

An exquisite tiara glinted on her head.

But when she'd look back on all the stunning aspects of this turning-point day, *he* would always be the best of them.

Epilogue

Mid-February had arrived and, with it, Jeremiah and Remy's wedding day.

Their forty guests had parked a distance away and been transported through the snow by a convoy of horse-drawn sleighs. They'd ended the ride at a small, stone chapel in the woods with just enough seating to fit their group. Max had to admit that Fiona had done a phenomenal job with the planning. The chapel glowed with warmth and white candles. Pine greenery had been spread everywhere. Jeremiah and Remy were at the front, and the pastor was speaking about marriage.

Max sat next to Sloane, his arm stretched behind her back on the top of the pew.

Today, Jeremiah looked like the rich celebrity he was in his tux. Remy had chosen to wear a simple white gown with Eugenie's tiara. Her blond curls fell loose down her back. Remy enjoyed reading science fiction. And as a bride, she really did resemble an Elven character from *Lord of the Rings*.

Remy had one bridesmaid, her sister, standing beside her. Max's attention slid to Jeremiah's best man, Jude. Max's oldest friend happened to catch Max's eye and a pulse of understanding traveled between them. They were both deeply pleased for Jeremiah.

From there, Max's attention moved to the pew where Felix sat. For a long time, the sight of Felix had stirred animosity in him. It didn't anymore. He might share some personality traits with this man, but he'd never follow his example.

Next to Felix sat Gemma, wearing the engagement ring Jude had recently given her. Next to Gemma was Fiona, beaming, one arm wrapped around the elbow of her boyfriend, Burke.

A soloist began a song. Max took advantage of it, knowing the sound would mask his whisper. He inclined his head to Sloane's ear. "I want to marry you."

"I want to marry you," she murmured back.

Her statement brought him an intense rush of satisfaction. "Next month?"

"No."

"Fine. Next week?"

"Maybe early next year."

She'd continued to live at his garage apartment after Ivy moved home. Which was good, but still not close enough. She was paying employees to teach her established courses in LA and had expanded her course offerings and private lessons throughout the Northeast.

"Early next year is much too far away." He'd found that if he kissed her in a certain way, she became dazed and agreeable. He'd try kissing her that way later and see if he could convince her to marry him before the year was out. "But you *will* marry me?"

"You haven't officially asked me."

"But if I did officially ask you sometime soon, you'd say yes?"

"I guess you'll have to wait and see."

"Sloane," he growled.

"It's not proper etiquette to pressure a woman regarding her affection."

He chuckled. "I'm impatient."

"I noticed." Sloane had been receiving a steady diet of his adoration for more than three months. He loved seeing her this way, the way she'd always had the potential to be, so confident and serene. "I do believe I'll say yes if you officially ask me. But I'm not in a hurry. We have the rest of our lives ahead of us."

It was true. He woke every morning full of anticipation, itching to see her, to learn what the new day held.

The song ended and Jeremiah and Remy began exchanging vows.

He, Jeremiah, and Jude had come a long way. All three of them had been the sons of scandal, forced to exist beneath a storm cloud of interest and gossip. Max wouldn't have chosen that path for himself, and he'd guess Jeremiah and Jude wouldn't have chosen it either. But their character was the better for it now. They'd persevered. They'd chosen to put good into the world and good had found them in return.

Jeremiah and Remy were proclaimed husband and wife. The groom kissed the bride as the audience broke into applause. Music rang out. Holding hands, the couple made their way down the aisle.

Max gave Sloane a quick kiss. "Love you."

"Love you, too."

Their gazes held. In her eyes, he saw the promise of a lot of years.

A lot of life.

And a lot of joy.

*"In everything, do to others
what you would have them do to you."*
—Matthew 7:12

Acknowledgments

Thank you for journeying to Maine with me within the pages of the three Sons of Scandal novels! I loved Max, Sloane, Fiona, and all of the other characters. So, as is always the case for me, I'm finding it bittersweet to bring this series to a close. On the one hand, it's hard to say goodbye! On the other hand, I couldn't be more grateful and glad that I completed the series I set out to write.

Eugenie's tiara is real! If you're curious to see what it looks like, run a search for Empress Eugenie's meander tiara. The details I shared about its origin, including the fact that it was sold at auction, are accurate. Tiffany purchased 24 of the 69 lots at that auction, so it wasn't too much of a stretch to imagine that he brought the tiara to America and sold it to a Gilded Age Camden ancestor.

You no doubt noticed some interesting spelling and capitalizations in the quotes spoken during the Boston history tour scene. That's because I stayed true to actual quotes from Abigail Adams' letters.

Thank you to the team who worked with me on *Uneasy Street*. Charlene Patterson, my excellent editor. Joy, Crissy, Amy, Shelli, and Jennifer—my generous friends who served as Beta Readers. Reba Buhr and Ryan Hudson, audiobook narrators. You blow me away with your ability to bring my books to life.

I feel like the luckiest writer in the world to count fellow authors Katie Ganshert and Courtney Walsh as dear friends. They keep me from feeling lonely while doing this solitary job.

All my love to my husband, kids, and family. You are my greatest treasure.

Finally, all praise to God, who guides and equips my novels. So long as He keeps calling me to write, I'll keep sitting at my computer and pouring out His stories.

About the Author

Becky's a California native who attended Baylor University, met and married a Texan, then settled in Dallas with their three children. She loves writing sweet contemporary romances filled with sizzling chemistry, twisty plots, faith, banter, and humor. Her novels have received Carol Awards and landed her in the Christy Award Hall of Fame. When she's not writing, you'll find her power-walking her neighborhood, driving carpool, eating chocolate, doing yoga, or admiring her Cavalier spaniel.

To learn more about Becky and her books, visit her website at www.beckywade.com. While you're there, subscribe to her free quarterly e-newsletter for updates about upcoming books, exclusive giveaways, and more!

You'll find Becky on Facebook as Author Becky Wade and on Instagram as BeckyWadeWriter.